The DOWN EAST MURDERS

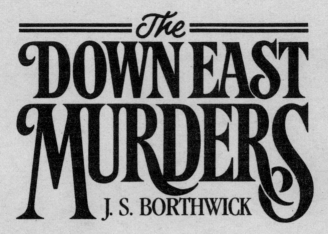

THE DOWN EAST MURDERS

J. S. BORTHWICK

A Critic's Choice paperback
from Lorevan Publishing, Inc.
New York, New York

Reprinted by arrangement with St. Martins Press

ISBN: 0-931773-58-X

First Critic's Choice edition: 1986
Second Printing 1987
Third printing 1987
Fourth printing 1987
Fifth printing 1988
From LOREVAN PUBLISHING, INC.

Critic's Choice Paperbacks
31 E. 28th St.
New York, New York 10016

Manufactured in the United States of America

For Maria and Alec, and Jim, again.

Cast of Principal Characters

SARAH DEANE ... Teacher, graduate student from Boston
HARRISON PETTY ..... Director, Godding Museum of Art
DORIS ORDWAY ..... Secretary, Godding Museum of Art
NATE HARWOOD .... Artist
MARIAN HARWOOD .... Wife of Nate
ROGER HARWOOD .... Artist, son of Nate and Marian
GIDDY LESTER .... Cousin to Alex McKenzie,
niece to Elspeth
ALEXANDER McKENZIE .... Physician from Boston
ELSPETH McKENZIE .... Artist, mother of Alex,
aunt of Giddy
SYDNEY PRIOR .... Owner of Prior's Gallery
RUTH BAKER .... Visitor from Missouri
TINA COBBLE/COTTLE ..... Friend of Alex's from Boston
RACHEL AND LYDA SEAVER .... Longtime Weymouth
Island residents
LEM WALLACE .... Harbor master, Weymouth Island
MIKE LAAKA .... Sheriff's Deputy Investigator
SUSAN COHEN .... Deputy Sheriff
SGT. GEORGE FITTS .... State Police CID

ONE

The end of July on the coast of Maine

"Alas, poor souls, it grieved my heart to hear what pitiful cries they made to use to help them. . . . "

"Alas, the sea hath cast me on the rocks,
Washed me from shore to shore. . . . "

—*Pericles*, Act II

The Godding Museum of Art in the little town of Rockport was a bulky Victorian number, once the private house of the prosperous and often contentious Godding family. It sat a few hundred yards from Route 1 on Pascal Avenue behind a sun-scorched lawn and the stumps of elm trees and, like an overweight old lady, loomed in a benevolent if confused way over her more modest neighbors, the Greek revival, the Gothic, and the Cape.

Even a room with an ocean view in the tallest tower of an old Victorian house does not make up for the fact that heat rises, and Sarah Deane, toiling over the final page proofs of the art show catalogue, suffered accordingly. At Sarah's feet, enjoying the breeze from a portable fan aimed at his face, lay a gray rough-coated dog, one that almost bettered the maximum height of thirty-four inches at the shoulder suggested by the American Kennel Club for Irish wolfhounds. The dog, paws extended, slumbered noisily next to the desk by Sarah's bare feet, his bearded chin resting on one of her discarded sandals.

July on the coast of Maine had been breathless, and August, just over the horizon, promised to be more of the same. It wasn't only the heat, thought Sarah crossly, as she deleted two dashes and substituted a semicolon; it was the bustle and fever of the approaching annual show that promised to destroy whatever peace and order she had been able to impose on her job as general typist and handmaiden for the Godding Museum of Art. Although the opening was not for a good two weeks, Harrison Petty, the museum director, was already showing signs of instability.

Mr. Petty. Sarah could hear him now, trumpeting about below, the bare floors and open stairway making his voice racket from room to room as he issued instructions and complained loudly to his staff. But at least he had air to breathe; the rooms below were large and opened into each other. Sarah looked resentfully about her room, glared at a provocative coal grate, and then, with a sigh, stared out of the window toward the distant shore and the haze of the harbor.

For fully five minutes she stayed at the window, and then turned reluctantly back to her desk, pulled the limp cotton material of her yellow shirt away from her overheated skin, reached for the last page of the proofs, and sighed again. Heat and tedium. Tedium and heat. And Mr. Petty. Now he was calling her name. She bent over a long paragraph. Absolutely indigestible. It needed to be broken into at least three bite-sized pieces. I suppose, she thought, this is what usually happens to needy English teachers in the summer—correcting the works of a person who should never have been let loose with a pencil. There he was again, right at the bottom of the stairs.

"Sarah," called the voice. "Sar-ah. Is it ready? Can you bring it down? Right now?" There was a pause, and then, "Sarah. Can you hear me? I want you. Now."

It was too hot, thought Sarah, to get up and bellow back down the stairs. Let Mr. Petty wait a minute. "Patsy," she said to the dog, "if you want to bite him today, go right ahead." She turned back to the introduction, knocked down two exclamation points, killed the second "de-acquisition" in the same sentence, and put a line through "prioritize" and "museumwise." Then she pushed the proofs together, strapped on her sandals, and began making her way down the steep staircase, Patsy following, his nails clicking on the bare wood.

At the foot of the second landing, in the center of the Godding's permanent collection of nineteenth-century portraits, stood tall, angular Harrison Petty, the recently appointed director of the museum, and behind him the patient figure of Doris Ordway, the museum secretary. Mr. Petty extended a bony hand for the proofs. "Ah, good. Sarah, our trouper. Not many corrections, I'm sure."

"Some words should be changed, Mr. Petty," said Sarah, "and the photographs haven't turned up. You know, the Winslow Homer for the front cover and last year's prize winner for the back."

"They're in my office," said Mrs. Ordway. "Roger Harwood's prize painting is fine, but the Homer is a little dark."

"You both realize, don't you, that this will be the Godding's most important publication ever, and hopefully"—Mr. Petty smiled, little knowing that Sarah had extirpated a number of "hopefullys" from his manuscript—"it will start a tradition of top-drawer catalogues."

Sarah nodded. Mr. Petty often saw the world in terms of drawers: top drawer, not-so-top drawer, middle drawer, and on down to bottom drawer. His mind, she felt, must be a warehouse of bureaus, chests, and file cabinets, all with numbered drawers. "Yes, Mr. Petty," she said, and then "No, Patsy," for the dog was now sniffing closely at the cuffs of his gray trousers.

"Good dog, Patsy," he said uncertainly.

"You know he won't eat you, Mr. Petty," said Sarah. "He just knows you're nervous."

"I'm not nervous," said Harrison, backing away from the dog. "And now, Sarah, I have a most serious subject to dis-

· 3 ·

cuss with you. A matter of security. Something affecting all of the Godding Museum family. Mrs. Ordway, may I have that bulletin from the Sheriff's Department."

Lord, thought Sarah, someone's cleaned out the gift shop, and we'll all have to take lie detector tests, and then, remembering her tiny salary, wondered when she had been elevated to membership in the Godding family. More like slave, she thought, but she reminded herself that she had really needed this job. There hadn't been many summer openings that would have allowed her dog to be part of the deal. Then she became aware that Mr. Petty was looking at her reprovingly, waiting for her complete attention.

"Yes, Mr. Petty," she said.

"Loss after loss," said Harrison Petty, flourishing a mimeographed sheet. "The Sheriff's office has circulated this bulletin . . . and about time, I may add. The midcoast has been losing paintings and valuable objects all summer and from what I hear for the past three or four years. We at the Godding are so very vulnerable. Mrs. Ordway will concur, I'm sure."

Mrs. Ordway, a stout, gray-haired woman of firm and reliable aspect, nodded.

"And we cannot afford extra security," said Harrison plaintively, "because I am absolutely hamstrung by our budget."

"We're over the budget now even without adding an extra guard," said Mrs. Ordway. "The catalogues are costing a mint. You could choose a cheaper printer. We've always had them done locally."

"Local. There you are. In a nutshell." Mr. Petty sighed deeply as if feeling the weight of the museum, the art thefts, the catalogues on his shoulders. He swept his hand in a circle indicating "local" as taking in a large portion of New England. "Local," he repeated.

"One Winslow Homer, an unsigned George Bellows, and a John Marin can't turn us into the Fogg or the Gardiner," said Mrs. Ordway. "Or even the Farnsworth." Doris Ordway knew her museums.

The mention of the Farnsworth—the old established rival in neighboring Rockland—brought Mr. Petty back to his subject.

"The Farnsworth lost a Hopper," he said in an anxious voice. "In broad daylight. Talk about security. But we must be vigilant. Thieves are working the whole area. The police want us to watch visitors, anyone strange."

"You mean with a razor and a rolled-up carpet," said Sarah.

Mr. Petty looked at her as if suspecting levity. "This is a serious matter, so be on the watch because who knows where they'll strike next, and, Sarah, I'm afraid that after the show opens we won't have anything more for you. It's been an agreeable association." Here Mr. Petty did a quick tango step away from Patsy, who was now showing a lively interest in the director's suede shoes. "We'll look for you to come in as a visitor, won't we, Mrs. Ordway? Tomorrow we'll start planning the reception. I want it to be so very nice, because touristwise . . . "

Sarah quivered.

* * *

On Thursday, the next to last day of July, the Weymouth Island ferry, the *Robin Day,* had just disgorged its passengers and was taking on its return load when Nathaniel Harwood burst out of his studio door and, like a stakes contender coming off the pace, pounded toward the public landing. Since it is impossible for a familiar figure to move violently through a small village without attracting notice, Nate's furious progress was remarked by several onlookers.

Rachel Seaver, the eighty-five-year-old Weymouth librarian, looked up from her weeding and addressed her sister, Lyda. "There goes Nate. On the warpath again, I'd say."

"Going to the mainland never agrees with him," observed Lyda. She hitched her wicker chair further into the shade.

"He's worse and worse," said Rachel, reaching for her cane. "He was ugly enough when Marian was with him, but now she's gone, he's a terror."

"Let's not think of Nate Harwood for the rest of the day," said Lyda, who was of a tranquil disposition. She pointed to the garden. "If you cut that honeysuckle back, the hydrangea might do something this year."

Two other of Weymouth's elder citizens also found Nate's charge toward the public landing of interest. They sat together on the bench outside the post office, where they were in much demand by tourists wanting photographs of the genus "Old Maine Codger." From their bench they had a fine overview of the sandy path leading down to the wharf and of the receding stern of the *Robin Day* as she headed out of the harbor.

"Nate's come out of his stall mad," said Amory Satterfield, the senior of the two. "Yellin' his head off about some painting."

"Just come off the afternoon boat, and now he's bustin' to get back on. If I was Marian, which thank God I ain't, I'd stay away from that fellow. Sit up, Amory, they're comin' to take our picture."

By the time Nate Harwood reached the public landing, he had left a trail of curious residents and elbowed tourists and could now be made out standing in front of a stack of lobster traps, an agitated figure waving what appeared to be five arms all terminating in fists—these being shaken in the face of Lem Wallace, constable and harbor master.

"Stolen. Robbed, goddammit. Walked right in and took it off the easel. Goddamn thieves. Get that boat back, Lem."

"Can't, Nate. She's cast off and under way."

"Call Rockland and get the police. Stop the people on the dock in Port Clyde and have them searched. Get that lousy Sheriff's Department on the phone."

"Lord, Nate, you've been gone three days. That's how many boatloads plus a whole raft of pleasure boats, cruise yachts, windjammers, the seaplane on day trips?"

"Christ—call yourself a constable?"

"Hold it, Nate. Go on back to the mainland and make a proper statement."

"It's one of those lousy tourists. Crawling all over the island."

"Hell, Nate, you sell paintings to those tourists. Don't go chewin' off the hand that feeds you. Shows someone can stand the stuff you turn out." Lem grinned and began coiling a tangle of heavy docking line. He enjoyed Nate-baiting; it was a pleasant, established island sport. The Weymouth residents had long accepted Nate as a local fixture, and, since he had been born on the island and had years of summer residence under his belt, the fact that he was an artist of considerable reputation, with shows in Portland and Boston, was not held against him. He was an irritant, but a familiar one.

As Nate Harwood was clamoring at the public landing, Elspeth McKenzie in the front hall of her cottage was fending off the attentions of her two Sealyhams, who barked and jumped, their stubby paws tearing at her stockings. "Down, both of you," she ordered and shoved the dogs into the kitchen, closed the door, and, with fatigue weighing down her limbs, made her way into the bedroom. Slowly, she unfastened her wrinkle-proof dress, worn always for shopping in Rockland, pulled on her old white cotton pants and her faded blue Mexican shirt, and, avoiding the bedroom mirror, walked into the living room. She knew that all-day shopping in August when one is sixty-two does not encourage covert looks at one's face. For a weary moment she looked at the shopping bags she'd left by the living room door. It hadn't been a complete waste. She'd found those straw place mats on sale, and, thank heaven, the brushes and watercolor blocks she'd ordered at Sydney Prior's shop had come in.

Only two weeks before the show. It was really too bad about exempting certain artists such as herself from the jury selection process. Otherwise, her blasted painting would have been framed and delivered, and she wouldn't be tempted to fiddle with it. All the way over on the boat she had wondered whether the weir in the picture was done with too much definition, pointed to itself in a way that negated the somber sense of the opening sea. All right, she told herself, go in and confront the picture as if you've never seen it before. If it's all wrong, it'll hit you immediately . . . smack.

What hit Elspeth McKenzie "smack," as she walked into her studio, was the empty place on the easel. She stopped, stared, shook her head, and then looked wildly about. Had she moved the painting before she left for the morning boat? Forgetfulness, senility? It was happening to some of her friends. But after a hasty tour of the small many-windowed room, a search of the supply cupboard, she knew it was gone. Suddenly winded as if she had been punched in the stomach, Elspeth sat down abruptly on an old blanket chest, and since, unlike Nate Harwood, she could not find relief in profanity or violent action, she only sat there, breathing rather fast and staring at her easel.

* * *

Roger Harwood shouted that his father did it. Coming home to Port Clyde from his part-time job on Ted Bassett's lobster boat, he confronted his vacant portable easel and then kicked it so that it spun around on its three legs and collapsed on the floor.

"It's my father," shouted Roger, sounding remarkably like his irate parent, Nate Harwood. "He'd do something shitty like that."

"You're crazy," said Giddy Lester, Roger's live-in companion. "Your father doesn't steal. And he's not out to get you. It's just because you bombed out of his dear old Bowdoin, and," added Giddy, whose greatest fault was an often unasked-for honesty, "I didn't think much of that painting anyway. I know the design was pretty strong, but all those spots and lumps like someone threw up on it. Your old style, Roger—well, it was more coherent, and you were saying something, you know, in a real visual way."

"My old stuff was representational crap. I see everything differently now. So where the hell is my painting? You didn't take it just because you didn't like it, did you?"

"Of course not." Giddy shook her head, thinking Roger certainly needed some outside direction. Giddy had tried before with no success, but the zeal of a reformer is not dampened by a little hostility. "Look, Roger," she said, "representational painting doesn't mean worn out. The new realism . . ."

"New realism! Oh, Christ, Giddy, that's on the way out. Let me paint the way I want." Roger's face, startlingly handsome with its dark eyes, heavy lashes, and long planes, had now worked itself into a series of elongated knots. He jerked his head as he spoke, so that a shelf of brown hair fell over his forehead.

"The new realism," said Giddy doggedly, "is still happening, and you were right there. I heard someone say that you were a coming artist with a special sort of insight. Anyway, the museum will be asking for a substitute. I think that tempera you did last fall in your old style of the Broad Cove Church is pretty good. You used to sell a lot of that sort. It's like that prize picture of the grange dinner that's going on the catalogue."

"Prizes! Who needs prizes?" said Roger, his voice rising, apparently forgetting the ecstasy he had felt when hearing of last year's award. "Commercial shit. Artists change. God, they don't sit on their asses painting the same stuff all their life. I'm into abstracts now and you, Giddy, couldn't recognize one with any meaning to it if you spent a year on it . . . so where's my painting gone?"

"I didn't take it and I don't know." Giddy, a cheerful-looking girl, sturdy and broad-shouldered, with a mop of straw-colored hair, was built for throwing the javelin. She studied Roger, now leaning against the wall of their tiny kitchen that also served as studio and dining quarters. Giddy had known Roger all her life—all her summer life anyway. Summers on Weymouth Island, Roger six years older, a tall skinny boy in cutoff shorts and basketball sneakers, sailing, going on picnics, scraping the bottom of the family skiff, and always Giddy tagging after. Little Giddy, being allowed to carry Roger's paint box or bring him fresh water for his brushes, and sometimes, when she was older, being allowed to go sketching with him. Of course, Roger was always sort of a loner, on the edge of things a lot of the time, but Giddy always felt she understood. Keeping yourself separate was what an artist had to do. And this year, Giddy at eighteen, having finished her first year of college, thought it was time to start living as an adult, an adult artist, who, like Roger, had a vocation. It had been part of her summer plan to move right into the world of turpentine and canvas, and meet and argue with other artists on all sorts of interesting topics having to do with color and tone and what the word "painterly" actually meant. She felt she should soak herself in the spiritual life of art—this from an imperfectly understood reading of Kandinsky—and by trying for physical joy at the same time, why, she would really come of age. In some confusion about these excitements, Giddy had taken Roger as a lover; to be more accurate, Roger had allowed Giddy to move into his two-room shack on the edge of Port Clyde to cook his dinner, mop his floor, and pay his rent from her small salary, all for the privilege of sleeping with him and listening to his equally confused ideas on art.

And now Giddy was being accused of not understanding what Roger was doing, of being an enemy of the abstract. This hurt, largely because it was true. All Giddy's efforts in that direction had resulted in paintings that looked like beef stew. But then so did Roger's, just more skillfully made stew. Which was why Giddy was almost glad to see the empty easel. It was as if some divinity had flown down the stovepipe and seized the work as a reproach to such falseness. So Giddy said aloud that it was a lucky thing, "even if you don't have to go through the jury business the way I do because of winning the prize last year. The new painting just didn't have it."

"Stuff it, Giddy, and shut up," said Roger, his voice rising again. "You know what, you've been working for Sydney Prior and his dump of a gallery too long. Art-store gift junk and all his eighteenth-century antique garbage. Old cracked oils of dead ducks and rotten apples and green bottles and bowls of grapes."

Giddy saw that Roger's lip was trembling, so she turned away, quietly set the easel back on its legs, and then went over to the old soapstone sink and began pumping water for the kettle.

After a rather meager supper at which Giddy had been silent and Roger had been sullen, he said, "I guess I could enter the prison one . . . the big oil."

"The one with all the lines and squares?" Giddy swished her tea bag back and forth in her cup and then, without looking at Roger, said, "I know you think I'm always being negative, but that one doesn't say anything to me about isolation or punishment or confinement. I know I'm not so sharp on abstracts, and I know prison is grim and so is the painting, but there should be more. And no one will like it."

"Art is not to like." Roger was now shouting. "Christ, Giddy, how irrelevant. What a shallow mind you've got. You're so hung up . . . I mean, way hung up. A little preppie art student. God, start thinking. Detach yourself."

Giddy, biting her lip, dropped her sodden tea bag into the sink, and then with great control said softly, "I think you've detached yourself, all right, but I don't think you've attached yourself to much of anything else. I think you're yelling at me because you don't really know what you're doing." She took a long sip of tea and decided that Roger was really coming apart at the seams. And besides, she hadn't known that Roger could be so mean. Take the hot water, for instance. She put down her teacup.

"We need a better way to heat things than this hot plate. Are you listening, Roger? The nights are getting colder now, so maybe a wood stove. We could look for a used one."

But Roger sat, not speaking, with his hands around his mug of coffee, staring at the kitchen door.

"And we need more than two lights and an extension cord, because no one can see to do anything. I don't know how you can paint in here, and I can't put any more money in this place because I don't have it, so honestly," Giddy rushed on, "why not do a few more churches or lighthouses . . . not forever, just for now. Maybe sell the 'Grange Supper.' You don't have to paint like your father, but . . . "

Roger blanched and his face twisted with rage. "Screw my father and screw his paintings and lighthouses and churches. And who the hell needs hot water and a stove in summer? All that crap. Christ."

Almost two months had passed since Giddy had moved in with Roger, and now she looked at him with something like active dislike.

"Say that all again."

"I'm not going to sell myself for some damn stove and some damn light bulbs. I'm not going to turn myself into some kind of prostitute."

Giddy stared at Roger for a full minute and then nodded. "You know, Roger, neither am I. Not anymore." She carefully put her cup of tea down on the table and then walked to the tiny chamber that served as a bedroom and with great deliberation began to fold her clothes and place them in her suitcase.

* * *

The news of theft among the Godding's invited artists sent Harrison Petty spinning. By Thursday he had hired an extra guard, called the Sheriff's Department and the State Police, and inspected each museum visitor with a suspicious eye. Now, feeling the need of a support group, he collected Sarah from her tower, marched her into Mrs. Ordway's office, and brandished a sheaf of newspapers in the secretary's face. "Have you read these? . . . Shocking. We're turning into Dallas." Mr. Petty unfurled a front page and read in a scandalized voice, " 'Work of gang suspected. New art heist brings the total to over fifteen paintings, plus other rare antiques and silver taken this summer. Nathaniel Harwood, noted New England artist, called the theft an outrage.' "

"I'll bet he said more than that," said Mrs. Ordway, who had endured much from Nate's museum visitations.

" '. . . Roger Harwood, son of Nathaniel and winner of last year's Godding Prize, could not be reached for comment, but another victim, Elspeth McKenzie, well-known Massachusetts artist and longtime Weymouth summer resident, was described as deeply distressed. These three missing paintings were to be shown at the Godding Annual Show.' Now listen to this. 'Godding connection suspected.' Now I ask you," cried Mr. Petty. "The Godding connection. It will ruin us. They'll think we're into drugs."

"Actually," said Sarah, "it will probably bring visitors in droves. There's nothing like crime."

"Attracting exactly the wrong class of person."

"It might help sell catalogues," Mrs. Ordway pointed out.

"And that's another thing. Three pages of the catalogue shot. Call the printer, Sarah. Tell them to hold everything."

"We'll have to pay for any changes," said Mrs. Ordway. "The cheapest way is to have the printer insert an errata sheet for each of the missing paintings."

"Cheapest . . . oh no." Mr. Petty almost wept. "The catalogue is the crown of the show. Errata sheets are tacky, second class. Sarah, remember to call the caterers, too. I hear there's a problem with the Newburgh." Mr. Petty lifted a stack of file cards from the secretary's desk, shifted them out of sequence, and began to prowl the perimeter of the small office. He reminded Sarah of an animated and poorly connected set of bed slats—albeit bed slats dressed by the likes of Pierre Cardin.

"We've always served afternoon tea and sandwiches at the members' reception," said Mrs. Ordway, rescuing her file cards.

"Bottom drawer," said Mr. Petty. "We're out to show the Farnsworth it isn't the only museum around. Evening reception, black tie, champagne, lobster, and the Fagin String Quartet."

"Good grief," said Mrs. Ordway.

"We need positive publicity. The Godding connection indeed! Act big and there you are. Bequests, loans, shows."

"Debt, bankruptcy, penury," said Doris Ordway, drawing a line through an entry in her copy of the catalogue proof set.

"How long have you been at the Godding?" asked Mr. Petty, as if seeing a bottleneck to progress clearly for the first time.

"Long enough," said Mrs. Ordway, and she heaved a sigh that rose all the way from the crepe soles of her brown oxfords.

"I think," said Sarah, seeing a need for peace, "that I'd better find out what substitutes the stolen artists are going to send in."

"Good suggestion," said Mrs. Ordway. "I'll send a note to Roger Harwood. He's living in some dreadful little shack in Port Clyde. Then you see if you can find his father and leave a message for Mrs. McKenzie at the Weymouth store—no private phones on the island."

"That's Alex McKenzie's mother, isn't it?" said Sarah in as offhand a voice as she could manage.

"Yes, do you know him?" said Mrs. Ordway. "I've watched Alex grow up. A perfect devil when he was little, and Roger Harwood quiet and sensible, but now . . . "

"I've seen some of Roger's new things," said Harrison. "Very negative. He should never have been invited. I know it's the rule about the prize winner, but I do feel we should do something, and about the jury luncheon . . . Sarah, you'll have to work late tonight and . . . "

While Mr. Petty fumbled forward, Sarah crept out to do her calling, wondering what had possessed her to bring up Alex McKenzie's name when she might not even see him this summer.

Mrs. Ordway returned to the study of her day's calendar. She was tired of junior curators from urban centers who advanced on small unprotected museums with ideas beyond their station or the museum's means. However, like the veteran pilot she was, she was prepared to stand by the wheel, ready for shoal waters.

Four hours spent working late at the museum brought Sarah to a new level of fatigue. She fought her way through mailing lists, addressed invitations, and helped haul pictures of the permanent collection to the basement to make gallery room for the expected show entries. And tried to dodge Mr. Petty. Sarah hadn't known that he was such a gossip. Even Mrs. Ordway, in the role of a wet blanket, could do nothing to stem the questions and speculations about the art thefts and the artists in question. Nate Harwood, in Mr. Petty's opinion, was an abomination, his son Roger uncouth, Mrs. McKenzie charming but headstrong, the Sheriff's Department hopelessly lax.

Sarah finally escaped at nine and drove her wheezing old VW slowly toward her boarding house on the edge of Port Clyde. A fingernail of a moon had slipped into the sky, and the houses showed as dark boxes against the darker lines of pine and spruces. She braked coming into the almost empty village, swung left onto Horse Point Road, and accelerated in the dip so that the old car could make the rise without shifting. Then she saw in the rearview mirror the headlights of a car and, without thinking, further increased her speed. Somehow she wanted the road to herself—solitude after the irritations of the day. She shot to the top of the rise, but just before she lost the headlights in the mirror she saw the car swing off the road and disappear. That's funny, she said to herself. I didn't know there was a house there . . . just that old wharf.

Coming from the center of Port Clyde, the blue Ford Fairmont had turned behind Sarah onto Horse Point Road. Following the curve of the harbor, it reached the top of the rise, traveled along a level stretch, its headlights first lighting the Volkswagen, and, as Sarah's little car disappeared, its high beam picking up the line of gateposts, picket fences, and silver mailboxes that stood along the margin. Then, as the widening of the road on the harbor side indicated something more than a private driveway, the blue Ford swung sharply into the entrance and with increasing speed rolled down the steep decline.

Under the single light at the end of Lloyd's Wharf, Ted Bassett, stacking lobster traps by the bait house with his partner, Guy Watts, saw the car turn and accelerate. He had time to shout "Stop," time to hear muffled answering screams, and then, grabbing Guy, shoved him aside. The two men, backs flattened against the wall of the building, felt the shack shudder as the automobile glanced off its side. Running forward, they watched it launch itself into the air like some metallic mammal at a nocturnal marine park, saw the dark shape hang for a second against the ink-blue evening sky, roll slightly on its side, hit the water, linger for a moment as if it meant to float, and then, nose first, with a sucking noise, disappear. But even as Ted Bassett, yelling to Guy to get help, raced to the end of the wharf, kicked off his shoes, and dove, great gasping bubbles from the sinking car began erupting on the broken surface of the water.

* * *

Deputy Investigator Michael Laaka of the Knox County Sheriff's Department arrived at his office a good twenty minutes early that next morning. He moved with caution, looking several times over his shoulder, and then gently closed the door before flicking on the light. Mike was not, however, up to some form of civic skullduggery. He had a matter at hand that demanded his attention before the morning reports arrived.

Pushing aside a weighty folder marked "Art Thefts, June, July," Mike unfolded a newspaper and brought out a pad. The last of July and the start of August were always challenging times, what with Saratoga cranking up with the Schuylerville

Stakes and the Whitney, and then the sprint test at Suffolk Downs. Just time for a few selections and a call to his cousin in New York who handled Mike's Off Track Betting assignments.

For a few moments Mike's pencil traveled happily up and down the entries for Saratoga, a mile-and-a-half race on turf. . . . Break Dancer looked good at that distance, and nail down Satin Slew in the allowance for two-year-old fillies. . . . She looked good breaking her maiden last month, and then . . .

A sharp tattoo sounded on the glass panel of the office door.

"Hell," said Mike Laaka, his pencil hovering between Halo Again and Spectacular Prince in the feature race.

The tattoo was repeated and the doorknob shaken.

"Okay, okay, wait up, will you?" Mike furled the *Daily Racing Form* and stuffed it into his desk drawer. "Come in, Susie," he called.

A small, uniformed, brown-haired person came to a halt before Mike's desk. Deputy Sheriff Susan Cohen was all business.

"Oh, relax, Susie. You're too early. What's up? The art people still shaking and trembling?"

"Not what's up, it's what's down."

"Down?"

"On the bottom. Bottom of the harbor in Port Clyde. Two of them."

"Jesus. Two cars in?"

"No. One car, two people." Deputy Cohen cleared her throat and read from the report in her hand. "On or about nine-thirty P.M. a two-door Fairmont with Missouri plates containing two persons turned off the Horse Point Road onto Lloyd's Wharf drive and proceeded into the water, the tide being about one hour and a half before high."

"The car proceeded? The hell it did."

"I'm reading from the report," said Susan reproachfully. She squared her shoulders as if to overcome small size by military bearing. "After it was ascertained by two witnesses that an accident had occurred, one left the scene to call the Rescue Squad, and the other proceeded into the water . . . "

"Never mind the formal report," said Mike sympathetically. "Did anyone get out?"

"No," said Susan. "It was horrible. The car went upside down in the harbor and one of the doors buckled, and the other was against some old pilings. Ted Bassett jumped right in and the rescue people got there fast, but it was no good." Susan shook her head sadly. "By the time the diver got there with equipment, they were both gone. An older man and a woman. The ID information is in the report. They're raising the car now with a crane."

"When did you get there?"

"About ten minutes after the call. I was patrolling with Wayne Jones . . . we both worked on the report. Anyway, Marge Bassett said Ted told her it was just awful. They were both floating in the back seat, and they'd screamed all the way down the drive."

"Jesus," said Mike again. "That's a rough one."

"It wasn't the big docks at Port Clyde, you know where the Monhegan or the Weymouth ferries come in. Horse Point Road is off the main route. Ted thinks the people, being from out-of-state, got mixed up and took a wrong turn and panicked. Hit the accelerator instead of the brakes. Older people sometimes don't coordinate the way they should."

"Sounds like an accidental death to me. Nothing to pull in the State Police. Send me the medical examiner's report when it comes in. Any more bad news?—because I don't need that kind of excitement." He leaned back in his chair. Mike's style was relaxed—some of his associates said that "laid-back" was hardly strong enough for the easygoing Sheriff's Detective. But Mike had a theory—if the police keep their cool, then somehow this outward and visible tranquillity will be caught, rather like mumps, by the community at large, and everyone will be the better for it. Susan Cohen, who believed strongly in the authority conferred by a trim uniform, often wished that the tall, long-jawed, blond Mike could be forced into one.

It might, she thought, arouse him to at least the appearance of constabulary zeal. Now she cleared her throat and returned to her report.

"Breaking and entering summer cottages in Owls Head, four fender benders on Route 1, a brush fire in South Thomaston, and that motorcycle club harassing Camp Merrilark by South Hope Pond. And a painting has been taken from the Weymouth Island Library that was supposed to be by someone called Church, only it wasn't signed. Rachel Seaver, that's the librarian, and her sister, were away all day on the mainland for the dentist." Susan lowered her report sheet. "That Rachel, she is one tough cookie."

"I know," said Mike, who had barked his shins on Rachel Seaver before.

"Well, we found out that Sydney Prior—you know, that fat man with the gallery in Port Clyde—told Rachel to get the picture insured, and she said she wasn't going to waste money that way and that she'd never liked the painting much but it covered a big waterstain on the wall."

Mike reached for his art theft folder. "This whole stolen painting thing is driving me up the wall. I've got that Harrison Petty from the Godding on my back, and now Rachel Seaver. When life could be so simple." He sighed. "Now my real problem, Susie Q., is to choose between Halo Again and Spectacular Prince."

"I suppose those are horses," said Susan, who knew Mike's newest passion. "Well, I don't like either of those names."

"Just choose one."

"Then find a horse called Deputy, because I've got to get back to work. Sir," she added with no particular conviction.

Mike pulled his racing form from the drawer and ran his finger down the entries for the sixth race. There it was—Deputy's Boy by Deputy Minister. And look at those odds. Mike reached for the phone.

TWO

The Friday evening two days after Elspeth McKenzie had confronted her empty easel found her son, Dr. Alexander McKenzie, preparing for his summer vacation. It was the end of an exceedingly difficult hospital day, in which patients and staff had locked themselves into a contest as to who could be the most unreasonable, but now Weymouth Island stood on his horizon. He began rolling up his wool socks and pushing a disreputable collection of shirts and trousers into his old hockey duffle. This pleasant work he interrupted from time to time to dribble a pungent sauce of his own invention over pieces of chicken slowly baking in the oven.

Alex wasn't quite sure why Tina was coming for dinner. Had he asked her—after three Scotches—or had she invited herself after X number of martinis? That's what happens at large boring hospital parties. You eat too many little liver things wrapped in bacon and drink too much and start running off at the mouth, and pretty soon you're making dinner for some strange female when all you have in common is that she works where you do and goes to Maine in the summer. And now he remembered in a fuzzy kind of way some talk about Tina's car being in the garage and what a coincidence that they both were about to head down east for their holiday.

Alex, looking for an escape route, picked up the letter that had just come from his mother on Weymouth Island. That might do it. A mother's urgent letter. He was called away and would have to leave tonight. Right after dinner. Tina wouldn't be ready for that because she certainly wasn't going to arrive at his apartment with her suitcase. Was she? Damn, what *had* he said to her?

Alex, searching for one or two anxious sentences that could be read to Tina, unfolded the thin sheets heavily crossed with his mother's strong script. Unfortunately, she was more inclined to divagation than to entreaty. "Dearest Alex," it began, "Lots of news at this end . . ." and there followed a report of his sister's pregnancy, his youngest brother's summer job, his father's visit to Oslo, his cousin Giddy living with Roger Harwood, and inquiries about his own hospital work. Then came the matter that was obviously the *raison d'être* of the whole:

> . . . not that I've been robbed of any great work and I wasn't happy with the light, and even if it's a compliment, I'd rather have my painting back because it was my entry for this year's Godding show. So what I wonder is could you manage to be here by Monday because I know you did a bit of detecting during that wretched affair in Texas. That nice Mike Laaka is some sort of investigator deputy, but he and the police are quite dense when it comes to paintings. Of course, I know it's your vacation and you need a rest . . .

"Of course," said Alex, turning to the last page.

> . . . so I'll just borrow an hour or so of your time and then you can spend all your time sailing and bird watching. Both Gilchrist girls will be in the Moody cottage for August. Sandra seems unattached now, and, as I predicted, Heather has broken off with that cousin of the Abbotts.

And here Elspeth McKenzie spent several sentences on the need for an older person, "not old, Alex, but thirty-four is getting up there," to settle down and take a mate.

Well, not much in all that to send a loyal son hurtling out into the late Friday night Boston-to-Maine traffic, and Alex began to consider inventing a family medical problem when the buzzer from the outer door sounded. He pressed the release button and raced to check on the chicken.

The pieces of chicken, gleaming in a dark chestnut sauce, proved almost ready, and by the time Tina was being relieved of her suitcase and tennis racquet, Alex had someone else on his mind.

"Great getting a ride all the way to Maine," said Tina, who was fair of face and hair, strong and long of limb, and looked ready for action. "I've called Mother and she says you're to spend the night and go to the yacht club party Saturday night. We can use *Moondust* for the big race. God, it'll be heaven to be away from the hospital."

Alex smiled warmly—only the corners of his eyes suggesting colder weather—settled Tina in his one respectable chair, put a well-diluted martini in her hand, excused himself, went into the bedroom, and began putting in a call to Sarah Douglas Deane at her crowded and often noisy Port Clyde boarding house.

After a period of misunderstanding on the party line shared by Pete's Service Station, Alex heard an irritable voice say, "Yes, who? Okay, hold the line." There was a period of silence following competing cello and violin passages, and Alex hummed to himself until he heard Sarah's breathless "Hello."

"Catch your breath."

"What?" Sarah whispered.

"Is that you, Sarah? This is a terrible connection."

"Tony?"

"It's Alex. I'm not your brother or your father or your mother."

"Oh, Alex. Hi. How are you?"

"Do you have to whisper? Is someone listening in?"

"It's the quartet practicing. The Fagin String Quartet."

"Sarah, couldn't you have found a place with your own phone?"

"Pete's Service Station here," said a deep voice.

"Sarah?"

"Be nice to Pete's. They put my car back together every week. It's a party line. The telephone's next to the practice room so I have to whisper."

"I'll start again. Hello, Sarah. How are you? I miss you. Will you come and visit me . . . or us . . . my parents' house? On Weymouth?"

"But I'm still working at the Godding."

"Almost finished?"

"Yes, the catalogue is done and I'm being laid off after we get the show juried and hung. 'Terminated,' as Mr. Petty says."

"And then you'll come?"

"I guess I can. Yes, thank you very much. I mean after I've stayed a few days with my grandmother in Camden. She expects me."

"How about the fifteenth? That's a Friday," said Alex, consulting a wall calendar.

"It just stopped dead," said a worried female voice. "I'm stuck on Limerock Street in this fog. Maybe it's the transmission."

"What?" said Alex.

"That's Pete's again," said Sarah. "He does night emergencies."

"I give up," said Alex, "but I'm looking forward. Look, I'll see you then. On the dock at Port Clyde in time for the three o'clock ferry to Weymouth.

"I hope," said Alex, as he returned to his guest, "that you like well-cooked chicken."

Tina smiled and tossed her blunt-cut, never disordered blond hair away from her face. "It's hard to ruin chicken completely. So, Alex, did you hear about Mrs. Schuster?

She'd been out of the ICU for about ten minutes when all hell broke loose . . . and I suppose you can guess the rest, dammit. Down the tube."

Sarah climbed the stairs, the sounds of Beethoven draining away in the distance. So Alex had called after all, was coming back into her life again . . . or rather she was coming into Alex's life, the part about which she knew so little. He had told her that Weymouth was the summer pasture of the McKenzie clan, who had been spending time there practically since the first summer cottage went up. And, of course, she knew that Elspeth McKenzie was one of the Godding's invited artists.

Sarah had seen Alex off and on during the past winter and, since that trip to Texas a year ago, had maintained a warm but sisterly relationship with him. Keeping it light and easy. That was it. No pressure . . . a movie, a concert, a hike, a valentine with a dog on it, a new leash for Patsy. But as she toiled up the last few stairs to her bedroom, she turned her mind to the last piece of editing to be done before the show opened. She gathered the proofs of the errata sheets, the lists of works selected by the jury, and picked up her pencil.

* * *

"We have the last corrections," said Mrs. Ordway, as she and Sarah presented themselves before Mr. Petty's desk. "The printer will bind the errata sheets into the catalogue and ink out the titles of the stolen works." Here she paused and took note of the anguish on the director's face. He had lost the battle with several outspoken trustees, so that the catalogues were being repaired in the cheapest way possible. Really, Mrs. Ordway thought, he's not going to last. No meat on him at all. Just string and nerves.

"Did Elspeth McKenzie come through?" asked Mr. Petty, oblivious of the scrutiny that found him wanting.

"Mrs. McKenzie," said Mrs. Ordway severely, "will send in a watercolor called 'View of Portree.' That's Cornwall. It's being framed by Mr. Prior right now. And Roger Harwood left a huge oil titled 'Strong Walls.' The state prison."

"You should see it," said Sarah. "Like oatmeal with stripes."

Doris Ordway adjusted the tilt of her reading glasses, which were attached to a beaded chain hanging from her neck, and turned the page of her small notebook. "No painting from Nate Harwood. He came in two days ago while I was trying to serve the jury their lunch. In a terrible temper. He said he might have a substitute or he might not, and that he didn't turn out secondhand trash like some young so-called artists. I suppose he means Roger. It's too bad about those two, they used to be quite close. Perhaps Nate feels threatened. Anyway, nothing has come in. We can hope he skips the opening. He usually manages to pick a fight with half the membership."

"Dear, oh, dear. The man is a menace. Now let's see about the sculpture." Mr. Petty unfolded the first-floor plan of the museum on his desk and weighted the edges with four small votive figures. Sarah thought that they appeared to represent some kind of fertility gods or goddesses, and she wondered whether they also represented accomplished fact or only wishful thinking.

Mrs. Ordway indicated a page of jury selection titles. "It's too bad about that one, 'Maine Woods-Man and Timber.' The jury was unanimous but it's going to take up half the center gallery."

"Oh, my God," cried Mr. Petty. "What will we do? It's a complete space hog. George Segal by Disney World. Well, damn."

The sculpture, a vast assemblage of logs and plaster figures spattered with greens, chrome yellow, and umber, had been the subject of controversy for some days, and Mrs. Ordway had viewed it with disapproval since its delivery, but in the interest of harmony was glad to try and explain it to Mr. Petty.

"That central lump is a sort of lumberjack with a real ax

stuck in behind and the rest is just trees." Mrs. Ordway, whose literal view of art on the hoof had probably helped preserve her sanity these many years, added helpfully, "You can put it in the entrance hall and if you don't spotlight it, people may walk right past."

"Perhaps you're right," said Harrison. "Keep it dark, a mystery. The forest primeval."

" 'The murmuring pines and the hemlocks,' " said Sarah.

"Yes," said Mrs. Ordway, "we had it in eleventh grade."

But Mr. Petty, lacking a firm decision-making process of his own, now began to find the jury's unanimous vote irresistible. "I see it now. Mass against mass, challenging, impacting on the observer. The primitive forces of the forest and tool-using man. The wildwood."

Mrs. Ordway sidestepped the wildwood. "The price of lobster has gone up fifteen cents a pound. You'd better skip the Newburgh and have tuna fish."

* * *

Sunday morning was well advanced when Alex McKenzie came out onto the screened porch, settled himself in a decrepit rattan armchair, and surveyed the strip of ocean just visible through the stand of white pines. The dark trunks of the trees broke the horizontal line of green water, and in the field by the porch the flatheaded Queen Anne's Lace, the slender brush-topped hawkweed, and the spikes of evening primrose moved in the southwest wind in patterns of yellow and white. The sky was cobalt and almost cloudless, and the air was spicy with salt, bayberry, and fir balsam. Alex sighed with the peace given by a good night's sleep next to a tranquil ocean and a breakfast of hot, crisp, and savory things.

He could have wished that the big old shingled cottage had a wider view of the sea, but his mother said that if she had waves coming and going all day she wouldn't paint a stroke, it was too distracting. Alex's father, of a steadier temperament, had built his boathouse and study on a ledge over the stone beach and claimed that the ocean view helped his research into the Anglo-Saxon epics.

It was good to be back on the island, good to be away from the pressured world of medicine, good to put up one's feet and catch up on last month's magazines. Of course, his mother was still up to her game of trying to find herself a daughter-in-law and so add to the supply of grandchildren. She usually made a flank attack on the subject by reminding Alex of scenes of past family happiness, such as, "I remember when I was thirty-four. Your father and I took you four children to Nonquit for July because the swimming was so much warmer and you'd all had those sore throats. Remember? Kate and Ellen went to Camp White Oak and Angus cut his head on the wheelbarrow, and you joined that junior Audubon group, and I put you all into red striped bathing suits so I could keep track of you on the beach." His mother smiled at her firstborn, carried away by her memories, and murmured again, "And I was just your age."

Alex sat calm and firm. He knew that these nesting impulses on his behalf usually gave way to the pull of her current painting project. He also recalled the summer at Nonquit, but this did not stimulate a wish to father four children in red striped bathing suits, only the remembrance of a whopping case of poison ivy—face, arms, hands, and backside covered with blisters, calamine lotion, and sticky bandages.

His mother now came onto the porch holding an oversized coffee cup aloft with one hand and the skirt of her blue caftan with the other.

"Here's your second cup. It's so good to have you here, Alex." Elspeth placed herself at the end of a long cane settee and looked brightly at her son. And he smiled back, seeing that her white hair, which sprang from her head in little tufts and curls, was fastened back from her face with what was certainly the remnant of a man's foulard necktie. Elspeth believed that everything on earth had at least two uses, and since her husband, packing for his trip, had tossed his neckties around the bedroom . . . well, he had only himself to blame if one ended about his wife's brow.

An outsider studying the two would certainly have concluded that they were mother and son. But in the mother's face, the planes of the cheeks, the long thin mouth, the gray eyes were modified by age, by small explosions of wrinkles at strategic places, and by a loosening of skin on her neck and chin. With her, humor, pride, intelligence, deviousness, and patience had long since made their peace, and the face was all the stronger. On the son, the skin still stretched tight over the cheekbones and along the jaw, the hair was dark, almost black, and the heavy brows that rode high over the eyes were open, not slightly hooded as were the mother's. Only in the man's nose was there a departure from the maternal stamp. What was a slender but undeniable beak in the mother was aggressively straight in the son, suggesting the possibility of a paternal gene.

But mothers are blind and Elspeth, contemplating Alex, thought how much like John he looked, and then she thought of her husband, off in Oslo giving some incomprehensible seminar in Old English metrics and remembered he'd now been gone almost four weeks. Her eyes filled.

Alex, observing these symptoms, moved the subject to neutral ground. "What's up on the island? Any excitement besides having an art thief on the loose? Is Rachel Seaver still ruling the library?" Rachel, he knew, resigned with great ceremony every fall and returned every spring, she being the only one who understood the Rachel Seaver catalogue system and knew a nonreturner from a reliable borrower.

"Yes, Rachel's back but she's quite lame. Both she and Lyda on canes. And Rachel is absolutely furious about the library painting. I do wish burglars would stick to TV sets and the silver."

"Taking your painting is like making off with a child, isn't it?" said Alex, taking a long sip of coffee made the way he liked it, strong and milky.

"Exactly. It makes a hollow space." Elspeth indicated a

middle spot in her anatomy. "But I'm putting in that little watercolor I did at Portree last fall. Sydney is double-matting it in white, and I think it's going to be rather nice. I certainly hope you can help the police, because we'd all like our paintings back. Now how was the trip down? You must have come in late."

"I left Boston late Friday," said Alex, "and I gave a friend a lift and spent Friday at her house. And yes, Mother, the friend, Tina, is young, blond, handsome, and probably fertile. I see her around the hospital. Very efficient. Her parents offered me a bed and I accepted. But I'm not planning a wedding."

"Alex."

"Nor am I going to take the Gilchrist females sailing or bird-watching. Not my type. Besides I've got something in mind . . . quite different."

"How do you mean different? Married? Oh, Alex, I hope not."

"Different. Not like the Gilchrists. How would you and the Sealyhams like a visit from a full-grown male Irish wolfhound?"

Disappointed, Elspeth subsided on her settee. "A dog. Well, I suppose you can bring an Irish wolfhound, dear. It might be good for the Sealyhams. Stupid will love a male around, but Seymour may turn territorial and bite someone. You haven't gone and bought a big dog like that, not in that little apartment?"

Alex was enjoying himself. "No, I haven't bought a dog. Patsy will visit with his owner, who is right now finishing up a job at the Godding. She's Sarah Deane. I've known her for over a year. She was down in Texas during that murder investigation I've told you about. She's a fervent supporter of women's rights and lost animals. You should get along."

"Yes, Alex."

"And don't make noises like a brood hen or go on about children in striped bathing suits, or you'll frighten her right off the island."

"No, Alex."

"I just want her to relax, look around, enjoy herself. If Father gets home, they ought to have a fine time talking about the decline of language since *Beowulf*. She's doing graduate work and teaching at a day school in Boston."

His mother looked at her son from under her hooded eyes and smiled. "Yes, Alex."

THREE

August was well under way, the annual Seafood Festival faded thankfully from memory, and Knox County was beginning to crank up for the choosing of the Blueberry Princess and the upcoming Union Fair. The big coastal schooners, the *Adventure,* the *Stephen Taber,* the *Mattie,* the *Victory Chimes,* having picked up their new load of passengers (referred to in an unkindly way by the local people as "cattle") in Rockland and Camden, and pushed by the prevailing southwest wind, scattered among the islands of Muscongus and Penobscot Bays.

By the second week of August there was a sense that summer could end. The goldenrod spread through the fields, the children began to look at displays of school lunch boxes in store windows, and when an actress giving a recital at an outdoor theatre told her audience in a throaty voice that "summer's lease hath all too short a date," her listeners stirred in their seats and knew it was so.

For Giddy Lester, as August lengthened, so did her sense of frustration. The month was almost half gone and here she was laboring fruitlessly in the service of Sydney Prior and his gallery store. She now advanced toward her employer, clutching a stack of watercolor blocks and mat boards, and dumped them on the counter.

"Grace. Please. Hold the mat board by the edge. You know what fingerprints do to a surface," said Sydney Prior. "I can't think why your family started calling you Giddy. It's taken hold."

"It's into August, Mr. Prior, so I wish you'd teach me to cut the mats, and then I could do my own properly."

But Sydney Prior shook his head. He hadn't thought it would work, but Elspeth McKenzie told him that her niece wanted a summer job connected with art, and Elspeth was a neighbor on Weymouth and a valued customer. So here he was, stuck with Giddy, who with her big hands and her sheep-dog haircut, right over her eyes, reminded Sydney of an over-grown child, always bumping into some carefully arranged display.

"Grace, you know that my workshop is off limits," said Sydney, for, he felt, the hundredth time. "It's not personal. My customers are particular and I can't afford mistakes. I run on a very small profit margin."

Giddy didn't believe this. The markup on prints and art-ist's equipment seemed substantial, and as for the antiques in the Parlor Gallery—all those ship's paintings and Chinese tea sets—well, I bet he siphons off a bundle on that stuff, she thought, as Sydney, a large ovoid figure in his pale summer suit, made a stately progress to the front door of the shop and disappeared. Giddy, with a sigh, began to sort through the watercolor blocks, wishing she could afford the heavy French paper. Nothing was working out. Moving in with Roger had been a bummer, and now this, her first job in the art world, was turning into another. This world as represented by Prior's Art Gallery (Quality Art Supplies, Custom Framing, Fine Antiques and Works of Art) did not fit her mental picture of the place where artists gathered during the day and into the night, drinking espresso or ouzo and talking about tonalism and rectilinear mobilities and architectonic landscapes—all expressions that Giddy had heard, never quite understood, and yearned to discuss.

"I should have taken that job at summer camp teaching

basket making," said Giddy loudly and resentfully to a carved heron glued to a piece of driftwood.

"I told your Aunt Elspeth that this was not a glamour job," said Sydney, reappearing suddenly at the back of the shop. "You have a big responsibility just keeping the art supplies in order." Sydney had a habit of circling around and coming in through the back and finding Giddy daydreaming. "Now go into the storeroom and check on that order from Winsor and Newton and don't lose the packing slip." Here Sydney turned toward the door, and Giddy heard his dry little cough receding toward the Parlor Gallery. Although she was of an optimistic and equable nature, she felt again that the combination of Sydney Prior and Roger Harwood had done serious damage to her whole personality. Giddy shook her head, went into the storeroom, and began pulling at sealing tape.

*　*　*

On Monday the eleventh of August, Elspeth McKenzie, with a view to her coming houseguests, spread her red and blue diamond pattern quilt on the guest room bed and folded an old rug on the floor, together with a crock as a water dish for the expected dog. She noted, as she went about her affairs, that her son was more restless than she had seen him for some time, and these symptoms she regarded with interest.

Alex, at his mother's behest, spent Monday off-island, visiting the Rockland police station, calling on Mike Laaka in his basement office, and consulting with a host of antique and fine art dealers about the stolen paintings. "Probably out of state by now," he was assured on all sides. "Stolen art usually gets to a fence fast and is shot out of here in twenty-four hours."

The remaining days Alex filled with strenuous and repeated hikes about the five-mile perimeter of Weymouth Island, as if it were a confinement. He swam in the frigid waters of Tinker's Cove far out past the sheltering shoreline rocks, set up his telescope on the deck of his father's study, and marked the waves of shore birds flying back from their northern nesting grounds. He returned to the house, announcing ruddy turnstones, black-bellied plovers, a Caspian tern, and two pilot whales, and then told his mother that bird-watching was beginning to be a bore.

At intervals Elspeth appeared with a new mystery or a section of the *Boston Globe* and shook her head over him. She felt that at thirty-four a man should have learned how to relax even if an Irish wolfhound and its owner were impending. She found him now standing on the lawn gazing at the patch of ocean.

"I'm not really restless," said Alex crossly, as if in answer. "It's just that I'm wound up from the hospital routine and it's hard to unwind. I think I'll go for another swim."

"I know you may have given up bird-watching, but Rachel Seaver said someone saw a lark sparrow on the island. An immature."

"Too early for accidentals," said Alex. He was trying to wring the residual salty moisture from his bathing suit before putting it on again.

"Well, then," said Elspeth, casting about for another subject of interest, "did you know Marian Harwood's back on the island?" She settled herself in a lawn chair and reached for her knitting bag.

"I thought you said she'd finally left Nate."

"She did, but she came back on the late-afternoon boat last Friday. She's been staying with Rachel and Lyda, but because she's afraid of running into Nate, she's not going out anywhere."

"She's hiding out at Rachel's? Why? I mean Nate can be a real rat, but he wouldn't hurt her."

"He almost threw her out when she said she was going to leave him. Hardly time to take her own clothes. Just a few things tossed in a suitcase. It was lucky she had on her new navy blue she wears for funerals and weddings the day she

· 34 ·

left. Rachel was in the garden and heard Nate yelling about getting out and not even putting a finger on the island again. Told her to go back to North Haven, where she belongs with all those snobs. Rachel remembers those little details. That's why she's such a good librarian."

"Poor old Marian. Life of the doormat."

"Well, the doormat stood up for a change, and Nate called her all sorts of names . . . even a bastard, and I always think of bastards as being men. Fitz-somebody. But Marian certainly isn't a bastard, because she has that Boswell nose and the Cooper chin."

"Back on the track, Mother," said Alex, interested in spite of himself.

"We've got a plan, Rachel, Lyda, and I. We've almost had to force it on Marian because you know how passive she is, except for leaving Nate. It's a defense, of course, being a doormat. Anyway, we decided it was time for Marian to stand up and be a real person. Nate is going to all lengths, we've heard, to make sure that Marian doesn't get any sort of a settlement, and the cottage is in his name—never mind that Marian's father paid for it. The place is just stuffed with Boswell furniture and china, so it seemed just the time, with Nate being off somewhere, for Marian to get hold of the things that belong to her family."

"I see," said Alex. "You have a plan."

"Rachel's worked it out. Marian is to lie low, not letting Nate know where she is, and then when it's safe, she will sneak over to her cottage."

"For God's sake, Mother, how do you know Nate won't turn up and haul you all into court?"

"We're taking precautions. Rachel's acting as lookout from their garden and Lyda will watch the road from the post office with her binoculars, and they both have whistles."

"One if by land and two if by sea?"

"Exactly. And three if by air—the seaplane."

"Organized crime comes to Weymouth," said Alex, now highly amused. He abandoned his bathing suit and lowered himself into an old canvas folding lawn chair with a canopy top, the whole of which was apt to buckle and trap its victim without warning.

"We've told Marian to be very sure to take only those things that came from her family. There's the desk and the green tea set from Edinburgh."

"You mean Marian Harwood has been trotting back and forth with tea sets?"

"You've no idea how we've had to push her on this. She was quite willing when Rachel saw her last Friday in Rockland, but now she seems to have a bad case of cold feet."

"Well, I've never thought of Marian as a double-oh-seven."

"Of course," said Elspeth, "no one should keep valuables in a summer cottage because you see how easy it is to take anything, and we won't let her go entirely alone."

"Oh, certainly not."

"I'll give a hand, but for the furniture we'll need a man."

"No, you don't. You all can run around and blow whistles and break and enter, but not me."

"I've already promised you. Rachel and Lyda are much too frail, I have that nasty back, and though Marian is very strong, she's not Superwoman."

"Unpromise me and forget the whole thing. You're asking for trouble."

"I've tried to make it clear, we're Marian's old friends and neighbors helping her move."

"And I'm not one of the moving men. Let Marian's lawyer settle who owns what."

"Do you want to know where the lark sparrow was seen?"

"Who confirmed it?"

"I couldn't say." His mother held up her knitting and began counting stitches.

"Okay. Okay. I'll probably lose my license for committing a felony. Where is this sparrow?"

"Mr. Bartbury from the Audubon saw it down next to the old ice house."

"Thank you, Mother." Alex sat up abruptly and was promptly grabbed by the chair, which folded neatly under him, bringing the canopy down over his head.

"Shit."

"I didn't hear that," said his mother. "And be ready by six-thirty tonight and wear gloves. We're being careful about fingerprints."

FOUR

Giddy Lester felt the Godding show would provide the only bright spot in a stale and unprofitable summer. She had found out early on Tuesday that her sepia-and-wash sketch of cormorants lined up on an ocean ledge had made it through the jury and was now hanging with the works of other notables of the artist community. This triumph, however, when reported by Giddy to Roger on a chance meeting in Port Clyde, did nothing to reconcile them to each other. Roger, whose state prison abstract had been hung in a dark corner of a far gallery, only looked daggers and departed without speaking. Then and there Giddy decided that not only should she be quit for good of Roger, but it might be a good idea to cut loose from Sydney Prior. She could stay on Weymouth with the McKenzies—Aunt Elspeth and Alex always seemed glad to see her.

The fever of preparation at the museum left Sarah Deane little time to think about her coming visit to Weymouth Island, but when she did, it was not Alex, but his mother, she thought about. She sounded formidable. "My mother looks like a benevolent hawk with white hair," Alex had said last winter, and now Sarah found this less than reassuring. However, as the show day drew close, she found hardly time to breathe, let alone worry about maternal raptors. It seemed to her that an octopus on roller skates would have been hard put to keep up with the crises generated at the Godding. As typist, copy editor, and handmaid, she raced about unpacking catalogues, checking labels, lists, prices, and fending off artists whose works either were rejected or were thought to be hung in unsuitable places. She helped suspend yellow and black banners from the ornate portico, typed publicity releases, coped with visitations from the local critics, and conferred with the plumber about the museum's balky septic tank.

Interference from Harrison Petty was a major annoyance. The director, sure that his opinion was indispensable, rushed about with revisions and corrections and new ideas for picture placement, bumped into a full tray of champagne goblets with ghastly results, and sent the caterer wild by a last-minute doubling of the Newburgh order and the substitution of pastry shells for toast points. But in the last hours Mrs. Ordway and Mr. Petty gave up confronting each other on the unhappy subject of stolen paintings and altered catalogues and began to pull together out of the troubled waters toward the Wednesday gala reception and dinner—that is to say that Mrs. Ordway kept her head and rowed with a steady oar and Mr. Petty caught crabs.

To everyone's surprise the long-awaited affair went off with a remarkable degree of smoothness; this was attributed variously to the lobster Newburgh, the champagne, the Fagin String Quartet's sticking to Mozart (with interlacings of Haydn and Vivaldi), and the absence of Nate Harwood. Nate had not sent in a substitute painting, and his nonappearance gave rise to a collective sigh of relief. Roger Harwood had also given it a pass, perhaps to protest the location of his entry. Elspeth McKenzie, too, missed the dinner, staying sensibly at home cutting up haddock, potatoes, and onions for her fish chowder. She had learned from her friend Mrs. Ordway that her watercolor of the Cornish coast had won the Asa Godding award for a painting that did not reflect a New England subject—Asa being the Godding family renegade, who spent his mature years drinking his way from one European city to another and finally returning home in time to drink up a sizable part of the Godding shipbuilding fortune.

Meanwhile, untouched by the goings on at the Godding, Deputy Investigator Mike Laaka faced yet another report of a missing painting. This came as a letter from one Miss Ruth Baker of Winfield, Missouri, thanking him for his expression of sympathy on the death of her parents in the automobile drowning accident and the package of their personal effects he had sent. These, Miss Baker pointed out, should have included an oil painting—a seascape—that her parents had written about in their last letter. "I will be in Maine as soon as possible," she concluded, "to find out about this, and I hope I will have the full cooperation of the police." Mike groaned. August was enough of a zoo without these continual intrusions from the art world, and now he had heaped on him the arrival of a bereaved and possibly angry Ruth Baker. He would have to cancel his weekend at Saratoga and miss the Sanford Stakes. A hot two-year-old, Felony by No Robbery, looked like a sure thing for a betting detective.

* * *

Sarah, exhausted by her efforts for the Godding opening, found that being without a job was not so painful as she had expected. She had packed her things at the boarding house on Wednesday morning before the great event, said goodbye to Mr. Petty, who thanked her in a distracted way, and nodded agreement when Mrs. Ordway wished her sunshine and good salt air.

The next few days at her Grandmother Douglas's large, partly closed house in Camden could hardly be called a period of repose. Her tiny eighty-eight-year-old grandmother, fragile in body, strong in spirit, kept to a regime established sixty years before, and Sarah found herself alternating heavy meals in a gloomy dining room with long sessions of reading aloud from *The Heart of Midlothian* and the more complicated books of the Old Testament.

Finally, on Friday, Sarah bade her grandmother good-bye and submitted to an examination of her vacation plans.

"This friend you propose to visit?"

Sarah had been waiting for this. Her grandmother, Edwardian born but a Victorian by preference, seldom allowed for any subsequent social developments. "Alexander McKenzie. He's a physician."

"I would not call that a recommendation, Sarah. Will you be staying alone at his house?"

"Grandmother, I'm twenty-seven and Alex is thirty-four."

"That is hardly an answer, but it is certainly time you were settled, because living with a large dog, teaching other people's children, is not what I call settled. Now is this Dr. McKenzie related to the Weymouth McKenzies? Elspeth, although much younger, is a friend. We have worked for the Godding. Her father was a Sinclair."

Sarah gave in. There was no point in having a face-off with the nineteenth century, and her grandmother was sounding more and more like Lady Bracknell. Sarah reassured her on as many points as possible, settled her grandmother in her bedroom, kissed the soft white cheek, rescued Patsy from a life of starchy handouts under the kitchen table, and set off.

Feeling an entirely unaccustomed sense of freedom, she drove slowly down the long tree-shaded back road to Rockport, past a field dotted with black and white belted Galloway cattle looking like carved toys against the bright green of the pasture, then curved around Rockport Harbor and over the bridge to Pascal Avenue. She checked her watch. Just past one-thirty. Plenty of time before the three o'clock boat. I wonder, she thought, what kind of present you take to someone's mother who is an artist and is described as looking like a hawk. Wine, sherry? Or did "McKenzie" mean Presbyterian abstinence? How about cheese? Yes, cheese was always safe. And then Sarah, driving slowly toward Route 1, saw the yellow and black banners hanging from the Godding portico and the building seemed to beckon like a fat, gaily bedecked old friend. Why not? Go in and see the show as it was meant to be seen, as a visitor, a stranger. Sarah pulled her car under the shade of a chestnut tree for Patsy's comfort and set forth.

* * *

Elspeth McKenzie consulted her son over an early Friday morning breakfast. "Do you think plain old fish chowder is too dull for dinner? I'm having salad and biscuits, and perhaps baked tomatoes."

Alex began to be sorry that he had sprung Sarah on his mother at all. They could have gone somewhere else. "Sarah will eat anything," he said shortly.

"And my blueberry buckle with the foam sauce or cottage pudding?"

"Sarah won't be expecting any great production. You'll make her uncomfortable."

"I always like to make a small special effort for a guest," said Elspeth. "And now, Alex, tonight Marian will need help with the highboy."

"No way. Last night was it. Besides, I didn't sense that Marian was one bit happy with all your efforts."

"The highboy was her grandfather's. Eban Boswell. Bird's-eye maple with a shell pattern. Alex, it's in for a penny, in for a sheep, or whatever the saying is. You're committed now. We'll take out the drawers and pack them with the Staffordshire."

"Where are you going to put it all? Look at that thing. It's taking up half the kitchen." Alex pointed to a Hepplewhite desk that he and Marian had wrestled into the kitchen the night before and that now stood in the corner shrouded in a poncho.

But Elspeth only smiled and began busying herself with the breakfast things, piling cups and plates into a large dishpan. "Don't go without the list," she called as Alex moved toward the door. "About six bottles of white wine, nothing fancy. California and dry. And ten pounds of sunflower seeds for the feeder, and Rachel says the library package—the used books from the sale—is ready at the church."

Alex began to object but then remembered that the penalty for leaving the island was that the return was always weighted with merchandise. He picked up his binoculars, a necessity on any pelagic trip no matter how short, hung a wool sweater over his shoulders, and turned at the door.

"No to the highboy," he called, and started down the path before his mother could regroup.

Once landed in Port Clyde, Alex devoted that Friday morning almost entirely to the intricacies of art theft. He had caught Sydney Prior opening his shop and, as an old acquaintance, was ushered directly into the Parlor Gallery for coffee and to hear Sydney's opinion on the local art world in general and art thieves in particular. The Parlor Gallery—actually three long rooms that opened into each other—reminded Alex strongly of the shop of Kim's mentor, Lurgan Sahib, with its profusion of rich and glowing and curious objects. Red, blue, green, wheat, crimson patterned carpets succeeded each other; walnut, mahogany, tiger maple, tables, chests, chairs, shone with reflected brown light; and in clusters on polished surfaces, silver tureens and samovars, the blue, red, and gold of Imari, the white of Chelsea, the blue and white of Staffordshire, and then a parade of stone china in salmon red and royal blue. The walls were covered, but not overwhelmed, with several small tapestries, marine oils in gold frames, and a line of sporting prints with strangely elongated jockeys and arch-necked horses—Troubadour, Firenze, Ben Brush, Imp—and set against the windows, luminous with the morning light, a succession of jade-green sandwich-glass candlesticks.

Sydney handed Alex a coffee cup and leaned anxiously forward from a Queen Anne chair. "Of course, I've suffered several losses myself, ones I could ill afford."

"Have you?" said Alex. "I didn't know you were a victim, too."

"Oh, in my business you expect it. Professionals and, of

course, light-fingered customers . . . though I do try and screen them before I bring them into the Parlor Gallery. But who knows? Perhaps they were evening break-ins. A ship's oil, a barkentine off Beachy Head." Sydney gestured at the fire-place, where there was an undeniable gap over the mantel. "Quite valuable. These extended Cape houses are easy to get into and no alarm system is infallible. Mine is always going off when I don't want it to. Besides, I'm open all day, completely vulnerable . . . " Sydney's voice trailed off mournfully.

"Have you reported what you lost?"

"I'm making up a list, but this happens all the time. I have my own methods of investigation. We dealers exchange infor-mation, advertise in the trade journals. And, naturally, I don't want my fine arts insurance to go one dollar higher. So annoy-ing. Acquisitions over which one has labored."

"You'd better tell the police everything," said Alex.

Sydney ran one finger over the glossy surface of a Shera-ton inlaid card table next to his chair, frowned at some invisi-ble imperfection, and shook his head. "It's difficult, my dear Alex. No thief in his right mind would allow his stolen goods to remain in Maine. Any piece of real importance shoots out to Dallas, Chicago, Miami, the West Coast." Sydney leaned gingerly back in his chair. "Do tell your mother we missed her at the opening. Her prize was well-deserved. A charming watercolor. All in all, quite an affair. But too expensive by far. Imagine! Lobster and a catalogue with color reproductions. Someone should tell Harrison that the Godding is not located in Boston. We are a modest community." And here Sydney let his glance rest affectionately on a Chippendale slant-front desk.

"Of course," he added, seeing Alex's expression, "by modest I don't refer to quality. Quality is always available in this area. The Godding—and this is between the two of us— is not quality. It is very small potatoes. And under Harrison, I'm afraid it will become smaller. Why, I can remember a time . . . " Sydney was off at a gallop, and Alex, an expert at fast exits, said he must be off, stood up, and, followed by

Sydney, sidestepped a table with an alabaster chess set in its center and made his way through the long passage to the shop in front. There, catching sight of the straw-thatch head of his cousin Giddy, who was disemboweling a large carton, Alex waved. "Coming over to see us?"

"How's Giddy doing?" asked Alex, as Sydney padded along with him to his car.

"I took Giddy as a favor to your mother, to whom I can refuse nothing. But her mind is not on the work, and I tremble at the idea of her in my workshop or the Parlor Gallery."

"That's too bad," said Alex. "Giddy may be a little on the casual side, but I've always enjoyed being with her."

Sydney shrugged. "Oh, well, I'll try to muddle along with her, but my nerves are at their absolute limit, and I have this little cough . . . "

But Alex, seeing a medical trap ahead, shook hands and said that the police were waiting.

* * *

Mike Laaka and Alex had played together as boys and had marched through seventh grade as best friends, breaking Mr. Laaka's barn chamber window with green apples, going off on clandestine fishing trips out past Rockport Harbor in Mike's leaky skiff, and together winning the eighth-grade science prize with a model solar-heated outhouse. But then Alex had gone off to school in Massachusetts and on to college and medical school, and Mike, after finishing high school and a course at the police academy, had taken up a law enforcement career with the Sheriff's Department.

"How do, Alex," said Mike. He closed a small green booklet with the title "North American Graded Stakes." "Well, I suppose you've come to talk arts and crafts again."

"That's right," said Alex, pulling over a chair.

"Told you the stuff's probably been bought and sold twice over."

"Any pattern showing up?"

"Nope. Nothing we can count on. Things have been taken any old time of day around the county. The objects stolen, they're usually small, portable, and valuable. The paintings? No pattern. Thieves aren't specializing, like taking only old ones or new ones or going in for landscapes or bowls of fruit. Seems to quiet down in the winter, except for a few big heists . . . mostly silver, furniture, china then. Hell, the only pattern I can see is that in summer the thieves don't do a clean sweep. One or two things and leave the rest."

"And this summer?" said Alex.

"Let's see." Mike whirled his chair around and rolled himself over to a low cabinet supporting a framed photograph of Secretariat winning the Belmont. He cautiously extracted a folder from a drawer and closed it gently. "Okay, early July. Couple of examples. Tenants Harbor: eighteenth-century ladle, porringer, eight spoons, and a strawberry set. Special forks just for eating strawberries. Would you credit that? And paintings: two framed family portraits, a sea captain and his missus. The owners had just inherited the pair from an uncle, and they didn't have a photograph. They'd been scheduled for a trip to Portland to be appraised. Then from Friendship, an oil done by the lady of the house. Just been finished and framed. She's well-known in Philadelphia circles, it says here. Again, no photos available. But in the same house the thief walked right by this other famous picture."

"What famous picture? If you don't mind telling me. I don't want to muscle in."

"Muscle on in. I don't know one painting from another. Sculpture. That's what I like. Something you can get your hands on." Mike rustled around in the folder. "Here you are. List of paintings *not* taken. Albert—no, that's Albrecht Dürer, with two little dots over the *u*. 'Virgin and Child with St. John.' A woodcut about eight by twelve inches. Little thing. Would've been easy to lift."

"But not easy to get rid of. That's a real treasure. Is it genuine?"

"That one has been appraised, documented, and authenticated. Sydney Prior was one of the experts, and the owner said that Sydney suggested an alarm system, but they didn't get around to it. Anyway, the Dürer is safe. Then there's the Weymouth Library's marine oil that might have been by this Frederic Church. Not much info there. Rachel Seaver says it was the gift of an anonymous donor and she never liked it. Taken when she and Lyda were off for the day at the dentist —a fact known far and wide because they called for a taxi a week in advance and alerted all their friends on the mainland."

"So what do you think? All separate hits by separate people?"

"Who's to say? No evidence left around. No prints. No big search-and-destroy scene . . . you know, drawers dumped, desks ransacked. Just a few things gone in each house. Look at Roger Harwood's report. Only his new painting taken, and the thieves left all his other stuff, like that big prize winner called 'Grange Supper.' "

"And father Harwood, only one picture taken?"

"Right, a selective thief. Like Roger's, it's this year's entry for the Godding. And one from the library, which has another oil and two watercolors. So put your gray cells to work, Alex, because I hear you're one whiz of a detective, Texas style."

"Who in hell have you been talking to?"

"You have a proud mama."

"I'll fix her. I don't advertise that adventure. I had a lot of help and we got lucky." Alex stood up. "So, shall I tell my mother you're hot on the trail?"

"I'm colder than a mackerel. The summer's been wild, traffic crunches, drunks racking themselves up, people driving into the harbor . . . and yes, wait up, Alex. One more thing. Another painting missing, maybe. Daughter of this old couple who drove off Lloyd's Wharf in Port Clyde back in July claims her parents bought a painting, and that it was missing from the personal effects we mailed to her."

"This was an accidental death?"

"Oh, hell, yes. And the painting—if there really was one
—may have just floated out of the car when the bodies were
removed and then gone out with the tide. No records found
in the car or on the bodies. The daughter's due any day now.
Hope there's nothing to her story. I've had it up to here with
art. Now can I interest you in the sixth race at Saratoga? Nine
furlongs for fillies and mares, and Terra Affirma has won her
last three starts."

"Lord, Mike, you're really into this. Two years ago it was
golf."

"Keeps my mind off crime." Mike grinned. "I'm a peaceful man. And horses are it now. I fell in love with one called
Adored. Just love to watch those sweethearts head for home."

Alex, driving down Route 1, reflected that had a horse been
stolen from the local citizenry, Mike might have conducted his
investigation with more enthusiasm. Then, turning down Pascal Avenue, he pulled his elderly red Volvo up in front of the
Godding and noted a familiar gray-bearded animal filling the
driver's seat of the VW bug parked under a tree.

"Hello, Patsy, old boy." Alex reached through the open
window and submitted to a vigorous washing of his hand and
forearm. Then, breaking into a run, he caught up with Sarah,
a slim figure in a red and blue cotton skirt and white blouse.
She stood in the front hall of the museum, confronting a vast
assemblage of planks and plaster whose label claimed that it
stood for the spirit of the the Maine woods.

"And what does that say to you, Ms. Deane?" Alex
touched Sarah lightly on the shoulder.

Sarah jumped. "Alex. You came out of nowhere." She
gave him a quick kiss and then pointed to the sculpture. "The
judges thought it was powerful."

"Meaning it could kill you if it fell on you?"

"It certainly needs more room."

"Like Fenway Park?"

"Or Mount Katahdin. I just came in here to use up time
before the boat. Besides, I haven't seen the whole show put

together. Just the chaos beforehand. Have you come to see your mother's picture, and does she like cheese?"

"Yes, to both. After we've cased the show, I'll help you through the rigors of the sea voyage."

"I can certainly use some fresh air," said Sarah. "That gallery job was murder. I galloped up and down three flights of stairs all day, and then visiting Grandmother Douglas isn't exactly a rest cure. I mean she's a wonderful person, but nothing has ever changed in that house."

Alex smiled and gave Sarah a quick and not entirely professional rundown. "You look as if you weigh about fifty pounds. We'll feed you up. Mother's mixing up a fish chowder and some sort of blueberry thing. My father's away, so she needs to hover and nourish. Patsy will be a great stimulant." He pointed to an arched opening. "Let's look for Mother's watercolor. She's won a prize she's trying to be humble about, and then she's one of the stolen artists . . . very select company. Have you heard about the goings-on in the local art world . . . besides the Godding entries?"

Sarah expressed interest, and Alex described his morning activities as they moved toward an inner gallery. He finished by saying, "I'm no great wonder as a detective, as you have every reason to know, but I thought we could look through some galleries on rainy days."

"That might be fun, although I should really be trying to pick up at least a part-time job for the next few weeks. I'm short of cash, and I have to start classes at B.U. by the middle of September. So you see, I can only come for a very short visit."

"Don't be foolish. As you said, July has taken its toll. You need sea bathing and fortified biscuits, and I need a companion."

Sarah, who was inspecting a large sculpture of what appeared to be a badly crushed 1950 Buick, turned to Alex. "Okay, I'll help you track down the family treasures and look for a job at the same time. Maybe one of the shops can use an untrained helper."

Alex nodded and drew Sarah's attention to a pen and wash. "It's my cousin Giddy's. I like the way she's done those cormorants. Marvelous profiles. They always look so sure of themselves."

"Which reminds me," said Sarah, "I know you're an incurable bird-watcher, is your mother?" She wondered if she could survive many days of intense bird-watching.

"Off and on. Mostly she paints. Right now she's into burglary as a sideline. We're both invited. Ever steal a highboy?"

"Not yet I haven't. Oh, look. Here's your mother's." Sarah pointed, and they both walked up to a small watercolor. Abrupt squares of white houses with orange roofs hung along dark ledges and cliffs—bold slashes of umber and sienna—and below wide dancing strokes of green and ultramarine sea. The picture was double-matted in cream board, giving a depth and distance to the scene, and the narrow silver metal frame held the whole in a timeless moment of sunlit coast.

"Oh, I like it very much," said Sarah.

Alex stepped back and squinted at the picture. "Yes, I think she's brought it off. Sydney did a good job with the framing."

"Who?"

"Sydney Prior. He owns the best art supply shop hereabouts, plus an antique trap. Says he's had some things stolen, too."

Sarah moved down to a darker end of the room and then stopped in front of a tall oil. "Here's one of the substitutes." She backed away. "It doesn't improve at a distance."

Alex peered at the title. " 'Strong Bars.' God, it's Roger Harwood. This must be a new style. Marian Harwood's son," he explained. "She of the highboy we're going to steal. So is that enough? I've seen Mother's painting, and I've found you. Shall we show Patsy the ocean? It's almost low tide. He can wallow in the mud flats."

Sarah, following Alex's car, turned south on Route 1 and then turned again and drove along the east bank of the St.

George River, which ran green and wide, its surface whipped into tiny waves by a fresh southwest wind. She was suddenly filled with a sense of well-being and the special excitement that comes when the first day of vacation coincides with perfect weather.

"A great day for a sea voyage," she said, reaching over and ruffling the coarse fur around Patsy's neck. But now Alex shot far ahead and she had to concentrate on keeping up along the curving road to Port Clyde and a parking spot over the hill from the town docks.

"Place is a nightmare in the summer," said Alex. "All the island people scattering their cars all over the place. Now I've got a few errands." He pulled a crumpled list from his pocket.

"I'll try the general store for your mother's cheese," said Sarah, "and then I'll look around in some of the shops."

"In no shop will Patsy be welcome. I'll take him and meet you back on the Weymouth boat dock in half an hour."

It was still fifteen minutes to departure time when Alex galloped up to Sarah and dumped his packages at her feet.

"Have you seen Patsy?"

"No," said Sarah, alarmed, "you had him."

"He got untied at the church where I was picking up books."

"Well," said Sarah, "he's hard to miss. I'll go across and check the waterfront, and you do the parking lot and the street."

At three minutes to boat time, Alex saw Sarah run down the length of the wharf, followed by a black and dripping beast. Patsy, distinguished only by eyes and his teeth, in which he clenched a muddy piece of something, had indeed enjoyed a good wallow and roll in the low-tide beach. A large quantity of this mud he had transferred in several hardy shakes to Sarah upon their reunion. For those unfamiliar with the dark rich quality of flats mud, it is enough to say that it is a cross between blue-black soup and tar and has some of the latter's adhesive qualities.

"Hello," said Alex. "Joy in Mudville. What on earth has Patsy got?"

"Aren't we lovely? Patsy has a trophy. I can't tell what it is because he won't let go." Sarah wiped her face with her sleeve, leaving an inky smear across her cheek. "I hope your mother's tolerant."

"She'll be glad to show you the best places in our cove for you and Patsy to have your ocean dip. The water is very bracing."

"I can imagine." Sarah gathered Patsy close and picked up her canvas bag with one mud-splashed hand. "When we were little and spending summers with Grandma, we had to take bracing swims every day. There was a forfeit if you didn't swim ten strokes."

"A sound woman," said Alex. "The boat's loading. Let's try and find a place in the bow. Small craft warnings are up and the wind's switching around to the northeast, so we should get there in a hurry."

"Why," asked Sarah, as she followed Alex down the gangplank of the *Robin Day*, "do people think cold water is morally good? Grandmother Douglas thinks the temperature in Maine is regulated directly by God."

Alex, arms full of packages, shouldered his way toward the bow. "Cold water keeps the devil at bay."

"And doth make cowards of us all or something like that," said Sarah, coming to rest against the bow rail.

"Do you think," said Alex, looking with distaste at the blackened dog, "that Patsy will yield up that object for an honorable burial at sea?"

"You try. He just hangs on and growls."

This proved to be the case, and after a losing tug-of-war, in which Patsy backed into two passengers in pale summer dresses, Alex gave up and leaned over the rail, and Sarah felt the throb of the engine under her, saw the last of the docking lines heaved off, watched the black water swirl and foam away from the hull as the *Robin Day* slipped away from the dock, and then, looking up, saw the gulls rise and soar overhead.

"Here we go," said Alex, his face lit with a half smile, the sort of smile, Sarah thought, that says *I'm going home.*

As if in answer, he said, "There've been McKenzies and their ilk going out of this harbor for years. We haven't always been summer people. My father's family came from Nova Scotia and my mother's from Scotland, and on both sides they married into people living around the Port Clyde area. That's Marshall Point Lighthouse on your left and Hupper Island off to starboard, but the old charts of 1788 show it as Muse or Mouse Island . . . now we're going through Lobster Fare or Herring Gut . . . must be a million Herring Guts in Maine. Port Clyde used to be one. That's Hart Island off the port bow."

Sarah nodded. Alex sounded like some sort of seagoing conductor calling off islands instead of stations.

"Now we'll go between Old Horse Ledge and the Sisters —they're clear enough now, you can see the surf breaking, but watch out when the fog comes in. That's McGee and Barter Island over on your right."

"Look at the lobster pot buoys," said Sarah. "Like confetti. More every year and, I suppose, fewer lobsters."

"It's a circle, more equals less, less equals more. Here's Thompson and Davis Island and Allen coming up. We'll slip between Burnt and Allen Islands. If you believe some of the records, Captain Weymouth settled down on Allen for a couple of months in 1605."

"But the people on Weymouth don't believe it?"

"Oh, they'll allow that the captain made it to Allen, all right, but only after he'd spent a night or so at Sailor's Cove on Weymouth. Monhegan has its claims, too, but all good Weymouth citizens know in their hearts that they were first."

"How about the Vikings . . . long before 1605?"

"Weymouth claims Vikings, too. We're a greedy lot. Now look ahead for Old Woman Ledge on your starboard. And there's Weymouth, just past the whistle buoy."

Sarah, braced on the rolling deck, saw the rising headland of Weymouth, watched the terns swoop to the water, counted two porpoises rolling off to port, and, looking over the rail, saw the lobster buoys bob past the bow, and then she looked at the horizon and began to consider the coming visit to Weymouth Island.

* * *

Her skin tingling from a plunge in the ocean followed by a warm shower, Sarah sat on a drift log at the little pebble beach of Tinker's Cove hard by the McKenzie boat-house. Patsy, in a like condition of cleanliness, sat beside her, his gray coat fluffed and drying in the late-afternoon sun and freshening breeze. Across his paws, in safe harbor, lay his trophy from the Port Clyde mud flats—now revealed after rinsing to be a much worn man's felt hat. Every now and then Patsy snapped at a deerfly or Sarah absentmindedly rubbed his ears, but otherwise the two were at peace.

Sarah reflected upon the past few hours. She had meant to drift into the McKenzie domain in a cool, detached sort of way, just a passing friend of Alex's, a woman of the world stopping for a summer weekend. But with her arrival in a windblown and mud-speckled state, she might just as well have come wearing a child's shirt and camp shorts with a tag around her neck saying, "Please wash me." And Alex's mother—a puzzle there. In Sarah's experience, mothers of marriage-age sons—be the sons ever so mature—reacted in one of two ways on beholding possible wife material. Either they became dangerously gracious while flashing signs saying, "Get lost, you aren't good enough for my splendid, clever son," or they puffed up like female quails and rushed the candidate about the house showing off family treasures. But Elspeth McKenzie had not yet revealed herself, speaking mostly of the Godding show and fish chowder. Nevertheless, although her tall angular figure contradicted the idea, her energy in the matter of towels and soap suggested she might turn into a quail.

The fact was that Sarah had not allowed herself, through

a rather difficult winter of teaching, to weigh her feelings about Alex or to ask herself how much her peace and happiness depended on his concern. Both the death of Pres, the love of her undergraduate years, and the loss of careful, kind, cautious Philip last year had urged the wisdom of hanging loose. She had had grand plans of giving up her teaching job at the day school, her master's program at Boston University, and sallying forth to minister to a suffering humanity—in what capacity was never clear—and finding her own stability and selfhood thereby. But reality, in the form of her signed teaching contract, the acceptance of her thesis proposal, and the presence of her adopted Irish wolfhound had all said no to change, and Sarah had, rather shamefacedly, settled back into her well-worn and sometimes lonely groove.

She picked up a small stone, crusted with orange lichen, turned it over and ran her thumb across the rough surface, and then tossed it into the small waves as they came hissing up over the stones. How long should she stay? She remembered the universal truth that fish and guests smell after three days. Besides, it looked like a storm coming up, the sky to the east was peculiar, the water was turning to slate, and there had been talk on the ferry of one of those hurricanes—Ginevra, wasn't it?—hitting this part of the coast. No one wanted a guest lingering in bad weather. Sarah picked up another larger stone at random and turned it over in her hand. Soon she would be back at Smith-Weston School teaching English —*Silas Marner*, *The Scarlet Letter*, the topic sentence and the paragraph. How safe. How dull. Sarah hurled her stone at the Atlantic Ocean.

A shadow fell over her shoulder, and Patsy gave a pleased whine.

"That stone was thrown with a certain amount of urgency. Something wrong. Has my mother been clucking over you?"

"No," said Sarah. "It's school coming up so soon. And your mother was quite nice about the mud."

"Oh, she's used to it. Seymour and Stupid are always

ending in the drink." Alex sat down on the log next to Sarah. "Patsy's still got his hat."

"Yes, I had to wash it while he held it in his teeth. Are you really going ahead with this highboy thing?"

"I finally said yes. If I don't help, I'll have slipped disks and wrenched knees and concussed ladies to deal with."

"Well, I'm game . . . I guess. But what's it all about?"

"Come on back to the house and I'll tell you." And as they slowly made their way up the path, Alex gave Sarah a sketch of the life and times of Marian and Nate Harwood, adding, "He's one of the world's growlers, and Marian has spent her life being trodden on. My mother and her neighbors, Rachel and Lyda, seem to think this project will develop backbone in Marian—something I doubt. Anyway, we go into action after dark. Rachel and Lyda to stand guard."

"Honestly, Alex, you're all crazy. It's Gilbert and Sullivan. *The Pirates.* I think island living has gone to everyone's head. But I do like your house here, though it's no cottage."

"Everything on the coast inhabited by summer people that's not a barn or a castle or a fish house is a camp or a cottage, be it ever so oversize," said Alex, gesturing at the weathered shingle McKenzie structure that rose up, extended out, bulged here, recessed there in true New England summer style.

It was just after nine o'clock that night when Sarah found herself, in the company of Elspeth McKenzie, Marian Harwood, and Alex, stumbling over a long sloping fold of granite, carrying one end of a maple highboy, its loot-filled drawers having been carried over earlier. From time to time Alex sang in a low voice, " 'With cat-like tread/ Upon our prey we steal/ In silence dread/ Our cautious way we feel,' " and Elspeth and Sarah joined softly in the chorus. Marian Harwood, however, was entirely quiet, and Sarah thought she hardly seemed to care in which direction the furniture traveled.

Set upright in the McKenzies' crowded storage room off the kitchen, even in the dim light the highboy was a handsome piece, of the quality and condition that excite antique dealers.

"It *is* beautiful," said Sarah, running her finger along the honey-colored wood. "It feels like satin."

Marian Harwood stood up straight and dusted off the front of her blouse. She was a short sturdy woman with a square face and a bush of gray-brown hair that looked like a kind of fur muff and did nothing to define the head beneath. And curiously for a woman who had led what Sarah had been told was a badgered and unhappy life, her face was unlined, her cheeks were full and smooth, and her blue eyes bland. She looked years younger than Elspeth, although the difference in age could not have been too great—Alex had told Sarah that the Harwoods had a daughter over thirty living on the West Coast. Marian's voice, too, lacked inflection. Sarah, going back and forth between the two cottages, had had little conversations with her, and once when Sarah had admired a fine Wedgwood pitcher, Marian had said, "Yes, it's nice, isn't it," in the same voice in which one might admire a dress without any intention of buying it. She spoke always in a low voice and her remarks gave history, not significance. "My Grandfather Boswell inherited the chest from his uncle; the umbrella stand was in the hall next to the walnut table in Aunt Letitia's house; the green plates were for everyday." Sarah felt Marian needed a bolt of lightning to bring her awake.

"You did pack the blue bowl, didn't you, Marian? The one from the sideboard?" asked Elspeth, who was solicitously draping a sheet over the highboy.

"No," said Marian.

"Then it's sitting right there waiting for you," said Elspeth, sinking back in a wicker rocker. "Now one of us can go back, but I think it's good for you, Marian, to do some of these things entirely by yourself."

"I suppose so," said Marian. "Or we could forget the bowl."

"Of course not. But if you'd rather not, I suppose Alex . . . "

"No," said Marian. "I'll go." And in a moment she had disappeared, and Sarah could see her flashlight from the kitchen window as it bobbed over the path.

"I think Marian's going to come out of her shell," said Elspeth. "Before she left Nate, I've seen her sit for a whole evening and not say a word, and all this past week she's been very down. But now, off she went for the bowl. Leaving Nate and this little exercise are just what the doctor ordered."

"Not this doctor," said Alex. "You've been reading too many psychology books, mother. Let Marian get proper help if she's depressed."

"How very stuffy of you, Alex. It's time you got away from Boston. And now it's almost bedtime." Elspeth moved to the kitchen counter. "Sarah, I always have cocoa before I go to bed. How does that sound?"

"Perfect," said Sarah. She looked around the pleasant kitchen, with its blue-painted chairs and table, the pots of fuchsia and white geraniums hanging by the window, and decided that she was feeling somewhat akin to Marian Harwood, rather numb and finding it difficult to react.

Elspeth thought, Sarah's easy on the surface, but she's holding back, waiting. But then Elspeth recognized this quality as one of her own and knew that old-shoe familiarity would not come easily.

"What's that?" said Alex, going over to the window.

"Someone calling, I think," said Sarah.

"It's a woman's voice," said Alex. "Listen." He pushed up the window and now footsteps could be heard on the porch and a woman's voice making little bleating sounds. Then Marian Harwood, eyes wide, face flushed, pushed into the room.

"I've hit someone," she said. "Over the head."

"Good God, Marian, get your breath," said Elspeth. "Are you all right?"

"I hit him with the warming pan. It looked just like Nate. The shape of his head. Right there in the living room."

"Now, Marian," said Elspeth, soothing her. "Take deep

· 58 ·

breaths." She reached out a hand. "You're shivering. I'll get a nice hot drink. Alex, won't you go?"

"It's all right, Marian," said Alex, leading her to a chair. "You just stay put, and I'll go over and see what this is all about. Is your door unlocked?"

Marian nodded. "I heard a noise. In the studio. I was leaving the dining room. I went into the living room, and I took down the warming pan—you know, it hangs next to the fireplace—and I hid behind the door, and then he came into the room, and I hit him. He went right down on the floor. He was opening drawers in the big chest."

"Be careful, Alex," said Elspeth. "There might be more than one."

"I'll come with you," said Sarah.

"All right," said Alex. "But just as far as the house."

They went, Sarah running behind Alex, half-falling up the steep path, pushing through the overreaching alders, tripping on roots and shelves of rock. Overhead, she could hear branches groaning in the tall spruces and remembered again the talk of gale warnings.

At the top of the path the half-moon showed well above the treetops, clouds gusting across it, and then Alex turned as they reached the Harwood lawn.

"Stay here by the birch tree. Don't move or call out unless there's a good reason. I'll go in and if I don't come out in ten minutes, go and find Lem Wallace. He's the constable and harbor master. House next to the post office."

And Alex was gone, crouching, moving to the windows, then onto the porch, the screen door open, and into the house. After five interminable minutes, a room in the cottage filled with light, and after a short interval, Alex reappeared at the front door, his arm around a dark drooping shape.

"It's okay, Sarah. Just our neighbor. I'll take him back to our house and go over him there. Only stunned, I think, with a cut over the face."

"It isn't Nate Harwood, is it?" asked Sarah. Somehow, she had had the impression of someone much younger.

"No," said Alex shortly. "It's Roger. Number-one son."

Back in the McKenzie kitchen, Roger Harwood, sullen and unspeaking, slumped in a chair, while Alex dabbed at his abrasions and fashioned a butterfly bandage for the larger cut on his chin. Then, producing his bag, Alex checked Roger's pulse, blood pressure, and the size of his pupils. Marian, after a weak clutching gesture and a cry of "Roger," had subsided and let Alex go to work.

"He'll do now, I think," Alex said to Marian. "It was only a glancing blow. Told me he never lost consciousness." Alex straightened and dropped a handful of little bloody cotton pieces into the wastebasket. "We'll put him into the room next to mine—my sister's room," he said to Sarah—"and I'll keep an eye on him tonight. Then tomorrow he may feel like telling us what he was doing crawling around in the dark in his own house and frightening his mother."

Roger lifted his head, and Sarah saw with distress that he seemed about to cry. "Look, I have to go back to Port Clyde," he said in a thick voice. "I'll explain later, Mother. I was just looking for something, something I'd left in the cottage." Sarah noticed that this was the first time that Roger had directly addressed his mother, and, even so, he avoided looking at her.

"You might have a concussion," said Marian. Her color was better now, and she seemed to have pulled herself together.

"You can forget about Port Clyde," said Alex. "We're in for a slice of that new hurricane, Ginevra. You stay here, Roger. You'll probably be starting one hell of a headache. Marian, you look ready for a dose of bed. I'll bet Rachel's waiting up for you."

"Cocoa all round," said Elspeth, "and then, Alex, I wish you'd check the dock and put an extra line on the sailboats."

They drank their cocoa in silence—all but Roger, who refused. Alex then told him to go to bed. "I'll look in on you later."

"You're not my boss," began Roger, and then thought

better of it. "Oh, hell, okay, but I'm leaving in the morning. I've got work to do."

Some time later, Alex and Sarah, having labored securing the dinghies, doubling mooring lines, and fixing chaffing gear on the McKenzie and Harwood twin catboats, the *Peg* and the *Molly,* climbed to the top of Tinker's Cove and stood listening to the sea rumbling over stone beach. They faced into the increasing wind, their clothes and hair tumbled and wet from the salt spray.

"Why on earth was Roger wandering around in the dark in his own house?" asked Sarah. "Is he looking for old family china, too?"

"God knows. Like Marian, he's on the outs with Nate so it's probably as he said, he's looking for something that Nate wouldn't let him have. Anyway," said Alex, as a branch above them gave an ominous crack, "we seem to be in for a real blow."

"I like storms," said Sarah, raising her voice against the clamor. "Especially from bed with the blanket pulled up."

Back in the kitchen they found Elspeth putting away a bottle of brandy. "For Marian," she explained. "The cocoa wasn't enough. I've walked her back to Rachel's. She's had a real shock."

"Yes," said Alex. "I suppose alcohol was called for. I didn't know Marian was so intrepid. Furniture heists, attacks with lethal antiques."

"But it was the second shock. I thought she was going to pass right out. She turned absolutely white. I had to put her head down."

"What are you talking about?"

"That old felt hat. The one Patsy's so crazy about. It's Nate's. He wears it everywhere. On the island, in town, fishing. I hadn't recognized it, of course, because it was such a mess when I saw it first, and now it's all out of shape with that hole in the middle. But Marian knew it right away. Patsy let her look inside, and there were Nate's initials stamped in the band. *N.P.H.* Marian almost collapsed. She couldn't even speak, but she must have been thinking that Nate has been hiding on the island, watching everything she's been doing. I tried to tell her that Patsy found the hat in Port Clyde, but she wouldn't listen."

"Nate may have lost it on the ferry, or on a trip over in his Whaler, and it came in with the tide. I've lost three that way."

"And now that Patsy's so fond of it," said Sarah, "I hope Nate Harwood forgets it and buys a new one."

"I agree," said Elspeth, "but Nate hangs on to everything. Well, quite an evening. Really. Hitting your own son over the head with a warming pan."

"Gilbert and Sullivan," Sarah said to Alex. "Or P. G. Wodehouse."

The storm, constituting a sizable piece of Hurricane Ginevra's skirt, had up until eleven o'clock remained just within the bounds of civility. Now she showed her true colors and just before midnight hurled herself at the shores and islands of midcoast Maine.

A few minutes after twelve the wind-tattered yellow and black banners celebrating the annual Godding show tore loose and whirled about the nearby telephone pole. These were immediately followed by five slates from the Godding's roof, which sailed across the street and broke a window in Marilyn's Trash & Treasure Shop. At the same time in Owls Head, as if sensing trouble, Mrs. Ordway, faithful pilot of the Godding, moved in her sleep and dreamed of flood and cataract. At one o'clock, in an extra spasm of wrath, the wind wrenched Sydney Prior's gallery sign from its bracket, lofted it past the general store, and slammed it down in front of the Dip Net, the popular luncheon counter of Port Clyde. Across on Weymouth Island, the old birch tree by the post office split in two, its larger section falling across Amory Satterfield's bench, and at the same time Rachel Seaver's gate blew loose and slapped and spun wildly.

At one-fifteen, Weymouth harbor master Lem Wallace, who had stayed up dressed and ready, looked out of his front parlor window, took the measure of the wind now changing to the northwest, woke his sixteen-year-old son, and together in boots and slickers they went down to the public landing and began checking on the skiffs and dinghies they had secured earlier in the evening. There they found Captain Seth Lamson of the *Robin Day* adding to his already doubled-up mooring lines.

Elspeth McKenzie lay awake and thought anxiously about her chimney, which over the winter had developed a decided list, and about the fragility of the five old apple trees behind the house.

Sarah slept off and on through the night, felt the old cottage shudder, heard the branches of the big white pine next to her bedroom window rap on the glass, and listened to the surf sounding one long crescendo. "It's not a fit night out for man or beast," she said to Patsy, who together with Nate Harwood's hat had long since sought safety with Sarah on the blue and red quilt.

Alex had set his alarm to check on the well-being of his reluctant patient. Between these intervals he slept the undisturbed sleep of a man long used to being turned out of bed. Shortly after Alex's four o'clock visit, Roger Harwood, taking advantage of the general bluster, kicked the glass out of his bedroom window and left the cottage by way of the roof and drainpipe. At five-forty that morning, Nate Harwood's dock broke into six pieces and vanished, and the lobster boat, the *Helen C.*, pulled away from its mooring in the harbor and fetched up on Abbott's Ledge.

So well past daybreak the winds cried havoc, and then the storm moved snarling in an easterly direction and pointed toward Nova Scotia—but not until, in one last departing spasm, it hurled the battered body of one of Weymouth's summer residents at the island, where, in a tangle of ocean debris, it was held fast by the shore.

Elspeth McKenzie, wrapped in a flannel dressing gown, came late to breakfast, heavy-eyed and worried.

"It's all right, Mother," said Alex, who was doing things with a wire whisk and a bowl of eggs. "The chimney held together."

"And the apple trees?"

"Survived but took a beating. Lots of branches down. I've been listening to the battery radio. The electricity's out and the whole coast is a mess. Nick Scott lost his lobster boat and Thorn Lurvey's dory broke up, the town landing's rim-racked and half the sailboats at the boat club are on the rocks. And Roger took off."

"Roger? He's not upstairs?"

"No. I'd gone to look in on him at four o'clock and all was well, but he was gone when I went in at six. Broke a window, damn him. Well, I wasn't about to chase all over the island in this storm."

"Oh, poor Roger."

"To hell with poor Roger. He'll turn up. No boats or planes going out, so he can't leave unless he swims. I told Lem to keep his eyes open. He can live on blueberries and sea greens and reflect on his sins. I'm doing my puffed French toast with cinnamon special learned at my mother's knee. Where's Sarah?"

"Not up yet. Alex, I do like her."

"Fine," said Alex, dipping a slice of bread into the beaten egg.

"But I don't think I'll get to know her easily. Really know. There's a protective shell."

"And don't you try and pick away, Mrs. Hen."

"But of course I know her grandmother—because of the Godding. One of the founding spirits. Old Mrs. Anthony Douglas. You know that huge Queen Anne house in Camden out on Bayview Street, the one with the stone hitching post

· 64 ·

and the curtains always pulled? A real tartar, but frail. I wonder if Sarah's anything like her."

"Back off, Mother."

"And Deane. It's a common name, but I wonder if she's related to those Deanes in Concord. There was a Douglas in my class who married a Deane."

"I said down, Mother. Heel and stay. Lay off the family research act, or I'll take Sarah away and bring a soft porn film star to the island."

"You've become much too prickly, Alex, and turn down the flame under that toast. I've said nothing to annoy you."

"But you're in there trying," said Alex, pointing his fork at her. The kitchen door opened, and he looked up. "Well, there you are."

"And about time," said Sarah. Her face was flushed with pink from yesterday's sun, and she wore a yellow shirt tucked into faded jeans with a soft gray sweater tied over her shoulders. "What a wind. Everything shook," she said, coming over and inspecting the French toast now turning brown in an iron skillet.

"After breakfast, Ms. Deane," said Alex, "I'll take you and Patsy out to Captain's Head to see the surf, and we can look for Roger. He gave us the slip last night."

Sarah and Patsy—the dog decoyed from Nate Harwood's hat by a piece of burned toast—stood with Alex below the east side of Captain's Head. "Too windy to go right to the top," said Alex. Sarah agreed. They were quite high enough. She could look back along the length of the island and see one line of waves after another smashing in. Directly below, the sea foamed in over the glistening sable rocks and boiled into pools between the clefts, and Sarah remembered what the pamphlet "Welcome to Weymouth" had to say about hikers who wandered too near the edge of a cliff or who climbed down on the shore rocks. She backed away from the edge.

Alex was busy with binoculars. "Might see some gannets

with this blow . . . or some fulmars," he shouted over the wind.

"It's wonderful," Sarah called back, "and terrible," she added, remembering what Yeats had called the "murderous innocence of the sea."

"I can't hear you." Alex lowered his glasses and looked at Sarah, who was facing into the gale, as a dark wisp of hair that had escaped from the blue bandanna tied around her head blew across her reddened cheek. At her throat he could see that her slight tan ended in a high circle, the terminus, no doubt, of a workday blouse. Suddenly, Alex felt he couldn't stand it a minute longer. It was as if the wind were blowing away a year's worth of self-restraint, a year of brotherly walks and visits, of treading gingerly on the edge of Sarah's sensibilities, outside Sarah's castle walls. He wanted to pull his arms tight around her so that she couldn't breathe or protest or argue about Philip or Pres or any other damn past event or man.

"Sarah, Sarah. I love you," he found himself shouting.

"What?" Sarah called against the wind.

"Sarah, do you hear me, I love you. Come and live with me. Or, goddammit, marry me." Alex glared at Sarah as a burst of wind cracked through the trees behind them.

"I can't hear you. You look like you're going to bite someone. Live where? You mean the rest of the summer? Back at the boarding house, I guess. Or with my grandmother."

"I can't hear you either. Hell, this is impossible. Come down out of the wind." Alex grabbed Sarah by the arm and, with Patsy trailing, steered her onto the narrow path that led to the trail in the woods. "That's better," he said. But now that he could say it all without yelling, he hesitated. He might drive her right off the island with that roaring-bull approach. Damn, he'd waited all this past winter for Sarah to get her bearings; well, he could wait a few days more.

"Alex, what on earth's the matter?" Sarah pulled off her spray-soaked bandanna and peered at him.

"Stubbed my toe," lied Alex, pointing to a rock on the

path. "Come on, let's look at Sailor's Cove. That's where Captain Weymouth was supposed to have anchored the Archangel. We can hike inland." Nothing like history to cool you off, Alex told himself as they made their way across the island, the path crossed with uprooted spruce trees. "You see," he said after Sarah had dutifully examined the less roiled waters of the cove, "they think that on May seventeenth Weymouth brought his ship into the mouth, where it shelves to fifteen feet. We know from the journals it was blowing a gale, but they must have risked putting a boat ashore to look for wood and water, and then the next night anchored at Monhegan Island, and the following day sailed north and found an anchorage between Allen and Benner and Davis islands."

"Isn't this all disputed?" said Sarah.

"None of the early writings mention this island—not called Weymouth then, naturally. An Indian name. But there's a rock above the cove with the name of one of Weymouth's crew carved on it. Thomas King and a cross and a date, and it matches an inscription on a mainland rock. There's a big celebration, Landing Day, held every year at the end of August."

"Why August if they landed in May?"

"Tourists and good weather. The practical spirit of New England at work. It's a big thing. They reenact the landing and have a two-day bash, clambakes, games, races, fireworks."

"It sounds like fun," said Sarah doubtfully.

"It's quite a scene. Pageants and costumes and everyone pretending good fellowship. Patsy can go as a seventeenth-century wolf—there were tame wolves then. Sydney Prior is a sort of hereditary marshal and the history buffs go all out in proper getup, but most of the men just put cardboard buckles on their shoes and roll up their trousers and call them breeches, and the women put on aprons and caps."

Sarah nodded. She was rather breathless from the fast pace, scrambling after Alex, who, from a seeming surfeit of energy, had charged along the trail, jumping fallen trees and sprinting in the clear places. Now he took off again and hustled her through the midriff of the island, coming out at last by a chain of overlapping boulders and ledges that made rudimentary caves.

"Where are we now?" panted Sarah.

"On our way to the Bucket. That's a sheltered cove over here on the east side. I thought we could look around in these caves for Roger. They're great places to hide in. We kids always thought bears slept here."

But an inspection of the caves yielded nothing more exciting than a cache of empty beer cans and a skeleton sneaker. "Of course," said Alex, emerging from under a boulder and brushing Spanish moss from his shoulder, "in good weather we could have taken the scenic route, the lower trail that runs from the lighthouse to Captain's Head just above the high waterline. Too dangerous today. They had to take it off the tourist map. Too many visitors getting into trouble. Now, we'll climb up and look over the Bucket and then along to the south—that little indentation—that's the Pail."

Sarah climbed out to the rim and looked down into the shelter of the Bucket, whose rocky arms acted as a partial breakwater. "The wind's really going down," she said, and then pointed at the shore. "Look at those pot buoys and lobster traps and all the other junk that's been washed up."

Alex clambered up beside her and lifted his binoculars. "A lot of hard cash shipwrecked. I'll climb down and grab the ones I can reach before the tide takes them. The yellow and black ones are Lem's and those red ones are Nick Scott's. See those sticks out there. That's what's left of the old weir, the one Mother painted."

"Her stolen picture?"

"That's right, only she painted it on a calm evening. Now it's jammed with stuff caught in it from the storm."

Sarah watched as Alex, Patsy wiggling and slipping after him, started down the steep path to the cove. Alex's almost black hair was standing up in places, stiff from the salt wind, the collar of his tan chamois shirt was up around his neck, and his sleeves were rolled; he looked, Sarah thought, quite the man of action as he reached for overhanging branches and swung himself over the boulders. Perhaps he'd missed his specialty and should have gone in for surgery instead of internal medicine.

Today, anyway, he seemed to require constant motion. In fact, the whole course of their friendship had had a frenetic quality. It had begun in the middle of a murder, and even their winter meetings had had a tentative quality, often rushed and unsatisfying. And now look at Weymouth. Furniture heists, finding Roger, and now the storm. Of course, there was another side of Alex—the Alex who gently wiped and bandaged Roger's face, who got up every two hours to make sure he didn't have a subdural something or other. She shook her head. Any real understanding of Alex would have to wait until things quieted down.

And then Patsy was back, the fur of his legs and belly soaked, and Alex behind him holding a clutch of rescued pot buoys by a handful of tangled pot warp.

"What a mess. More buoys caught in the weir, parts of a dory, tons of seaweed everywhere, toggles and floats all over the place. I'll leave these here and come back when the tide's gone out and see what I can save. Let's hike back by way of the lighthouse. Roger might be there."

"In it?"

"Could be. It's supposed to be locked, but kids get in from time to time. Hey, look there. Old Buster. He's one of our local ospreys." Alex pointed to a tree by the edge of the cove.

"Is that heap of sticks his nest?"

"Yes. There's always been an osprey nest at the end of the Bucket."

"And the osprey's always been called Old Buster, and he lives with Mrs. Buster in a nest by the Bucket next to the Pail. Quaint."

"Don't you go sneering at island ways, Ms. Deane." Alex

lifted his glasses and watched the big bird rise to the edge of the nest, take off, and, angling into the wind, disappear on steady wingbeats.

"Almost an eagle, isn't he?" said Sarah, to make amends, but Alex didn't answer, and she saw that he had fixed his binoculars on the irregular outline of the weir. The wind was fast subsiding and the water of the outgoing tide was departing in swirls and eddies. Now more of the weir was exposed, so that the tall sticks pointed high in the air. She yawned, suddenly hungry in the salt air, but Alex stayed, staring, adjusting his focus.

"What do you see? A bare-breasted phoenix?"

Alex lowered his glasses. "No, I don't think so."

"I was trying to be funny."

"Yes. So let's skip the lighthouse for now, shall we? It's lunchtime and I've got to see Lem Wallace about something."

"What *do* you see out there?"

"I don't know." Alex sounded puzzled. "I really don't, and I'm not going to try to talk myself into anything either."

Back at the cottage, Elspeth looked up from a cauldron of steaming stew. "You must be starved. I've done cornbread, too."

"Great," said Alex. "Feed Sarah. I've got to catch Lem."

"He's being mysterious," said Sarah, as Alex departed. "I think he's found contraband or bags of cocaine from the hurricane." She accepted a large bowl of stew and a square of hot cornbread and thought comfortably of a long post-luncheon period of reading one of the novels she had found in the guest room bookcase.

Alex returned two hours later, soaked to the waist, smelling of brine, and smeared with flats mud. His mother looked at him with disapproval. "You're dripping all over everything. Go and wash. I've kept the stew warm."

"Sorry, Mother. I'm afraid we've found someone in the debris that came in with the storm."

Sarah, curled in an alcove with *Mansfield Park,* closed her book and sat up. "So that's what you saw." She shivered. It was exactly what she had been trying to hide from herself since they had stood at the top of the cove.

"I wasn't sure at first. All that kelp, broken spars, part of a net."

"You're quite certain?" Elspeth held her hand to her throat.

Alex pulled over a chair and sat down. He looked exhausted. "Lem and I went out to Bucket Cove. The wind's down, and it's almost low water now. A man. Caught in the weir. We brought him in." Alex did not furnish the unwholesome details, which involved a gaff, a rope, and a blanket. "He'd been in the water for quite a time . . . well over a week, I'd guess, and the storm battered him about. Lem's called the State Police on the radio, and when they have a chance they'll come over and take the body to the mainland."

"How awful. A man, you said. Who?"

"Impossible to tell. Lem will go over with the police and make a report, and I'll go over tomorrow and make mine." He smiled ruefully at Sarah. "I'm sorry. I'm afraid it's just one of those terrible ocean facts. Probably some poor devil fell overboard, got caught in a line, maybe . . . something like that."

But here Alex was not being entirely candid. The ropes that circled the wrists and ankles of the corpse did not point to any entrapment by a fouled anchor line or a suddenly taut length of pot warp. Although the rope was loose now because of the breakdown of the flesh, it was obvious that it had been wound and knotted with care and with a seaman's knowledge of how to make an object fast.

Later that afternoon, following Alex's rehabilitation by shower, stew, and good brown ale, he marched Sarah off on another island tour. "First, we'll stop in at Rachel and Lyda's. Tell Marian we're going Roger-hunting. She'll have been worrying."

"Except she didn't exactly rush over this morning to see how he was," said Sarah.

"After all, Roger's caused a lot of grief in the past, what

with washing out of Bowdoin and his wars with Nate. Marian's been a buffer through it all. She's probably had it with both of them."

"She reminds me of those little wooden people that come with toy farms or Noah's Arks. You know, shaped like a bottle. Mrs. Noah."

"Nature probably meant Marian to be everyone's favorite relative. Aunt Comfort. But nature also gave her Nate and Roger. Now come on and meet Rachel and Lyda . . . the backbones of the island."

"Your mother told me that Lyda's an artist and a plant expert."

"Right. Lyda once identified a variant of sea blight that she'll tell you about, and she'll show you her paintings. Rachel rules the library, but don't try and borrow *The World According to Garp* or *The White Hotel*. Somehow, they're always out."

Sarah was led into the tiny gray clapboard house, heard from Lyda the details of the variant sea blight, inspected a row of framed watercolors, soft colors rather like Beatrix Potter's of fungi, she thought, admired Lyda's phlox, and put down three dollars for her pamphlet, "Artists of Weymouth." Next, at the small salt-weathered shingle cottage library, she met Rachel Seaver, contributed another three dollars to the children's book fund, and was shown the water stain on the wall once covered by the missing painting.

"They're amazing," said Sarah, as they left the library. "How do they keep going? Rachel's arms and legs are like twigs and Lyda's almost bent double."

"That's it," said Alex. "They do keep going. They've never heard of the word 'leisure.' It wouldn't be proper for them to sit back and relax."

They made their way around the little village, behind the white community church with its square bell tower, and into the little churchyard behind. Here Sarah lingered, kneeling and scraping away moss and lichen to read the epitaphs. A granite table with a scroll top: *Here Lyes Inez Seaver, Beloved and Virtuous Wife of Elephalet Seaver*. Beyond a leaning Celtic cross:

In Memory of Cap't. Enoch Starbox, AE Twenty-Five Years, In the Dread Bosom of the Wave, I Found Myself a Watery Grave, 1824. Then across by the wooden fence a Doric column covered with stone ivy, the resting place of Royale Abbott, 1836–1915. The column, Sarah saw, inclined in a protective way toward the stones of his three wives laid at his feet: Joanna, Olive, and Eda, who in turn sheltered three little lichen-covered lozenges, *Our Willie, Baby Dear,* and *Little Lucinda, Her Rest Is Sweet.*

"That's enough," said Alex. "We're going to meet Amory and Clara Satterfield. There's Amory's father over there, that big cenotaph. Captain Halvah Satterfield. I remember him making sailboats out of shingles for the children to sail in tide pools." And Sarah followed Alex down a path, over a brook, to a small white farmhouse to shake hands with Captain Halvah's son. Alex then stalked ahead through a long sloping meadow knee-high in grass, tansy, goldenrod, and purple asters. He pointed out this barn, that cottage, that fishhouse, a studio, a stand of white pines, a marsh. He exclaimed over storm damage—a birch cracked, a roof ripped, a shed toppled.

"Now we're going across Satter's Field. The cows won't bother you." He pointed to several solemn-faced Guernseys.

"Satter's Field as in Amory Satterfield."

"No one knows. Was the family plain Satter and owned a field or did people get tired of saying 'Satterfield's field'? You see both versions in the cemetery." He pointed ahead. "That's the art school where the trees begin. Started by Sydney Prior's father. He was an artist from Kentucky who found Maine and liked it. Summers anyway. Now it has a hired director and some of the larger cottages are rented out."

"I know," said Sarah. "Harrison Petty rents one. Mrs. Ordway told me."

"And there off to the west is the old ice pond."

"Alex, stop it. You don't have to imitate a tour guide. I know what you're doing. You're trying to distract me. Well, I know all about those who go down to the sea in ships and how fishermen are lost every year, but it's more than just finding someone drowned, isn't it?"

"I guess so."

"And you don't want to upset me because of the bad time in Texas."

"I remember you said once you might be a fatal friend, that things happened to people around you, and I said that was crazy. So now I don't want you to make idiotic comparisons."

"You're the one being idiotic," said Sarah. "No, I don't mean that. You're trying to be kind, but that was a quite a time ago, and I think I can face things. That man wasn't just someone who fell off his boat, was he?"

"No."

"And there's something fishy . . . sorry, I didn't mean fishy."

Alex, remembering the condition of the corpse, shook his head. "If you must. The body had been tied hand and foot. By someone. And there was a stainless steel chain around his neck with a disk."

"And?"

"It said the man was a diabetic, which may not mean a damn thing."

"But?"

"Nate Harwood was a diabetic."

At that moment, Patsy, who had chosen to stay in the McKenzie kitchen waiting for a chowder handout, came, curved tail waving, bounding through Satter's Field, his head high and, in his teeth, Nate Harwood's hat.

FIVE

One of the best things about the McKenzie household, Sarah thought on Sunday morning, was the eat-what-you-can-find breakfast policy. The sun was coming through the windows in bright patches, and a radio station from Boston was giving out with a Bach cantata, while Sarah moved peacefully about, squeezing oranges, assembling tea, Grape-Nuts, honey, and yogurt. Later, well fortified, she walked down to the town landing with Patsy, who sniffed and snapped at fishy bits tossed up by the storm. There she found Alex sitting on a coil of docking line, looking out over the harbor into the bluest of skies.

"Everything's so clean and washed," said Sarah. "I can see for miles. Right out past the harbor, right to Monhegan . . . and then almost to Spain."

"Spain?"

"Yes. Such a wonderful open feeling. I'd like to sail off in a straight line on and on, and then, one day, there Spain would be." Sarah's finger sketched a rising land mass.

Alex smiled. "If you sailed on and on in that direction you'd hit Miami Beach."

"What a spoiler. Doctors are so logical."

"Sorry, but I can't think much farther than the mainland." He gestured at the harbor mouth. "There goes the

State Police boat with the body. We can take the early ferry over so I can give my report to the State Police, then we can spend some time being art theft detectives to satisfy my mother."

The first trip of the day on the *Robin Day*, now restored to service after the storm, was notable for the large number of visitors who appeared with luggage ready to depart the island. "Rats leaving," suggested Sarah, as she, Patsy, and Alex made their way to the bow while the boat, rolling slightly, poked out between Katherine Point and Mac's Mote.

"I suppose Katherine Point is named for some poor woman who threw herself into the sea when her lover deserted her," said Sarah.

"Wrong," said Alex. "Katherine was a midwife, early nineteenth century. Had a house on the point."

"And everyone said, 'Go find Katherine out on the point.'"

"And don't say, 'How quaint.'"

Sarah smiled but did not pursue the subject. Island folklore was beginning to wear. Time to find that job, finish the summer on her own. Remember about fish and guests. And the Weymouth people—Alex, as well—all wound up into their special island world, and now the murder, well, she felt like a member of an audience who had accidentally become involved with a longstanding theatre company where everyone has private jokes, pet names, can recite the repertoire back for twenty years and name the stars, the ingenues, the walk-ons. Why, even the discovery of a body in the weir wouldn't knock a hole in the Weymouth script for August—in fact, it would be added to the legends of the island. She could see it as a thriller, all in caps: Beloved Doctor McKenzie returns Home to his White Haired Mother to solve the Mystery of the Stolen Paintings. Braving a Tempest, the Doctor discovers the Body of an Unknown caught in a Fish Trap. Who has done this Foul Deed? Act II opens with the Doctor (Ta-ran-ta-ra, ta-ran-ta-ra) on his way to the Police to Tell All. (He's got a little list.) Why did Fugitive Artist Roger Harwood break into his own

· 76 ·

cottage under the Cover of Night? Why did Abused Wife Marian Harwood try to Slay her Own Son with a Warming Pan? Is Rachel Seaver, Aged Librarian, secretly reading *The White Hotel*? Will Sarah Deane, Summer Visitor, stuff this and think about Getting a Job?

Well, she really didn't have time for more than a walk-on in this particular soap operetta . . . or did she? Sarah leaned far over the rail to stare into the bow waves and was rewarded by cold spray splattering her cheeks and stinging her eyes.

When she opened them, Alex was scanning for sea birds. *I mustn't decide too much about Alex yet. Still too soon. See how it goes this winter. I can't bounce from man to man, from Pres, to Philip, to Alex. But Alex was alive, and Pres and Philip were like two photographs left in the sun, ghostly images fading away to the back of her memory.* Sarah watched over the rail as two logs passed from the bow to the stern of the boat, one after the other, half submerged, then, bobbing in the wake of the ferry, disappearing. *Come on, now, Sarah,* she told herself, *think about Alex. Had she ever given him a spare room, even a cupboard, in her head? What did Alex want or need? Be objective. What he needed, obviously, was a woman. One not all hung up with shaking off the past and trying to fend for herself. Let's see. A bird-watcher, a science-oriented person. A blonde, perhaps, for contrast. Call her Sonja, sturdy, calm-minded Viking type, ready for clambakes, sailing races, ready to put on homespun and an apron for Landing Day. Sonja would be one of those "doctors' wives" who cheerfully kept the casserole warm when he was called out, who knew what to say when a patient called up about spots or diarrhea.* She saw Sonja dressed in a pastel skirt and matching sweater. Sarah picked up an imaginary telephone. "I'm sorry, but doctor is on an emergency"—Sonja might be one of those females who called her husband "Doctor." *She would like to hear all about things like liver function tests and spinal taps and what the CAT scan showed and grand rounds. What were grand rounds anyway? They sounded like something Louis XIV did with his court. Sonja would be good in bed, an imagi-*

native lover. Would she? No, dammit, she'd be lousy. Alex couldn't have everything.

"Wake up," said Alex. "We're docked. Move it, Patsy."

Sarah came to and saw the real and present Alex McKenzie, his eyebrows lifted in mock exasperation, his hand reaching out for Patsy's leash.

"Alex, what are grand rounds?"

"Grand rounds are something I'm trying to get away from. Shake a leg."

While Sarah took Patsy on a tour of the bushes by the Sheriff's Department parking lot, Mike Laaka went over the question of the Weymouth corpse with Alex.

"It's the State Police's baby now," said Mike. "They have jurisdiction over homicides. As for the ID, that'll have to wait for a dental check, but hell, it's Sunday in August and every dentist for miles will be off somewhere."

"And the medical examiner?"

"The chief's coming in from Augusta. The body's in the hospital morgue. No proper facility in the state yet. This guy's been in the water so long another twenty-four hours won't make much difference. Besides, I've got that Missouri couple business to worry about."

"What's that?"

"I told you the other day. Man and wife from the Midwest who went into the harbor. Their daughter's trying to find a painting they bought but hasn't any proof . . . checks, receipts, sales slips."

"I remember now," said Alex. "So here's my report, and a question. Has anyone seen Nate Harwood lately? He's not on the island, and he's a diabetic. The body had a diabetic tag around its neck, and Nate's hat washed into Port Clyde."

"Lots of diabetics around, lots of hats washing in," said Mike. "We'll take things as they come. Clothes, dental records. No one's reported Nate missing, and hell, he drives all over the state, making trouble usually. Blew me up a couple of weeks ago for not finding his painting right off the bat."

"Mind if I ask around for him?"

"Go ahead, but why stir up a hornet's nest? No one wants to find Nate. I like him a lot better missing."

At that moment Sarah stuck her head in the door, and Alex made the introduction. Patsy, at home in palaces or police offices, trotted in, his tail dislodging a bronze horse and rider from a low bookcase.

"Hell," said Mike. "That's John Henry. Excuse me." And he knelt on the floor and peered behind the bookcase.

"We're leaving." Alex stood up. "It's dangerous in here, and Mike"—Alex raised his voice as Mike crouched scowling over a headless jockey—"another missing person. Roger Harwood. He's probably on Weymouth, but if he turns up on the mainland, will you let me know?"

"Matter of fact," said Mike, rolling the jockey's head between thumb and forefinger, "Nate wanted me to watch Roger. Thought he might be into drugs or something. Called him a cheating s.o.b. Fine thing for a father to say."

"Have you watched him?"

"No. Why should I? I asked around town and the State Police, but no record. Nate was just being ugly as usual. Hell, he's in here twenty times a year asking me to sink a gaff into some poor creature he thinks is out of line. And listen to this. Nate wanted me or Lem to set a guard on his cottage. Said his wife might try and lift some stuff from the place. Now can you imagine proper Marian Harwood doing a thing like that?"

"You never know," said Alex, not looking at Sarah, who had turned away to the door. "See you, Mike."

Driving bumper to bumper through the city of Rockland on Route 1, the air freighted with the mingled odors of hake, haddock, and old bait, Alex and Sarah returned to the subject of the absent Nate.

"My grandfather," said Alex, "had a collection of boys' books on which I cut my teeth. They would have called Nate a 'bounder.' He has a genius for touching someone's sorest point."

"Like?"

"Like trying to replace Rachel as librarian on the grounds of old age, trying to enlarge the post office into Lem Wallace's back garden, wanting to tear down the lighthouse because it's been out of operation for fifty years."

"I get the idea," said Sarah. "A public enemy."

"His one strong point, aside from marrying Marian, used to be his interest in Roger, helping him learn to draw and paint, but that's all gone to hell now. So let's forget Nate and get on with our tour, cruise the antique shops and galleries. Lucky I'm with an expert."

"No expert. I typed and ran around, but no one trusted me with art."

The tourist lanes of Maine are thronged with galleries, antique displays, and the more dubious "trash and treasure" shops, and Sarah and Alex, and a restive Patsy, visited, questioned, peered into back rooms, turned over stacks of pictures, framed and unframed, flipped through drawings, engravings, oils, pastels, and watercolors.

Dusty and hungry, they came to rest at the Sail Loft Restaurant overlooking Rockport harbor. Each had added to his household possessions: Alex with a foxed print of the sidewheeler *Katahdin*, and Sarah with a slightly damaged sweetgrass basket.

"I think we should give up this amateur search business," said Alex, after they had ordered.

"I agree," said Sarah, eyeing with interest the approach of her crab cakes and blueberry muffins. "Everyone says stolen stuff leaves the state right away. But, really, isn't selling stolen paintings anywhere terribly risky? They're so easy to identify."

Alex, now busy with his stuffed sea bass, shook his head. "Not so. Local artists have local reputations. Mostly."

"You mean these stolen paintings are small-time stuff."

"Sure. Take Eakins, Homer, Hopper, Porter, the Wyeths, the well-known old marine painters and luminists. A thief would have a hell of a time because they have international reputations. But my mother, the rest, just regional artists.

Successful around New England, the Atlantic coast maybe, but face it, no one in Chicago, L.A., Dallas, let alone London or Paris, would have heard of them. Of course, there's that so-called Church taken from the library, but no signature and Rachel says it was never listed in any of his catalogues."

"I don't see how there could be much money in all of this."

"Money, but not wads of it. Just a good addition to one's income and tax free. Mike went over the list of summer thefts and said if they're all by the same person, it may come to between twenty and sixty thousand a year profit. Maybe more, but you'd have to subtract the middleman, the fence. A nice painting done of a popular subject sells. And don't forget that some of those pocket-size objects fetch a big price—silver ladles, sugar shakers, snuffboxes, old pewter, and so forth."

"You mean you're looking for a modestly greedy thief. But it's peanuts really. Look at football pools, horse races, Atlantic City and Las Vegas. Cocaine sales. What's sixty thousand these days? A lot to you or me, but to an operator taking risks, nothing."

"Then look for someone whose budget is a little out of whack, maybe. Come on, one more stop. The Godding. It's open Sundays. See if anyone there has a new idea."

* * *

Mr. Petty, when cornered in his office on the subject of stolen art, was fretful. "It's a matter of security. I'm doing my best on very little money and almost no support. We need a full-time guard. The trustees don't realize the threat. We're trying to be responsible here at the Godding. Not like the Farnsworth, losing a Hopper in broad daylight."

Sarah stood with Patsy at the back of the director's office, trying to keep her eyes from the picture hanging behind his desk. It was a large framed reproduction of Monet's "The Pheasant," in which the featured bird lay in a very broken-necked sort of way across a white tablecloth. It had come, she knew, from the gift shop collection, and although it might be an attempt on Mr. Petty's part to reach across for donations to Maine's hunting population, it might also say something about Mr. Petty himself.

"Have you seen Nate Harwood lately?" asked Alex.

"Thank the dear Lord, no," said Harrison. He picked up the show catalogue from the glossy pile on his desk and began flipping the pages. Grimacing, he looked up. "But he's going off the board. His term is up. How he was ever chosen . . ." Harrison let the catalogue slip back to his desk. "But I wasn't here when he was elected." After a moment's silence, Mr. Petty, as if seeing Sarah for the first time, waved. "Hello, there. You're certainly looking better. When you were with us, I told Mrs. Ordway several times that you didn't look at all well. No color. 'Our waif,' I called you."

"Is that noise you're making a snarl or a growl?" said Alex, as they left Mr. Petty contemplating his pile of catalogues.

Doris Ordway's office was not much larger than a commodious broom closet, but it was a miracle of organization. Calendars, show schedules, docent lists were all marshaled in tidy rows on the wall.

"Doris," said Alex. "We need help. What do you know about stolen paintings?"

"Sleuthing, are you?" Mrs. Ordway nodded her approval. "Well, I've never heard that the Godding's been stuck with a hot painting. Our collection, such as it is, comes from private donations, or galleries where the provenance of the work is established. So I don't know much about the dealers who live on the fringe. I think it would be just luck if you stumbled on any of these missing paintings."

"Then I'm about to call it quits," said Alex. "Oh, and one more thing. Have you seen Nate Harwood around?"

"Not lately. He came in here like a Roman candle during the jury selection period, Wednesday the sixth, I think, but he wasn't at the reception, and I haven't seen him anywhere else."

"Thanks, Doris. Hope we'll see you on the island for Landing Day."

"I wouldn't miss it, but I refuse to put on a costume."

"Not even a bonnet?" said Sarah.

"Nor yet a linsey-woolsey skirt," said Mrs. Ordway. "And speaking of paintings, are you on your way back to Weymouth?"

"On the three o'clock boat. I thought Sarah and I would try for a sail."

"Do me a favor. There's a woman in the gallery library. I've just finished seeing her. A Ruth Baker from Missouri. It's a grim story. It was her mother and father who drowned in that Port Clyde accident."

"And she needs a ride to Port Clyde?" said Alex.

"No. Just lead the way, if you will. Mike Laaka sent her here. She's visiting the local galleries, trying to find out something about a painting her parents bought. I've given her a partial list of local dealers, but a complete one is hopeless. Think of the artists who sell from their own studios. I told her to try the Port Clyde Arts and Crafts Gallery, and, of course, Sydney."

Mrs. Ordway stood up. "Come along, I'll introduce you."

Ruth Baker, sitting on the edge of a leather wing chair in the museum library, proved to be a slightly built, anxious-faced woman with a snub nose and short brown hair mixed with gray. She sat in her blue and white cotton suit, knees together, feet in their white T-strap sandals square on the floor. She was marking a copy of *Antique Digest* with a pencil. Sarah thought that she had a very determined mouth and chin.

"I'm checking dealers not on your list," she told Mrs. Ordway.

"Do you think your parents' painting was taken from the car?" asked Alex, going directly to the matter as the three left the museum.

"I don't know exactly." Ruth Baker hesitated. She had the rather flat midwestern accent, but spoke in a low husky voice, soft to the ear. "Anything might have happened. One of those fishermen, the diver, even the police could have taken it. The car's windows were rolled almost to the top, but when the diver broke in, the painting might have floated out." She paused, then went on, her voice even huskier. "The police said that's what probably happened. Or that it fell out of the car when the car was raised and went out with the tide."

Sarah saw that Ruth's eyes were full, tears almost ready to spill down her cheeks. "Why don't you tell me about it," she said. "I'll drive down to Port Clyde in your car."

And this week, thought Alex resentfully, as he ran Patsy down to his car, was supposed to be the quiet time for Sarah and me to practice being together.

For a while, Ruth, at the wheel, was silent, concentrating on following Alex's car as it threaded its way along the Old County Road past the water-filled lime quarries that pitted the land on both sides. Then, as if aroused by the sight of these, she pointed. "Look. I could understand if they'd gone off into a quarry at night. Regular death traps. But to drive down onto a wharf right into the harbor, why, that doesn't make sense."

They turned toward Port Clyde, and Ruth, as if to make some effort at being pleasant, gestured at the St. George River lying like a great green ribbon on their right hand. "What a pretty river."

"Yes, isn't it," said Sarah, watching the river going past with only the smallest eddies visible where the channel buoys broke water, as if sudden death were foreign to such peaceful movement.

"I had a letter from them the day they died," said Ruth. She frowned into the sun-speckled windshield. "It was written on a paper place mat from a restaurant—a place called Damariscotta. I'm the only child and not married. Mother and Dad always sent postcards, notes, souvenirs, a balsam pillow, a key ring . . . you know. I've got the letter right here." Ruth reached with one hand into the straw handbag and produced a folded piece of paper. "There. See what you think."

Sarah opened it, carefully smoothing the folds. She could

see that the scallop-edged paper was decorated along the top with a line of ships—sloop, ketch, yawl, schooner, bark. "They were having a late lunch," explained Ruth, "because they'd been driving all over the place, and they just loved Maine. It was their first trip to the East Coast. Go on. Read aloud. Start at the third paragraph."

" 'You'll never guess what Dad and I have done,' " Sarah read slowly, the handwriting clear but cramped.

> We've bought a painting. A real oil and it's a beauty. An island scene with a little bit of shore and a fence and the ocean to remind us of this part of Maine. Nine hundred dollars! Pretty steep, but we said just this once let caution go to the wind. We paid for it right on the spot. Dad had just cashed some traveler's checks; I had that emergency money pinned you know where.

All at once Sarah could see it. An elderly woman in a gallery backing off modestly, asking if there was a ladies' room, or retiring to the car for a moment, then her hand fumbling at her dress front. An old-fashioned cotton print or maybe a summer pastel pantsuit, the kind Sarah had seen on older women on bus tours. Then the money, rolled neatly, would be brought out from some subterranean garment and counted out anxiously.

Ruth nodded. "Mother always did that . . . pinned money all over herself, her bra, down her girdle, her slip. Go on, finish it. I'm used to it by now."

Sarah didn't believe it. Ruth's hands were fastened so tightly around the steering wheel that the knuckles stood out as hard as marbles. She read on, however, hesitating when the meaning became clear.

> Dad says you only live once, so let's enjoy it. Besides the painting was perfect and all framed. You can help us choose a place in the house for it. Now here comes Dad with the second surprise.

Sarah saw that on the bottom half of the place mat the firm blue ink gave way to a trembling pencil scrawl. Ruth, anticipating, said, "Dad had a tiny stroke last year, only Mother called it a 'spell.' His hand shakes. Can you make it out?"

> Mother and I [read Sarah] have been sitting here eating clam chowder, and we've decided that we like Maine so much that, darn it, we're going to turn back to one of those pretty little towns and see if we can rent a cottage on the water somewhere for next summer. We were on our way back home, but we haven't a tight time schedule.

Here the handwriting changed again and Ruth's mother was back, the writing now crammed into the bottom of the paper mat, dodging around the scalloped edge.

> A little place but with a bedroom for you. Aren't we the gay old things?

Ruth nodded. "I'm the librarian at one of the elementary schools, and I usually take part of my summer vacation with them. And 'gay' doesn't mean anything funny to them."

All at once it hit Sarah. This wasn't like that accident she'd read about last week, skimming over the details—"Elderly couple perish in freak accident." These were Mr. and Mrs. Baker, who had loved Maine and had bought an expensive painting to remind them of their trip, and who were going to have a summer cottage here, just as her own Grandmother and Grandfather Douglas had had sixty years ago. "Ruth, how awful," she faltered.

"I should have gotten it into my head that they're gone," said Ruth, "but I haven't. And I'm going to try and trace that picture. It was almost the last thing they did before they died, and I think it's wonderful that they suddenly kicked loose and bought something beautiful and impractical. They were always so careful."

"The description's pretty vague," said Sarah. "An island sea scene isn't much help."

"I suppose there are lots of islands in Maine."

"Over three thousand, I'm afraid."

"I don't have to search the whole coast. Mother wrote that they didn't go any further down east than Searsport and that they didn't start visiting shops until they were in the midcoast part. Of course, I did get postcards from the big islands, Vinalhaven, Monhegan, Weymouth."

"That's still a lot of territory."

"I have all the rest of the summer and the fall, too, if I need it. I've taken a leave of absence. The police have been kind about the accident, but I don't think they're very interested in the painting, which I think might have been stolen."

"That's going to be hard to prove," said Sarah.

"If I have to, I will," said Ruth, and again Sarah noticed the determined chin, the firm mouth.

"We're coming into Port Clyde now," said Sarah. "Slow down for the turn. Alex is up ahead in front of Prior's Art Shop." She reached over and touched Ruth's hand. "I'm so sorry."

"Thank you, Sarah. It helps just talking to an ordinary human about it." She smiled, climbed out of the car, and, together with Alex, hurried up Sydney Prior's brick walk. Sydney himself was at the door, and Sarah, walking behind, saw Alex perform introductions to a very stout bald-headed man in a white suit. He reminded her strongly of someone misplaced from the tropics. She was about to join them when she was halted by a large placard in the shop window. "Wanted through Labor Day—Art store assistant. Duties: clerical and sales." Okay, there it was. The job she'd been talking about. Sarah smoothed her hair, buttoned the top button of her blouse, and, seeing Alex about to turn away, presented herself to the proprietor.

"I've been working at the Godding," she finished, "and Mrs. Ordway knows me." Somehow she was sure that Mrs.

Ordway was known far and wide as a person of sense and probity.

"Sarah," said Alex, "you need a vacation. You heard Harrison Petty call you a waif."

It was absolutely the wrong thing to say. "Thank you, Alex," said Sarah in a freezing voice. "I can take care of this." She turned to Sydney Prior. "I'd really like this job. I'm not long on organization, but I'm pretty good with people."

"Well, Alex," said Sydney, "your cousin Giddy has left me in the lurch, and if Miss Deane can help me out, I'd be delighted."

It was all concluded in a minute. Sarah would start work first thing in the morning, taking the early boat from Weymouth. "So helpful you've been at the Godding. Now I'll have some free time for Landing Day. My annual chore." Sydney smiled, shook hands with Sarah, and beckoned to Ruth Baker. "Come in where we can talk. Perhaps I can interest you in a cup of tea, a China blend or a Darjeeling." Ruth nodded, and together they disappeared into the shop.

Sarah, her chin lifted, her mouth rather small, drew Patsy close on his leash and swept down the path of the shop and toward the waiting *Robin Day*. But there is a fate waiting for those who try to sweep, and Sarah caught her toe on an uneven surface and sprawled face down, her elbow rasping on the road. Alex helped her to her feet. "Go into Sydney's and wash," he said quietly. "That's a mean-looking elbow, and I didn't mean 'waif.' It just came out."

"Because you thought 'waif.' Just like Harrison Petty. Sarah Deane, little Orphan Annie batting around through the world with Sandy."

"Your elbow."

"I'll clean it on the ferry. There's a bathroom."

"It's called a head."

"You're impossible. Petty, a good name for you both." And Sarah stamped off toward the boat landing, a little line of blood trickling down her arm.

Alex followed with Patsy, eyebrows up, mouth tight.

Since unreasonable behavior often begets more of the same, the clean-up session in the tiny head of the *Robin Day* did not bring Sarah to a pacific frame of mind. The truth, of course, not easily admitted, was that she didn't want a job at all; she wanted to relax, hike, go sailing, swimming, and spend time with Alex, perhaps even stay past the prescribed three-day limit. But she needed money . . . or did she? Come off it, she told herself. You're not going to make that much in a few weeks. It was being called a waif. Twice. A sort of childlike derelict in need of protection. Sarah scrubbed her elbow with a piece of paper towel with unnecessary roughness. Well, she'd pack up as soon as they hit the island and go and stay with her grandmother. She'd read *The Heart of Midlothian,* work on the background of her grandmother's needlepoint, and listen to strictures on Christian conduct. By the time she ducked out of the head, Sarah was bubbling like a witch's cauldron.

Alex stood, Patsy beside him, at his usual place by the bow, looking taller than his six feet, perhaps because he was flanked by three elderly, dark-dressed women who, like the Three Fates, huddled at the rail gazing seaward. Sarah arranged her face into a well-tempered smile. She would be extremely courteous. She would thank him for the interesting visit, hope they would see each other in Boston this fall, had enjoyed meeting his mother, all great fun. Here she stopped short. What was great fun? Capturing Roger with his trembling lip, finding a corpse in the weir, hearing Ruth tell about her drowned parents? Okay, Sarah, she said to herself. Shape up. I may not be a waif, but I'm pretty damn trivial. Me and my little dignities.

"Alex," she began uncertainly, focusing on a point below his chin. "I'm sorry . . ."

But Alex took her hand and forced her to look directly at him, and the scarcely held emotion in his face shook her—his lips like a slash, the muscle at the corner of his mouth a knot, his hand so tight over hers that she felt her pulse beat against his grip.

"Sarah, for Christ's sake."

"The Gulf of Maine," announced a guide as he herded his flock to the port bow. "The Gulf of Maine is named after the state of Maine." The guide was now shouting against the throb of the diesel as the *Robin Day* labored out of the harbor. "The Gulf is formed by three major banks, the George's Bank on the south, the Nantucket Shoals to the southeast, and the Brown's Bank on the east. The Nova Scotia current runs southwest . . . "

Sarah looked helplessly at Alex. They were now separated by a man in a flowered shirt setting up his camera on a tripod. "I'm sorry," she called.

"Excuse *me*," said the man.

Alex, not a lip reader, shook his head. He might as well try and make love to a nurse in the middle of the emergency room on Saturday night. He reached again for Sarah's hand. "Let's try it back in the stern."

The aft cabin and the outside benches proved to be hot in the full sunlight and as crowded as the bow. Alex, using Patsy as an offensive linesman, managed to find an outside corner next to a chest marked LIFE JACKETS: ADULTS 32, CHILDREN 8. "Sarah," he said, "you're not a waif."

"No," said Sarah, "but I'm sort of hung up on not being one. I'm always overreacting."

"We'll get away from everyone. Go sailing . . . all the way to Spain."

"That sounds good. It's so hot today and . . . "

"Alex!" A cry from behind, and Sarah saw a large shock-headed girl in bib overalls fling herself out of the crowd of passengers and throw her arms over Alex.

"Hello, Giddy," said Alex with such marked lack of enthusiasm that Sarah almost laughed. He lifted Giddy's arms free.

"I'm coming over to Weymouth," said Giddy. "I've quit Sydney Prior, and I'm staying with you. Our own cottage is rented, and Aunt Elspeth always says 'any time.' "

"Sarah, this is Giddy Lester, my wild and woolly cousin. Giddy, this is Sarah Deane, our houseguest."

"It's really Grace, but I never could stand it." Giddy paused and added in an offhand voice, "Have you seen Roger anywhere? Since the storm, I mean. Not that I care, but he can do such totally stupid things, like taking a skiff out in the middle of a hurricane."

"He's hiding out on Weymouth," said Alex shortly.

"On Weymouth. Hiding out. What for? What has he gone and done? I mean he's been impossible most of the summer. But he's okay?"

"As far as we know," said Alex. "You can help look for him."

"It's not that I care a damn . . . but anyway. I'll be here for Landing Day. All the good old fun and games and . . . what's the matter? Honestly, you look peculiar, Alex. Are you seasick or getting the flu or something? Doctors never take care of themselves." Here Giddy paused, seeming to remember that Sarah was attached to the party. "You look sort of funny, too. You're not going to throw up, are you?"

"No," said Sarah.

"Well, that's good because a lot of people do even if it's absolutely calm. It's the combo of the diesel and the motion. Is that your dog? I mean do you take him visiting, because Aunt Elspeth can be pretty fierce sometimes, particularly if she wants to get on with her painting. Some of my friends are absolutely turned into jelly by her."

"Everything's fine." Sarah managed a level voice, thinking, Have I cleared it up with Alex? I can't let him think I'm like the princess and the pea. And then she was aware that Giddy was looking at her expectantly.

"I said," repeated Giddy, "how about sailing when we get in? We can take out one of the catboats. How about it, Sarah? There's room for three if we scrunch up."

"Giddy," said Alex in a repressed voice. "Would you take this dog for a walk? His name is Patsy and he has claustrophobia. All the way to the bow."

"It's all right," said Sarah. "There's no room for Patsy anywhere. And you two go sailing. I've got a headache coming on—all this sun." It was true. Sarah was now aware of beating temples and a pounding in the back of her skull.

"Alex, did you know I had a picture accepted for the Godding show?" began Giddy, and Sarah leaned back against the cabin and closed her eyes.

Elspeth McKenzie was on the town landing talking to Lem Wallace when the *Robin Day* docked. Her impression as she hurried up to them was that all was not right, something about the way Alex strode ahead of Sarah and Giddy, but she reminded herself that no one would thank her for solicitous questions.

"Hello, Giddy. Coming for a visit? I suppose you've walked out on Sydney. Alex, we're organizing a search for Roger. He hasn't turned up, and I've begun to think he might have had a concussion after all and passed out. Of course, it's hard to find anyone, with all the visitors milling around and . . ."

Giddy tumbled into the conversation. "Oh, that dumb Roger. What on earth does he think he's doing and why should he have a concussion?"

"Giddy here," said Alex, "would love to search. She's a Roger expert. Sarah and I have had a tough day and will now take at least three hours off. Mother, if you'll watch Patsy, we'll disappear and give you a hand tonight. Sarah, come on. I need you." And Sarah found herself again held by a hand that closed completely around her wrist and drawn up the path toward the cottage.

Changed into a bathing suit, Sarah walked into the icy water through floating pieces of seaweed, and then dove, opened her eyes underwater and saw an apron of kelp, a line of boulders pockmarked with barnacles, and felt the cold water carry her headache away and out to sea.

Later, leaning back against the gunwale of the little catboat, a shirt pulled over her wet bathing suit, Sarah watched Alex steer out of Tinker's Cove and turn along the western shore of the island, trying to catch the falling afternoon breeze. He reached over and let down the centerboard.

"Have to wait and get by Tinker's Ledge. At this tide we've only got a foot in some places. We'll tack out and then run back."

Sarah nodded, placed a boat cushion under her head, and fixed her sunglasses more firmly on her nose. The sun that had been like a flame on land was now lower in the sky, and a mild sea breeze freshened her face. This, and the sail filling, luffing, and filling again, the boom swinging over as Alex brought the *Peg* about on each new tack, all seemed to leave the foolish and petty human broils behind. Sarah repeated the word "petty" to herself and was able to smile. She felt the boat heel to a quick puff and let her hand fall over the gunwale, letting the cold water stream between her fingers.

Long afterward she looked back on this late afternoon on the water as a moment of absolute refreshment that Alex had lifted out for her to frame the end of the day.

Coming about for the last time, Alex pulled up the centerboard, let out the sail, and they ran before the wind, gently rocking from side to side, the water running softly under the bow. Alex silently pointed, and Sarah saw three sloops, one after the other, spinnakers blown full—yellow and red, green and white, and the palest of blues. They floated like great balloons drawn by an invisible string, passed northwest behind the islands, and disappeared.

"Do you know those lines about one of the Maine islands?" said Sarah. " 'The ocean shows no scar from the cutting of your placid keel; care becomes senseless there . . . ' " Alex smiled, and Sarah finished to herself, " 'Pride and promotion remote; you only look; you scarcely feel.' "

After the *Peg* had been tied on her mooring, they both stood for a moment on shore and saw the islands hanging like dark green and purple pincushions in the water, and then Giddy stood at the top of the cove and called. It was dinnertime; it was search for Roger Harwood time. "Life as a Mardi Gras," said Alex angrily.

"We had this afternoon," said Sarah.

And somehow, without Sarah's actually agreeing, it was decided that she was to go on staying with the McKenzies and each morning take the eight o'clock ferry to work.

"Sydney's an old fusspot," said Giddy thickly, her mouth full of boiled beef. She swallowed and took a lusty gulp of milk. "But maybe you'll get along, probably because you're not me."

Sarah, who had been in a warm daze since coming in from sailing, answered questions at random and ate her way through boiled cabbage and corned beef without really tasting anything. After dinner she found herself equipped with a flashlight and joining with Giddy and Alex in a futile search of Satter's Field, the graveyard, and sundry unmarked swales and marshes.

"Here's Mother," said Alex, pointing to the road.

"Good news," said Elspeth. "Rachel's missing two rhubarb pies she'd put out to cool and some lettuce and carrots from Lyda's garden. We guess it's Roger."

"And he's getting his vitamins," said Alex dryly.

That night, leaving the rest to a Landing Day planning session, Sarah fell into bed, unable for once to think, question, or worry over past events. She slept at once.

SIX

Sarah departed Monday morning on the ferry, leaving Giddy and Alex arranging a wire run for Patsy. "Those sheep of Tom Satterfield's," said Elspeth. "We can't have an incident. After all," she added, illogically, "Patsy's only human. Now Seymour and Stupid seem to have lost the hunting instinct."

"Just overfed," said Alex unkindly.

Sydney Prior welcomed Sarah, produced coffee, and led her about the shop. "Miss Deane . . . or Sarah. May I call you Sarah? . . . A friend of the McKenzies and Doris Ordway. . . . Here are the brushes for oils, the prices are on the handles. These are the watercolor brushes. Try not to touch the brush end. I carry golden sable as my finest grade. You dropped from the sky at exactly the right time . . . so much to do for Landing Day. I'm the chairman. I'm always the chairman. My father before me. I tell everyone it's a hereditary post. Here are the turpentines, the fixatives, and the linseed oils."

Sydney led the way around the room, opening cases, touching watercolor blocks, racks of poster board, and mat board, and pointing out the gift objects, carved birds, paperweights with imprisoned seashells, ceramic mugs with hand-painted marine scenes. "Very popular items," said Sydney. "And here are the inexpensive prints." He held up a little woodcut of a harbor seal. They moved on to the supply of scratchboards. "Landing Day," repeated Sydney. "I'm absolutely on the rack. The preparation alone . . . thank God for Labor Day . . . my vacation."

"Your father used to run Landing Day?" said Sarah.

"For many years. It was part of the art school pageant in the beginning. He started the art school. Quite an achievement in those days, a summer school on an island. Here are the oils. I give a ten percent discount to local artists. Winsor and Newton with the London label for students, and the Rembrandt and Van Gogh as the top of the line, and here"— Sydney moved to a large V-shaped bin—"are the reproductions. Only artists with a New England connection, plus a few inexpensive originals by local artists.

"But you do sell more valuable things," said Sarah, remembering the sign promising "Fine Antiques and Works of Art."

"Indeed, my inner sanctum, the Parlor Gallery. Come, I'll show you." Sydney seemed in an expansive mood.

I hope, thought Sarah as she followed him, that I can keep from knocking the place to bits. And sure enough, like a trap for the ungainly, a gold and red tea service was set out close to the door of the gallery on a fragile-looking table.

"Some rather nice things here. Take these chairs." Sydney rested his hand lovingly on the back of an uncomfortable-looking armchair. "Scrolled feet, crest rail, middle eighteenth century. And the Windsor chair. Wonderful condition. See the balled feet, the seat with the comb back . . . and this Sheraton chest." Sydney ran a finger around the maple veneer banding. "Original brasses . . . and this side chair. See the six slats and the ball finials with the double ogee curve in the front slat."

"Marvelous," murmured Sarah, afraid to speak or move.

"I take care of the customers back here myself, but I

might ask you to shine some silver, do a bit of careful dusting and polishing, perhaps help show paintings to customers. Things I never dared ask Giddy to do, but I can tell by the way you move you won't be dangerous"—Sarah by now having restricted her profile to a shadow line, arms and elbows against her body.

"My workshop's through that door—where I cut my mats, make my frames. Off limits because I just cannot have orders, materials mixed up . . . not that I don't trust you, my dear, but it's easier that way. I'm quite a creature of habit. Beyond the workroom, storage rooms, and my living quarters, though in summer I do try and spend as many nights as possible on Weymouth."

He led Sarah back to the shop and pointed to a small button by the cash register desk. "If you have a customer who, in your opinion, doesn't, shall we say, look like the run-of-the-mill tourist . . . you know, the five-to-fifty-dollar sort . . . or who asks questions that show a real interest"—here Sydney almost whispered—"in making an important purchase, press that button, and I'll come and take them back to the Parlor Gallery. Sometimes a glance out of the window, a Mercedes, a BMW, the better American makes, an antique model." Sydney nodded at Sarah's expression of distaste. "But this is a business, my dear, and there's no point in having people in my parlor who will be perfectly happy with a print of the Flying Cloud or large families with greasy-fingered children ruining my treasures."

"Yes," said Sarah submissively. Well, she supposed it did make sense in an unpleasant sort of way.

"Now it's almost ten o'clock, and I see someone pulling up. A last year's Citation, and the driver's quite ordinary. Your first customer, Sarah."

It wasn't until late afternoon that Sarah remembered the woman who had lost her parents in the drowning accident. "What about Ruth Baker?" she said.

Sydney, who had been popping in and out of the front

shop all day, stopped and shook his head. "Who did you say?"

Sarah explained, adding, "I think it's hopeless. A sea painting."

"Oh, yes. Of course. The poor woman. I gave her a list of galleries to check. I wonder if it was an original oil . . . so many copies these days. Quite exhausting for her, the mid-coast and the islands, too. I told her that Weymouth has only a few small art shops with a very limited selection, but they might be worth a try." And Sydney lifted his shoulders to suggest the futility of Ruth Baker's search, and then turned, alert, as the little brass bell above the door tinkled.

*　*　*

Alex was at the end of an active morning making minor repairs to the McKenzie dock, when his mother called to him from the top of the bank that Mike Laaka was waiting on the phone at the Weymouth general store.

"Okay, Alex," said Mike. "Just got it from the State Police. Death probably due to drowning or head injury. Some of the skull damage doesn't fit with an after-death battering in the ocean. The medical examiner will be here this afternoon, and then we'll know more. And I hate to give you credit so early in the game, but you were right."

"About what?"

"Don't be modest. Nate Harwood. Dental confirmation this A.M. Hey, Alex, you there?"

"I'm still here," said Alex in a grim voice.

"So now it's roundup time. Where's Nate been? What's he been up to, getting himself knocked off like this? The Sheriff's Department is helping out . . . we always do. So now I suppose someone had better tell Marian Harwood the bad news. Or the good news."

"Oh, God, Mike, shut up. I'll tell Marian if that's what you want."

"Yeah, that's what I want. Take Lem with you to make it official. You can stand by for support. The State Police will want to question her when she's up to it. And you, can you make it over on the noon boat? Another statement."

"Okay," said Alex shortly.

"And Alex. Watch Marian. See how she takes it."

"Oh, Christ."

"So long. I'll pick you up at the dock."

Marian Harwood took the news without blinking. Alex, together with his mother and Lem Wallace, found Marian kneeling in Lyda's garden, helping to tie up the phlox that had been beaten almost flat by the storm. She looked up, a bunch of paper ties in one hand, a straw hat tied under her chin.

"It's Nate," she said. It was not a question.

"Yes," said Elspeth, bending down to her. "Oh, Marian, I'm so sorry."

"As soon as I saw his hat I knew. I've been waiting. Like a bomb ticking." Marian got slowly to her feet. "Just like a bomb," she repeated.

Lem Wallace soberly shook Marian's hand and left, and Alex followed, leaving Marian to the care of his mother and Lyda. These last two, he decided, appeared more shocked than the bereaved wife, an observation he did not intend to report to Mike. After all, a woman in the process of divorcing a difficult husband might be forgiven for not showing grief.

* * *

"You can't deny there'll be universal rejoicing," said Mike as he guided Alex to a booth at the Claw, the diner next to the Sheriff's Department. "People might not want to help much. I can hear the cheers over at the Godding. That Harrison Petty was over last month talking about Nate and defamation of character or some such crap. Couldn't make any sense out of it. Told him to find a lawyer."

"Nate has two children," said Alex, accepting a crab roll from an interested waitress. A daughter, Joyce, in L.A., and Roger, currently a missing person on Weymouth."

"We'll be helping you smoke him out. After all, he's number one on the wanted list. I hear he's been living with your cousin Giddy."

"Not anymore. She's left her job and is staying with us now. If anybody can find Roger on the island, Giddy can."

"We'll be having Giddy in as well." Mike delicately removed a bone from a piece of halibut. "The body's off to Augusta for tests, and the samples for the more complicated procedures are off to Washington—the F.B.I. labs. Maine hasn't the money for a decent forensic lab or morgue. In the meantime, we can worry about how Nate made it to Bucket Cove. Dumped from a boat? From Weymouth, from Port Clyde? From where?"

"Difficult."

"Jesus, don't I know. They won't be able to figure out what the storm did with the body if they study tides and currents all year."

"And the rope used to tie him?"

"Looks like regular lobster pot warp to me. Three strand manila and been used before. The kind of stuff anyone can pick up along the shore after a big blow, or have around for hauling traps."

"Do you think the art thefts figure in? Nate was one of the stolen artists."

"Could be. We'll dump all that on the State Police's plate. They're setting up a command post trailer in Port Clyde. So now, Alex, getting ready for Landing Day? I hear Lem Wallace got roped into playing Captain Weymouth."

"No," said Alex, irritated. "What with Nate being dead, and Marian next door, and Roger playing hide-and-seek, I doubt if we'll be doing much about it."

"Oh, hell, of course you will. Marian can sit on her porch in a black dress if she wants, but damn, having Nate gone is the best break that woman's had. Now she won't have to go through the divorce. Yeah, I know about it, Marian filing, Nate contesting. I hear from Lem that Marian's staying over at Rachel Seaver's, so tell her to stay put. The police are closing the cottage, keeping a guard there. Same with Nate's Thomaston house. The crime lab will be along on the double to check for latents—prints to you—and all the usual crap. We're lucky one way. Nate had a complete inventory of both houses brought up to date after Marian walked out. The insurance people have copies, so it'll be a piece of cake to see if anyone's helped himself to the Harwood goodies . . . whether Roger's been anticipating his inheritance."

"I think," said Alex, "that I'd better tell you about the Weymouth Island reclamation gang," and he described for Mike the raids made by Marian, his mother, and himself, leaving out Sarah, who after all was an innocent guest—what was the cliché, an unwitting tool? "The upshot," he finished, "was that Marian was after some bowl when she stumbled on Roger. Had a terrific fright, apparently thought it was Nate or an intruder, and brained him with a warming pan."

Mike leaned back in the booth, his broad ruddy face stretched in a wide smile. "Jesus, Alex. Let's add this up. Breaking and entering, conspiracy to commit a crime, commission of a felony, assault with a deadly weapon, harboring stolen goods, not to mention Roger, who must be guilty of something."

"Enjoy yourself."

"The fingerprint guys are going to love this."

"Marian just took some things that were hers, and we tried to wear gloves," said Alex defensively, thinking, God, I sound just like my mother.

"Beautiful," said Mike expansively. He produced a cigar from his shirt pocket and rolled it back and forth in one hand. "Well, old Nate's in no position to complain this time and that's something to be grateful about."

"Stop rejoicing, Mike. You knew Nate, you know Marian, the whole family. This is real, not some damn horse race."

"Look, if I'm going to be sorry about anything," said Mike, "it's wasting the taxpayers' money trying to find someone who did the whole county a favor. Okay, so that's not professional and it's off the record, and we'll work like hell to clear it up. But listen, old buddy, my sympathy is being saved for someone like that poor Ruth Baker, whose parents drove themselves off Lloyd's Wharf. Losing both parents at once. She's a nice lady, and I'd like to help her find her missing painting if I had any time away from the Harwood mess . . . which I don't." Mike lit his cigar, pulled at it, and blew an angry cloud at Alex.

* * *

It was just closing time when Alex walked into Prior's Gallery shop. He stood at the doorway for a second looking hot in his long khaki pants and rumpled blue shirt with the sleeves rolled. Then he walked across the floor to Sarah and told her that Nate Harwood had been found. "Positive identification of the body," he added for Sydney's benefit. "No mistake."

"You thought so, didn't you?" said Sarah soberly. "Poor Mrs. Harwood."

Sydney was silent for a moment. He stood turning a small bottle of rectified turpentine over and over in his hand. Then he looked at Alex and shrugged. "I'm not going to be a hypocrite and say I'm full of regrets . . . except for Marian. She doesn't need any more trouble in her life . . . although this may put an end to it."

"Hell, Sydney," said Alex, "you sound just like Mike Laaka."

But Sydney only pursed his lips and began sorting through the day's sales slips.

Later, standing on the crowded stern of the *Robin Day*, as it made its five-fifteen run, Alex described his lunch with Mike while Sarah, holding a bag of doughnuts, tossed little chunks to the gulls that hovered screaming over the wake. "It's just as well that the State Police are managing the case," he said, "because Mike isn't exactly extending himself. He sees Nate's death as the happy removal of a big fat burr from under the community tail."

"Charming expression," said Sarah. She held her hand up and a gull swooped and nipped away a piece of doughnut. "Do you think Mrs. Harwood and Roger will be hit hard by this?"

"In a way. For what might have been but wasn't. I remember Nate from when I was little. Tough, cantankerous, a disciplinarian, but not impossible. Marian must have seen husband and lover potential when she married him. And you know, once upon a time, Nate was proud of Roger, taught him to draw, took him sketching. Didn't pay much attention to Joyce—she's quiet like Marian. Anyway, for a long while Roger was a reasonable approximation of the fair-haired son. But that was B.B., Before Bowdoin. Then, after Roger was given the ax, there was hell to pay. You know, how sharper than a serpent's tooth it is to have a son flunk out of Father's college. And, after that, Nate seemed to be angry and bitter most of the time."

"And his painting went sour?"

"It seemed to. Nate's early work was strong. The critics seemed to think he painted on the edge of being, well, remarkable. Marvelous with light, great flat planes of paint laid on with a pallet knife. But then, instead of going on, he retreated, and his work turned hard and set."

"Did he drink, do drugs? Go mad, try and kill himself?"

"No. Nate was almost abstemious. He seemed to have a sort of rock sense of himself as an artist. I don't think he'd have tried to destroy himself, his talent, like that. I'd say he took his disappointment about himself, about Roger, out on other people. His son gone, his creativity drying up. Mother tells me his last things were tense, almost stillborn."

"But he sold well?"

"Oh, sure. Nate had a solid reputation in the Northeast, and the technique was still there. And Sarah, let me say again how very sorry I am that you've been on the outskirts of this. You've had enough of sudden death."

"It's odd," said Sarah, "but I feel quite separate. It's as if I read about it all somewhere. Pres, Philip, they were different. Part of me. It sounds horribly selfish and hardhearted, but I didn't know Nate Harwood, I hardly know Marian Harwood, let alone Roger. And the whole island scene seems remote from real life, mainland life. Ruth Baker touches me more, her parents disappearing like that. I've been thinking that the island is like a stage set with quirky characters doing quirky things."

"That's the trouble with English teachers. They fly off into fiction."

"But these last few days, pure theatre. I wouldn't be surprised when we dock if everyone on the island troops down to the harbor in costume singing and tossing their hats."

"*Pirates* again?"

"With a touch of *Ruddigore,* which reminds me, the next act is coming up. Tonight at the historical society. Your mother said we ought to go."

"Why on earth?"

"It's an art lecture, and your mother thinks we might learn something to help with the art thefts, plus support the community at the same time."

"No community on Weymouth," said Alex. "Never has been. Undeclared warfare. But here we are. Land ho."

They made their way through the platoons of boat arrivals, and up the worn rock path. Just ahead, apparently fellow passengers, a poorly matched couple made their way; he tall and angular in a cotton cord suit, holding a bulging briefcase, she, short, sturdy in a summer print dress holding a shoe box under one arm.

"It's Harrison Petty and Mrs. Ordway," exclaimed Sarah. "You don't suppose he's the feature tonight, and she's got the slides."

"Cross your fingers," said Alex. "Maybe they're going to the Inn or the Lodge." But depression deepened when they saw Mrs. Ordway indicate a path that climbed off toward Tinker's Cove.

"Only three houses up there," said Alex gloomily, "and in view of Nate's death and the size of Rachel's house, that leaves the lucky McKenzies. Though I'm very fond of Doris Ordway," he added.

"But only in a solo," said Sarah making a face.

"I had to ask him," whispered Elspeth, as Sarah and Alex slipped in through the back door. "No one else would, or could." She turned back to the kitchen, lunged at the oven, and removed a tray of dark crackers heaped with some sort of burnt offering. "We'll call them smoked sardines, and, Alex," she said, "please water Harrison's drinks. He doesn't make much sense even when he's sober. Sarah, would you rescue the gingerbread? I've sent Giddy into the living room because she doesn't care what she says."

The dinner was somewhat redeemed by Elspeth's crab and broccoli dish and by her seating arrangements, which isolated Harrison at the end of the table between Giddy and old Mrs. Edna Wallace, Lem's mother, who was none too certain of her surroundings and kept asking Mr. Petty why he had given up hauling traps. Patsy, joining the guests during dessert, sat close to Mr. Petty's knee and barked from time to time as the museum director guided his gingerbread to his mouth.

As they filed out of the front door, Elspeth delayed Alex and Sarah. "A memorial service for Nate. Tomorrow night, six-thirty at the church."

"But," said Alex, "the medical examiner is just beginning . . ."

"I said 'memorial,' not the body. Marian wants it over as soon as possible. Come along, Giddy, we'll be late."

"Count me out," said Giddy firmly. "I've done my bit. I'm going for a walk, and besides, I can't sit on those hard little chairs."

No one could, thought Sarah, trying to find a comfortable position on her folding metal chair, a piece of furniture designed without regard for the human shape. And the room was absolutely airless. She looked resentfully at the closed casement window beside her ear, and then, Alex beside her, rose with the audience as Rachel Seaver at the front of the room indicated an American flag hanging limply from a pole, placed one hand over a flat plum-draped bosom, and led them through the Pledge of Allegiance. The audience subsided and the houselights dimmed. Harrison Petty unfolded himself and made his way to the front of the room, while Mrs. Ordway illuminated the screen with a blank rectangle of light.

Sitting there well to the back of the room, Sarah, breathless with the heat, saw through the window that a half-moon had risen into the evening sky. She turned back and saw Mr. Petty indicate on the screen a painting showing a ship listing in turbulent waters. "The Currier Gallery of Art in Manchester, New Hampshire," said Mr. Petty, "has one of the finest examples of late baroque in this exciting scene of 'The Storm' by Claude-Joseph Vernet. I wonder if you sense the tension between the figures on the shore, the twisted tree, and the distressed ship . . . " Sarah let her mind wander away as Mr. Petty's voice faded and rose, so that she was only dimly aware of passing ships, rocks, vessels, and surf, collections, galleries, and museums, on and on, until, with the announcement of the William A. Farnsworth Library and Art Museum, Sarah began to hope that the end was coming. She sat up and listened as Harrison skimmed rather too quickly over Homer's "Girl in a Punt," and Heade's "Storm Clouds on the Coast," but then, as the first marine painting from the Godding collection appeared on the screen, Sarah, who knew it all too well, turned again to the window.

Since the historical society building sat atop a ridge that rose behind the church, Sarah could see the library roof, the outline of Rachel's cottage, the irregular bulk of the McKenzie house, and beyond, along the tops of the spruce trees, the gambrel roof of the Harwood cottage. She was about to turn away, when she saw a dim shape rise up from the McKenzie side of Satter's Field, vanish into a shadow, reappear by a patch of ground mist, then disappear into the trees that marked the path leading to the Harwoods. She waited and now, as if this were an old-fashioned magic lantern show, saw a second figure detach itself from the McKenzie cottage and in its turn move toward the path. Then the ceiling lights went on, and the scene beyond the window was lost. It was intermission. The audience, like galley slaves released from their chains, rose to its collective feet, and Alex's arm was taken by Amory Satterfield, who seemed to be mistaking Alex for his own father. Sarah turned, looking for Elspeth, but saw that she was now surrounded by a circle of women in pastel dresses.

Sarah—it was the easiest thing in the world—moved up the wall aisle, toward the door, and out to the plot of rough-cut grass at the back of the building, where a grove of birches like white fingers marked the edge of the field. Grateful for the cool air, she walked along the marshy edge of Satter's Field, squelching in the mud, her canvas shoes and skirt soaking up the dew from the long grass, and then turned toward the Harwood roof. After climbing a slippery embankment, she stopped and asked herself what in God's name was she up to, but there seemed to be no proper answer, except that the little shiver of excitement she had first felt on seeing the two shadows was now more intense and urged her forward. Sarah, scrambling up a long ledge, saw a car parked in the road opposite the Harwood front door, a vehicle she recognized as the island's all-purpose emergency car, one of two on the island. Of course. Murder had been done, and the car was standing guard, its occupant commanding a view of the front of the house and its entrance. So where had those two figures gone? Well, she remembered Marian talking about china stored in the cellar. And cellars had cellar doors, hadn't they? Half crawling, Sarah worked her way through a thicket of alders, a clump of mature thistles, and a patch of wild raspberries, and, bent double, plunged across the side lawn toward the back of the house. Then, almost to the shelter of a lilac, she caught her foot in a hidden croquet hoop and sprawled flat. Her breath knocked out, she could only open and close her mouth like a beached fish.

For fully five minutes, she lay on the soaked grass gasping and calling herself an idiot who should now rise up and call the police. But instead she stayed on the grass, increasingly chilled and stiff, waiting, listening. For a long while nothing but night noises, unidentifiable creaks and peeps and the raucous whoop of a heron in the cove. And then from the blurred outlines of the lilac, a soft rasping . . . the cellar doors opening exactly where Sarah had imagined them to be. And now two shapes moving across the lawn and stopping at the margin. Unmistakable, the voice of Giddy.

"I said, you turkey . . . you absolute turkey. Now get out of here fast."

"God, Giddy, keep it down."

"Roger, how dumb . . . " Sarah lost the next few words, and then Giddy's voice rose again: " . . . and everyone's working their butt off searching. What were you doing in there anyway, breaking in and throwing papers around? Don't you know about your father?" Sarah again lost the flow, and then, " . . . so I tried to clean up. Now go on, we shouldn't be seen together. There's a service tomorrow, didn't you know? Oh, you make me so . . . " And then Roger suddenly swiveled about and came directly at Sarah, a menacing figure in the shadow.

Sarah stood up. "Giddy, it's me," she called softly.

Giddy flung herself around. "Who in hell?" Then, gesturing at Roger, "Get out of here fast." And Roger was gone, a dark shape twisting through the trees.

"Giddy," called Sarah again. "It's me, Sarah Deane. Over here."

"Well, shit," said Giddy, coming over. "God, what a night. Listen, it's bad enough my trailing Roger around to see what he's up to you, without you . . . "

"I saw you from the window at the meeting, two people going by."

"And you followed. Damn, Sarah, don't start in like Alex

with his half-baked detective routine, snooping around when he's practically middle-aged. And that Roger," added Giddy angrily, "crazy. Anyway, you can't tell."

"But you've found him now and I've seen him."

"I promised. I'll shut up about finding him and you do about seeing both of us."

"But the police," said Sarah. "Fingerprints."

"I used Marian's gardening gloves, and Roger's are all over anyway."

"I skipped out of the meeting, what am I going to say?"

"We'll make up something. Look, honestly, I was doing Roger a favor by following him. I think he needs help, and if he finds out you saw us, well, he does have a temper. Things might get complicated."

"But Roger's father is dead, murdered," said Sarah with increasing exasperation. She was suddenly very tired. "Go to the police, Giddy, and let them decide what's important."

"I will if I have to, but now I think Roger's just looking for something that belongs to him. Tell everyone you left the meeting for fresh air."

"And that I got lost and rolled into a raspberry patch?"

"Sure," said Giddy. "You're just a visitor and didn't know where you were going. Visitors are always falling into holes or off some cliff. Alex said you're an English teacher, so use your imagination. Just wing it."

"I get the picture," said Sarah irritably. "But Alex and your Aunt Elspeth are pretty sharp."

"Make an effort," said Giddy. "Now go on ahead. I'll take another route."

Too weary to try to navigate the marsh, Sarah turned and walked south down the road within three feet of the watching police car. Just a mixed-up summer visitor going by, she said to herself.

At the McKenzie picket fence, she stopped and looked across the misty swale to the lighted windows of the historical society building and heard muted voices singing, "Oh beautiful for spacious skies, for amber waves of grain."

They're finishing, thought Sarah in a panic. I'd better clean up. She hurtled through the back door and into the kitchen. Alex was seated at the table holding a glass of beer. Patsy lay at his feet, a square of gingerbread between his paws, Nate Harwood's hat having been taken as evidence.

"Hello, Sarah. Look at you." He studied Sarah for a moment as she stood in the doorway, disheveled, a triangular tear hanging down from the sleeve of her shirt, lines of dried blood criss-crossing her legs. "Been for a little walk? Lovely night. I was hot, too. Slipped out just after you did. Thought I'd find you somewhere. Down on the dock, maybe."

Sarah shook her head.

"To the beach for an evening swim? No? Up at the Lodge for a little night life? No again? I give up. Your turn."

"I went for a walk . . . around the graveyard, on past the church."

"I don't remember any roses or raspberry patches along there," said Alex. "And I think you've been in a patch of something. Hungry perhaps? A little smackerel mackerel of something?"

"I don't like sarcasm," said Sarah. She turned to the sink and ran water over a paper towel, just as she had aboard the *Robin Day* only the previous afternoon. Her legs now looked as if she had walked into a wall of barbed wire.

"Soap's behind the sink," said Alex. "Now my mother's used to my disappearing at these things, and she might be willing to think that you had an attack of the vapors, but you'd better think of something to say. She'll think you tangled with our fugitive, Roger." Here Sarah abruptly bent over the sink.

For a moment she scrubbed furiously and then said, "I'll tell your mother I fell into some thorny things . . . which I did, dammit. Summer visitors do things like that, don't they?"

"Yes, summer visitors do peculiar things. Take off, go exploring, scratch their legs. You sometimes see summer visitors doing detective work without asking their old friends to come along. And look now, here's Giddy and Mother."

"Alex, I don't see why you couldn't have stuck it out," said Elspeth. "Giddy turned up and walked me home."

"Have some gingerbread," said Alex. "Sarah here is just washing up. She fell into some raspberries and into the marsh."

"Oh, Sarah," cried Elspeth. "Your poor legs."

"And her poor blouse," said Alex.

"I lost my way," said Sarah. "I was trying to take a short-cut."

"To where?" said Alex, looking up, interested.

"That's the trouble with tourists," said Giddy, stepping forward. Sarah saw that her hair was combed, and she looked as fresh as if she had just come down for breakfast. "Tourists always get into trouble. Do you remember last year, Aunt Elspeth, when that woman from Pennsylvania fell into the ice house pond, and I gave her mouth-to-mouth, and then that man on the Ocean Trail hike went into the bear caves and had a *grand mal* fit, and the girl from the Eider Inn climbed Light-house Point and her body was never found?"

"That's enough," said Alex. "I know collaboration when I hear it. I see you didn't fall into the raspberries."

"I know my way around. I went for a walk around the harbor. Lots of light. I like to see what cruising boats are in."

"I must have missed you," said Alex. "I was down there for quite a while."

"I didn't stay there the whole time."

"Went up Lighthouse Trail, did you?"

"As a matter of fact . . . the view is terrific even with only half a moon."

"Too bad, I must have missed you there, too. The Eider Inn? Did you . . . "

"That's enough, Alex," said Elspeth. "You sound like one of those Ionesco plays."

"Yes," said Sarah. "Stop it." It was, she felt, a scene that had been repeated many times when a younger Alex had teased and badgered his little cousin.

"Here's something to think about," said Elspeth. "Harrison Petty left me with a whole stack of catalogues to try and get rid of. The Inn and the Lodge will probably take a few, but not enough to get him off the hook." She picked up the top catalogue from a stack left on a chair. "That picture of Roger's. 'Grange Supper.' I do like it. A real sense of design that I miss in his new things. And it reminds me of something, though I suppose there are millions of paintings of people eating at long tables."

"It's because it's a Saturday-night bean supper," said Alex. "You've been to too many."

"It does look familiar," said Sarah, glad of a change of subject.

" 'The Last Supper,' " said Alex, finishing his beer. "Or 'Salome serving the head of John the Baptist.' "

"That's not very helpful," said his mother.

"It's not meant to be," said Alex. He stood up. "Good-night all. Sarah, I'll walk you over to the boat tomorrow and make sure you don't get lost again."

"Now what's the matter with him?" said Elspeth.

"I can't imagine," said Sarah untruthfully.

Later, climbing into bed, she was once more too tired to sort out the evening: truth from falsehood, danger from accident, necessity from promise. Alex's in a temper, she thought, smiling a little. He's not the man on the spot for once. But what kind of a spot was it? A silly incident with a couple of over-age adolescents, or real trouble? Maybe she'd better not try any more night solos, because if Roger wasn't doing anything wrong, why was he acting like someone in a crime series? All right, she told herself, I'll tell Alex I saw Roger but not Giddy.

* * *

Which Sarah did as she and Alex sat on the chest of life preservers in the stern of the *Robin Day*. "So I thought I'd take a walk around Satter's Field, and I saw this man running along by the trees, and I thought it might be Roger, so I followed right through all those raspberries and roses, got all muddy and tripped, and Roger disappeared . . . and I guess that's about it."

"Sarah, you're one hell of a lousy liar. I know you . . . you have great powers of specific description, and that little scenario isn't worth a C-minus."

"I'm sorry."

"No, you're not. You're enjoying yourself. English teacher turns lone sleuth."

"I did promise."

"Yes, you probably did, but you may be sticking out your neck, and I love your neck just where it is—attached. Listen. Nate Harwood was murdered. Roger Harwood went into hiding after being trapped in his own empty house. Why? How did he know that Nate wasn't around? Murder, Sarah. Shall I spell it? Nate may not have been a favorite in these parts, but he was a living, breathing man a few weeks ago. Roger might not be involved, but I don't think you should be trying to find out, alone, at night. So what really happened, and how does Giddy fit in? I don't want one of my favorite cousins hamstrung either. And did you know that, according to Mother and her spies, Giddy was living with Roger earlier this summer, so she may have been having a lover's reaction or a motherly spasm? Giddy's strong on the underdog."

"Okay," said Sarah, abandoning loyalty. "Here's how it went . . . " And she gave in careful detail the sequence of events. In the retelling it sounded to her ears exactly like a school adventure story.

Alex listened quietly and then said, "All right, I'll talk to Giddy and clear you of treason. The police will have to heat up the search for Roger. Then I've been asked to round up some people for the memorial service tonight. I'll pick you up at Sydney's at five. How's it going there?"

"Oh, he's not too bad," said Sarah, "but the art supply and gift business isn't exactly thrilling. I haven't broken anything yet, but then I only sell the cheapies. Ali Baba's cave is off limits most of the time."

Mike Laaka met Alex outside the newly planted State Police Command Post—a somewhat used-looking trailer set up on blocks by the side of the Port Clyde public landing. "This," said Mike, as if exhibiting a rare specimen, "is George Fitts, State Police CID. George here tells me the medical examiner thinks Nate's head was stove in somehow."

"Morning, Dr. McKenzie," said Sergeant Fitts, moving his head slightly on its vertical axis. He was a slight, neatly dressed, smooth-faced, bald-headed man with thin lips and narrow elliptical eyes. He looked, to Alex, rather as if an electric light bulb had been mounted on the neck of a department store mannequin. He now carefully unfolded a notebook. "We're waiting to hear about the manner of death. He was dead before he went into the water. Microscopic exam of the lung tissue confirms that."

"Lots of problems there," said Mike. "God, the salt water. That guy was completely pickled, and the fish had been helping themselves."

"Yes," said Alex, "I helped pull him out."

"So," said George, his pencil poised above his notebook, "we're glad you're helping us in this, Doctor. We need someone who knows the island. Keep your eyes open. Mike thinks the art theft series may be tied in. I don't. Not yet. Right now I want to hear about Mr. Harwood." George angled a hand in the direction of the trailer door, and the three men trooped inside.

When Alex finished with his summary of what he knew of the life history of Nathaniel Harwood, Mike nodded. "Like I told you, George, Mr. Amiable. Anyway, we've got to start finding out where old Nate was and when. He gyrated all over the map, and he didn't announce his plans in advance. Think of all the places he might have stopped to go sketching."

"I have the following," said George. He had a voice as thin as his lips, and he had a way of finishing his sentences by pushing his lips together as if afraid that an unnecessary word might escape. He held a time sheet close to his rimless glasses. "Tuesday, August fifth, Harwood came over on the noon boat from Port Clyde to Weymouth. He'd been off the island for three days, movements pretty well accounted for. Three nights spent in Thomaston, his winter house with the big studio."

"Whole parcel of people saw him," said Mike. "Your mother, who was on the same boat, and Rachel, Lyda, Lem, and Amory Satterfield, who all saw him after he landed. He was mad as hell about his painting being stolen. Same afternoon your mother reported her Godding entry gone, and later Roger in Port Clyde found his painting gone. We put it down to just three more stolen paintings. Art stuff has been disappearing spring and summer for at least three years without anyone getting knocked off. But now I sort of wonder about a connection."

"To go on," said George, "because at this stage I don't speculate, the museum suggested that each artist send in a substitute work to the Godding show and Mrs. McKenzie and Roger did so. Nate stopped in at the museum some time before noon on Thursday, August seventh, but didn't commit himself to another entry. He borrowed Mrs. Ordway's phone, and she heard him call Sydney Prior to ask about an overdue order of palette knives. Then we have a neighbor's confirmation that Nate turned up Thursday evening at his winter house in Thomaston."

"And Friday?" asked Alex. He pulled off his sweater. The little trailer office was heating up with the morning sun.

"Friday it was boom-boom all over," said Mike. "In Rockland in the A.M., Nate and Roger slammed into each other right in front of the bookstore and had a big shouting match. Clara Satterfield heard them and was so embarrassed she ducked into the five-and-dime store. Nate turned up next in Port Clyde for a late lunch at the Dip Net and complained that the lemon pie was all gone. Then up turned Roger in that old wreck of a pickup he drives. Takes one look into the Dip Net and backs off. Waitress knows both of them and guessed that the place was too small for the two of them."

"Here's where we need Giddy Lester's statement," said George. To Alex, the two policemen were like a comedy team, passing the recitation back and forth, breezy Mike and smoothie professional George.

"Sydney's statement gives it that Giddy waited on Nate in the morning before Nate drove to Rockland. Nate came back after lunch and this time Sydney handled him. Nate wanted to go all through Sydney's supplies and was told to butt out. Not in those words . . . you know big juicy-mouthed Sydney. Anyway, Sydney said good-bye, that he had to leave for a meeting in Portland."

"Confirmation on Sydney Prior in Portland that Friday afternoon and evening," said George.

"Next," said Mike, "Nate goes off toward the public landing, and by God, wouldn't you know, there's Roger down by the shore. The kid takes one look at Dad, drags a skiff into the water, and takes off rowing like mad into the harbor. As far as we know, Roger wasn't seen for the rest of the afternoon, and from what I hear has been missing since Saturday on Weymouth, after being conked on the head by his mother."

"He's been seen recently," said Alex, and he filled the two men in on the night meeting of Giddy and Roger.

"Will I ever blister that boy's balls," said Mike.

"Not helpful," said George. He unfolded a white handkerchief and delicately blotted his forehead. "You always come on too strong, Mike."

"Bullshit," said Mike. "I get along good with kids and, hell, I've known Roger all my life."

"So it's fixed that Nate was alive and well in Port Clyde Friday afternoon," said Alex, seeing breakers ahead.

"Right," said George. He refolded his handkerchief and examined it for flaws. "Nate also turned up at the Port Clyde Arts and Crafts Gallery and signed the register, and then around three o'clock he came into the general store, which means he wasn't on the three o'clock run of the *Robin Day* to Weymouth."

"Almost another collision at the store," said Mike. "Marian Harwood was there when Nate came in, so she dodged into the side room where they keep the bulk stores. Got down behind some dog kibble bags and stayed there until the coast was clear. This from one of the clerks. He noticed her because she got her dark blue dress covered with dust. Damn silly, a grown woman acting like that."

"And where did Marian go from there?" said Alex.

"Hold it with Marian," said Mike. "Finish Nate, because now we have the case of the missing groceries . . . that's a pun, George, so smile, live a little. Nate bought two cartons of groceries, canned stuff and perishables, lettuce, peaches, so forth. Paid cash and told the clerk—a kid called Jerry—to mark his boxes with 'Harwood' and put 'em on the five-fifteen boat. The store does this for its island customers. Nate said he had some business and left and, as far as we know, was never seen again. Jerry put his groceries on the ferry and they were off-loaded at Weymouth. Nate never turned up to claim 'em and Lem Wallace finally carried the stuff up to Rachel's. He knew Marian was staying there and must have figured that with 'Harwood' marked on, they were for her."

"Mrs. Harwood herself came over on the five-fifteen boat and says she didn't see her husband," said George. "But she isn't a reliable witness because she stayed in the cabin—this confirmed—and Harwood usually stayed on deck."

"How about all the old boys on the post office bench?" said Alex.

"No help," said George, "what with a big weekend crowd disembarking Friday. If Harwood was around, he didn't do anything to attract attention."

"Except not pick up his groceries," said Alex.

"And not keep an appointment," said Mike. "A man from Vermont wanting to buy a painting. Set up for seven o'clock at the Inn. Nate wouldn't have missed that one. He loved making money."

"We did have a report of lights going on and off in the Harwood cottage last Friday," said George.

"The furniture caper, I'm afraid," said Alex, looking at Mike.

Mike grinned. "That's a little wrinkle I'll brief you on, George, so you can arrest half of Weymouth's leading citizens."

"What about Nate getting over to Weymouth in his own or a private boat?" asked Alex, moving the discussion to safer ground.

"Possible," said George. "Or a seaplane. But we've checked. Nate's boat was in for repairs and we've no reports that he used any other one. Now, Marian Harwood. She says she shopped in Rockland and has sales slips to prove it, had lunch by herself at the Salad Patch, about one-forty or so. She then drove to Port Clyde, saw Nate at the general store, ducked into the side room, and after he'd left, she went out without buying anything. Claims that she was too upset. She checked her watch, saw that she'd missed the three o'clock ferry, and so decided to drive out to Spruce Head. No particular reason, just to kill time. Then says she returned to Port Clyde, parked her car, boarded the five-fifteen to the island, and went directly to the cabin. Everything confirmed but her Spruce Head expedition between three and five."

"And Saturday?" said Alex.

"Big zero on Nate," said Mike. "No substitute painting sent in to the Godding. No one saw his car come or go from the Port Clyde parking lot he uses behind the boat docks. Of course, the whole place is a nightmare on weekends, so that doesn't mean much."

"More important," said George, "Harwood failed to meet his Portland dealer for a long-planned date to talk about a one-man show. So, though it's tentative, we're taking Friday midafternoon as the last time Nate was seen alive."

"Next," said Alex, "you've got the scene of the crime."

"Listen to the expert," said Mike. "That Texas business

went to your head, Alexander McKenzie. What scene of what crime? Christ, a body stuck in a weir is no scene."

"It's all you've got," Alex pointed out.

"Correct," said George. "Our people will go over the whole cove and the beach and rope it off from the public."

"But," said Alex, "if Nate had been dumped in the waters around Weymouth over ten days ago, wouldn't he have washed in sooner? Maybe the body was weighted and the weight came loose in the storm."

"Possible," said George. He laced his long fingers together and seemed to ponder the point. "Possible and probable. I'd say he was thrown in, tied and weighted from a boat, not dumped from either Weymouth or Port Clyde. Too many people around in both places for that sort of operation."

"Weapon?" said Alex.

"Maybe old faithful, the blunt instrument," said Mike. "Man's best friend. The lab people said the skull fracture suggested it."

"And motive?" said Alex, and immediately regretted it. "Never mind, I can guess motive."

"Which brings us to young Roger Harwood," said George. "The alienated son is always a sound bet. As is the wife. I always say start with the family. Violence begins at home."

"Don't go neglecting the alienated public," said Mike. "Hey there, Susie"—this to a neat brown head in the doorway—"what's doing?"

"I have a person on the premises," Susan announced. "She claims to have been here before. Ruth Baker."

"Aw, hell, Susie, you know she's been here before. So what does she want?"

"She wants to see the vehicle. The vehicle in question."

"I'll leave you to this, Mike." George rose, a swift, perfectly oiled motion, and, reaching across the deputy's desk, swept his cap neatly from underneath John Henry's hooves.

"What vehicle, Susan?" said Mike, sighing.

"The wrecked one . . . you know, the car her parents were drowned in. Port Clyde harbor."

Mike groaned. "What a frigging nuisance. It's at some damn junkyard. She signed the release. Okay, send her in. No, Alex, stick around. Maybe we can cut this short."

Ruth Baker stepped into the room, took off her sunglasses, and blinked in a nearsighted way at the two men.

Alex stood up. "Hello there, Miss Baker. Still looking?"

"Oh, it's Dr. McKenzie. Hello, Mr. Laaka. I've had this idea. It's about Mother and Dad's car. I never did see it."

"Please sit down, Miss Baker," said Mike. "You've been thinking that the painting might have been overlooked? But you must know that something like that, even if it's wrapped up, is pretty noticeable. No one could miss it unless it washed out when the diver got the car doors open, and in that case, it might be gone for good. I think you're just troubling yourself for nothing. Honest, Miss Baker, why not call it quits, and if that picture shows, we'll be in touch right away."

"I didn't think the painting would be in the car . . . but maybe a sales receipt, a note, something that didn't seem important to the police." Ruth's hands fastened around the top of her white handbag, and she snapped the catch open and shut.

Alex was reminded of some tawny little field animal, a rabbit, a prairie dog, with bright eyes and a nervous nose, ready to jump if danger threatened. "Look, Mike," he said, "was the car actually searched?"

"Our guys cleaned it out, but not like a forensic lab does."

"So something might have been left?"

"Yeah," said Mike, "I suppose it might. See here, Miss Baker—can I call you Ruth? Okay? Now, Ruth, we've got upwards of fifteen hundred unattended deaths in Maine, which is peanuts, I know, when you look at New York or Chicago, but we haven't the cash or the facilities to research every case. Our local medical examiners aren't forensic pathologists, just ordinary garden-type physicians like Alex here. They rule on death. If anything looks offbeat we call in the State Police and the Chief Medical Examiner in Augusta."

"And my parents' death was ruled accidental," said Ruth.

"Right. It was even witnessed. We guessed that your father may have felt faint—you said he had spells—or that your mother, if she was driving, panicked. Who knows? We couldn't identify the driver since both bodies were recovered from the back seat. You know all this and you authorized the cremation. Deputy Cohen and her partner checked out the car, emptied it, and we sold it, like you asked, for junk."

"It was just an idea," repeated Ruth. "If I could just see the car, to go through it once, then maybe after I've visited a few more galleries, I'll go home."

Alex could stand it no longer. "Come on, Ruth. I'll show you the way to the junkyard. Where is it, Mike?"

Mike reached for a file marked, "July, Accidental deaths," turned several pages, and pulled out a card. "Ford Fairmont, 1980, $600. Tim Potter, Auto Parts, Potter's Field—sort of a sick joke, I guess. Over by Union off Route 17."

* * *

Even the dust and the crumpled metal did not hide the fact that the Baker car had recently been a mint ready-to-go machine. But it had a blind, defeated look, its headlights hanging out on wire stalks, like the compound eye of some space age arthropod. Ruth stood for several minutes looking at it, then, visibly bracing herself, bent to peer in through the driver's window.

Alex, thinking that at such a moment he should take himself off, wandered down one of the rutted dirt roads. It was a sea of destruction. Cars, pickups, a tractor, a school bus, bodies without wheels, wheels without bodies, metal pleated and twisted, car seats covered with dirt and giant slivers of glass. Alex stopped by a yellow Honda Accord, its rear body whole and new and its front gone as if sheared by clippers. The hole in the driver's windshield was almost completely round. Alex, feeling sick, walked back to Lot 16 and found Ruth Baker sitting in the Fairmont's driver's seat.

"Watch out for broken glass," said Alex.

"The brakes don't work."

"It's been in an accident, in salt water. Nothing will work right. The junkyard just bought it for parts."

"Oh," said Ruth. "Well, I suppose."

"You were thinking the brakes were defective?"

"I guess so. I still can't believe they let themselves go right into the water like that."

"A car that goes into salt water would have to be dried and lubricated immediately, and Mike said there was too much damage to make it worth the expense. The brake fluid probably leaked out on impact."

"I didn't want the car anyway. A reminder like that around."

"Did you find anything?"

Ruth indicated a small heap next to her on the seat. It was a pathetic collection. A lipstick, eight pennies, a quarter, a ballpoint pen—"all in between the seats," said Ruth—a folded road map of New England, and a small brown notebook, these last two the worse for immersion.

Ruth held up the notebook. "It's lucky it's in pencil because I can still read most of it. Just gas expenses and mileages. Dad always kept track on trips. There are some notes about inns and restaurants at the end, and places to visit. See for yourself."

Alex turned the pages, fragile and furred at the edges. Miles per gallon were marked in a shaky hand against a column of figures, and then Galena, Gary, Toledo, Hudson, Erie, Niagara Falls, Utica, Lenox, Portsmouth—a fuel log of the trip. Other notes followed—art galleries, museums, L. L. Bean, Wiscasset, Pemaquid Point. Then, a last notation, "rental cottages?"

"You see," said Ruth, "that proves they were serious about finding a place."

"Ruth," said Alex, "you're just going to make yourself twice as miserable with this. It's over. Perhaps your parents asked directions for a cottage, took a wrong turn, got mixed up. No one would want to hurt them. And they weren't robbed, were they? Did you get their money, jewelry, from the police?"

Ruth nodded, her face unhappy. "Yes, Mother's engagement ring. I have it with me. A ruby with diamonds. It's old-fashioned but valuable, I guess. And Dad's lodge ring, the cash, Mother's new camera, though that's ruined. Only the painting missing."

"Perhaps it was lifted from the car when they stopped somewhere."

"But the painting would have been wrapped, don't you suppose? Not looking like a painting. I think the note about the cottage is important. They might have stopped at a real estate agency along the way and told the salesman about loving Maine and buying a painting. Mother was like that, friendly, always talking. She'd give someone her life history in the first five minutes. Maybe I should look for a dishonest real estate person."

"You can suggest it to Mike, but don't be surprised if he isn't enthusiastic."

"That might be because the police themselves are involved," said Ruth, ready to leap down another path. "That would explain why they're not hunting for it."

Alex saw that Ruth Baker was made of sterner material than he had at first thought. "Okay, Ruth," he said. "But if you're going to visit real estate offices, I wouldn't start by suggesting they employ light-fingered salesmen. And I wouldn't go to Mike and talk about dishonest deputies. Local people are a little touchy about suspicious out-of-state people."

"You don't know how many people have said 'out-of-state' to me," said Ruth angrily. "You'd think it was a disease."

The rabbit turns, said Alex to himself. He reached over and squeezed her hand. "I'll bet everyone is a lot friendlier in Missouri."

"Well, you've been very nice," said Ruth, "and I'll try not to do anything stupid . . . but I am going to learn about brakes and summer rentals."

Alex, driving back from Potter's Field, suddenly remembered Giddy, who at that moment might be making her statement at the State Police trailer. She'll think Sarah betrayed her, he thought, and shoved down the accelerator.

He found Giddy flanked by a stenographer, Mike Laaka, and George Fitts. Giddy's face was red, her hands in fists, and her blunt chin thrust out, so that altogether she reminded Alex of a Shetland pony the McKenzies had harbored when they were children. That animal, with hooves planted forward, neck arched, hindquarters set, could rarely be persuaded to move ahead in a straight line or tolerate a rider for more than a few minutes.

"Hi there, Giddy," said Alex. "How's the statement going?" He reached for a folding chair, opened it, and sat down.

"Giddy here—" began Mike.

"That's Ms. Grace Lester to you, Deputy Laaka," said Giddy.

"I am telling Miss Lester," said George, "that we know she visited the Harwood cottage Monday night and spoke to Roger Harwood, and later asked Sarah Deane not to discuss the incident."

"And Sarah's a traitor," said Giddy loudly.

"No, I am," said Alex. "You gave yourself away Monday night . . . too helpful. So I put the heat on Sarah and made her tell me. Come on, Giddy, you can't hide things like that. How long have you been meeting Roger while we've all been beating the island for him?"

"I haven't been meeting him. I'm completely finished

with Roger Harwood. It was . . . " Giddy fumbled for some comprehensive expression. "It was one of those life misjudgments everyone makes. Roger isn't always totally in control, but that doesn't mean I'm going to sneak on him."

"Even," said Alex, "if he's broken into his murdered father's house twice . . . and his mother's trying to face this alone?"

"I know what I should do, which is more than some people. I don't go crying to the police every time I accidentally bump into a friend. You never used to be such a law-and-order creep, Alex, going around messing up other people's lives." Giddy's face was increasingly flushed, and Alex didn't know whether she was about to hit him or burst into tears.

"Leave Roger Harwood for now," said George. "Tell us, Miss Lester, about Nate Harwood coming into Prior's Gallery on the eighth of August."

"Oh, okay," said Giddy, subsiding. "But you've got most of this. I was alone in the shop just after we'd opened—that's after nine-thirty—and Mr. Prior was on some errand, and Mr. Harwood walked in."

"Was he wearing his hat?" Alex remembered Patsy and the flats mud.

Giddy screwed up her face in an effort at recall. "I think so, because he didn't take it off the way some men do. He wanted action on his order. I told him that the palette knives came through the West Coast and be patient." Giddy, Alex reflected, would have told Lenin to be patient. "So," she went on, "he wanted to look over the whole place, the Parlor Gallery and the workroom, but I said no way, that Mr. Prior would have my scalp if I let him loose in the whole place. By that time some customers were stacking up, so I said we'd call him and good-bye, Mr. Harwood."

"And he left?"

"Finally. I can usually handle mean people. They just need someone to talk right back to them. That's Roger's problem. He's really freaked out by his father . . . " Giddy suddenly halted and stiffened. "That's all. Can I go now?" She stood up and stuffed an escaped tail of her T-shirt into her jeans.

Mike tried once more. "Give us a break, Giddy. What was Roger doing at his cottage? What did he say to you?"

Giddy reached for her rucksack, started for the door, and then turned. "That's what I asked Roger. What was he doing there? Well, you'll just have to work on it."

* * *

Sarah, on arriving at work that morning, had found she was to be given an outdoor assignment. Sydney, in shirt-sleeves, was kneeling over several open boxes filled with stacks of brochures. "The Landing Day programs," he said, holding one aloft, its blue cover handsomely decorated with a woodcut of Captain's Head. "We never used to have any, and it was all a terrible scramble. Children's games, pageants, Captain Weymouth—whoever played him—and his sailors wandering around eating clam rolls. No sense of history. My father began working on an orderly protocol, and, naturally, I became involved. I set the cultural guidelines, readings from Captain John Smith and from James Rosier's Journal plus a library display, though Rachel Seaver can be extremely difficult."

"I can see why you need a program."

"Indispensable for the tourists, and this is the biggest yet."

Sarah turned over the pages and found a full-color picture of how an artist imagined Captain Weymouth's vessel, the *Archangel*, to look as it rode at anchor off what was now Sailor's Cove. The reproduction, she thought, compared favorably in quality with those in the Godding catalogue. "You *are* a benefactor," she said.

Sydney seemed pleased. He pressed the tops of his pudgy fingers together and rocked gently back on his heels. "Weymouth means a great deal to me. Almost every summer of my life spent there. I'm a widower now, and no children. What better way to spend my money?" Sydney's voice had a proprietory ring, and Sarah could see that Landing Day was for him the culmination of the year, a self-wrought apotheosis.

"And now, my dear," said Sydney, "you must help me with the distribution. Count out about three hundred—they're in packs of twenty—and leave a pack at the motels and shops along the coast. Use your judgment. No bars or grills, nothing too ramshackle. You have your car? Fine, I'll hold the fort."

It was almost two o'clock when Sarah, driving north on Route 1 with her diminished supply of programs, caught sight of Ruth Baker coming out of a roadside real estate office. She turned her car, pulled alongside, and called out, "Any luck?"

"I'm off on a new tack," said Ruth. "I'm trying to find out if Mother and Dad actually started looking for a cottage."

"It's something to try," said Sarah, "but I suppose the police . . ."

"The police, even if they're not implicated themselves, which I think is likely, have made it clear that they're too busy to bother with my parents' painting, and that the case is closed. But I haven't closed it." Ruth stamped a white sandaled foot.

Sarah, talking over the scene later with Alex, agreed that they had both been wrong about Ruth Baker. "I think she's the pioneer type," Sarah had said. "Quiet and stubborn and keeps trekking west no matter what. I can see her in a wagon driving a mule team with her family china packed in a flour barrel. She's the sort who hides the children and meets a grizzly with a frying pan."

Sarah now nodded encouragement as Ruth leaned into her car window and described seeing her parents' car. "I found a note about a rental cottage, and the brakes don't work."

"What?" said Sarah. "You drove the car?"

"No. I just sat in the front seat and pushed and pumped the brake pedal. It went right down to the floor."

"But you can't think someone fooled with the brakes to get at a painting. The brakes probably got smashed when the car went into the harbor, or maybe they were defective. I'm sure the police checked it all out."

"But what if that painting had been done by some really famous artist or was one of those stolen ones that everyone's talking about? Then the gallery owner would have to get it back. Because of his reputation."

"No," said Sarah, frowning. "A gallery owner, even if he'd sold a stolen Rembrandt, wouldn't try to get it back by fooling with the brakes. Taking a chance on causing an accident is a great way of making sure the painting is damaged. It's crazy, Ruth."

"You can't discourage me," said Ruth stubbornly.

"Another thing, if the brakes were tampered with, how could anyone know where or how they'd fail? Your parents could just as well have gone off in a ditch or hit a tree, or even tried the brakes in a safe place. It was just terrible luck they turned off down toward that wharf."

"Crazy or not, I'm going to find out what salt water does to brakes, and I'll keep after the real estate people and the police. And the galleries, of course. People from Missouri are like mules. You've heard that, haven't you?"

Mule is right, thought Sarah, as Ruth headed for her own car. But, after all, Ruth's tenacity was admirable, an example to them all. Ruth knew what she wanted and, in spite of grief and in the face of official skepticism, was going forward. I think I'll help her if I have some time, she told herself. Somehow, Ruth's project was infinitely more appealing than the distasteful Harwood affair.

Sydney Prior welcomed Sarah back. "I've been run off my feet. Come into the parlor and help me unpack the china that's come in. A Meissen dinner service and the Crown Derby I've been waiting for."

Sarah followed Sydney as he, huffing and puffing and coughing his dry cough, led the way to the back parlor. I'm certainly trading on the fact I'm not Giddy, she thought. Otherwise no one would let me loose in here—this as she caught herself from stumbling over a doorstop shaped like a basket of fruit.

It proved to be a long afternoon, punctuated by Sarah's returning time and again to deal with front shop customers —Sydney having had a bell wire installed in the Parlor Gallery to warn of such. In the parlor she fetched and carried paintings, many in heavy gold frames, but finally the last purchase was concluded, and an oil by Jonathan Fisher, documented and tenderly wrapped by Sydney, was carried off by a young couple whose visible attributes in the matter of clothes, jewelry, and automobile were all that a gallery owner could desire.

Sydney subsided in a wing chair and wiped his forehead. "Drudgery. Pure drudgery. No one knows what a day I put in. Harrison Petty has nothing like it. The Godding is an ivory tower."

Sarah, done in from program distribution, with arms that throbbed from lifting outsize paintings, did not answer. Instead, she finished unwrapping the last Crown Derby piece, a little eight-inch bowl, and held it to the window, seeing the pattern in gold and white, deep blue, and crimson glow as if it had caught fire. She could see how one could become fond of such things. Then, putting the bowl down, she asked on impulse, "Mr. Prior, if you wanted to steal something valuable, how would you do it?"

Sydney sat up and stared. He looked too astonished to answer.

"I don't mean you," Sarah said hastily. "I mean anybody. I'm thinking of Ruth Baker and her parents' painting, and all the others taken this summer."

"But I wouldn't," said Sydney. "I think art theft is . . . " He seemed bemused by the question. "My gallery," he went on. "I've always tried . . . "

"No," said Sarah. "Just pretend. I'm curious, how would you go about it? Of course, first, you'd have to be sure the house or studio was empty."

"I think," said Sydney, recovering, "that first of all, stealing art is insane. Paintings are, or should be, original. One of a kind. Think of the disposal problem. Paintings are easily traced and recognized, hard, often impossible, to get rid of."

"But paintings are taken," said Sarah. "All the time."

"Well," said Sydney rather grudgingly, "if I were that foolish, I'd move away to some place no one knew me . . . take a new identity. Then I suppose I'd . . . what's the word . . . case the area, find out who owned what galleries, what houses were vulnerable. I'd take a job as a janitor, a security guard, or a yardman and wait my chance. But, to repeat, I wouldn't. If I turned larcenous, I'd go in for cameras, watches, jewelry, things like that. What are you up to, Sarah? Helping Mike Laaka?"

"Oh, I ran into Ruth Baker again, and then as you know I'm staying with the McKenzies and I've heard all about the thefts."

"And Ruth Baker thinks her parents' painting was stolen?"

"It's just that she's upset and can't trace the picture, and then she thinks—it's absolutely wild—that someone might have tried to kill her parents to get at the picture. Anyway, I began to think about stealing things when I was admiring that Crown Derby bowl, and I thought that since you're in the business you might have an idea. I mean you've had things taken, haven't you?"

"I'm afraid that being a victim doesn't tell me how it's done or how the objects are disposed of. I've been fortunate, small things mostly, silver, last month a cloisonné dish, a paperweight, things that slip into a pocket, under a coat. So Sarah, tell me how you'd go about it."

Sarah shrugged. "I'm afraid I'm like you, Mr. Prior. I think it's a stupid way of making money."

"I think we'd both be caught in our very first heist . . . is that the term? I'm too conspicuous, and you'd look guilty. Now let's close early, it's almost four-thirty." Sydney got laboriously to his feet and unbuttoned his double-breasted white suit jacket; Sarah could see his stomach comfortably overlapping his belt. "You know," he said, "I'd despaired of getting my price for that Fisher. A good day's work. And now off to Weymouth."

"But the boat doesn't leave until five-fifteen," said Sarah, "and Alex was going to meet me here."

"We'll leave him a note. Say I've kidnapped you. Beginning my career of crime." Sydney chuckled so that his cheeks moved softly up and down, and Sarah thought, not for the first time, of Charlie Chan. He only needs a white Panama, she said to herself, and lo, Sydney reached behind a door and produced a vintage Panama.

"My father's," he said. "Sentiment plus comfort. We'll go in the *Tempest Queen* . . . my boat. Her last run. She's been sold."

"Why? Does she leak?" asked Sarah.

"No, but I'm having a new one delivered this weekend that will be heavier and a little longer. I'm no swimmer and at my age I want to feel secure. I'm going over to Nate Harwood's service. It's the least I can do for Marian. What a life she's had. Besides, I haven't been over to my cottage for several days—too busy."

So it was that Alex found Prior's Gallery closed and a note on the door from Sydney suggesting in rather coy terms that he had spirited Sarah off to Weymouth. Alex slowly made his way to the boat dock, where he found Giddy surrounded by grocery bags.

"For tonight," said Giddy. "Supper after the service. I think your mother's asked Sydney, so I'll duck out. Things are certainly hectic this summer. Your house is a regular circus and I came for a little peace."

"So," said Alex, "did I."

SEVEN

The Weymouth Community Church stood on a rise in the middle of the cluster of buildings that made up the little town's center, a location that would have given its congregation a commanding view of the harbor, had not the founding elders arranged for the box pews to face sternly north and its windows to be fixed too high for anything but heavenly contemplation.

The service for Nate Harwood had been set for six-thirty to accommodate the schedule of the *Robin Day,* but the wide wooden steps to the church were thronged by five-thirty. Nate Harwood in life had pleased few and aggravated many; Nate in death—even if not bodily present—was a star. His arrival in the weir, the fact of foul play, the appearance of the Sheriff's Department in strength, plus the greater glamour of the State Police CID, and the cry after the murdered man's missing son, Roger—all these ensured the popularity of the service.

Lyda Seaver wiped the last drops of water from a large bowl of white phlox. "I think we should just have the flowers grown on the island in the church," she said to Rachel, who in the role of church organist was engaged in putting her music in order. "It feels just like Sunday," she added, beginning on a vase of asters.

"Hardly," said Rachel. "Nate Harwood never went to church."

"But," said Lyda in her soft voice, "the service might help him—wherever he is." Unlike her spare, sharp-featured sister, everything about Lyda was soft. She was built on the lines of a sofa cushion, her arthritic joints hidden in pads, her rosy face circled by a fine cloud of white hair.

Rachel looked up. "You know perfectly well where Nate is. Don't be a fool, Lyda."

"We can hope," said Lyda. "And pray."

"Pooh. All this is for Marian. I wonder if Roger will stop this nonsense and come and support his mother. What an extremely foolish boy." Rachel sounded quite animated and, forgetting her cane, began going from pew to pew to see if the hymnals were in place.

"Here's Elspeth," called Lyda.

"Good," said Rachel. "She can deal with the minister."

Elspeth came up the aisle in navy blue, carrying white gloves bunched in one hand. "They don't match," she explained.

"Mr. Leggett's coming over," said Rachel in an extremely loud whisper. "I don't think he'll do at all, but he's the only minister we could find at short notice. He's a guest at the Inn. Our Reverend Sharper is off-island."

Elspeth looked up to see a young man with a black robe over one arm, emerging from a recess. She hurried over. "Mr. Leggett. How nice of you to fill in, and on your vacation, too. We were desperate. Now, Mrs. Harwood just wants to get this over, so keep it all very general. Mr. Harwood was so difficult. Have you a safe text?"

Mr. Leggett, a young man with a large head of black hair and a severe sunburn, changed his expression from one of practiced condolence to perplexity.

"Do the one about in my father's house are many mansions, though I suppose the new translations say apartments or condominiums," said Elspeth. "And don't talk about Mr. Harwood as a lost sheep."

"Psalms," said Mr. Leggett, clutching at straws.

"Yes, of course, and do hymns at intervals because the singing will take everyone's mind off Nate."

"A memorial service," began Mr. Leggett.

"And remember to keep it short because it's dinnertime for half these people, and now we'd better open the doors. I do hope my son—he's a doctor—makes it in case someone faints."

At six-fifteen, Sarah, now changed into her only somber costume, a dark green jumper with a ruff-necked blouse, came through the door with Alex and Giddy, but then, as they started down the aisle, stopped and whispered to Alex, "Please go on. I mean it. They'll want you up front with your mother. You're almost family." Alex, seeing Sarah set, nodded and strode ahead to Giddy's side.

Sarah settled herself next to a large lady in a black and red flowered dress and tried to listen as Rachel Seaver on the old organ dealt out Bach in wheezes and groans. As was only suitable, Sarah at first tried to think about Marian Harwood, but soon the parade passing down the aisle proved too much of a distraction. Here came Amory Satterfield leaning on a cane, in a thick-looking dark suit, and behind him Mrs. Satterfield in lavender with a pearl pin. Clara, wasn't she? Not many Claras anymore. And now Lem Wallace, hair wet and combed, in a gray suit, followed by three teenage children, and then Harrison Petty in light tan, Mrs. Ordway in gray check, and Sydney Prior, bulky in his ice cream suit, Panama in hand, inclining his head slightly to the left, to the right. Charlie Chan goes to church, thought Sarah, stifling an impulse to giggle, then wondered suddenly if she had seen, without knowing, in the flow up the aisle, the person most properly interested in the service—Nate Harwood's murderer. It was a sobering idea.

But now Rachel, on the organ, had switched from Bach to "Come Thou Almighty King," which faded into "Abide With Me." The stream up the aisle turned to a trickle, and here came Marian Harwood, moving along with her support group from the Boswell family. Marian, her square, ruddy face expressionless, holding her handbag in front of her stomach like a package about to detonate, was wearing a too short, rather creased green and white dress with a red belt. Was that a statement? I've no sense of her as a person, thought Sarah. She never seems to act—except in the warming pan incident —just reacts to events like a benign lady robot. Was it all part of the battered wife syndrome? she wondered.

And the whole scene, like one of those quasi-sociological studies made in one of those rare moments that brought the different, often warring elements under one roof. The old-timers, Weymouth bred and born, Amory Satterfield with his kith and kin, Lem Wallace, the other islanders, fishing, lobstering, farming, enduring winters of Northeast storms and isolation. And Rachel and Lyda, leaders of the moral minority. And the next layer, old summer people, the Harwoods, the McKenzies, Sydney Prior; then the Weymouth Boat Club group, usually found talking about tennis ladders and the weekend regattas—all in impeccable gray or navy today; and the next circle, the art school people and the regulars at the Inn and the Lodge; then the solid friends from the mainland, personified by Mrs. Ordway, and the not so solid in the shape of Harrison Petty. Castes within castes, plus, of course, the houseguests like herself, temporary satellites in the summer orbit. And there was Mike Laaka over on the left, born on the coast and knowing almost everyone here. He must be looking over the house.

But now, breaking into Sarah's speculations, Mr. Leggett stepped forward, looking like a very small crow in his robe, and said in a high voice, " 'I-am-the-resurrection-and-the-life-saith-the-Lord-he-that-believeth-in-Me-though-he-were-dead-yet-shall-he-live.' "

Though he were dead, thought Elspeth McKenzie. Really. It sounds as if no one is sure. Oh dear, I always cry at funerals. Think of something else. Marian is holding up. Amazingly calm, but then she always is. Why did she wear that dress? It's far too short; I can see her slip. Where's her new blue one she got in July for her Uncle Howard's funeral? Why isn't Sarah sitting with us? Still keeping her distance? Is that Alex's fault, because summer will be gone and nothing will have happened? Alex says Sarah's lost two suitors. No one says suitors anymore. He says both men died suddenly and Sarah's just coming out from under.

"Aunt Elspeth, stand up." Giddy pulled her arm. "Hymn 71."

Rachel gave warning with three measures and two chords, and the mourners in ragged chorus sang, "For the Beau-tee of the Earth, for the Glor-ee of the Skies . . . "

Why didn't Roger come? thought Giddy, humming absently. I don't suppose he's really done anything awful, but he's certainly being weird. Maybe Sarah couldn't help telling Alex about seeing me. He may have some hold over her. But they're not sleeping together, at least I don't think so. Alex's off in his old room. Is Aunt Elspeth being stuffy? Alex's getting pretty old now, so maybe there's something wrong with him . . . or with Sarah. Maybe it's psychological with her. God, was I stupid about Roger . . . all that time wasted and I thought I was in love. And there are a lot of things I never knew about him, so why am I trying to protect him?

Now it was Elspeth's turn to poke Giddy. "The hymn's over."

" . . . Therefore," said Mr. Leggett, "we will not fear though the earth be moved and though the hills be carried into the midst of the sea, though the waters thereof rage and swell."

That's a good text for storms, thought Rachel. We can use it for the Wednesday prayer group. She took a tiny gold pencil that was suspended from a chain around her neck and made a note on the edge of her music.

Mrs. Ordway, seated beside Harrison Petty, was counting catalogues. So many to sell before they broke even, so many more before a profit. But now it looked as if next year's budget would be a shambles, and Mr. Petty would have to accept a Xerox catalogue instead of that fancy printed affair.

She stared down at Harrison's shoes with irritation. They had arrived from Wildsmith's in London last week and must have cost a mint . . . and those suits and ties . . . Dior, Pierre Cardin. Money through his fingers like water. Mrs. Ordway sighed for the future of the Godding.

Alex, sitting by Giddy, was broiling in his tweed jacket, the only suitable garment he had with him. Poor Nate, he thought. Never went near a church if he could help it and now he's the feature attraction. Why did Sarah have to go and sit by herself, and oh hell, here he was with another homicide. Had the whole Maine coast conspired to get rid of Nate as a public menace? Think it out. How about Roger? What was he looking for in the cottage? The police must have gone over the whole place, through Nate's things, his desk. Good God, Nate's desk! Why, he himself had staggered back and forth, carrying filled drawers of Nate's desk . . . and then that high-boy. More drawers. Christ, half of Nate's and Marian's—and possibly Roger's—household goods were sitting right there in the McKenzie house. Alex got to his feet.

"I've remembered something," he said to his astonished mother. Alex pushed his way past Giddy and strode toward the church door, pursued by whispers that rolled like a wave after him: "He's a doctor . . . an emergency . . . someone's sick."

Mike Laaka, sitting to the side under the shadow of the choir loft, had been occupied counting heads and wondering, as had Sarah, about the possible presence of the murderer, but the sight of Alex speeding toward the entrance was of greater interest. Mike put down his hymnal and followed.

Sarah, now busy testing her distance vision by trying to read a brass plaque fastened to the east wall, "In Memory of Aeneas"—or was it Phineas?—"Satter, Minister of This Church 1829–49," saw Mike moving down the aisle and turned in time to see Alex disappear through the door. It was like one of those old-fashioned thrillers. The doors would be bolted. Someone, perhaps Sydney Prior in his Charlie Chan role, would step to the altar and say, "People not to leave seats, please. I have unworthy idea concerning murder." From this exciting reverie, Sarah was jolted by Mr. Leggett, saying, "Think now of our departed brother, Nathaniel Harwood, husband, father, artist." Oh dear, she thought, he's getting personal. She tried to think of Nate Harwood as a husband-father-artist, but all she could see was the weir that morning with the dark mass that must have been Nate. Only one more hymn to go before the end of the service and the official end of Nate Harwood. The end made acceptable through ritual, though not perhaps the end if you believed that Nate was in some appropriate circle of hell. Would it be the one with the fiery wind? Or would he be in purgatory? Sarah considered what Nate might have done or not done to have made it safely to purgatory. Did Catholics still believe in it? An act of contrition was needed, wasn't it, but Nate didn't sound like the type . . . or maybe there'd been no time. Sarah could only imagine purgatory as an oversize teeming canvas by Pieter Brueghel or Hieronymus Bosch . . . people with multiple arms and legs and bodies made like jars.

And then Sarah was on her feet again, sharing her hymnal with the stout lady in the flowered dress who smelled of Old Spice and had the voice of a sea lion. "Jesus, Lover of My Soul, Let Me to Thy Bosom Fly," roared the woman. Sarah closed her eyes and tried to conjure some other place, some salubrious pastoral corner . . . a meadow, a clean running brook, but unbidden into her head marched stacks of Godding catalogues. She frowned, trying to exorcise the vision— the Godding logo in black Gothic letters, the Winslow Homer on the front cover, Roger Harwood's "Grange Supper" on the back. And instead of fields and streams, in a sudden synthesis of past and present, she had it. Of course. History of Art, second year. European paintings of northern Europe, Bosch and Brueghel. Miss McBrennan pointing with her ruler. "Sarah Deane, please stand and explain to the class how this painting contributes to our understanding of the term 'genre.'"

Alex first strode, then broke into a run, taking the fast route around the library and cutting in behind Lyda's garden. He was just opening the back door to the squeals of the Sealyhams and the pleased howl of Patsy when Mike Laaka tapped him on the shoulder. "I've got mud all over my best shoes."

"You do get around," said Alex in a resigned voice. "I've thought of something."

"I thought you thought of something."

Alex opened the door. "Come on in and tell me if anything's turned up yet from the Harwood cottage search."

Mike hung the jacket from his dark brown suit over a kitchen chair and pulled his tie loose. "George isn't very forthcoming even with me, but I gather only Nate's sales and show records have turned up. Nothing else. Nothing having to do with Roger."

"Okay," said Alex. "Then we've a job to do before everyone piles in here. It's the furniture. God, I was sitting there in church, and I realized that half the Harwood furniture is packed in here. The desk's over in the corner and the highboy is in the back hall—both stuffed with papers and china."

"I suppose," said Mike, "we should wait for George, but what the hell. Let's go. I'm here and George isn't. Find some gloves. We'll try not to leave more prints than you and your gang did. I'll take the highboy and you do the desk."

Ten minutes later, Alex, on his knees, straightened and flourished a brown envelope. "Mike, get in here."

Mike appeared, dusting his knees. "I've dug out recipes, sewing patterns, and little decorated plates wrapped in tea towels. And you?"

"Letters. Three of them, each marked 'copy,' all to Roger. Imagine a father a few miles away from his son writing him formal letters. Here's number three, dated August third. Nate starts in about Roger not answering the first two, '. . . if you do not take immediate and appropriate action . . . ,' with the key phrase, 'for deliberate plagiarism without acknowledgment of the original.' Plagiarism? Of what? The first two letters are in the same vein and each refers to some face-to-face meeting they had."

"Looks like Roger's been a bad boy," said Mike, "and Nate caught him. Oh, damn, here come the others. Take off those gloves." And Mike and Alex, snatching at their fingers, stood up to face Elspeth, Giddy, and Sarah as they came through the back door.

"What are you doing with Marian's desk drawers?" said Elspeth. "She *will* be upset. Mike, how nice. You'll stay for dinner, won't you? Turkey and green beans from the garden. And Sarah has an idea, and I think it explains a lot about Roger."

"We could use an idea," said Mike.

"Well," said Sarah, "I was trying to think of something pleasant and then the Godding catalogue came into my head, and I thought of history of art and Miss McBrennan, who was a real generalissimo. I remember being made to explain a Brueghel painting. The slide was on the screen, but Miss McBrennan had put in backwards. Left to right, and there it was. Roger's painting."

"Roger copied a Brueghel?" said Alex.

"Not exactly, but the figures are the same, in the same position. The 'Peasants' Wedding.' Roger did a mirror image, kept the background shapes, modified the colors—more black and white, used modern clothes. Try it and see. Hold a catalogue up to the mirror."

This was done while the admiring group agreed that here indeed was Brueghel in modern dress.

"Even I know that painting," said Giddy, "and I've just started art history."

"And I do," said Alex, "and I'm an art idiot."

"No comment," said Mike, "but I like it, copied or not."

"Strange we didn't catch it," said Elspeth. "It seems so obvious now. Oh, heavens, the turkey. Giddy, will you? Damn, a little overcooked"—this as Giddy wrestled a large brown bird onto a platter.

"I think I'll go out," said Giddy. "I don't need Sydney for dinner."

"He probably feels the same way," said Elspeth, as Giddy flung out of the door. "Now about this Brueghel."

"There's no law against it, is there?" said Sarah. "Isn't everything in art derivative? And Roger didn't make an exact copy. There are just so many subjects, so many scenes. Like literature. Shakespeare swiped most of his plots, and musicians take off from someone else's theme. Look at those 'after Giotto,' 'after Titian' things," said Sarah. "And homage paintings. 'Homage to Goya.' Not plagiarism. All Roger had to do was put 'homage' in his title. I mean where does something original begin, the jump into a new world, a re-creation? A sea change."

"Yes," said Elspeth, "if you're a Mozart or a Picasso, you can pull it off . . . which Roger isn't." To herself, looking at Sarah's face, flushed from her little speech, she thought, now I'm seeing more of her, the person thing coming out a little.

"Putting all this high-class speculation aside," said Mike, "the point is that Nate took a dim view of Roger's copying the painting, judging from the letter I've got here." And Mike produced letter number three, holding it by the corner. "You see," he said when he had finished reading, "it's what Nate and Roger thought that counts, not whether Roger was pulling a fast one in last year's Godding show. Because this Brueghel must be what Nate is so hot about."

"Which adds up," said Alex, "to a big reason for Roger to be looking through his cottage for copies of the letter."

"Which couldn't have been done safely unless Roger was damn sure Nate wasn't going to show up and catch him," said Mike in a hard voice.

"You mean Roger knew then that Nate was dead," said Elspeth.

"Not necessarily," said Alex. "Roger could have checked around, found Nate was off the island, and so hopped over to have a look."

· 141 ·

"But," Sarah protested, "why destroy letters if your father's still alive? He'd just write new ones. He could expose Roger any time he wanted to."

"To be fair," said Mike, "and that's my middle name, Roger might have come over Friday trying to have some last showdown with his father. Maybe pleading with him . . . 'Forgive me, Father, I won't do it again.' Then, when he didn't find Nate at home, he decided to have a look around, and had to sneak in because Lem Wallace had been asked to keep Roger away from the cottage."

Elspeth reached for a stack of dinner plates and turned toward the dining room. "It seems to me that Roger's new style—everything nonrepresentational—makes sense now . . . his backing away from the Brueghel mode. Well, since Sydney's coming for dinner, we can ask about plagiarism."

Settled to a dinner of turkey with apple dressing, green beans, and cucumbers in sour cream, Sydney Prior considered the evening's question. "It's customary for an artist to acknowledge the source of his inspiration unless it's so obvious that it would be redundant. I suppose anyone can tinker with the Mona Lisa without a complaint." Sydney moved his wineglass back and forth between his palms and took a tiny sip. "One is, of course, free to dip into what I'll call the universal subject pool—dawn, hell, *ecco homo*, Virgin and Child, the rape of the Sabine women, one's mother in a chair, a lily pond with a bridge. But if one wants to spin off a very specific scene, say 'The Night Watch,' Picasso's 'Guernica,' Homer's 'Cracking the Whip,' then I believe there should be a polite nod in the original artist's direction . . . though it isn't always done. Whether the Brueghel falls into the Mona Lisa class, well, who is to say?"

"To repeat," said Mike, "that's not the point."

"Oh, I agree, Mike. The point is, did Roger feel threatened and decide to take steps . . . fatal steps?" Sydney shook his head and then brightened. "An excellent domestic Chablis, Elspeth."

"I'm glad you're not a wine snob, Sydney," said Elspeth,

and a general attention to food and drink followed until Sydney, wiping his lips carefully with his napkin, said, "I hope you'll forgive me, but I'm going to talk out of turn because this is a murder case, and we are all friends together in common cause."

"Have you been holding out?" said Mike.

"It's about Nate and Harrison Petty and may mean nothing at all. But, you see, Nate and I were both members of the search committee for the Godding's new director, and, of all the candidates, Harrison had the most experience in museum work, which," said Sydney in a regretful voice, "isn't saying much. We had no really top-drawer candidates."

Sarah, as Sydney produced Harrison's own favorite figure of speech, suddenly saw the museum director as a long, awkwardly articulated marionette being taken out of a lower drawer along with other tag-end imperfect candidates. She bent her head hastily over her plate.

"Well, we had just about agreed that Harrison would have to do when Harwood burst a bomb. Said he'd done some investigating on his own and that Harrison had once been implicated in some scandal when he was in his last position—assistant director at some small-time art museum in Chicago. Said he was never charged or convicted of anything, but that it was something to make us hesitate about the appointment. Nate indicated that he could supply details, but everyone told him to be quiet, that the matter was over. But unhappily there was a delay in confirmation and Harrison found out why. He sent word to the committee saying that he'd been the victim of false charges a long time ago. It was all very unpleasant and I doubt whether Harrison ever forgave Nate."

"Nate Harwood sounds worse and worse," said Sarah. "He deserved being caught in the weir."

"Join the club," said Mike.

"Harrison is fairly competent and he knows his collections," said Sydney, "but he spends too much. Of course, the Godding, as I've often said . . . "

"That's enough, Sydney," said Elspeth. "I love the Godding."

"The State Police will be having Petty in," said Mike,
"but we sure as hell don't need any more people with motives."

"And the art thefts," said Elspeth. "Anything new
there?"

"Things are quiet, though I expect that Ruth Baker to
turn up any minute and put me in handcuffs. I wish she'd
forget about her parents' picture and go home to Missouri.
And thanks, Mrs. McKenzie," said Mike, standing up. "That
was some fine supper. I was hollow as a drum. Now I'll go over
to Lem's and see about smoking out Roger."

"Okay, Sarah, a walk," said Alex, after the dishes had been
dried and stacked, Sydney had departed, and Elspeth had
gone to bed.

"Over and over I have this theatre feeling," said Sarah,
as together they wandered down the sandy path to the town
center. The moon, nearly full, had risen, and the bleached
buildings seemed almost one-dimensional. Sarah gestured
ahead. "Sea village by moonlight. Two inconsequential
figures walk slowly and without purpose toward the water.
Sound effects: small waves washing, feet on loose stones,
dinghies knocking against the wharf. Action."

"If you feel inconsequential, it's probably from sitting
alone at a funeral service."

"I do feel as if I'm sort of palely loitering outside of all
of this—Nate Harwood, the island precedents and connections. What are those things, electrons, that whirr around
away from the nucleus? I can only pick up hints and scraps.
I don't know how to help you with the Harwood thing. Even
Ruth Baker's case makes more sense."

Alex, not answering, looked down at Sarah. The moonlight made her seem almost as unreal as the buildings beside
her, and he felt that if he reached to hold her she would
disappear like ectoplasm in his arms. Then, while he was

wondering whether to try the experiment, Sarah walked ahead to the end of a dock and looked out over the moon-splashed water.

"I think," said Sarah, "that you're all too close to this—your mother, Giddy, Mike Laaka. How can you be objective about people you've known all your lives, all snarled into years and years—two hundred at least—of associations?"

"So," said Alex, "since you're feeling like an electron, tell me what you see from out there. Nate Harwood, art thefts, Ruth Baker."

"It's like someone dumping jigsaw puzzle pieces out on the table. Is it all one puzzle or is it two or three? I think you've got to start sorting out the pieces, find the edges. And I'd start with those paintings. They might tie the whole mess together."

"Stealing art is a major industry. The missing paintings may just be part of the usual stolen traffic scene."

"I heard Mrs. Ordway talking once, saying that fall and winter were usually the prime hit times, when the summer cottages were empty and the full-time residents had gone south, and that it was odd that in these last few years more things disappeared in the summer, when it's harder to get away with it. Someone must know the whole summer scene like a book."

"Your point being that it takes more nerve and a lot of inside knowledge to get away with stuff in the summer."

"Yes, who's going where and taking what boat. Island comings and goings, who's going to a wedding or a funeral or shopping for the day, who's in the hospital, and, of course, who has paintings and little silver collectibles."

"Mike has checked on everyone he can think of during the theft periods, and it seems that the entire population of Knox County was on the move, in boats, on ferries, back and forth, shopping, and no one was seen sneaking out of a studio with a painting under the arm. As for inside knowledge," said Alex, "only Rachel and Lyda know everything. And you have to eliminate people like them."

"Why? Maybe I can see better from the outside because I don't see everyone as beloved old Weymouth characters, or Marian Harwood as the poor abused wife, or Roger as the misunderstood son."

"I didn't ask you to turn into the D.A."

"Or Sydney Prior as everybody's favorite art dealer, or Harrison Petty as everyone's unfavorite museum director. And Doris Ordway. She's got a great cover for keeping an eye on the art world. Maybe she's saving for a trip to Paris."

"Stop it."

"And the murder. What if Nate caught the thief stealing a painting and had to be eliminated? And Ruth Baker. Her parents could be snatch artists from the Midwest cutting in on local turf and the local gangs snapped their brakes or whatever you do to brakes. And their painting? It was stolen and they were acting as their own fence, which is sad because I like Ruth."

"You've gone mad in the moonlight."

"I'm a little light-headed. Church and that big dinner." At which point, Patsy, regrettably damp and redolent of seaweed and old fish, ran up from the beach and shook himself. Sarah reached for the dog's collar. " 'All I have to say, is to tell you that the lanthorn is the moon; I the Man i' the Moon; this thorn-bush my thorn-bush; and this dog my dog.' "

"What the hell? Damn you, Patsy, down. What did you say?"

"Unrelated except to madness," said Sarah. "I just felt like a moon quotation with a dog in it. Frivolity."

"I don't think you can get away from Nate in the weir. Work from the murder and just maybe you can bring in the paintings."

"I suppose," said Sarah sadly, "it won't ever be possible for us to have an ordinary conversation or be frivolous about the moon."

EIGHT

The following Wednesday and Thursday mornings spun by so quickly that it seemed to Sarah as if the small patch of the Maine coast represented by Prior's Gallery had been wound into a cassette and set on fast forward. She discovered that art shops can indeed turn into pressure tanks. Customers in the front shop pushed in, fingered, dropped, paid for, returned, and exchanged. Sydney padded back and forth between the low-price and the high-price zones, and several times herded Sarah into the Parlor Gallery to help set paintings on easels, wrestle drawers open, and upend chairs so customers could examine for dovetailing, saw marks, and square-headed nails.

On Thursday noon Alex met Sarah at the shop for lunch. "Try to make it back in forty minutes," called Sydney, "and remember, we've got inventory tonight."

"Inventory?" said Alex, as they headed up the hill to the Ocean View Hotel.

"Oh, he's all wound up," said Sarah. "He thinks that with these art thefts, plus the usual shoplifters, he'd better count stock. I'll stay through dinner until it's finished and go back in his boat. Alex, you've no idea how complicated the antique business is. Serpentine chests of drawers and reverse-serpentine ones, and chests-on-chests and highboys and lowboys and probably middleboys."

"They all sound expensive," said Alex, as the hotel screen door slammed behind them.

"That gallery is simply stuffed, not only the big things, but little china dolls and doorstops, things Sydney calls 'teasers.' Inventory will be horrible. Well, it all makes me very hungry, and I could eat a serpentine chest. Let's start with soup and you can tell me what's going on in the crime world."

"So you see," said Alex, as he finished the last of his soup and reached for his ham sandwich, "the exact time of death is unknown—due to things like water immersion that I won't go into. But the police are taking Friday midafternoon until the five-fifteen departure of the *Robin Day* as a working hypothesis. No one saw Nate after boat time, he didn't pick up his groceries, he missed an appointment with a buyer at the Inn."

"Cause of death?"

"Blow on the head. Details unpleasant. Some hints about fragments, metal maybe, imbedded in the skull. Reports due any day. Listen, this is going to ruin your lunch."

"I'm tougher than you think. So who was in Port Clyde that afternoon?"

"Some members of the hate-Nate society . . . except Sydney, who seems to have got himself safely to Portland while Nate was still alive. Now it's a matter of footwork, telephone calls, interviews. All the sweat that usually solves a case. I'm going over to the field office this afternoon to see what plans they have for grabbing Roger."

"If he hasn't made a raft and floated away. He must look like Ben Gunn by now with a scraggly beard."

"My mother says she won't search anymore. She's going on about cruel and unusual hounding of a neighbor's son, and she'll stick to her painting, thank you."

"Speaking of painting, I'm learning more than I ever wanted to know. You should hear Sydney going on about paints, everything in perfect order. Cadmium orange, chrome yellow, Indian yellow, Naples yellow, cadmium lemon, cadmium lemon pale, cadmium yellow, new gamboge, yellow ochre."

"And your perfect yellow? That's impressive. Sydney may never let you go."

Sarah stood up and slung the strap of her handbag over her shoulder. "That was a good lunch. Now I can face chests-on-chests. No, we'll split the check and the tip," she said firmly as Alex reached for the bill, and then, glad of a distraction, pointed at the window. "Across the street. Ruth Baker. Still looking, I suppose. I told you she was tough." Sarah reached the door, waved, and called.

Ruth, Sarah noticed as she crossed the street, was now deeply tanned, her nose freckled, her hair cut into a shorter bob, her once crisp summer suit creased; and sneakers had replaced her traveling shoes. She's really getting down to it, thought Sarah.

Ruth greeted her briskly. "Oh, Sarah. Good. Do you know a garage mechanic?"

"Try Pete's Service Station. It's just outside Rockland and my car lives there half the time."

"You're not thinking of putting your parents' car in working order, are you?" asked Alex, who had joined them. "You'd better get two opinions if you are."

"I just want the whole car gone over," said Ruth. "Then if everything checks out and if I don't find the painting by the end of the week, I may give up. I hired a diver yesterday to go down by that wharf, but he didn't find anything."

"Let us know if there's anything more we can do," said Alex. Privately, he told himself that it was high time for Ruth to head home.

"Ruth Baker's certainly persistent," Sarah said to Sydney when she returned from lunch. Sydney, now well into his inventory, was counting through his collection of pewter porringers. "Who did you say? Ruth Baker? Oh, dear, is she still looking?"

"She's been told it's almost hopeless, but now she's into the car angle. She thinks the police were careless in going over it."

The little bell tinkled, and Ruth, as if she had heard her name, stood on the threshold of the parlor. "I came through the front," she said. "Sarah, I've called your garage and then I talked to Mr. Petty at the Godding. He gave me the name of the Ocean Body Shop because Dr. McKenzie said to get two opinions. Mr. Prior, could I just ask you one or two more questions, and it will be the very last time I bother you."

Sydney sighed, nodded, rose heavily to his feet, and indicated a chair by the window. Sarah left them and returned to the front shop to finish counting brushes. I hope he's not going to try and sell that poor woman anything, she thought. Taking advantage of her, maybe pretending that he's found her painting. Sarah scowled and decided the idea was an unworthy one. It's because I'm trying to find guilty people and Sydney looks like a character in a mystery story. Then, sitting back on her heels, she reconsidered Sydney, but this time—Sarah was a fan of old movies—Charlie Chan dissolved into the white-suited bulk of Sydney Greenstreet, a large and sinister figure who wheeled and dealt in an international art theft ring. She saw him sitting in a basket chair under a slowly revolving fan. There would be palm fronds, louvered doors, and a beaded curtain. He would be toying with a paper knife and saying to Ruth, "Come in, my dear. I've rather been expecting you."

At which point, Ruth Baker, rather flushed, emerged from the back room. She was carrying a small rectangular brown paper package—obviously a painting.

How despicable of him, thought Sarah.

Ruth pulled the string and paper away from an oil framed in a narrow gold-leaf frame. It showed a dark gray sky and a large glistening umber and black jagged headwall, its base rocks licked by a tongue of white foam. "It's Captain's Head on Weymouth Island," she explained.

Unforgivable, thought Sarah angrily. Aloud, she said in

as neutral a voice as she could manage, "It's very nice, Ruth, but it's not . . . "

"No, it's not like having my parents' picture. I know that. But Mr. Prior was so nice about it."

I'll bet, said Sarah to herself. Worse than Sydney Greenstreet.

" . . . for nothing," said Ruth, carefully smoothing the paper back around the frame and retying the string.

"What?"

" . . . because of losing Mother and Dad. He wanted me to have something from Maine that didn't remind me of bad things. His father painted it. It's an original," she added proudly.

Sarah felt as if someone had punctured her in a vital place. Evil to him who evil thinks. "It's a beauty," she said to Ruth, and indeed it was.

"He said it wasn't really valuable because it's modern, and his father wasn't that well known. But I don't think it matters if you like the picture. And Sarah, thanks for everything. I'll be coming out to Weymouth before I go home. To visit the galleries and see Captain's Head, where this was painted. You're lucky to be working for such a nice man." And Ruth was gone, the little bell sounding behind her.

Sarah, considerably deflated, began to count boxes of charcoal sticks, and Sydney, as if to rub it in, arrived with a large pitcher of lemonade. "Must keep our worker's spirits up," he said.

Later that evening, Sarah sat on the floor and chewed on a turkey sandwich, the texture of which seemed to have much in common with a white rubber bathing cap. She listened as Sydney held forth on the importance of taking regular inventory, " . . . keep the stock up to date . . . deterioration . . . long-term deduction . . . all this humidity . . . problem with the glue . . . boiled oil . . . varnish . . . trestle table."

"And shoplifting," murmured Sarah between bites, thinking to move the conversation into a more lively vein.

"Common thieves." Sydney finished his sandwich and wiped his mouth with his silk handkerchief. For someone who professed to know about life's finer things, he seemed quite oblivious to the failings of the sandwiches. "It's a game," he said. "Ripping off old Sydney Prior. Stuffing their pockets."

"It's not all kid stuff," said Sarah. She lifted her clipboard and read, "Snuff box, silver sugar caster, two gravy spoons, one mustard pot . . . all eighteenth century. A porringer, a tankard, both early American pewter. A doorstop."

"Anything not glued down. I'd just bought that mustard pot in London last spring, and I was fond of that doorstop. Now I suppose I'll have to watch the floor," said Sydney crossly. "That one was in the back hall by the barn. Some doorstops bring a nice price. I sold an unusual sailor boy last year."

"Aren't dogs common?"

"Some are, but this was a Jack Russell terrier."

"You're missing a painting, an oil of Criehaven. I don't remember seeing it."

"Before your time. It was behind that screen. Probably taken when I was in my workroom. After all, I can't lock the place like a prison during the day. I will tell the police, but it will be an exercise in futility. This is not an area where they have special men who work exclusively on fine-art theft. And now, Sarah, it's time to weigh anchor for Weymouth. Just leave the inventory lists in my workroom, will you? On through that door." Sydney indicated a passageway.

Sarah, holding a stack of clipboards, opened the door to the workroom, thinking, I'm actually in the forbidden place. She remembered that Giddy had complained of never being allowed there. Well, it was hardly mysterious, simply a businesslike chamber with long shelves and tables with glass cutters, framing equipment, and tools all set in orderly array. Lists of orders were pinned on a large cork board, and finished pictures, tagged and dated, were set into a floor rack.

She put her clipboards on the table and then, glancing around, was interested to see that Sydney, the art expert, had mounted not a special group of preferred watercolors or prints, but a long series of photographs of boats. Old-fashioned launches with awning tops, one tublike sailboat, a long-nosed speedboat, a rowing dory, and several variations on the lobster boat. Each was neatly framed in dark wood, matted in a moss green with a small brass label centered on the frame: *Dewdrop, Blue Girl, Running Water, Ocean Bound, Fluvanna,* on through *Misty Morn, Furl Sail,* and the present owner's *Tempest Queen.* Not much imagination, thought Sarah, and all rather pompous.

"Are you coming, Sarah?" called Sydney.

"I was admiring your boats," said Sarah, emerging from the workroom.

"Yes," said Sydney in a pleased voice. "Mine, my father's, and even two of my grandfather's old launches. I remember many with great fondness."

"And now it's good-bye to the *Tempest Queen,*" said Sarah, as they headed for the wharf.

"Yes, my new one is being painted and having radar installed, which I hope I can master."

"Have you named it?"

"Here we are," said Sydney. "My dinghy, but more of a dory, really. With my weight, I can't use a pea pod. Yes, I've thought about the name, and I think she'll be the *Christmas Past.*"

"But that's not a nautical name. Is *A Christmas Carol* a favorite story?"

"Of course," said Sydney, lowering himself cautiously into the dinghy.

Sarah's experience in coastal piloting had been confined to an occasional glance over someone's shoulder at a folded chart. Usually, by the time she had located a spindle or a buoy, the boat had slipped past and was heading for another marker. Now she marveled at Sydney, standing at the wheel of the *Tempest Queen,* spinning it this way and that as the dark irregular island shapes loomed, menaced, and receded, and finally the greater bulk of Weymouth rose up dead ahead of the bow. Sarah began to thank her employer, but he waved her quiet. "No trouble. And be careful walking back to the McKenzies', my dear. Stick to the main path. Moon or no moon, you never can tell. After all, Nate Harwood . . ." He left the sentence unfinished.

* * *

"Splinters," said Alex. "Metal splinters?"

"Look at the report," said Mike.

George Fitts cleared his throat, a tidy little opening of his upper respiratory system. He picked up the sheaf of papers, knocked them into alignment, and wrote "August 22" at their head. "Provocative, I think," he said. "Some of the head damage is, of course, compatible with surf slamming the corpse against the rocks, but there is an indication of a severe depressed skull fracture with enough damage to the temporal-parietal area to cause instant loss of consciousness and very probably death. The lung tissue shows that he was dead before he went into the water."

"And the splinters?" repeated Alex.

"Microscopic fragments, iron particles, embedded in the skull, so deep they didn't wash out. The injury suggests a very hard blow downward, the object being almost driven into the skull. The size of the fracture almost fits the torn section in the crown of Nate Harwood's hat, the one found by the dog."

"You mean," said Alex, "that the hat floated into Port Clyde and the body into Weymouth. Well, I suppose that's possible, currents taking the hat in and the body out to sea."

"Full report still to come," said George. "Meanwhile we can look for the weapon, something weighty that could go through the hat and into the skull with such penetration."

"A splitting maul, maybe," said Mike. "Or an ax."

"Speculation without facts wastes time," said George. "Here's a fact. A lobster trap recovered from Bucket Cove by the diver, with rope still attached that matches the type used to tie the body."

"Nate certainly wasn't stuffed inside a trap, was he?" said Alex.

"Not in, on," said Mike. "Tied on by the pot warp, we think. And we've found extra ballast in the trap. Nate was meant to stay down."

"Remember," said George, "I'm from off the coast. We have potatoes, not lobsters. This is my first seacoast homicide, so some of the terms are new."

"Okay," said Mike. "It's not often I have a chance to instruct the State Police. For rope, we say warp, pot warp. And it wasn't one of the new wire traps. She's an old-timer, wooden with oak lathes. By ballast, I mean those poured cement slabs at the bottom of a trap—although a few old men still use rocks. This trap had the usual cement slabs plus two extra rocks. And no toggle."

"Toggle?" said George.

"Flotation for the warp," said Alex. "The warp is attached to the pot by a kind of bridle and halfway up the toggle line is fastened to the mainline and has a toggle at the end."

"They used to have glass bottles for floats," said Mike, "but now, mostly, they've Styrofoam doughnuts. Keeps the line from fouling on the bottom."

"I don't want a history of toggles," said George. "The point being that no toggle means either that it was lost in the storm, or none was attached, to avoid attracting attention."

"Especially not with Nate as bait," said Mike. "No buoy recovered with matching warp, but that storm was a real trap smasher."

"So," said George, "we're looking for a lobsterman who uses old traps."

Alex grinned and Mike hooted. "God, George," said Mike, "everyone on the whole goddamn coast can get his mitts on a wooden trap, not just lobstermen. People use 'em for flower planters, make goddamn coffee tables out of 'em. And every storm washes in pot warp, too. Lot of people put out a few traps just for their family. Anyone can haul traps because the courts knocked down the residency requirement, but the amateurs better not get too busy, or they'll have their trap lines cut. Cowboys don't like the sheep ranchers muscling in."

"Nate always put out a few traps," said Alex, "and I think Sydney has one or two down in his cove on Weymouth."

"You've made your point," said George. "Still, we have to check around and see if anyone's missing a wooden trap or if anyone was seen lowering a trap Friday afternoon or evening."

"You mean one with a body attached," said Mike. "Come off it."

"Or someone going out who isn't known to set traps."

"Okay," said Mike. "That makes sense. Fishermen keep an eye out for freebooters. We'll help you ask around. But Nate must have been dumped after dark, because why advertise? Out of the harbor, behind some island, maybe. Fog was coming in that night, so it wouldn't have been hard."

"Hauling's done in the daytime," put in Alex. "A boat going out at night might have been noticed."

"Yeah," said Mike. "The local people are pretty sharp about boat engines. They get to know the sounds, internal combustion, diesels, cranky outboards, auxiliaries, the draggers and the seiners. But in the A.M., forget it. Even with fog there's a lot of action."

"And I'm for action," said Alex, rising and stretching his hands to the top of the trailer. "I've a date with a hungry lady."

"An ax?" said Sarah.

"Or a splitting maul, or a barbell. You name it."

"How about a kettle? One of those iron cauldrons, or an old smoothing iron, the kind you heat on the stove."

"It's good to talk to someone who knows about domestic blunt instruments," said Alex. "I'd never have thought of a smoothing iron."

"Sydney has a lot of expensive blunt instruments. Umbrella stands, soup tureens, whale-oil lamps. There's a Chinese vase that must weigh twenty pounds. And he's missing some things, too."

"Blunt instruments or paintings?"

"Both, including an oil of Criehaven. He's turning the list in to Mike. And I've only half an hour for lunch today."

"A quick picnic," said Alex. "The Dip Net can make up some sandwiches, and we can eat down by the harbor and watch the world go by."

But they had barely settled to their lunch when Alex suddenly stood up and stared down the line of dinghies and tenders tied by the landing.

"That's the *Molly*," he said. "I'd swear it. But what the hell."

"The *Molly*?"

"The Harwoods' catboat. It's the twin of the *Peg* and is supposed to be sitting in Tinker's Cove. Marian doesn't sail much anymore and definitely not to the mainland."

"Roger!" exclaimed Sarah.

"Yes, damn it. He's sailed off under everyone's nose."

Sarah stood up, took two last quick bites of her sandwich, and brushed the crumbs from her skirt. "I've got to get back, but I'll keep an eye out. But I wouldn't think he'd hang around Port Clyde."

"Here's Giddy," said Alex. "Wouldn't you know? I smell a rat."

Giddy, a canvas bag over her shoulder, appeared before them, tousled, T-shirt damp, the bottoms of her jeans rolled and wet.

"Hi, Alex. Sarah. Taking a break? Have you broken anything at Sydney's yet? Because you will sometime, even if you're not me. You know that law, objects that can be broken, will be. Alex, I sailed over in the *Molly* because I thought you might want to take out the *Peg* today. Mrs. Harwood said okay."

"From Weymouth? That's too far in that peanut."

"God, Alex, you sound like my mother. It's no big deal. The wind's just right, and I've done it lots before."

"I doubt that. Damn it all, Giddy . . . "

"I've got to go," said Sarah, seeing a family broil ahead. "Sometime, Giddy, take me with you and give me some pointers."

After Sarah had departed, Alex advanced on his cousin. "Listen, you dumbhead, are you helping Roger? Because if you are, it's no kindness. All he's doing by hiding out is pulling a lot of suspicion down on his head. The police aren't fools, and they know all about Roger and his father's unfriendly relations."

"What a regular old-maid wimp you're turning into, Alex. I like sailing alone, and Roger means absolutely nothing to me anymore, and now I'm going to bail out the *Molly*. We took on water on the way over."

"We?" said Alex.

"Yes, we. The *Molly* and me."

"And Roger makes three."

"Oh shut up. Go over and look. I don't have Roger hidden in the boat. Why don't you buzz off and go play with the police? There's the Sheriff's car and the State Police diver. Your scene, isn't it? Well, I'm just fine. I'm going to sail back, because the wind's switching to the northwest, which is perfect."

"You win," said Alex, "but I'll keep my weather eye out for you." Alex had to confess to a weariness with Giddy and her apparently bottomless fund of energy for devious activities. He betook himself over to the general store landing, where the State Police boat was now standing by with a diver on board.

"Hi," said Mike. "Crap city. Bet you're glad you're not going down in that muck. They'll start looking around in the pilings and then go around to the other boat docks. Hate to think of all the garbage we'll have to go through, plus a million rusty old blunt instruments."

"I hear Sydney's turning in a list of stolen objects, including a painting."

"He probably took them himself to collect the insurance. He's too rich for my blood. You'd think we'd have something in common, too, what with his being from Kentucky and my being into horses, but no way. He's only into curly furniture, not a decent chair to sit on in the whole place, and china that breaks if you sneeze at it. Well, Sydney is George's baby in the Harwood murder business, which is okay by me. I don't want to set foot in the place again."

* * *

"I have Saturday off from noon," announced Sarah, as she and Alex squeezed into their now familiar notch by the bow of the ferry. "Mr. Prior's closing shop. He's all wound up in Landing Day, dress rehearsals for a school pageant with Queen Elizabeth yet. They're doing the outfitting of Captain Weymouth's ship, Lem Wallace as the captain."

"Poor Lem, he's got enough to do without putting on a ruff and a velvet suit," said Alex, "but now, look at that fog bank over there. I was hoping to catch Giddy redhanded with Roger as a stowaway, but with fog, forget it. We'll be running at half speed, and Giddy will blow into Weymouth like a leaf, and Roger, if he's in the boat, will slip away again."

Sarah shook her head. "But why come back when he was home free in Port Clyde?" And then, even as she spoke, the fog rose around the ferry, swathing the islands ahead, and she heard ahead the two-note guttural *ooo-ah* of a foghorn and the *Robin Day* sounding the single warning blast.

Giddy was waiting for them at the dock of the *Robin Day*. "Beat you in," she said. "And look at the fog. We're going to be socked in for a while. I sailed right by the ferry and could hardly make her out . . . and I don't suppose," she added, "you could see me."

"No," said Alex, "we couldn't see you or anything in your boat."

Giddy looked gratified and, as the three trudged up the

road toward the McKenzie cottage, cheerfully expounded on the pleasures of long-distance solo sailing in a fourteen-foot catboat.

Established on the McKenzie porch with gin and tonics and a bowl of fresh shrimp, Giddy, Sarah, and Elspeth listened as Alex said that it was high time to see if there wasn't some sort of common denominator that helped explain the art thefts. "And let's stick to the paintings and forget about the portable silver and china."

"What I don't understand," said Elspeth, "is why any of our paintings were taken at all. Contemporary paintings mostly, nothing really valuable or old, except for some old family portraits and that possible Frederic Church from the library."

"Exactly," said Alex.

"Did Mr. Holmes say exactly?" said Sarah.

"To repeat," said Alex, "exactly. No really well-known contemporary artists in an international—or even a national —sense have been robbed. And note this. Mike gave me a copy of the victims' statements. Roger Harwood: 'The paint had just dried.' Nate Harwood: 'The paint was hardly dry.' My mother: 'I'd about finished it.' Two others: 'Not even framed'; 'Just took it off the easel.'"

"But," protested Sarah, "the library painting must have been old and dry."

"Then you've got one thief who likes wet paintings and one who likes dry paintings," said Giddy. "So what?"

"In all cases," said Alex, "you've got some valuable works or exhibited works like Roger's prize winner and the Dürer woodcut left behind."

"It must make sense," said Sarah, taking a long sip of her gin and tonic.

Elspeth stood up and walked to the screen door. "The fog's in," she said. "I can't even see the apple trees."

"What," said Sarah, "do the painting of the weir and the library painting have in common?"

"Both marine paintings," said Giddy.

"None of the stolen paintings," persisted Sarah, "has been recorded or shown. But then we have Ruth Baker's parents' painting."

"About which we know nothing," said Alex. "So forget it."

"No," said Sarah. "I think it fits somehow, but the point is that none of the missing paintings is easily traced. No records. Perfect robbery bait."

"But who on earth," said Elspeth, coming to rest on a blue-painted sea chest, "could have known that much about which paintings had just been finished, which ones had been exhibited, which ones were old undocumented family favorites?"

"Harrison Petty!" exclaimed Sarah.

"Sydney Prior," said Giddy.

"Roger Harwood," said Alex.

And then, as if under the baton of a conductor, they all said, "Nate Harwood."

Later, at a dinner of pleasantly scrambled-together leftovers, Alex pointed out that they had to keep quiet. "Guesswork just causes trouble."

"You started it," said Elspeth, "and I can't believe it's a friend, someone we've known all our lives. Of course," she added, "Harrison Petty is new here."

"Both Sydney and Harrison know all the upcoming shows, the recent past shows, know the art community, do appraisals . . . and so did Nate," said Alex.

"But not Roger," said Giddy.

"No, certainly not Roger," said Alex. "But he knows a hell of a lot about the midcoast art scene, and as far as I can see, is as free as a cloud to go where and when he wants. And he probably needs money."

"Roger isn't hung up about money," said Giddy, thinking of the poorly heated little shack. "It could be anybody. They all move around all over the place and have boats to get to the island."

"Only one thing," said Sarah. "If Nate was the thief, who killed Nate?"

"Simple," said Giddy. "Nate had an accomplice who double-crossed him."

"Like Roger?" said Alex. "Their antagonism was a front?"

"No," said Giddy, stung. "They wouldn't have worked together—not since Roger got kicked out of Bowdoin."

"How about Sydney and Nate, then?" said Alex. "Nate as leg man and Sydney as mastermind—except Sydney was in Portland that afternoon. Well, you two figure it out because Sarah and I are going to get lost in the fog."

"Good," said Giddy. "I'll come too. I need the exercise."

"I thought you wanted me to go over your portfolio," said Elspeth to Giddy. "This is just the time."

"Get Patsy and put on a slicker," Alex told Sarah. "It's really dripping out there."

"It's like being inside a vaporizer," said Sarah, her rubber boots slipping on the path, Patsy pulling ahead against his collar. "The fog doesn't come on little cat feet or rubbing its back on windowpanes, it's like fifty wet blankets."

"My favorite fog description," said Alex, reaching over and successfully getting possession of Sarah's hand, "is something about fog everywhere, fog up the river, fog in the marshes, fog lying out in the yards, hovering in the rigging of great ships, drooping in the gunwales of barges and small boats . . . "

"I keep forgetting that you probably do read something besides *The New England Journal of Medicine*."

"Approbation from Ms. Deane."

"New game," said Sarah. "How many fog quotes can anyone think of in any given fog?"

"English teacher to be given a handicap of ten quotes. I like O. Henry's London fog thirty parts, malaria ten parts, parts of gasleaks and dew drops and honeysuckle all equal a Nashville drizzle."

"On a Maine island it would be coastal fog fifty parts, wood smoke fifteen parts, sour smell from split wood ten parts, balsam and salt spray ten parts each, fish fifteen parts, bayberry twenty parts."

"You're over a hundred. Hey, watch where you're going." This to a small shape that hurled itself at him and then tripped at his feet. "Hello. It's Jimmy Wallace, isn't it? What are you doing out in the soup, Jimmy?"

"Dr. McKenzie?" A small boy wearing enormous rubber boots got to his feet. "My father said I'm supposed to find you. He's opened the store, and you're to call Mr. Laaka. He's the one in plain clothes."

"Yes, I know," said Alex in a resigned voice.

"I'll go on and meet you by the public landing," said Sarah and, with Patsy lurching ahead and looping back, she made her way down through swirls of gray moisture, at times feeling with her feet for the path. Once she wandered off behind the church that stood like a ghostly shard in the fog, so that Alex caught up with her before she reached the harbor.

"That was Mike with information," said Alex. "Among the junk brought up by the diver was one interesting object."

"I know all about interesting objects."

"Which is all it is until the lab tests are finished, and that may take a while, the airport is socked in. It's an old-fashioned doorstop. Heavy as hell . . . almost eight pounds. A dog."

"Oh?" said Sarah. "And doorstops don't usually turn up in harbors." Sarah put her head down against Patsy's neck. "Go on."

"Sydney Prior has identified it as one missing from his gallery. It was on the list turned in to the police—as you know."

"I can guess what comes next."

"Yes. Sydney has turned in his entire collection of doorstops, as well as some other cast-iron objects. But you can see that a doorstop is more than an adequate blunt instrument.

The weight is right, the bottom is rough and cracked, so I suppose fragmentation is possible."

"Okay," said Sarah. "So be it. But let's skip murder for the rest of the night. I'll cast a spell over this whole blessed island, and we'll vanish . . . doorstop and all." She turned away abruptly. "Let's walk to the lighthouse. I still haven't been up there." She looked toward fog-shrouded Lighthouse Point and suddenly had the sense of a tiny spot of light, the smallest point of yellow moving in the gray mist. "The lighthouse doesn't work anymore, does it?" she asked, puzzled.

"Not for years. Are you seeing things?"

"I have spells on the brain, I think. You said the lighthouse was locked?"

"And that kids break in. Lem has the key."

Sarah started to climb the path, feeling somehow that the lighthouse was leaning down on them, blurred and menacing. Arriving at the wooden door, she was aware that her breath was coming faster than the climb warranted.

"It's locked, all right," said Alex, shaking the door handle. "I think we'd . . . "

But the sentence was never finished. Patsy suddenly pulled forward on his leash, barking, and Sarah found herself being dragged back down the path."

"Wait up," called Alex. "Shut up, Patsy," for the dog was now issuing hard staccato barks demanding attention.

"What's across here?" shouted Sarah, hauling Patsy to a standstill. "A keeper's house?"

"Torn down years ago," Alex shouted back. "It's probably a raccoon."

"Or Roger?" Sarah put her hand over Patsy's muzzle. The dog's hair was stiff, his throat rumbling.

"If it's Roger," said Alex, joining her, "he'd take off with all this racket. Or duck into the tunnels."

"What tunnels?"

"A series running to the lighthouse from below. Left over from a World War II spotting station . . . it's dismantled now. Lem said the police have checked them at least twice. Anyway, we haven't a flashlight, so let's say it's a raccoon. What Patsy needs is a good dose of Mrs. Woodhouse," he added as the big dog whirled around his legs.

"But of course it's Roger," said Sarah, "and Patsy smells him," and Patsy, suddenly peaceful, came over to Alex and, in the role of a model dog, offered a paw.

"He's never done that before," said Sarah in admiration.

"Marvelous," said Alex, "but it isn't getting us forward. Roger," he called into the fog, "if you're hiding, come out. We're friends." He paused and then shouted, "And stop being such a goddamn bloody fool." He turned back to Sarah. "To hell with it. Let's go back. I'm soaked, and we can't see two feet ahead."

Elspeth, wrapped in her old flannel dressing gown, met them at the door. "Sydney came over and said Sarah can have all of tomorrow off, because if the weather stays this way there won't be too many customers driving along the coast. He said he'll go over for a little while tomorrow if the fog burns off."

"Sarah," said Alex, "that gives us the whole weekend."

"Not quite," said Elspeth, as she led the way into the kitchen for the cocoa ritual. "You've forgotten that you signed up as a leader for tomorrow's midcoast Audubon trip. Joe Bartbury is at the Lodge with the group."

"Oh, Christ."

"They particularly want you to find some crossbills and a black-backed woodpecker, and don't glower, you did this yourself."

"I'll help," said Giddy, coming in from the hall. "I saw two boreal chickadees early yesterday on the Ocean Trail."

"Skip the cocoa, Mother," said Alex. "Oh, Christ," he said again and marched to the refrigerator and produced a sweating can of beer and pulled at the tab. "Sorry, but this week's been impossible. Oh, all right. I did promise. Look, Sarah, will you come? It will only be about four hours in the morning."

"Thanks," said Sarah, "but I've got a school syllabus to worry about. I'll meet you for lunch."

"I'll do the marshes and ponds first, then Captain's Head, and meet you there around twelve-thirty. Giddy, you can take them back and show off your chickadees."

"No one is drinking cocoa," said Elspeth sadly. "We used to have such good times. It tied the whole day together."

"And now we're old and unstrung," said Giddy.

"Speak for yourself," said Alex. "I'm for bed. Bring sandwiches, Sarah."

My God, thought Giddy, as Alex and Sarah went their separate ways, how do they stand it? I think they're both sexless. Alex used to be normal and bring all those girls here, but he's probably taken some sort of a vow or picked up a disease or something. Maybe he's scared Sarah or she's scared him. I'm glad I'm not made that way, everything repressed.

* * *

Alex was long gone by the time Sarah made it to the kitchen on Saturday morning. The radio on the counter was sounding a Mozart horn concerto, and the bright trembling notes seemed to be bouncing from one wall to the next. Beyond the kitchen curtains she could see that the heavy ground fog still hung over the garden, but a light rim to gray sky and an orange glow in the east suggested later sunshine.

Sarah finished her breakfast, checked the time—past eight—and read a note from Elspeth saying that she was off to do some sketching while the fog held. Loosed from Sydney Prior's shop, she should have felt free and easy, but she could settle to nothing. Her school list, the business of choosing among *Jane Eyre, Huckleberry Finn,* and *The Norton Anthology of Fiction,* she shoved to the edge of her mind. The cottage was strangely still, full of lamps unlit and furniture in waiting: faded flowered covers on lumpy sofas and stuffed chairs, wicker in various stages of unraveling, hooked rugs with loose loops for the unwary, and on the walls, framed photographs, many brown with age, and here and there an old print with stained edges. Obviously, Elspeth's interest in design did not extend to the family living quarters. The room was not tasteless; it demonstrated a total lack of interest in something as soulless as taste. Sarah walked up to the mantelpiece and examined a crowd of tarnished cups and trophies from canoe races, tennis matches, the Camp Wyonegonic war canoe team prize. The photographs showed family picnics, sailing scenes, children in drooping shorts and middy blouses. There was a younger Elspeth McKenzie with startlingly dark hair, standing next to a tall man with an untidy mustache—John McKenzie, no doubt. Sarah recognized Alex's nose. Then a large photograph showing a group by the shore. They stood beside a large kettle and held lobsters over their heads with triumphant smiles. The picture showed the infant Giddy, easily recognizable in a disordered romper suit, Alex, all knees and elbows in a sweater with a large A on its chest, and beyond, Alex's father standing next to, yes, Marian Harwood. A younger Marian, less stocky, standing in the center scowling at the camera, and beside her, that must be Roger, the thin face and that shelf of hair. But the man next to Roger, one arm around the boy's shoulder, looking so bland . . . could that be the notorious Nate Harwood? The photograph upset her whole idea of the Harwoods, as if Marian with her scowl and Nate with his mildness had exchanged personalities for the camera.

For a minute Sarah stared at the photographs, as if trying to bring the past images into some sort of relationship with their present manifestations. Then she turned. Come on, she told herself. Go on out and do what you've been wanting to do and stop spinning your wheels. And she marched into the hall, pulled on her yellow slicker, stuffed a bandanna in her pocket, snapped on Patsy's leash, and began walking rapidly down the path. She skirted the library, jogged past the church, past Clare's Diner, and began the long climb to the lighthouse.

The fog was lifting over Weymouth Harbor, and Sarah,

pausing halfway up the Lighthouse Point path, could see the outline of Mac's Mote with its clump of wind-twisted spruce trees, and beyond that the hump of Little Mote. In the harbor all was a-bustle. Small boats twisting about, sail covers coming off, auxiliary motors starting, moorings drooping off. Down below, she could pick out a troop of people fresh off the *Robin Day*, moving through the row of shops near the diner. One figure in a light red raincoat ducking into a gift shop reminded her strongly of Ruth Baker. Gathering Patsy close, she pushed ahead through a knot of visitors who were debating the wisdom of climbing to the lighthouse.

"You won't see anything," said one. "All this mist, and besides I heard that it's locked."

"I told you," said another. "Let's get coffee. The diner's open." And they retreated.

Sarah took her way alone up the rock-lined path, seeing the lighthouse just above her, its head caught in a wreath of fog. Arriving, she tried the door handle, as had Alex the night before. Locked. Cautiously, she made her way around the base of the lighthouse, Patsy trailing, apparently indifferent now to the place that had so excited him. Well, what had she expected? Roger sitting on one of the outside benches waiting to be discovered? And then she heard it. Music. Banjo and bluegrass seeming to come from under her feet. Madness. She covered her ears and then listened again. Now it was fading, and Sarah, as if following the Pied Piper, went down along the path until she came to a broken square of concrete off to the left. Beyond, three or four concrete steps descended to an open wooden door.

"Christ," said a familiar voice.

"It's you, Roger," said Sarah, recovering. "I heard the music." She pulled Patsy to her knee, wishing that her unpredictable dog would at least growl. She reached down and picked up a fist-sized rock. But when Roger emerged into the light she had a surprise. She had been used to thinking of him as a shaggy-haired bearded castaway, but now she saw a stranger in a clean blue denim shirt and tan corduroy pants, with a clean-shaven face, his brown hair neatly trimmed. And in his hand a duplicate to the stone in hers. "Drop that," she said, trying to control her voice, "and I'll drop mine." Both stones dropped and rolled together down the slope.

"Alex and I were here last night," said Sarah. "Did you hear him call?"

"I heard him," said Roger. He examined his feet for a minute and then lifted his head defiantly. "And who are you anyway? Alex's latest female?"

Sarah, in an almost automatic reaction, began to bristle, then realized that it was important to take nothing personally. "You've shaved," she said. "We thought you'd be almost overgrown by now. Everyone's been looking for you. All over the island."

"You sound just like Giddy," said Roger. "Which I don't need."

"You sailed with Giddy to Port Clyde, didn't you?" said Sarah, and then because it puzzled her, "If you didn't want to be found, why did you come back to Weymouth?"

"My business," said Roger. "And suppose you move off now . . . and take your dog." For Patsy, suddenly awake to duty, was pulling forward, whining.

"But why haven't the police found you?" persisted Sarah, addressing another problem. "They searched here and in the tunnels."

"Easy. I've got a key to the lighthouse . . . half the people on the island have copies, and I'm only here on a one-day stand. Plenty of places to hide on Weymouth. Those Sheriff's Deputies call themselves police."

"But you gave yourself away with the music just now."

"I took a chance. Looked too foggy for tourists and that last bunch turned back. I didn't hear you. Giddy picked me up a tape deck and some cassettes when she was in Port Clyde. Got me a razor, cut my hair, and found some clean clothes."

"Helpful Giddy."

"Sure. Why not? We're old friends. So go ahead back to

town and yell you've found me. I know a lot more places on the island."

"I don't know what I'm going to do," said Sarah honestly, "but," she added, feeling suddenly that she understood, "if all this hiding out has to do with your painting, you know, the 'Grange Supper,' well, your father's letters to you have been found . . . copies anyway . . . and I don't think it matter all that much. Using the Brueghel, I mean, because I don' suppose you intended to do anything dishonest."

"Shit," said Roger, his face contorted. "Shit."

"We've all talked about it. Lots of artists work from some other artist's idea, but they usually say so. All you had to do was mention the 'Peasants' Wedding' in your title . . . say i was a variation. It's still an interesting painting. I mean it. like it a lot."

Roger digested the statement, then stiffened.

"And who in hell are you to like it or not to like it?"

"I'm not an artist, but I worked at the Godding on the catalogue, and I kept seeing the reproduction of your paint ing. All you have to do is take a bow to the original. You father's wrong. It wasn't really plagiarism . . . just one of those 'after' paintings. And," said Sarah, warming to her work "why not let Giddy alone? She's going to end in jail with al the lying she's doing."

Roger exploded. "You stop telling me what to do. Get out. Get the fuck out of here. You don't belong here, and you don't know anything about Giddy. Or my father, or my family What are you hanging around for, anyway? Just another of Alex's shitty girl friends. Number thirty-three. Another little bit of pussy looking for a free bed and free meals. So just you butt out. Okay? Butt out." And Roger, tears running down his cheeks, his fist lifted, moved a step closer.

Sarah did not wait. She turned and ran stumbling and slipping across the ledge, dragging Patsy in headlong flight. She did not stop until she had come down from the lighthouse path and turned north on Ocean Trail and was almost to the

boundary of the Eider Inn, where she came to rest against a
rounded boulder a few paces off the path.

Damn, damn. Goddamn Roger Harwood, and damn the
Harwoods and the McKenzies, and all the incestuous families
with their cute little customs, and goddamn Weymouth Island
with its stupid Landing Day, and Alex with his little bits of
pussy. She supposed she was simply another in a long line of
females who just loved to look at birds or crew in the *Peg* or
wear an apron on Landing Day and then snuggle down with
him under the red and blue quilt at night. And damn you,
Sarah Deane, playing snoop woman. What do you care about
Roger Harwood or Giddy or who's hiding from what?

For a moment, cheeks hot, hands in fists, Sarah fought
down a choking sob, but then, biting her lip, sniffing furiously, she took hold of herself. Well, that's progress, she
thought, reaching down and pulling at Patsy's hair. A year ago
I might have been upset, really upset. I might have let Roger
get to me, but now, she told herself, taking a gulp of air, I can
take this whole scene. Or leave it. What was I trying to do
anyway? Show the police . . . and yes, Alex . . . that I can have
ideas, find something right under their noses? Well, so she
had. Roger. And she'd damn well report him, too.

She stood up straight and began a brisk march past the
Eider Inn. All was peace there. The long line of rocking chairs
was filled with guests reading, talking, knitting, waiting for the
fog to lift. Sarah, emotions under a double wrap, her chin
high, walked past the Inn and down along the east side of
Satter's Field to the beginning of the woods, where a rustic
sign spelled out "Weymouth Summer Art School—1920."
Beyond, Sarah could see the art school cottages spread in a
loose curve in a clump of pines. Which was Sydney Prior's, she
wondered; and Harrison Petty, he'd rented one. Small world.
But boring. Sarah repeated "Boring" aloud, as if to remind
herself that nothing on the island held any real interest.

And now, walking ahead along the trail, Sarah saw, just
off the path, a clump of people searching the lower reaches

of a marsh. There was Giddy, setting up a telescope, and there was the villain McKenzie himself, holding forth on the Wilson's warbler. "Look about waist high . . . watch for the black cap in the male."

"I call it his yarmulke," said a voice straight from Flushing.

They hadn't seen her, and Sarah quickly moved on and passed the bank leading down to the Bucket and came up to a sign that repeated the now familiar injunctions against letting dogs run free and wearing improper footgear, and indicated that part of the Ocean Trail that led to Captain's Head. This Sarah selected as the most proper place to clear her head, but hardly had she turned around the first boulder and through a pack of hikers than, oh hell, there, off the trail was Harrison Petty, sitting on a log and bent low over a map. Reining in Patsy, who was disposed to greet his old friend, she tiptoed past, and Harrison did not look up. Safely around another turn, she thought, he really isn't that bad. In fact, he probably had a few good points. After all, he had tolerated Patsy at the Godding, when he was obviously scared witless by the dog, and further, she doubted if he collected summer women on anything like the scale attributed to Alex by Roger.

In this charitable frame of mind, Sarah came to a second sign, larger and lettered in red. It warned visitors not to climb to the lower rocks nor attempt to swim at the base of Captain's Head. Beneath was a painted map indicating the location of two rescue rope stations. To the right of the sign, fastened to a large shelf of rock angling toward the sea, she saw a bronze plaque: "To the Memory of Miss Agnes Bloom and Miss Dorothy Hardy, Lost from Captain's Head, August 23, 1895. *Ora pro nobis.*" August 23, thought Sarah. Why, that's today. Oh, dear. Rather soberly, she continued up the now much narrowed path that twisted through the rising folds of metamorphic rock, and then, Patsy leading, followed the trail where it led over a bald rise marked by a small cairn. Here Sarah passed a woman kneeling beside a child examining lichens. Beyond, three steps led straight up, and Sarah came out on a flat table that, through some freak of wind, stood completely clear of fog.

Standing alone on the wide tabletop of Captain's Head, the ocean and sky around her, Sarah found that she was no longer preoccupied with the important business of not being hurt by the likes of Roger Harwood, nor the possibility that for Alex she was just one in a long string of summer diversions. She had never been so high on the island before. That Saturday after the storm, she and Alex had climbed only halfway up the trail. Now the path ahead seemed to lead directly into space. Sarah had a problem with space; whenever she looked over anything that dropped even fifteen feet, her joints dissolved. Moving cautiously forward, she saw that the path curved out and around the Head, and that a series of stanchions connected by rope guarded the outer rim of the trail. Holding Patsy tight, Sarah took hold of the nearest of these and made herself peer over the edge, and her legs immediately responded by sending electric needles of alarm. There, at what seemed a mile below, the dark water rose and curled against the rocks, while along the cliff the gulls wheeled and screamed.

Character training session over, Sarah backed up and followed the path, which now dodged away from the edge and took a safer course to a lower-level outcropping. Here she stopped, looked back up at high cliff, and unbidden into her head came the figures of Agnes Bloom and Dorothy Hardy turning in the air, falling like overdressed dolls to the rocks below. 1895. She saw it clearly: straw hats spinning off, high boots with buttons, long skirts—perhaps fatally long—flying up. Had their skirts caught under a heel? Had they been improperly shod? Or were they schoolteachers, botanists looking for lichens, or artists seeking an unusual perspective. Why had they fallen together? A suicide pact . . . lovers caught in a forbidden relationship? Or, perhaps, Miss Agnes first, on a ledge, slipping, sliding, losing her handhold and Miss Dorothy to the rescue. One after another, hands outstretched in surprise, in supplication. Going, going. Sarah found her cheeks wet with tears. *Ora pro nobis.* Pray for us. She craned again toward the rocks below, trying to banish their ghosts—ghosts that surely rode the surf, clung to the rocks, cried out against the tide.

Shading her eyes, Sarah traced the far shoreline along to a point where two triangular rocks rose against the cliff base. Now, indeed, she was seeing ghosts. No, it was only someone's sweater or raincoat, a rose-colored slash above the tide line. Or a dress. A dress crumpled up. But why would anyone throw their clothes over Captain's Head? She squeezed her eyes trying to make it out. The dress had a shape. It was filled with someone, someone bent in such a funny way that it looked more like an awkward laundry pile than a person.

Sarah found herself scrambling back up the path shouting. But Captain's Head was empty, and she ran like someone distracted, first to the edge of the high east cliff and then back along the trail toward the western curve, Patsy following, leash trailing, barking. The rope. Those rescue ropes. Where were they and did you rappel down or throw them? Sarah had had a one-week survival course at camp years ago, but now could she even tie a safe knot? And the tide. Was it coming in? Alex, how to get Alex? But running, calling down along a hundred yards of the Ocean Trail, brought no one. "Find Alex," she told Patsy, but the dog just stood and barked. But now there was one of those life rings fastened to a post with its coil of rope. Right in front of her nose. Lifting it down, she found it so heavy that she had to detach the life ring and roll the coil along the bank. Hoisting the coil around her body, heavily overbalanced, she worked her way to the overlook where she had first seen the rose-colored shape. Now the end of the rope around a stanchion in a bowline . . . that damned rabbit around the tree. Or a square knot? Sarah pushed the rope around and under and around in a sort of a wild tangle and then threw her weight against it. It held.

Now to get down. Pretend it was gym class. She had climbed those long ropes often enough in grade school. Over you go, you coward. And Sarah found herself sliding fast down the rope, hands on fire. Trying to keep her legs wrapped around the line, she pushed herself past one jutting rock after another, slipping, sliding, while above her head, along the top ledge, Patsy raced back and forth barking and barking.

A resting place, a tiny foothold by a dead bush. Now the next drop. Steeper. Sarah did not dare look down, afraid that fear would loosen her hold. Down she went, twisting like a puppet on a tangled string, until at the very end of the rope she found herself on a widening shelf with only a scramble of fifty feet or so of scattered rocks. Now she could judge the tide. It was coming in. The foam was almost up to the rose-colored shape.

Sarah, bleeding hands held away from her side, looked for a moment back to the top of the cliff and saw at the edge a cluster of figures, hands pointing, binoculars raised. The bird-watchers. "Here," yelled Sarah, but her voice sounded as a squeak against the murmuring ocean. Patsy, where was Patsy? Alex would know that something was wrong if he found the dog running loose. But no, there was Alex with his head up, searching the sky. "Alex," screamed Sarah. And Alex looked down. Directly at her. She saw him turn to the stanchion, then back to her. He tugged at the rope, and then in what seemed like one smooth extended motion he swung himself over the edge, hands high on the line, feet against the rock wall, coming so fast that he went to his knees on landing.

"In God's name . . . " he began.

Sarah pointed. "The tide's coming in . . . not much time."

Alex stared and then nodded. "Okay, if I wave, the person's alive. You get help . . . send someone back. Lem Wallace, the Coast Guard, a boat. What you can manage. We may need a chopper. A stretcher from the cottage hospital and an emergency kit. IV fluids, a backboard, a blanket. The works. Got that? I'll need someone back down here to help me."

"Yes," said Sarah.

"Give me your sweater, I'll need a covering." And Alex

clambered over the wet rocks and bent over the crumpled figure. Then, without looking back, he waved.

In defiance of the rules of physics, going up, even with damaged hands, proved to be easier than going down. Momentum was not a problem, and firm ground was the destination. At the top, arms reached out and Sarah found herself standing in the center of the bird-watchers, the subject of anxious inquiry.

"Dr. McKenzie, he just went down that rope. Did he see a nest? An osprey nest?" And then Giddy pushed her way to the front.

"Someone's hurt down there," said Sarah.

"I'll go down," said Giddy. "I've climbed here lots of times."

"Wait," said Sarah. "Someone's got to go for help," and she explained what Alex wanted done.

"Okay," said Giddy, "get going. You'll find Lem out by the harbor."

"No," said Sarah, deciding. "You know your way around, where everyone is. I'll climb back down." To a worried-looking woman in the front of the group, Sarah said, "Please take the rest back to their hotel," and to Giddy, who had taken hold of the rope, "No, damn it, Giddy. I'm the one that's going down. Give me your jacket. Has anyone got gloves? Good. And sweaters and belts? I can make a bundle and tie it around my waist." And then, with the borrowed pair of leather gloves on her hands, she was over the edge again, trying not to hear the ocean below.

"Yes," said Alex, "she's still alive, and it's Ruth Baker." He was kneeling by a tide pool, his hand on the woman's twisted arm. "She's unconscious. Head injury for sure. And shock from internal bleeding. I thought Giddy would come, she's had first-aid training."

"No," said Sarah, feeling his words like a blow. But then she made herself kneel next to Alex. "Giddy's better at finding help. Now what do you want me to do?"

"Wait up," said Alex. "I've some more checking to do." And Sarah watched as Alex's hands traveled up and over the broken terrain that was Ruth Baker's body, pressing here, adjusting there. To Sarah, only the fact that Alex said it was Ruth Baker made it so. Otherwise the heap of material on the rocks could have been any of a hundred persons who chose that day to wear a light red raincoat. Because how could this object have any particular identity? The red swollen features, the jaw askew, a tooth poking through a bloodied lip. One of Ruth's eyes was closed, but the other was half open as if Ruth were winking from her comic, off-center face, letting Sarah in on an obscene joke. And the blood leaking into the raincoat from some important center of her body decorated the fabric with a growing circle of carmine that looked like a grotesque magnification of a swatch of brocade.

"Okay," said Alex, "that's good." Sarah saw that he was fishing again in Ruth's throat. "Upper airway's still clear. Sometimes the tongue falls back into the throat. But she's got a fast pulse . . . losing blood. Got to stop that. Give me your bandanna," and Sarah silently unknotted it from her neck and handed it over.

"A.B.C.," said Alex. "Airway, breathing, circulation. Here, after I've tied this cloth, you keep pressure. There," and Sarah found her hand opened and its palm pressed into a warm sticky piece of material . . . Ruth's underpants.

"Hell," said Alex, "she may be losing too much . . . she's tachycardic. And we'll have to stabilize her cervical spine." Again to Sarah, "Go look for a board, a plank that's washed up. I'll keep the pressure now."

It seemed to Sarah that a century of bleeding, of living and dying, must have passed before she dragged a long splinter-edged plank into place, and Alex, holding Ruth's head with its crazy one-eyed stare, showed Sarah how to log-roll Ruth onto the board and fasten down her chest, her pelvis, her forehead with belts and the sleeves of sweaters and jackets.

And now a lobster boat heaved itself around the cliff and,

lurching and rolling, came in by the rocks, and Sarah watched a concert of careful forward motion . . . a wire stretcher, lines, Lem Wallace, a man in the Sheriff's Department brown uniform, a nurse in a white suit soaked from spray. Sarah stood back, feeling useless. She heard Lem Wallace say, "We've got a chopper coming in from the Naval Air Station," and then Alex, as he climbed into the boat, "Let's get that IV going . . . what have you got? Normal saline? Okay, where's the needle? We'll run it wide open, and I want a pressure on her. Now. Where's the cuff?" And they were gone.

The tide was coming in fast. Sarah, her head throbbing, held her fingers, stuck together with Ruth's blood, away from her sides, felt the cold water surge around her ankles, and for a moment thought how easy it might be to slip into the green water and rest as the tide pulled you in and then out and far away.

Wearily, she turned back toward the cliff and saw Giddy climbing over the rocks toward her.

"Come on, Sarah. I'll help you back. It's a tough climb if you're not used to it, and you've already done it twice. You should have let me come down. I'm on the rescue squad at college. Rinse your hands and then take my arm."

And Sarah to her chagrin found that she needed that arm.

The battery radio on top of the laundry hamper was playing "September Song," and a steaming mug of spiced tea sat within reach on the toilet seat. Sarah lay deep in the bathtub, bubbles of pine-scented Vitabath up to her chin, her muscles and bones all dissolved into something like noodles, her hands, anointed and bandaged, hanging over the sides of the tub. Elspeth had insisted on the radio because, as she said, "You might just fall asleep and go under. I'll send Giddy up now and then to check. And Patsy's fine. He came back by himself. Now take a long peaceful soak."

"I'll be okay," Sarah told her. "I've got a long peaceful book." It was certainly useful to have a rack across the tub if you had damaged hands, and in truth there was no more peaceful reading than the pursuit of Fanny Price, anxious, mild, dutiful Fanny, and her adventures in the intricate domestic circle of Mansfield Park.

But Sarah soon found that no book could distract her from the memory of Ruth Baker's shattered body and broken face. "It's a long, long while from May to December . . . September, November," mourned the radio, telling her that time was short. Very short, perhaps, for Ruth. She saw Ruth again, sunburned, dogged, as she trudged from shop to gallery to real estate office. And if Ruth died, would the end to it all be just another bronze plaque near Captain's Head? Ruth's would be in up-to-date language, no Latin tag, but maybe with some cautionary note. "In Memory of Ruth Baker, who walked too close to the edge . . . who wore improper shoes . . . or, who didn't notice someone walking up behind her." Or had it been that Ruth had felt dizzy? Had she, like her father, been subject to spells, and had she at the cliff's margin, like Cortez and his men, stood in wild surmise, and then fainted at the grandeur of it all? For who would hurt Ruth? Who indeed? Well, Sarah knew now that the summer world of Weymouth Island was just another jungle masquerading as a quaint New England backwater, a world where . . .

"Sarah, hey, Sarah. Are you awake?" Giddy thumped on the door. "We've had a message from the store. From Alex. He's at the hospital. Ruth Baker is critical. Stable but very critical."

NINE

On Sunday, the twenty-fourth of August, Sarah slept late for the second day in a row, and when she arrived in the kitchen she found the breakfast dishes washed and put away. Giddy and Alex were sitting at the table; Giddy making a pen sketch of an ear of corn, Alex reading the sports section of the *Boston Globe.*

"You look better," said Giddy.

"Ruth Baker?" said Sarah, pulling up a chair.

"I called the hospital this morning," said Alex. "Stable. Fractures of the jaw, shoulder, arm, femur. We won't know the extent of the head injuries until the reports are in . . . or guess at a prognosis. She's on support." He was serious, unsmiling, and Sarah remembered that yesterday noon—it seemed an age ago—she'd been furious with him. Now she felt dull, emptied of emotion, as if he were a mere acquaintance, just a physician making a report.

"What do you mean," she said, "on support?"

"They're helping her function. Taking care of breathing, excretion, fluid loss, trying to get her into balance. You know."

"Yes," said Sarah. She remembered Pres, her lost love from her college years. His last scene in the hospital had introduced her to the mysteries of the ICU. "Yes," she repeated. "Maybe I do know."

"I've some questions about yesterday," said Alex. He put down his paper. "Ruth Baker. Let's go over the Captain's Head business."

Sarah looked at her hands, swollen, red, patched with Band-Aids.

"No, not down the rope again. Mine are in bad shape, too. Just a review of the period before you found her."

"You've got an unhealthy mind, Alex," said Giddy, looking up. "Everything's crime with you. You know that people are always falling off Captain's Head."

Sarah poured herself a glass of orange juice and took a sip. "I've been thinking about it and really it must have been an accident. Ruth was harmless. No one could have taken her seriously as an investigator. And she wasn't the sort to jump off, to try and kill herself. She's a fighter. She was just looking around the island."

"Humor me, please," said Alex. "Go over your route. From the beginning." He took up a pad and pencil.

"I walked to the village and to the lighthouse trail. Midmorning. I saw someone who looked like Ruth coming out of that gallery near Clare's Diner."

"You didn't try to speak to her?"

"No, I wasn't sure it was Ruth."

"Too bad."

"I didn't think I had to," said Sarah. Alex's judicial tone annoyed her. He sounded almost as if he were trying to fix the blame for Ruth's fall. "Ruth had told me that she was going to visit some galleries on Weymouth, perhaps take a look at Captain's Head."

"So she wasn't keeping the visit a secret."

"I don't know. Not from me anyway. Besides, Ruth is exactly as she described her own mother. Half the people in Port Clyde and on the ferry probably know her whole story. She's so, well, absolutely open."

"A good quality," said Alex, "but maybe not healthy in the circumstances."

"I agree with Giddy," said Sarah. "You're too suspicious."

"Doctors are like that," said Giddy. "They can't conceive of anything normal." And Giddy stood up from the table and reached for her pad and pen. "I'm going out and do some sketching."

Alex watched Giddy bang out of the room and then turned back to Sarah. "Remember that Ruth thought something was wrong with her parents' car and was calling up garages? We should check that out fast."

"That means you're beginning to think that her parents' accident wasn't one. But I told her how idiotic it was from any point of view to try and kill someone by fooling with the brakes. Be logical," said Sarah, feeling that for once logic—logic without the muddy waters of emotion—was hers. "Ruth's parents were unknown here. Visitors. Everyday elderly people. Ruth told me her father managed a hardware store and her mother was a housewife. You remember housewives."

"I know this sounds off the wall, but what if Mr. and Mrs. Baker were, as you once humorously suggested, employed as fences? Harmless-looking mom-and-pop fences. Back and forth with paintings and silver spoons to Cleveland, Chicago, and points west."

"Alex!" Sarah shouted—it felt good to shout—"I'm the one with the runaway imagination, but now I'm in control and you've gone crazy. Listen, this was their first, repeat first, trip to the state."

"But you were the one who didn't want anyone to forget the Bakers' lost painting. Now I'm trying to find some sort of a link . . . trying to fit together those puzzle pieces you were talking about."

"I refuse to think that poor Ruth was tossed over Captain's Head. She probably got dizzy and tripped. I was dizzy just looking down."

"Start at the beginning. Describe your walk from the village and tell me what you saw. And who."

"All right," said Sarah. "If you think there's a point."

"I wouldn't ask if there were no point." Alex was beginning to sound like George Fitts. "Did you see Ruth again? Anywhere?"

"No, not after that one time . . . and, oh, I forgot. I went up to the lighthouse, and I ran into Roger."

"You forgot! Just like that. And haven't told anyone? Sarah, for God's sake, are you working with Giddy?"

"I forgot because of everything that's happened. Roger said he was staying there for one night. And frankly, I can't stand him."

"No one's asking you to, but I'll have to let someone know in a hurry. It's time he was flushed. Stay here, I'll be right back."

I'm right, thought Sarah, a surgeon's personality, and then the memory of her encounter with Roger and her craven flight from the lighthouse came sharply back, and Sarah felt her face turning hot.

Alex returned and took up his pad and pencil. "I told Lem," he said. "He'll nail Roger if anyone will."

Sarah, despite a complete lack of sympathy for Roger, was smitten with a sense of revulsion. "Thanks to Sarah the sneak."

"Not a sneak. This isn't a game, and it's no time for delicate feelings."

Once, Sarah thought, she might have risen like a trout to that remark. Now, older, she only glowered.

Alex seemed to take note of Sarah's increased color. "Anything the matter? Did Roger say something, do something?"

"He was insufferable, but it was nothing to do with Ruth." To her fury, Sarah felt her face more and more like a furnace. "It wasn't important." And in a businesslike manner she described the highlights of her walk, the Eider Inn, the art school, the trail to Captain's Head. "I suppose I saw Sydney

Prior's cottage and the one that Mr. Petty is renting, but I don't know which is which."

"Sydney's is the gray shingle one between the Bucket and the Pail on the ocean side, and I think Petty's rented the small one with the two chimneys near the school. More important, did you see either of them?"

"Not Mr. Prior, but Mr. Petty was reading a map just off the trail near the Head, and then," continued Sarah in the coolest voice she could manage, "I went along to the top, passing your group and someone with a child. Captain's Head was empty. You know the rest. I climbed down the path and there she was."

"You didn't hear anyone cry out, scream, the sound of a struggle?"

"Of course not. The sea gulls were yelling their heads off, but that's all. Did you have any stragglers in your group?"

"Giddy and I ran a taut ship. The idea of some of those people—some in their eighties and none too steady—wandering alone to the edge of the cliff is pretty frightening."

"So it seems to me," said Sarah seriously, her anger subsiding as her thoughts gathered again around Ruth Baker, "that it was just a horrible accident, just like her parents' horrible accident. I don't know if the lost painting fits in, but I'm going to work on that angle. I've just decided. For Ruth. You work on getting her better, okay?"

"It's pretty much out of my hands now," said Alex. "I'm not a neurologist. And you'd better write out a description of the people you met on the trail for the police. They're the ones to decide about accidents or homicides, but I'd say that neither George nor Mike wants to add anything to the mess. And Sarah, what's the matter? All morning I've felt that I've been talking to a refrigerator . . . or a broiler oven. I'm not sure which. Oh, Christ, Giddy, what now? I thought you'd gone sketching."

"Aunt Elspeth grabbed me," said Giddy, stamping into the room. "She's invited Mrs. Harwood for lunch, and I'm supposed to make potato salad. She thinks Mrs. Harwood is completely round the bend."

"Who could blame her?" said Sarah, thinking that a trip around the bend might be something in the nature of a rest cure. She could use one herself.

"Marian's been pretty good always about working off her frustrations," said Alex. "Gardening, weeding, getting in the kindling, pruning. She may not have been happy, but she kept busy."

"And I just can't imagine her going to pieces," said Giddy. "Doesn't seem in character."

"Well, here's news," said Elspeth, coming into the room. "They've picked up Roger. No resistance. He's being taken over to Port Clyde for questioning. Marian hardly batted an eye. She is *not* acting natural. Alex, won't you suggest she see someone?"

"She's still functioning, isn't she?" said Alex. "Sleeping and eating. Because if she is, I'd better stay clear. Marian's never acted as if she wanted my medical advice."

Certainly at lunch Marian showed no signs of fragmentation. She sat placidly, one hand in the lap of her seersucker dress, the other back and forth to her mouth. It was, Sarah reflected, an absolutely deadly meal. They sat at the table like members of an international conference, none of whom had quite mastered the others' languages. Alex was extremely polite and every now and then had something to say about the Red Sox. Elspeth began animated little sentences about Landing Day and stopped in the middle. Sarah concentrated on passing dishes and avoiding Alex's occasional inquiring looks, and even Giddy made little effort to keep the conversation afloat. As for Marian Harwood, she might have been a Guernsey cow invited for a cud-chewing session.

In the middle of dessert, Elspeth put down her spoon. "Marian, you're being wonderful, everyone says so. But control can go too far, and although Nate wasn't easy . . . I mean, of course, you're relieved . . . but don't you think a good cry would do you a world of good? Then after you've had a *complete* checkup, I think a trip. One of those tours, the kind that takes care of everything. France . . . or Greece." Elspeth waved vaguely in the direction of Europe.

Marian carefully squeezed a wedge of lime along her slice of melon. "Oh, Elspeth, I don't believe so. So much trouble."

"You could go with Joyce," said Giddy. Joyce, the Harwood daughter in Los Angeles, had been told not to come to the memorial service. "Too far," Marian had said, "all those plane connections."

"Joyce is too busy," said Marian without interest.

Elspeth stood up. "Let's call lunch over. We can all go outside." She added without much hope, "How about a round of croquet?"

But Marian stayed in her place. "I'm moving back to the cottage tomorrow," she said. "I need a change of clothes. The police are letting me. I'm asking them to stop."

"Stop?" said Elspeth. "Stop what?"

"The investigation. Nate's gone now. It's all over. I can manage. We've had the service."

"You can't do that," said Giddy. "The police don't just stop when it's murder."

"But I'm going to ask them to," said Marian. "If I can go back to the cottage they must be finished, mustn't they? What's the point in going on, all that trouble?"

"But Marian," said Elspeth, "don't you want to find out . . ."

"And thank you for a very nice lunch," said Marian, folding her napkin. "I must go back now. Roger's room should be cleaned. Fresh sheets. I hope the police let him go tonight. He may want to stay on Weymouth because it's all over, isn't it?" And Marian rose, smoothed a pleat back in her skirt, and departed.

"Totally spaced out," said Giddy, as Marian disappeared down the path.

"Marian has never been exactly lively," said Elspeth.

"Probably on drugs," said Giddy. "Valium maybe. What do you think, Alex? Did you look at her pupils?"

"I didn't notice anything like that," said Alex.

"Sarah," appealed Elspeth, "what do you think? You're an impartial observer."

But Sarah shook her head. "I've only talked to her really during the furniture lifting, and she was pretty calm then."

"God," said Giddy, "I'd have wet my pants. Carrying furniture around and thinking Nate was ready to grab me. I think she's schizo. In psychology we did a section on people who don't react. Something about affect."

"Reacting to Nate was a losing proposition," said Elspeth, "and Giddy, don't you go around saying that Marian's on drugs or losing her mind."

"I'll leave you psychologists to figure it out," said Alex. "I have a police session ahead of me. Not a free day after all, what with Roger and a check on Ruth Baker at the hospital. Sarah, do you want to come . . . for the ride?"

"Of course not," said Giddy. "Sarah, come sailing. It's your day off anyway. Who needs the police? I'll give you a lesson in the *Peg*."

"Sarah knows how to sail," said Alex.

"Not really," said Sarah, still not looking at him, "but thanks, Giddy. It sounds like fun."

"I'm off to see about the children's Landing Day art show," said Elspeth. "Three of them have submitted nudes."

Giddy turned to Sarah. "Let's get out of here, and I'll tell you what I studied in abnormal psych. Marian Harwood fits right in."

* * *

Alex arrived at the State Police trailer in the middle of what might have been a blazing row, except that George Fitts was the picture of control.

"The fact is," said George, tapping a newspaper, "you screwed up. The Sheriff's Department really screwed up.

Hello, McKenzie. No, don't go. Everyone in Knox County knows about it."

"Christ," said Mike. "So we screwed up." He was sitting hunched on a folding chair, shirt open at the neck, his almost white-blond hair disordered. "Okay, so someone blew it. My little deputy Susie Q. or her partner, Wayne Jones. Nothing's one hundred percent. Even the State Police CID falls on its ass."

"Simmer down, Mike," said George, "and let's see that it doesn't happen again." He picked up the newspaper and pointed out the headlines: " 'Accidental drowning possible homicide.' Okay, who's been calling the papers, Mike? Those garage mechanics?"

"It's no secret," fumed Mike. "That Baker woman was all over the county, getting people to look at her car. She might as well have been yelling murder. I'm not surprised the paper picked it up. They love to stick it to the police."

"And now Ruth Baker's unconscious," said George. "It almost looks as if we tried to keep her quiet. Unfortunate.'

"Fill me in, one of you," said Alex, who was perched on the edge of a table piled with folders and a collection of telephone books.

"God," said Mike, "it seemed like an obvious death by drowning. Susan Cohen and Wayne Jones signed the report saying the car'd been gone over. Wayne is on leave now and Susan's off this weekend, but one of them blew it . . . probably Susie. Women just don't care about how a car is put together no matter how many courses they take. They don't have a feel for machines. Anyway, when the car was pulled up, the brake lines were broken, the fluid gone. They must have figured that it happened when the car bounced off the bait house, or when it settled down against those pilings. After a phone call to Missouri to the daughter, they learned that the father had fainting spells, and it seemed likely that he was driving and lost control. Anyway, they didn't look any further into the brake failure."

"Tell McKenzie what the garage people found," said George, settling into his role as Roman father.

"Oh, Christ, Alex. The brake bleed nipples. Both off. The brake fluid would have drained right out. No accident. Both off from the same side of the car—dual braking systems in modern cars have diagonal fluid lines. Supposed to be fail-safe. Someone made damn sure the car wouldn't stop. And they . . ."

"Or he. Or she," said George.

"Whoever. They must have had time to do it on the quiet. I mean you can't lie down under someone's car and start unscrewing its private parts without someone noticing . . . no, George, I'm not trying to be funny."

"I hope not," said George. "It could have been done after dark, or in a garage, or on someone's property. It was after dark when the car went in."

"I'm afraid I come into this," said Alex. "I went with Ruth to the junkyard when she first had the idea of looking at the car, and I did my best to convince her to cease and desist. I told her that salt water and the impact would probably ruin the brakes and to forget it. But here's what bothers the hell out of me. Sarah said—to Ruth and me—that tampering with brakes as a way of killing someone, or as a means of stealing a painting, was nothing short of insane. How could anyone be sure of the sort of accident that would kill the people or allow access to the painting, assuming the painting survived the crash?"

"And how could the Bakers have been persuaded to go down to Lloyd's Wharf in the first place?" said Mike. "It's off the main road, no rental cottages available along there—mostly working people who are full-time residents. Yet someone must have given them directions."

"Lobsters," said Alex.

"What?" said George.

"Lobsters. What if the Bakers were looking around for a place to buy lobsters . . . or any seafood? It's what visitors here do. And someone told them about Lloyd's Wharf, innocently or maliciously."

"Scratch that," said Mike. "Tourists from the Midwest wouldn't cook lobsters from scratch. They wouldn't know how to eat them, most likely. Ruth Baker said her parents had never been to the East Coast before."

"That doesn't mean they've never had lobsters," said Alex. "It isn't a secret food. Maybe they thought they could buy cooked ones down at Lloyd's after they were told to go there by some real estate office where they were investigating rental cottages."

"And this real estate art collector locked the Bakers in the lavatory while he went out and drained the brake fluid from their car and lifted the painting. Forget it," said Mike.

"Stop guessing," said George. "We've checked on the Bakers. Hotels, inns, motels, cabins, rental condos, and no records, no reservations in the state. The daughter claims they were on their way home and then turned around to look for the cottage, but we've drawn a blank at every real estate office in the county. Now, let's review the facts. First, a series of art thefts over three or more summers from this part of the coast. Second, a stolen artist, Nate Harwood, is murdered by a heavy blow to the head by a doorstop that may have been taken or found at a local art dealer's shop. The victim is tied and put into the water. A number of local people disliked, hated, or feared the victim, including his son and wife."

"Not a number of people, the whole frigging county," said Mike.

"And now," continued George, without missing a beat, "we discover an earlier drowning homicide—or a vicious prank, the victims being, as far as we can tell, strangers to the area. The daughter claims a painting is missing from the car. Coincidence or connection? The daughter has been searching for a record of the painting and has begun to ask about the car's brakes. She has a serious accident. Coincidence or connection? Well, I, for one, am not jumping to conclusions. I'm going to chip away at these people. Where was everyone on the day of the Baker drowning, the day Harwood disappeared, the day Ruth Baker visited Captain's Head? Where were they on the days the various paintings disappeared?"

"Speaking of people," said Alex, "have you talked to Roger?"

"George did," said Mike, "and I hope he keelhauled him."

George put his fingertips together. "I think Roger may be lying about his movements on the Friday his father disappeared, and I'm not convinced that his hiding on Weymouth is related entirely to his breaking into his parents' cottage. But so far I haven't enough reason to ask the D.A. to hold him. We'll go on watching him. He can't remember where he was the evening the Baker car went into the harbor, and he claims to have been in the lighthouse tunnels during the period that Ruth Baker must have fallen. As for Sydney Prior, Harrison Petty, and Mrs. Harwood, we're just beginning to make up a profile of their activities. Prior, as I've said, is now confirmed for the greater part of that Friday afternoon and until early Saturday morning. His car broke down on the way home, and he didn't get in until four A.M. Witnesses all along the way."

"I have something about Harrison," said Alex, "not proven, but it may explain his feelings about Nate, who tried to block his appointment to the Godding. Sometime ago Harrison was involved in a scandal. Who knows what. Nothing came out for public consumption, but you know Nate, a mind like flypaper. He picked up dirt like that."

"Maybe selling paintings under the rug," said Mike. "Or had his hand in the cash register—that's a hard one to prove sometimes. Or maybe he was fooling around with little boys."

"What did I say about speculation?" said George. He took a sheet with a row of names and made a note. "For now it's enough to know that Harwood tried to use this to stop Petty's appointment and Petty knew it. We'll try and trace the charges."

"How about a Weymouth link?" said Mike. "Almost everyone tied into this circus has something to do with the island. Roger hides on it, Marian and Nate lived there and his body washes in to it. Harrison rents a cottage on it and Sydney Prior owns one, and Ruth Baker goes off the cliff there."

"But her parents were drowned in Port Clyde," said George. "You're swinging again, Mike. Stick to horses. You both may be interested to know that the fragments from the base of the doorstop are similar to the one embedded in Harwood's skull. I'm going to take another look at the Prior connection."

"A joke, George?" said Mike. "Because you gotta warn me. Well, I'll concede that a doorstop is one hell of a weapon and that Sydney has the heft to have used it, but God-a-mighty, if Nate saw old pussyfoot Sydney Prior coming at him with a doorstop, he'd have obliged by dropping dead from surprise. No need to hit him over the head. Sydney doesn't go in for the physical. Besides, Sydney himself reported the doorstop missing. Now that's too damn subtle for me if he's the basher on the head. And you just said that Sydney was whooping it up in Portland when Nate was alive in Port Clyde, so unless he has a private rocket ship . . . well, it won't wash."

"Patience, Michael," said George.

"Something I'm running short of," said Alex. "I'm going over to the Godding."

"To see if Petty's got sticky fingers or a loose fly?" said Mike.

"Shut up, Mike," said Alex. "Harrison may have had too many parking tickets." And he pushed himself away from the table and stalked out.

*　*　*

Sarah leaned back against the lee rail of the *Peg* and tried to listen to a summary of Psychology 102 as it applied to Marian Harwood. "So if Marian isn't a borderline psychotic," concluded Giddy, "then she's certainly got some weird neurosis. Now would you like to take the tiller?"

"I haven't done that much sailing."

"Then it's time you did. We're over Tinker's Ledge now, so just keep her off the wind and don't let her luff . . . flap her sail. And don't jibe, turning away from the wind. I suppose you always let the other people in your family do the sailing."

This hit home. "I wasn't that interested," said Sarah defensively. "And my brother, Tony, grabbed the tiller if my mother and father didn't want to do it. I usually went along for the ride and took a book."

"So you turned into an English teacher. Well, you're doing okay—just keep her steady. Now tell me, do you really like Alex?"

"What?" said Sarah, startled into letting the *Peg* luff.

"Like Alex," said Giddy, pushing the tiller. "You know, want him. To be a lover, to have him, live with him. Even marry him. I've been thinking about it because Alex is sort of a favorite cousin . . . though he certainly can be impossible."

"All that, Giddy," said Sarah "is none . . . " She stopped and then said with what she felt was a dignified smile, "That's really private."

"Oh, it's not a question I'm supposed to ask," said Giddy. "It's a fault of mine, asking what I shouldn't, but then I'm absolutely eaten up by curiosity, and Alex would chop my ears off if I asked him about it, so I thought I'd start with you, because you know, don't you, that Aunt Elspeth is absolutely salivating over you?"

Sarah hesitated, trying to erase from her mind the unlikely picture of Elspeth McKenzie salivating over anyone.

"Alex," persisted Giddy, "always brings women over every summer . . . sort of trial balloons . . . no"—seeing Sarah's face change—"not you. Anyway, I don't think so, because I've never seen him look at any of the balloons—we all used to call them that—the way he looks at you when you're not noticing. I mean he'd be all wrapped around some girl, but he'd have this faraway look." Here Giddy elevated her head and looked in a frozen way at the horizon.

"This particular balloon . . . " began Sarah, forgetting for the moment that she was mature, objective, and cool.

"Oh, don't be mad. You're not a balloon. That's what I'm trying to say. Hey, hold your bow steady. Look, even with all this crime and detective jazz going on, Alex sometimes looks at you as if you were both off in outer space. So do you really like him, because I'd hate to have him disappointed."

"He could always bring in more balloons."

"Oh, but they were always so boring. Only one or two with real possibilities. An actress once and a cello player and a couple of hospital residents."

"Of course I like Alex," said Sarah, thinking that a polite answer turneth away questions. "He and I have done things together. Concerts, hikes, and so forth. And he was very kind to me in Texas. I was in bad shape."

"Oh, shit, Sarah. Don't be so bloody formal. Take it from me . . . cousin Giddy, Alex is hot about you, but he's not the soupy type. Now bring the boat about without my help and say hard-a-lee. And don't get mad. If I didn't like you, I wouldn't sail with you. I only sail with people I like. Sometimes, when I was little and mad at Roger, I used to wonder if I could marry Alex. Of course, I was only ten or eleven, and he was just finishing med school. Later I realized you don't usually marry your first cousin, and that he was old enough to be my father."

"Not really," murmured Sarah, in spite of her intention not to be pulled into this conversation.

"I'll take the tiller now. It's tricky through these ledges."

Giddy and Alex, thought Sarah. Unlikely duo. Giddy, like a powerful Raggedy Ann, thatched hair standing up, peeling nose, big open blue eyes, tramping bang, bang, crash on everyone's nerve endings. Alex would go insane. Or would he? Someone like Giddy, loyal and open and with a shared childhood. If Giddy wanted to know something, she just up and asked. She made Sarah feel all nit-pickety, a bundle of trivial sensibilities. She closed her eyes and remembered how she and Alex had drifted about in the *Peg* in the late-afternoon sun, not saying much. Now with an inner jolt she knew she missed him, wanted him to be sitting at the tiller, his dark hair blowing over his forehead, his long mouth relaxed and easy, one hand folded lightly over the tiller. She was sorry she'd been so cool with him earlier . . . had not told him what Roger had said and cleared the air. Now she ached to tell him how comforted, how at rest she felt when he was with her, how much . . .

"Wind's switching," said Giddy. "We can make it back on a broad reach."

"That's faster?"

"God, Sarah, you're hopeless. Yes, faster. That or running before the wind. Tacking is slow, going zigzag. Do you want to go in the race on Landing Day? Sometimes I crew for Alex, but it's no big deal if he'd rather go with you."

"I don't know," said Sarah. "What I should be thinking about is helping poor Ruth Baker. She's left unfinished business. I've been thinking about being her stand-in and looking for her painting."

Giddy nodded and then, in a casual voice, said, "You bumped into Roger, I hear. Did he say anything in particular?"

"Not much," lied Sarah. "Just about hiding out."

"I know you probably think Roger is a real asshole and so do I sometimes, but if you'd had his father . . . especially after being sort of a favorite, well, you'd be pretty sour. He used to be okay. I've tried my best with him, but now . . . not that he's dangerous, but he overreacts." Giddy gave a sigh as if long used to the uncertainties of men. Then, shaking her head to indicate a new subject, "I'll tell you what's really bugging me. My painting. I can't seem to get off the ground in one piece. No style of my own. I'm so bloody eclectic. A little bit of Aunt Elspeth, a little bit of Roger, some of Dufy, and then I switch and fill in shapes like Braque or go in for black lines like Rouault."

And Sarah did her best to concentrate on Giddy, as she talked on about the troubles of the emerging artist who painted nothing that was her own, and began to think that this inchoate state was not too far from her own unresolved life.

Back on shore, Sarah walked slowly by herself up the path

from the beach, Giddy, the indefatigable, having decided on a fast uphill sprint.

I've got to put my mind in order, she thought, put Alex and his balloons on the shelf and start working on some sensible program of investigation. So preoccupied was Sarah that she was well within the cottage gate before she became aware of a group clustered about the granite block that served as a front door step. There was Elspeth in her painting pants and a wash shirt holding open the screen door, apparently inviting in a mosquito horde, and there was Giddy, a young Amazon in her red bathing suit, gesturing at a fair-haired woman in the crispest of green linen shorts, the tidiest of yellow rugby shirts, and on her feet the very whitest of boat sneakers. She was tan of face and limb, and her short hair circled her head like a honey-colored cap. Sarah took in all these details of dress and complexion in one glance and in the same moment knew herself to be dirty, perspiring, and wearing torn jeans and a too large, tie-dyed T-shirt left over from college days.

"Sarah," said Elspeth, "this is Tina. Her family's boat is in the cove. Alex told her we have a guest mooring. Which we do."

"It's no good," said Giddy in a forbidding voice, "if you draw over six feet."

"No," said Tina, "just a little over five, so if you haven't anyone coming in—"

"No," said Elspeth.

"Oh, great," said Tina. She smiled at Sarah. "I'm a friend of Alex's from the hospital."

"Oh," said Elspeth. "This is Sarah Deane, our house-guest."

"And a good friend of Alex's," said Giddy.

"Terrific about the mooring," said Tina. "I'll go and tell my father. We hate being stuck in a busy harbor, especially with all the Landing Day boats coming in. A little cove like yours is just what we're looking for. Alex told me the mooring might be free . . . well, actually I did ask if there was one. We had such a fun drive to Maine. My father wanted to kidnap him for our races. He's rapacious when it comes to finding crews for the August regattas. But Alex said no. He has this thing about Weymouth."

"We all do," said Elspeth.

"Everyone loves their own place," said Tina, "but it's fun to cruise around, and my father says he spent a lot of summers visiting on Weymouth when he was in college. He loves the island."

"Well, see you around, Tina," said Giddy abruptly, and turning to Sarah, said "Balloon" in a clear voice.

"Giddy," said Elspeth sharply, "won't you show Tina where she can leave her dinghy when she comes ashore?"

"I brought my racquet," said Tina. "Alex said there were courts. He's terrific. We won the doubles together last year at the hospital."

"I play," said Giddy. "We can have singles. How about now?"

"Or doubles if Alex comes soon," said Tina. "Sarah, do you play?"

"Not lately and I didn't bring a racquet."

"I'll lend you one," said Giddy. "Don't be stupid," she hissed at Sarah, and then, looking up, "Oh God, those shitty dogs!"

And there, trotting down the path to their own accompanying howls and yelps, came a canine trio—Patsy trailing a broken line from his collar, and the two Sealyhams beside him looking like abused stuffed toys. Each dog had a wreath of porcupine quills around his muzzle, and from time to time one or the other would pause to bat at its face with a paw or push its nose into the ground as if it were looking for truffles.

* * *

Alex climbed the stairs to the Godding and passed under the hanging black and yellow banners, now somewhat the worse for wind and weather. At the door he hesitated. To

Harrison Petty? That was the honest approach. Or to Doris Ordway, the back-door route . . . and possibly the more useful.

Mrs. Ordway's door stood open, and she herself was bending over a large floor plan. She motioned for Alex to come in and sit down.

"It's the sculpture show," she said, looking up. "A real worry."

"You mean how to arrange the pieces?"

"Goodness, no. Mr. Petty and the judges do all that. I'm thinking of someone bumping into the sculptures. You know, terra cotta, marble, glass. One knock and off the stand they go. Last year a glass box thing went into a million pieces, and a mobile was set too low and this absolute Goliath of a man caught his hairpiece in it. And now, Alex, what for you?"

"It's Nate's murder again, and the art thefts, and now the Baker drowning."

"But heavens, how could they all be tied in together? And that poor Miss Baker. I read about her accident. I suppose she was sightseeing. Captain's Head takes its toll. How is she?"

"Holding her own, I think," said Alex, thinking as he said it what an unsatisfactory expression—particularly for someone unconscious, for who knew what Ruth's "own" was?

"But you're here to ask me something," said Mrs. Ordway, folding her hands over the floor plan. "Something I probably shouldn't answer."

"Yes," said Alex, "it's about Harrison Petty. His work here. First, is he competent?"

Mrs. Ordway nodded. "He's quite able to handle any art-related problems the Godding's likely to present, though I do wish he'd realize just how small this museum is. The budget is in shreds."

"And he seems, well, normal? I mean, has there ever been a hint of anything not quite honest, or peculiar . . . anything out of place?"

"He's awkward," said Mrs. Ordway. "He knocks things

over. I'd like to lock him up during the sculpture exhibition. Of course, if you're built the way he is, all joints and bones and six foot five, I suppose it can't be helped."

"Anything else?"

"You make me feel like a spy, Alex, but I suppose it's in a good cause. One thing. He's not at ease with people . . . groups anyway. It's odd in a museum director."

"Does he shy away from any one subject or person? Does he seem attracted . . . oh, hell, Doris, is he gay?"

"Now how would I know, Alex? I just sit here and tend to my knitting and try not to drop too many stitches. But for what it's worth, I haven't seen or heard of anything like that. No male friends taking him out to lunch, waiting in the wings after work."

"Interested in children, boys?"

"Certainly not, he's terrified of children."

"Anything else at all? Missing office equipment, petty cash, odd letters going out or coming in? Liquor, drugs in his office? Anything offbeat?"

Mrs. Ordway stared ahead, hesitated, and then said, "It's such a silly detail."

"Shoot."

"He seems much too fidgety about these art thefts. I know he's worried about anything disappearing from the museum, but he's really off balance about it, and wants to hire two security guards now and put visitors through a sort of X-ray gate like the ones in airports. He acts, well, almost guilty. You'd think *he'd* lost the Hopper at the Farnsworth the way he's going on. But Alex, this is just a subjective impression."

"Harrison in a fidget isn't exactly bombshell information, but I'll file it away. One more thing. Do you know how he feels about Nate's campaign to keep him from being named the Godding director?"

"I see," said Mrs. Ordway. "Motive. Well, Mr. Petty felt, and still does, very strongly about it. He's always dropping remarks. But I don't know the details of the affair. Nor," she added firmly, "do I want to." Mrs. Ordway smiled her dismissal and bent again over her floor plan.

* * *

"These G.D. things are in like fishhooks," said Giddy. "I know," said Sarah, struggling with a raging Sealyham.

But it was Tina, behaving with the calm of a field surgeon, who took hold. She borrowed an apron, ordered pliers, alcohol, hydrogen peroxide, towels, and scarves to tie muzzles. Instructing the others in the proper restraint methods—tie dog A, lie across dog B, hold dog C—she dealt with each in turn, pulling quills and laying them like suture needles on a towel. Elspeth, Sarah, and Giddy were reduced to nurse assistants.

"Just like the E.R.," said Tina cheerfully. She ran her hand in a professional way inside Patsy's lip. "Here's one in the roof of his mouth. Sarah, the pliers. Giddy, keep his mouth open. Mrs. McKenzie, just hold his collar. Just a little one, but it can work in and suppurate and then you've got trouble. It's lucky I worked for a vet one summer. There, that's about it." Tina stood up, slipped off her apron, and stood forth becomingly flushed but unblemished. Giddy, Elspeth, and Sarah, however, looked like the survivors of a machine gun attack.

"Hello," said Alex, looming from the gate. "Don't tell me. It was an ambush."

"Hi, Alex," said Tina. "You've missed all the excitement."

"I think we'll have to go swimming," said Sarah. "Except Tina."

"And then, tennis anyone?" said Tina.

Sarah, having taken a quick swim and scrub with the others, shivered in a rising north wind and felt that, of all the places in which she might find herself, the tennis court was the least desirable. She had been coaxed into making a fourth, but now her head felt hot, her backhand, never distinguished, ceased to work at all, and she served doubles through her first two turns at service. Tina, her partner, smiled forgivingly and told Sarah she had a promising swing, while she herself stroked hard and accurately, going to the net to volley, a lean and smooth-muscled figure in very brief white shorts. Giddy, possessed by an inner demon, slammed the ball down the alley, at Tina, and frequently over the backstop. Alex played mechanically, without fire or error. He seemed abstracted and several times stopped to ask the score, or who was serving. Immediately after the last set concluded, he left to use the boat club telephone—one of four on the island.

He emerged frowning. "Ruth," he said to Sarah. "Still stable. They're calling in another neurology consult."

"She's still unconscious then?" said Sarah, now aware that her own head felt heavy and hot, her throat endangered.

"Your mother told me," said Tina. "What an awful accident." And Alex turned to her and launched into a highly technical explanation of Ruth's injuries. From this Sarah was able to salvage only a few phrases having to do with things like motor flaccidity, brain stem compression, mute tetraplegia, nonreactive pupils, and a particularly horrible expression having to do with the "doll's head maneuver."

Alex turned back to Sarah. "I'll go over tomorrow and see if I can do anything from a medical angle. The State Police will be going over Ruth's things at her motel, trying to find out what she was up to on Weymouth."

"Sarah, if you're free tomorrow, we could work on your backhand," said Tina.

"Thanks, but I have to go to work, and besides, I think I've got a cold coming on." Sarah swallowed with difficulty, and her teeth hurt.

"I'll play singles with you, Tina," said Giddy. "We can work on my backhand."

"You may kill someone with your backhand," said Tina.

"Okay, everyone," said Alex. "Coming, Sarah?" He

strode off and Sarah, feeling exactly like one of the Sealyhams, plodded along behind with the others and every now and then swung her tennis racquet halfheartedly at the rose hips that crowded the bushes along the path.

At the McKenzie cottage Tina departed, saying that she was free all tomorrow ". . . and the next day. Through Landing Day. We've been sailing for a week, and it's good to stop heaving. Lucky for me to have found Alex in place . . . and you, Giddy . . ."

"And Sarah," added Giddy in a belligerent voice.

"And Sarah, of course," repeated Tina, smiling, and to Sarah it was the smile of someone who had not once lost her serve and who was obviously not coming down with a cold.

Dinner that evening was a mixed bag. Elspeth frowned absently and put honey instead of chutney on her meat loaf, Giddy smoldered, and Alex, claiming preoccupation with Ruth Baker—something not quite typical—hardly said a word. Finally, after Elspeth had produced a slightly fallen cake and a bowl of not-quite-ripe peaches, Sarah rose and, pleading her cold, crawled off to bed.

She huddled under her quilt, too miserable to speculate either on the fate of Ruth Baker or on the fact that Tina closely resembled the woman—Sonja, wasn't it?—that Sarah had imagined as the perfect mate for Alex. Even more perfect, since it was obvious that Tina, along with her physical attractions and talents with perforated dogs, was a familiar in the medical world. Was she a nurse? A doctor? No matter, thought Sarah, gripped by a rising fever. Not my business who Alex plays tennis with or drives to Maine. Just another balloon coming to roost, she thought, woozily mixing her metaphors.

At which point there was a knock and Alex poked his head around the door. "How are you?"

"Just call me a sick balloon."

"I see Giddy's been talking," said Alex. "I hope she never works for the State Department."

"It doesn't matter," said Sarah, putting her head down on her pillow.

"Of course it matters. But first get well. Anything you need? Skilled nursing from a physician?"

"No, thank you," said Sarah in a hoarse voice. "Just sleep, please," and Alex quietly shut the door.

TEN

On Monday, the twenty-fifth of August, Alex, fresh from a rolling north-wind crossing, arrived at the State Police trailer. This, usually something of a sweatbox, today was shaken by gusts that caught desk papers and made the door rattle. George Fitts was alone.

"I'm going over to the hospital and see Ruth Baker," said Alex. "Anything new here?"

"They're finishing with her motel room, and Mike's helping us work the neighborhood, see where she touched base."

"If she's mixed up with anything off-color, I'll eat my socks. One thing I picked up. Harrison Petty's been having nervous fits over the art thefts. Maybe an overreaction, since he's responsible for the Godding's collection."

"Are you offering that as evidence?"

"Hearsay from Mrs. Ordway."

"I'm not interested in Petty's nerves, but we are trying for details on that so-called scandal involving him. It's not easy, since the whole affair was dropped and the art museum people there in Chicago are playing dumb. Petty won't tell us anything, just that Harwood maliciously tried to ruin his career. More to the point, Petty knew that Ruth Baker was looking for a garage mechanic. In fact, she asked him to recommend one."

"Probably everyone on the coast knew it," said Alex.

The door blew open, slammed against a metal cabinet, and Mike walked in, his light hair whipped by the wind. "Hi, Alex. George, here's the prelim of your lab team from Ruth Baker's room. Clothes, a suitcase, the painting Sydney gave her, toilet articles, but no toothbrush."

"False teeth," said George.

"None of that cleaning gunk or tooth glue around."

"I'll make a note," said George, reaching for a pencil.

"A few more bits and pieces," said Mike. "Harrison Petty was in Port Clyde until six-thirty Friday afternoon, August eighth. Visited the Arts and Crafts Gallery, the general store, and poked around in local antique shops. Nothing confirmed except the gallery visit. Doris Ordway left the Godding at five o'clock and says she has no idea why Petty was in Port Clyde. One odd note. Roger Harwood was seen standing at the end of the public landing that Friday at dusk. Someone thought he was fishing, then realized he didn't have a rod or line. He was just looking down into the water."

"What are you trying to say?" said George.

"Not that he was dropping the doorstop in the water after braining Papa, because I've had reports from twelve different people who claim they've seen twenty-four citizens drop objects into the drink. Someone's leaked about our heavy object hunt. Too bad about Sydney being away that afternoon. You know, I've even made up this little scenario where Sydney, before he leaves, rigs up the doorstop with a kind of counterweight and string and then sends word for Nate to come over and pick up his order."

"Setting up the doorstop where it could kill Giddy or a customer and letting the body lie there?" said Alex. "Try again."

"It'd make a good mystery," said Mike.

"It already has," said Alex, "with a cactus pot. Dorothy Sayers. Anyway, the doorstop in the water only a few hundred yards from Sydney's shop suggests that maybe Nate was killed there or close by, and that the murderer may have been in a rush, because why not take it out into the ocean and lose it for good?"

"If we assume that Nate was killed on land," said George, "then we've got the problem of how the body was carried off and dumped."

"Nate wasn't any great heavyweight," said Mike. "About one-fifty-five, five feet nine, all gristle. Mean beef on the hoof, but portable. No calls in from citizens who saw a body going off in a boat, though anyone who saw a harbor seal poke its head up that day now thinks he saw Nate's body floating by."

"How about boats at night?" said Alex. "You were checking."

"Nothing much," said George. "A dragger, two trawlers coming in. A couple of outboards zipping around after dark, probably high school kids. Nothing until the lobster boats started out around four-thirty and after, though not so many because of the fog."

"Does Harrison Petty own a boat?" asked Alex.

"God, yes," said Mike. "Wish he didn't. He's got a Starcraft with a seventy-five horse. He's cut at least ten traps loose and been hauled off rocks and ledges. Keeps it at Port Clyde or at Weymouth harbor."

"I can't imagine Marian Harwood going through the whole murder routine," said Alex, "weighting the body, tying it, and dumping it."

"She's a sturdy piece," said Mike. "Capable enough, I'd say."

"Come off it," said Alex. "She was on the five-fifteen ferry to Weymouth, and she'd been seen in Port Clyde an hour or so before, hiding from Nate in the general store."

"I think we'll have to cross Mrs. Harwood off the body transport list," said George. "She wouldn't have had the time, and after she landed on Weymouth her movements are accounted for."

"Roger had access to boats," said Alex. "Lobster boats, skiffs, dories."

Mike nodded. "Yeah, if he rowed the body out, he

wouldn't have been heard. You know, muffled oars. Hell, I think it's a frigging conspiracy. Marian acts as decoy, Sydney supplies the doorstop, Roger kills him and gets hold of the lobster trap, and Harrison Petty—he's tall and stringy—he carries the body to the boat."

"*Murder on the Orient Express,* ocean style," said Alex.

"Leave it now," said George, reaching for a pile of graph paper. "I'm collecting the Baker drowning and the daughter's accident data to see if it coordinates with any of this. Less imagination and more hard work is what I want."

"Pompous bugger," said Mike, as he and Alex headed for the parking lot. "Got microchips for a brain. So, Alex, you've been holding out on us. Who's this gorgeous Miss Tina-lovely-legs who came in on this gorgeous yawl all anxious to know where Alex McKenzie's cove is? I'm jealous. Me thinking you were a sex-starved doctor. Miss Golden Glow on deck with those knockers bouncing around in that soccer shirt. Hell, all I see at work is Susie Cohen buttoned up in her uniform."

"Shove it, Mike. She's just a casual visitor . . . a nice intelligent woman."

"Sure, sure. Two girls for the lonely doctor. Beautiful, Alex."

"I said stuff it. I've got to go to the hospital, and this," Alex glowered at Mike, "is still supposed to be my vacation."

* * *

Sarah woke well after seven, her fever diminished, her throat relieved, but her head like an overripe squash, and her voice, when she called to Patsy, sounding like an ailing bassoon.

The morning sun was pouring over the white-boarded walls in a great lemon wash so that the room appeared double its size. Elspeth McKenzie's painting of Tinker's Cove seemed by a trick of daylight to be alive and shimmering, the islands rising away from the water into a smoky distance.

She's really good . . . very good, said Sarah to herself, almost in surprise, and I haven't paid attention. Elspeth, Alex's mother, the community spirit, the friend of Marian Harwood, the maker of fish chowder . . . and Elspeth, the artist. Sarah thought back and saw now that perhaps in everything she had seen Elspeth do and say, albeit with humor and energy, there was a tiny holding back, some fraction of commitment withheld. Because here it was in this painting . . . passion. The painting was flooded with the love of light, of shadow, of viridian and azure and cobalt and white and yellow. It took a reality and gave it back newborn. And here it hung in the guest room, as if to say to the visitor that to the person, Elspeth, you saw in the kitchen, in the garden, with the dogs, there's more . . . find it here.

Sarah wondered if in her own life she had ever felt such a passion, such a single-minded loving absorption. Yes, perhaps. Now and then, a poem, a play, a magic paragraph, but it was all still a jumble, not yet part of her. And Elspeth's husband, John. Sarah couldn't know, but was his just such a passion for old words, epics, sagas, for forgotten Icelandic diphthongs and Anglo-Saxon vowels?

And Alex. Did medicine, the sick body made whole, brought back to its perfection, give him the same sort of joy that Elspeth must have felt when she pulled her loaded brush across that stretch of canvas?

But the thought of medicine brought Sarah abruptly back to her swollen head, her filled sinuses, and her dripping nose. And to the immediate need for something hot to drink. And Sydney Prior. Oh, Lord, she had to go to work. She pulled on her clothes and made her way to the kitchen. Elspeth looked at her with disapproval.

"Go back to bed, Sarah. I was going to bring a tray. You don't have to go to work. Alex sent word to Sydney that you were completely *hors de combat.*"

"Great," said Sarah, "but I don't need a tray. I'll just rummage around. I feel much better, so it's probably a twenty-four-hour thing."

Elspeth took off her apron. "If you're sure. Alex has gone ● meet the police and see Ruth Baker, and Giddy and I are ●ing painting. We're making Marian come with us because ● she does is mope and stare. I'm beginning to think she *eded* Nate to keep her stirred up. Says she wants to sell the ●ttage. Ridiculous. Now you just sit around today and drink ●ts of fluids, and oh, yes," Elspeth rushed on, "we've been ●vited by Tina and her parents to have a picnic on the beach, ● if you feel up to it . . ."

"Thanks," said Sarah. "Tina seems very nice," she added ●nnecessarily. "So good with dogs."

"Yes," said Elspeth, not looking at Sarah, "but it's not ●rprising. Besides working for a veterinarian, Alex says she ● a third-year resident at the hospital."

"No wonder," said Sarah, slicing an orange completely ●ff center. "We're lucky she showed up."

"Aren't we?" said Elspeth. She picked up her paintbox ●nd easel and, calling for Giddy, departed.

"The best cure for a cold and whatever else ails you," ●aid Sarah in her hoarse voice to Patsy, as she squeezed her ●ranges, "is crime." Liquids and aspirin were all very well, but ● keep the circulation going, criminal investigation, possibly ●azardous, was what the doctor ordered. Which doctor, Sarah ●asn't sure. Probably not Alex. But through her breakfast of ●iice and tea, Sarah was able to think only of the approach ●ow being suggested over in Port Clyde by Mike Laaka. It did ●lmost seem like a conspiracy in which everyone was responsi-●le for one bit of knavery. Perhaps it was an art theft ring ●volving burglars, couriers, fences, hit men, and then, finally, ● falling out among thieves . . . one of the oldest plot resolu-●ons in the world. And in the center, like a great white spider, ●ydney Greenstreet Prior, and like the honest-my-heart-is-●ure protagonist, Ruth Baker marching resolutely into the ●eb, talking of stolen paintings and faulty car brakes. So over ●he cliff she went.

"That must be it," said Sarah to Patsy. She felt better ●lready. One nostril seemed to be clearing itself. But what

could she do now on the island today except prove concl-
sively that she had a terrible backhand? Why, pick up whe
Ruth left off. Be, as she'd planned, Ruth's stand-in. She ima,
ined Ruth as she must now appear—weighed down, invade
by her support system of tubes and bottles and dials, even
coma, lying there with that stubborn look, her mouth purse
still searching, perhaps deep inside herself, still trying to fir
order and explanation in a random, accidental world.

First. Try and pick up Ruth's trail on Weymouth, perhap
pick up something about her search for the missing paintin
Had Ruth been going to spend the night on Weymouth,
had she been planning to go back to her motel? If on th
island, had the police tracked down her room and gor
through her things? One way to find out. The police were n
perfect, nor, she reminded herself, was Alex, even if he w:
now considered by all and sundry a sort of quasi-detective

Sarah went back to her room, her step lively. A showe
and a hairwash, because even if her hair could never be
honey-colored cap, it needn't look like strands of licoric
candy. Clean white shirt, best red canvas pants. To work.

The Dovekie Gift Shop, the Topsail Gallery, and the re
of the gift shops and galleries were thick with tourists, and
each Sarah was reminded that Saturday was foggy and rai
coats of every shade were abroad and that no shop or galle
on Weymouth carried original oil paintings worth over fi
hundred dollars. Only at the last shop, just out of the tow
did she hit pay dirt. The owner, a modish female with la
quered silver hair and matching nails, proved to have an a
tive memory.

"Little short woman from the Midwest. No makeup. Th
kind of face you can't do much with. Didn't know much abou
the art scene. Looking for a seascape, but I couldn't help he
'Look, luv,' I said, 'Weymouth isn't where it's at, artwis
Nothing with any real class here.' Told her to go look o
Monhegan or go back to the mainland, that's where the hig!
priced stuff was . . . artists as thick as thieves along the coast.

Sarah said that was an interesting expression and set he

course for the Eider Inn. There, after securing Patsy to a small tree, she presented herself to the desk clerk, a motherly-looking woman who put aside her knitting and nodded her head at Sarah's question.

"Ruth Baker," she said. "Well, thank heavens. We've been wondering. That poor woman. Captain's Head, they should fence it completely. Are you the police, because we have all her things, and," she added, frowning slightly, "her bill."

"She had reservations for the weekend?" said Sarah, trying to make her husky voice sound as she imagined an investigating officer's might.

"For Saturday and Sunday. A nice room overlooking Ocean Trail."

"And her things?" said Sarah, holding her breath. "Just to check."

"Well," said the woman doubtfully, "I suppose. And the bill?"

"Will be taken care of," said Sarah firmly. "Now may I?"

"Oh, yes, right back here in the office. You have a terrible cold, dear."

Sarah followed, praying not to meet any of George Fitts's advance guard. The woman pulled a small suitcase from under a desk and placed it on a table. "We didn't lock it," said the woman, "just folded her things and put in her toilet articles. She must have had her handbag with her."

"Yes," said Sarah, staring at the suitcase and wondering how to go about the search in a professional manner.

"You'll be wanting gloves," said the woman. "I've got some in my desk. Because I'm allergic," she added obscurely, leaving Sarah to wonder, to what? Guests, charge cards, suitcases?

"Here you are, dear," said the clerk. "I'll go because I know plainclothes people like to work by themselves. I've seen it all on TV."

Sarah, alone with Ruth's suitcase, stood for a moment appalled at what she was doing and then, remembering that her career in crime had begun quite a while ago with Marian

Harwood's furniture, slipped the rubber gloves over her hands.

Underwear, stockings neatly rolled, a garter belt. Ruth must be the last holdout from the pantyhose revolution. Pink pajamas, a pair of low-heeled navy shoes, a navy and white print blouse and skirt—probably for dinner; the Eider Inn was on the dressy side. Now a zip bag with toilet articles. Clumsy in gloves, Sarah tipped the contents out on the desk and in a panic scraped them into a heap. Toothbrush and paste, sun cream, and a prescription bottle of tablets. Aldomet. Wasn't that for high blood pressure? Sarah was sure that was what her own father took. Maybe Ruth did indeed suffer spells. Hastily, Sarah tumbled the things back into the bag and turned back to the suitcase.

A white cardigan, a blue scarf, and a little writing case with a tartan cover. Stamps, three new postcards, all Weymouth scenes, and, carefully folded into a pocket, the menu Ruth's parents had sent, telling her of their plans. And now underneath it a double sheet of writing paper, its top decorated with a garland of daisies. Sarah saw by the date that it had been written on the past Tuesday, so Ruth must have received it at her motel just before she left for Weymouth. Feeling more and more like a criminal snoop, Sarah opened the letter.

> Dear Ruth [it began], I'm sorry I didn't answer your note earlier, but your Uncle Fred had one of those kidney stone attacks . . .

Here Sarah skipped to the top of the second sheet and found matter to open her eyes.

> . . . Yes, I did hear. Only a postcard from your poor mother just before it happened. It seems your dad and she went just wild and bought a painting for a great deal of money though she didn't say how much. She said it was a view of the ocean with a fence or a fish trap, something like that. We've lost the card, I'm

afraid. I guess retirement had gone to your dad's head. He was always so careful with money. What a sad ending. All my love and hope to see you back home soon. Your loving Aunt Marta.

Sarah, almost shaking with excitement, replaced the contents of the suitcase, stripped off the gloves, and, trying to maintain a calm facade, returned to the front desk.

"All finished, dear?" said the woman. "You know if I hadn't watched all those old TV programs with women detectives wearing any old thing, blue jeans or bikinis, like 'Charlie's Angels,' well, I wouldn't have believed you were with the police."

Sarah, with admirable control, thanked her, adding that she would be sending the police lab team along as soon as possible.

"Which I will," she told Patsy, as she unfastened him from the porch and took her way north on the now too familiar Ocean Trail. Slowing her steps and feeling the excitement of her search subside, she asked herself what she had actually discovered. One more detail about the Baker painting, certainly. A fish trap, not a regular fence. A weir, of course. And all along she'd been thinking of farms and pastures. Well, Elspeth McKenzie's stolen oil had been a painting of the old weir across the end of the Bucket. But how many weirs, old ones, new ones, were there along the coast? How many kinds of fish traps? Did the Baker painting have perhaps a fence by land and a fish trap by sea? A weir, a purse seine. Was it a popular subject, in a class with lighthouses and surf crashing on rocks?

"Okay," said Sarah, hauling Patsy to a reluctant heel. "Table that one and go on. What next? The police." And returning Patsy to his wire run, she made her way to the Weymouth Store and, hoping that her cold disguised her voice, explained her find to the State Police.

"You didn't touch anything, did you?" said a cross voice —not George Fitts, Sarah was glad to note.

"Just a superficial exam," said Sarah, "with gloves." She hung up before she could be asked to identify herself. And now? She'd done her bit of investigation and broken several laws in the bargain. Sober reason told Sarah to go back to the cottage and deal with her cold, but then she came out of the store and saw a man on the landing reach down for one of the *Robin Day*'s docking lines. She broke into a run and made it aboard just as the last line was cast off. At that instant she knew, virus, sore throat, stuffed head or no, she was going to the hospital to see Ruth. Not to breathe on her, of course, not to give her pneumonia, but just to look at her from a safe distance, to draw from her something of her stubborn purpose and so try and help this appalling series of events to their end.

On making shore, Sarah slipped along past the Weymouth and Monhegan docks, trying not to cast a shadow lest Sydney Prior from his shop window catch sight of his truant salesperson skulking in the distance. She crept along the edge of the parking lot that lay at the turn of the tiny town's main street and noticed with a sidelong glance that both the windows of Sydney's Parlor Gallery and those of the shop itself on its rise of ground overlooked the length of the main street and the expanse of the parking lot. How handy. Ready for customers from every prospect . . . and ready to note the arrival or departure of anyone from the two ferry docks and the public landing. Sydney's gallery, in fact, commanded the whole blessed town. Did the police realize this? But then Sarah told herself as she worked her way through the rows of parked cars, the people at the general store had a partial outlook on the main street, plus an unparalleled view of sea comings and goings. How about the Port Clyde Arts and Crafts Gallery with its second-story windows—another fine view of the street and water. But neither place commanded the entrance to the parking area or the whole length of the street. Only Sydney Prior could see the works. But Sydney was on his way to Portland when Nate was alive and raging up and down the streets of Port Clyde, and she certainly hadn't seen

Sydney on the Ocean Trail the day Ruth fell from Captain's Head.

"Sarah!"

It was Alex in his car, the car directly in front of her, in fact in an excellent position to catch her up on his fender.

"Wake up. You walked right into me." Alex leaned out of the window. "You're supposed to be sick."

"I'm going to the hospital. I've got to see Ruth. It may not make sense, but I have to."

"It doesn't make sense."

Sarah shrugged and shook her head. "Still, I have to."

"Well, so do I. So climb in, and I'll tell you what happens to people who neglect colds and spread viruses." He opened the door and pushed a newspaper and a book to the floor. "I've lied to Sydney and told him you were out of action indefinitely with a dangerous variation of Legionnaire's Disease."

"And he's probably seen me," said Sarah, settling herself in the passenger's seat, her place in so many of their Texas travels and chases, but feeling today that Alex seemed much more of a stranger. "You know," she said, deciding to keep her mind fixed on the investigation, "Sydney Prior has absolutely the best view of everything in Port Clyde."

"A fact I'm sure the police are not neglecting."

"But he's the number-one art and antique dealer for miles around, and he knows everything about everyone, and he's got his own boat and can hit the islands as soon as he sees someone land in Port Clyde. Are the police digging into his records to see if he's got any funny bank accounts or stock operations?"

"The police are working up profiles on all likely people. That means banks, financial wheelings and dealings, the whole bit. But Sydney has run a reputable operation for years. Why steal art when you can sell the legitimate item at a wicked profit? And another thing, of all the people connected with Nate, Sydney kept on fairly even terms with him. Nate was a good customer, after all." Alex turned his car onto the main road and thrust it into the Route 1 traffic line. "I think," he said, "that we'd both better trust the experts. I'll stick to the medical angle, insofar as an internist can help a neurological team, and you try to get better and take some time off."

"Forget that," said Sarah. "You'd better hear about my trip to the Eider Inn," and Sarah described her search of Ruth's suitcase. "So I called the police," she finished, "and I've added 'fish trap' to my mental picture of the Baker painting."

"I hope you've got your bail money ready. And then I'll say it's damn well too much of a coincidence to think my mother's stolen picture ended up in the Baker car. I reject it out of hand."

"But 'fish trap' is one more piece of the puzzle."

"Agreed, and we'll have to let that aunt of Ruth's know about the accident. We all assumed she was alone in the world. And now you shouldn't talk anymore. You sound like Gravel Gertie and your nose is like Rudolf's."

"I can't stand that reindeer with the raw red bulb nose."

"Say hedgehog," said Alex. "As in 'prickly as a.' Colds make me impossible, too."

"I'm not being impossible," snapped Sarah. "I just want to see Ruth."

"And so you shall if I can fix it up. At a suitable distance in a gown and double mask."

"What's this?" said Sarah, picking up the book at her feet. "*Diagnosis of Stupor and Coma.* Don't you know all about stupor and coma?"

"Not anymore . . . never did, really. I borrowed the book from the hospital library. The field changes so rapidly."

Sarah read slowly, working her way from "consciousness" to clouding of consciousness, through to delirium, stupor, and assorted manifestations of coma, and then, skimming, found herself lost in a maze of terms like "spinothalmic collateral" and "midbrain tegmental reticulum." She closed the book, sighing for Ruth because, medical terminology notwithstanding, the string of cases presented in the book all seemed to end with the autopsy and the pathologist's report.

Alex seemed to read her mind. "It's not all that hopeless. There have been cases . . . " But he did not finish and they reached the hospital in silence.

"Go right over, Dr. McKenzie," said the charge nurse of the surgical intensive care unit. She pointed with her pen at the center cubicle shrouded with a green curtain. "Dr. Samuels has a teaching group in there, but it's okay. I'll find a mask and gown for Miss Deane and she can watch from here."

Alex ran the curtain back and saw that Ruth Baker was indeed the focus of a bedside lecture, and, standing at the curtain opening, he was once more impressed by the aura of tidiness and mechanical efficiency that surrounded the unconscious person. The blanket undisturbed, the sheet folded over its top in a sweep of smooth white, Ruth's arms extended along each side of her body, one held in a cast, the other accepting IV fluids and recording at its wrist her arterial pressure; from her midline, like the legs of some most delicate insect, the three silver-coated leads of her EKG monitor, and further down, discreetly emerging from the blanket, the line of the Foley catheter making its way to the urine collection bag. Near the foot of the bed, elevated by slings and pins, as if she had been arrested in the act of kicking, hung her right leg, while the other foot, incongruous in a sort of high-top basketball sneaker, stuck out directly at Alex from the coverlet. And Ruth's head, so neatly centered on the pillow, so properly raised to thirty degrees. How could that head seem even remotely human to those students leaning over her bed, their clipboards hugged to their chests—that head with its stainless steel bolt drilled into her shaved and bandaged head monitoring intercranial pressure, her eyes taped closed, her nose invaded by its naso-tracheal tube blowing oxygen into Ruth's quiet lungs?

No question about it, thought Sarah, taking one step closer to the cubicle, the perfect patient is one who is completely unconscious. Probably just as well, too, that so many here in these ghastly little units were out of it, because the probing, the intubating of their bodies—the effrontery of it all —would be more than any conscious person could bear.

The attending neurosurgeon, standing in his long white coat at the head of the bed, had just finished a sharp little lecture on the difference between stupor and coma.

"You mean not completely gorked out," said one of the students.

The surgeon nodded and then progressed in an orderly way from acute global aphasia on through to persistent or chronic vegetative states, and then, looking up, saw Alex.

"Hi, there. Alex McKenzie, isn't it? Want me now, or shall I finish with these people and meet you in the coffee shop?"

"Keep right on," said Alex. "I may learn something."

Dr. Samuels inclined his head and returned to his students. "This word 'vegetative' is used by Plum and Jennet to describe patients who keep going, maybe even for years, after a serious brain injury, without coming to in any meaningful way. Terms like 'neocortical death' or 'apallic state' don't cover all these patients, but everybody"—Dr. Samuels smiled around the group—"knows 'vegetable.' Very useful."

Alex and Sarah left and headed for the coffee shop. Why "vegetative" was better than any other term, he didn't know. It certainly took away any residual dignity the poor half-person had, and lent support to the three thousand and one "vegetable" jokes among the hospital staff. He remembered a six-bed nursing facility called the "squash court" and patients called turnip, cabbage, parsnip, and he could see it coming a mile off, "Ruth, the rutabaga."

"We'll be moving her after a while," said Dr. Samuels, sitting down opposite to Sarah and Alex and attacking his coffee cake. "We'll have to do the tracheostomy next week, run some more tests, and then, maybe, send her to Boston. They've got some newer scanners there, and then if nothing's going on, I suppose turf her to a long-term nursing place."

"How about wake cycles?" asked Alex.

"Yes, we're beginning to see signs of sleep-wake alternation, but she's unresponsive. I'm beginning to think about akinetic mutism."

"What on earth's that?" broke in Sarah. "It sounds horrible."

Alex and Dr. Samuels turned to her as if suddenly discovering an alien presence at the table.

"Oh, well," said Alex, "it means not moving or talking."

"How about later . . . moving and talking?"

"We'll just have to see," said Dr. Samuels in a soothing voice, a voice that Sarah recognized as one her dentist used when he was about to do some particularly nasty drilling.

"Head injuries are tricky," continued Dr. Samuels, "especially if the brain is grossly insulted."

"But it's sometimes temporary, isn't it?" said Sarah. "I read about people coming to after ages."

"One day at a time," said the neurosurgeon. He stood up. "I have to be off, six patients to see, and I'm presenting Miss Baker at rounds tomorrow. Call me, Alex, if you have questions."

"Really," fumed Sarah, climbing back in the car. "Doctors always beat about the bush. They're worse than lawyers. Never a straight answer. Where's that book? I'm going to look up that mutism thing."

"That was just a guess," said Alex. "It's not easy to understand, and you'll just be more depressed reading about it. No case is like the rest, but Ruth's in good hands."

"But tell me two things," said Sarah, as the car started. "Why is Ruth wearing a basketball sneaker and why have they taped her eyes?"

"The sneaker holds a foot without a cast into a position to prevent shortening of the Achilles tendon, and the eyes are taped to protect from corneal abrasions. Odd bits of dust and fluff float around. You can't depend on her blink response."

"But if her eyes are taped, how will anyone know if she wakes up?"

"Oh, they untape the eyes regularly, give her drops, and, of course, they'll be testing her responses."

"With pins?" said Sarah.

"Something like that. They call them 'noxious stimuli.' "

"I'll bet they're noxious. I hate hospitals, and I'm very lucky not to be in one, which is why it's a good reason for me to turn into Ruth for a while. Be her hands and feet. So, Alex, before you tie yourself into the tennis and cocktail events— you're invited by Tina's parents to a beach thing—no, let me finish"—as Alex frowned—"I want to try something out on you. First, I'll concede that the police with their teams and labs and computers probably will get to the center of all these goings-on."

"I agree," said Alex, "so that's why we should lay off."

"Wait up," said Sarah, "and do listen, please. Now I think I should . . . and you, if you want . . . work on the fringes. The trivia. All the little things that no one would think relevant."

"The quirky things?"

"Yes. The quips and cranks and the oddities and contradictions."

"Like someone buying a jogging suit who hates exercise, or patting a cat if he's allergic."

"That's the idea. Now can you think of anything at all, to do with anybody, that doesn't seem, well, fitting? Why are you stopping?"

"Ice cream. If you're hell bent on talking, I'm going to dose that throat."

"Raspberry sherbet, please, and thank you very much."

"Fussy, aren't we?" and Alex turned off the road by Dorman's ice cream booth. It was almost, Sarah thought, back to normal. Alex her special friend, and she, Sarah, not a trial balloon, but perhaps, as Giddy had said, something more.

Settled with cones, Alex driving with one hand, Sarah passing napkins, they drove south to Port Clyde.

"I'll start," said Alex. "Contradiction number one. Roger. Why did he come back to Weymouth after he'd made it safely to Port Clyde with Giddy, and then why did he let himself be found by you and the police, almost as if he wanted to be caught?"

"Not really trivia," said Sarah, "and the police are probably asking the same thing. I'd say he came back again to have another look for his father's letters, but after I'd told him everyone knew about the Brueghel, he gave up. Maybe, too, he was sorry for his mother going it all alone, though I haven't seen much sign of that."

"Mark it down, anyway," said Alex, indicating a small notebook on the dashboard. "Let's make it a rule. Each piece of trivia makes it on the list regardless. Number two. Why is Harrison Petty so damn anxious about the stolen painting business? According to Doris Ordway, he's in a continual lather, talks about frisking visitors and putting on extra guards."

Sarah considered. "What are you trying to say? That Mr. Petty's got your mother's painting under his bed . . . or sold it in the gift shop? I think it's genetic, he's just a natural nervous wreck. But I'll write it down anyway. Number three, why did Marian Harwood wear that wrinkled, too short dress with the red belt that didn't match to the service? Your mother noticed it and said she should have worn some new navy blue number she had."

"But remember, she couldn't get into her own cottage . . . or she did it as a mark of disrespect for Nate."

"Women that age don't usually make a point of looking their worst in public. Besides she'd been off the island so she must have had some clothes with her, and also she'd been able to get into her cottage all through the furniture lift. What did you see her wearing around when she first came to the island . . . before I came?"

"God, I don't know. I think you're making too much of the dress business, and, hell, I never notice female clothes, only"—he smiled at Sarah—"the absence of them."

Sarah arranged her face into an expression of disdain. "Men are so monotonous. The same knee-jerk remarks, the same stupid jokes."

"Sarah, please. Harmless male levity. Don't be such a schoolmarm."

"Men think anyone not carried away by *Penthouse* and *Hustler* is a schoolmarm."

"Let's get on with the list, shall we?" said Alex in a quiet voice. "We're both tired. I'm not at my best and am probably very close to the knee-jerk stage. Number three item, Marian's inappropriate costume. Number four, Ruth Baker's parents. Why did they pay cash for the painting?"

"Because they had the cash with them," said Sarah, turning and staring out the window at a view of an upcoming Exxon station. "Mrs. Baker carried the money in her bra and Mr. Baker had just cashed some traveler's checks. That's what their letter to Ruth said."

"People usually save cash for emergencies. Most art dealers accept credit cards or personal checks or certified bank checks."

"Who said it was an art dealer? It may have been one artist. You see signs saying 'artist's studio' everywhere. Paintings are hung all over the coast like laundry. You know, a moose or a sunset or waves breaking. Small-time artists and dealers might want cash."

"Since you've become Ruth's champion, why insist that her parents bought some trashy roadside work? Let's guess that their painting was at least of fair quality. It wasn't that cheap—nine hundred dollars—and may well have come from a reputable dealer. And even if Mrs. Baker had money fastened behind her teeth, it is not a folksy midwestern habit to pay cash for large purchases."

"Were credit cards and a checkbook found with their things?"

"That I'll find out, and you may write down that any dealer or artist of any reputation who asks for cash may have something to hide. Income tax dodger, perhaps."

"My turn," said Sarah, keeping her head a quarter turn away from Alex. "Sydney Prior. Why did he give Ruth a painting of Captain's Head done by his father? He's so money-hungry, trying to trap rich tourists in his back parlor, waiting for a Rolls or a Mercedes to pull up."

"Sydney's pretty generous when he wants to be. Funding half of Landing Day, closing his shop for the whole weekend."

"You're shooting down all my trivia and insisting on yours," complained Sarah. Her head was beginning to fill and ache. "Sydney just looks like a crazy hybrid between Charlie Chan and Sydney Greenstreet. He'd fit right into an art scam."

"And that makes him suspect? Logic, lady, logic."

"Logic tells me that he was much more likely to try and sell Ruth a painting than give her one—and by his father. Wouldn't you want to keep your father's painting? Didn't Sydney like him?"

"They were very close, and the grandfather, too. Sydney's mother died early on, and the three men used to come here from Kentucky for the summer. Sydney was married for a while to a mousy type, but she's been dead for ages. No children. Sydney's father and grandpa were considered oddities on Weymouth. They took day-long cruises around the islands wearing white suits and big white hats."

"Kentucky-fried colonels?"

"Something like. Of course, Sydney's father, August Prior, was a proper working artist. He used to preside over most of the classes himself, take students sketching all over the island. Grandfather Alfred was involved in some sort of family farm operation back in Kentucky. Tobacco, I think. On a fairly large scale, since Father August was able to buy the art school land with his own funds."

"Then why would Sydney give away one of his beloved father's paintings to a complete stranger?"

"The big gesture. Sydney is both a sentimental and a vain old coot. And it wouldn't be the first time. He gave one of his father's paintings of Lighthouse Point last year to be auctioned for a Landing Day benefit, and I've just heard that he's given another to replace the one stolen from the library."

"That could be a ploy. Isn't there anything off-color about the Prior family?"

"Not beyond the fact that not many people from the

Midwest settled into Weymouth life back in the first part of the century. Travel was quite complicated—trains, boats, ferries. August Prior had a reputation for irascibility . . . warning young boys away from the school. Life classes are a real drawing card. Boys, if you'll forgive me, Sarah, will be boys, so don't jump down my throat because I'm not at my liveliest, and, save for your presence and a few ocean hours, this hasn't exactly been a summer idyll. I see enough pathology at the hospital without adding a neighbor's body and a brain-injured woman to my collection. But okay, put down Sydney's present to Ruth as number five. Here's the next question. Why did Lem Wallace take those groceries marked 'Harwood' right up to Rachel and Lyda's cottage?"

"He must have known that Marian was staying there," said Sarah. "And I do think it's entirely reasonable that small boys want to sneak a look at nude models . . . it's the big boys. Never mind. Peace. I have my knee-jerk responses, too. So what about the groceries?"

"Did Marian see a chance to swipe Nate's groceries, knowing he wasn't on the boat, knowing he wasn't coming over, maybe knowing he was dead? Remember she said she didn't see Nate aboard, which isn't remarkable since she stayed in the cabin. Maybe she felt safe in hijacking the food."

Sarah shook her head. "That sounds too frisky for Marian, but I'll write it down. Here's Port Clyde. Ten minutes until the boat. One more question and this is really far-out. Why did Sydney Prior . . . "

"You have Sydney on the brain."

"Repeat, why did Sydney call his new boat the *Christmas Past*? All the other family boats—he has a framed row of them all the way back to Grandfather's launch hung up in his workshop—have classy-sounding ocean names like the *Tempest Queen*."

"There's no rational reason for boat names. *Christmas Past* may be Sydney's unconscious calling him Scrooge. I think you're reaching on this one. The only offbeat name the Priors chose that I can remember was a motor launch called he *Furl Sail,* which is a crazy contradiction. It was used for art school picnics."

"It goes on the list," said Sarah. "That's the rule. Now, we'll split the list. You take the Harwood groceries, the Baker cash payment, Mr. Petty's nerves, and why Roger came out of hiding, and I'll work on Sydney's giving a painting to Ruth, Mrs. Harwood's tacky church dress, and the *Christmas Past.*"

* * *

The white-hulled yawl *Moondust III* swung gently on its mooring in the darkening waters of Tinker's Cove, its sharp bow coming slowly up into the wind with each dying puff of air. On the beach all was jollity and good fellowship. Rum drinks in paper cups were passed from hand to hand: "Our own invention, we call them 'rum buzzes.'" Tina's mother and father, whose name was either Cobble or Cottle —Sarah's cold was making her deaf—moved to and fro among the McKenzie party, circulating celery and carrot sticks and a platter of cheese and biscuits. To Sarah's right, on a large driftwood log, Tina was talking hospital with Alex.

"Okay, so a spleen scan is useful," she said, "but God, after that red cell count, they should have looked around some more. They sent him home to play soccer. Soccer! Can you believe it? Well, back in he comes . . . "

"I know," said Alex. "I was around for the second admission, and everyone thought they'd missed an intraperitoneal bleed . . . "

It was a conversation that admitted no outsiders.

"I think that's pretty gruesome talk at dinnertime," said Giddy loudly. "Sarah and I don't know what you're talking about."

"It's all right," Sarah said to Giddy. "My voice is shot. I'd rather listen."

"But my voice is fine," said Giddy, who definitely seemed to have assumed the role of Sarah's defender and Tina's challenger. This Sarah regretted because modulating Giddy

would take more energy than she had to spare, and sh
wanted to pursue at least one piece of trivia before creepin
into bed. She shifted her seat to another log next to Elspeth
who was talking to Tina's mother. Sarah, who was beginnin
to be able to read Elspeth, saw that she was not really engage
in the conversation.

"Tell me," said Sarah, breaking a pause, "what does th
expression 'Christmas Past' mean to either of you?"

"Are you reading *A Christmas Carol*?" asked Elspeth.

"Is it a puzzle?" asked Mrs. Cobble/Cottle. "I always d
the *New York Times* one and stop halfway through. All thos
Russian rivers and kinds of fish."

"It's a sort of a puzzle," said Sarah. "The name of
boat."

"That is unusual," said Tina's mother. "But you see a
sorts. We tied up next to the *Blind Bat* at Northeast Harbo
last week. A terrible name."

"You're going to work on Sydney, aren't you?" sai
Elspeth. "We did wonder about the name because all th
Prior boats have had sea names."

"The water's ready for the lobsters," announced M
Cobble/Cottle, walking up to the group. "We hope you're no
sick to death of them, but we thought it would be fun . . .

And now there was much bustle in the melting of butte
and the cutting of lemons, while Tina and Alex and Gidd
lifted the lobsters from their seaweed-filled crate, each ta
fanned, claws splayed out, and dropped them one by one i
the boiling water.

Plain murder, thought Sarah, who dreaded the sound o
the creatures bumping around in the kettle, making the li
rattle. She retreated up the beach so that she could see th
group only as a blur by the fire and hear only the occasiona
rise and fall of voices. Suddenly, she yearned for the fla
no-nonsense voice of Ruth Baker, Ruth, who in her sturd
way would have been as at home here as in Zanzibar. Sh
would ask questions, find out how things were with thes

people to whom cruising yawls were the stuff of summer life. And how would Ruth have felt about Tina? No doubt about that. Ruth, untroubled by comparisons, would have found Tina, the young handsome physician, a person worth admiration, a woman whose work in the world made sense, who, like Ruth herself, firmly did what she had to do, went after what she had to have. And what Tina probably had to have was Alex. Sarah sneezed violently, once, twice, and again. It was time to leave the field and regroup, time to blow her nose and take aspirin. Sarah walked over to the party, extended her hand, smiled, and made her adieux. Alex made no attempt to stop her, only nodded his approval.

She lay in the porch hammock and listened to the faraway sounds of singing from the beach. Sea shanties and old college songs. *Blow the man down, Johnny, blow him right down . . My father was the keeper of the Eddystone Light, slept with a mermaid one fine night . . . With crimson in triumph flashing . . . Bull dog, bull dog, bow wow wow . . . Here's to all the happy hours, shout 'til the rafters ring . . .* Sarah gave a heavy sniff and turned back to essentials. *Christmas Past* so far was a dead end, so how about Marian Harwood's dress? Think, she told herself. And then she reviewed everything she could remember about Marian Harwood and tried to picture in detail the few times they had met or that Sarah had seen her around the island.

At last she isolated one extra-hot day on Weymouth. She had sat on a pine-shaded ledge above the McKenzie cottage and watched Marian Harwood carry an armload of split wood to a hollow clearing behind her house and then deposit a filled paper bag on the fire. Marian had stood, rake in hand, as the flames leaped out in little tongues whipped by the breeze that swirled around the clearing. She's going to burn down the whole island, Sarah had thought, but then as the fire had subsided and Marian had raked over the ashes, she had put the scene out of her mind.

Now she reconsidered. Yes, the day had been a real sizzler and something was very wrong about it. She closed her eyes and heard the voices from the beach rise in "Oh, they built the ship Titanic . . . "

* * *

The following day, Tuesday, the twenty-sixth of August, was notable for a marked increase in Landing Day fever. "It's right on our neck," said Elspeth, who, having blocked out a large oil of the churchyard hill, had begun to regret her role in the festivities. "I always say yes when it's months away and then I'm trapped."

This was true. The *Robin Day* was now joined by other ferries making special stops from coastal points. The Weymouth shops did a heavy business in lobster claw salt-and-pepper sets and balsam pillows while the Abenaki Lodge and the Eider Inn reported full houses through Labor Day.

Sarah, her cold waning, did not regret her return to work as Sydney Prior's assistant. She had no special feeling about historical reenactments and was glad not to be pulled into another tennis game. Besides, there was the trivia list to pursue.

"Didn't you hate to part with that painting of Captain's Head?" she asked Sydney when the crush of business had required both of them to stay in the shop for lunch.

"It was a nice little picture," said Sydney affably, "but I have several left. My father painted Captain's Head often. That one seemed like a very Maine-like scene for Miss Baker to help her remember something pleasant about her visit. Poor woman. Is there any news?"

"I think she's still unconscious," said Sarah.

"Tragic," sighed Sydney. "I feel quite responsible. She probably climbed up the cliff to see the view shown in the painting. I remember my father never liked heights, and he used to tie a rope around his waist and fasten it to a rock when he was sketching there. He had an idea that he might give in to an overwhelming urge to jump off. Poor woman," he repeated.

"Yes," said Sarah crossly. She was getting nowhere. She tried another tack. "How is the *Christmas Past* going?"

"Just fine. Such a relief to have a really sturdy boat and a reliable diesel engine. And a new dinghy, too. The old one sank at the dock, a seam opened right up. Imagine if I'd been off on the water in it."

"Has the new dinghy a name?" said Sarah, without much hope. "*Christmas Present* or *Christmas Yet to Come?*"

"It's *Yule Log*," said Sydney. "In keeping, I think. And there's your bell, Sarah. A whole charter bus load. I saw them pull up."

Alex met Sarah's boat. She had seen him from the ferry deck, standing apart from the welcoming crowd, tennis racquet in one hand, Patsy's leash in the other.

"Good tennis?" said Sarah, knowing this was an obligatory greeting.

"Good enough. We found a fourth. And no change with Ruth Baker beyond the fact that sleep-wake cycles seem more definitely established, but we'll have to . . . "

"I know. Wait and see. All right," said Sarah, all business again. "My trivia report. We may have to scratch Sydney's boat as a Christmas fixation. He's got a new dingy named *Yule Log.* Too cute for words. And his father did a lot of Captain's Head paintings."

"Mrs. Ordway checked the market value of August Prior's paintings for me. Oils bring from six hundred to two thousand dollars, depending on size and subject."

"Not a cheap present, anyway," said Sarah.

"I told you Sydney's eccentric. Want my trivia report?" Alex extended his hand in a companionable way, but Sarah, moving slightly ahead, affected not to see it. Alex dropped his hand to his side.

"Yes," she said. "The report."

"As follows." Alex's voice had a hard edge. "Lem remembers carrying the groceries to Rachel's but isn't sure if he offered to, or Marian asked him. But he says if there'd been a question about ownership he wouldn't have touched them. We must assume that Marian claimed them."

"Do you think she's so out of it, so much of a zombie, that she'd think they were hers . . . or wouldn't care?"

"Marian knew what furniture to make off with, so she probably knew what she was doing taking the groceries. Have you got anything else?" Alex was chopping his words into little metallic units, and Sarah with a sour little spasm told herself she was pleased that a proper working relationship was developing.

"I was thinking last night. We had one day just like an oven here on the island."

"How interesting."

"Please listen. First, what are the fire rules on Weymouth?"

"No fires."

"None?"

"Absolutely not. Not on land anyway. The whole island might go up. Fires must be made on the beach or on the rocks and only with permission from the fire marshal . . . like last night's picnic. Of course, in summer there's always a danger. Visitors, cigarettes, illicit cookouts."

"So an old island resident wouldn't burn anything in the middle of a clearing on a hot day with the wind blowing?"

"God, no. What are you driving at?'

"I don't know yet."

"You'd better tell me about it. It sounds like one of Roger's tricks. Anyway, we don't want an arsonist loose on the island."

"Not an arsonist and I'm not sure yet if it means anything. But what about Roger? Any new thoughts?"

"I don't have any leads on why he came back to Weymouth, and I plan to lean on Giddy until she squeals. Come on, we'll walk along the marsh—migrants coming through now—and I'll bring you up to date on what I do have. First, the question of Harrison Petty's nerves. The State Police have dredged up the following. Petty, out there in Chicago as an assistant curator of American paintings, had been, well, 'careless' is the official word. Seems a valuable Eakins sketchbook turned up in Petty's bottom desk drawer, Petty first saying it had been planted, then that he was using it for research, then he was recataloguing it. Egg on face, feet of clay, sticky fingers —all of that. A hell of a museum stink. Petty agreed to look for a new job if the art museum trustees out there gave him decent recommendations—which they did. Nate Harwood had a talkative cousin who was a trustee and there you are."

"So maybe that's why Mr. Petty's been so hung up on top and bottom drawers?"

"What are you talking about?"

"Nothing that matters. What does is that Mr. Petty has a big fat motive for murder. Why, Nate Harwood could have just trashed him anytime he wanted. Little museums like the Godding hate scandal . . . especially having to do with forgetful directors."

"I agree. Harrison's nervousness certainly makes more sense than it did. Now I've got more from the police end of things. Ruth's parents did indeed have a supply of personal checks and a Visa card, so that paying cash for their painting may have been at the request of the seller. Second, it's very doubtful that any of the suspect group could have murdered Nate and disposed of his body in the time such an operation would have taken—with the possible exception of Roger, who dodges in and out of the time frame. Your favorite, Sydney, no matter how well cast, could not have been in Portland and in Port Clyde at the same time."

"Have you thought that Sydney might have killed Nate *after* he got back from Portland . . . at dawn? What if Nate was a partner in the art theft scheme and Sydney caught him, tied him up or killed him, and went off to Portland? The falling-out-among-thieves plot."

"It won't work. Nate missed his groceries and an appointment that evening, so everything points to his being dead by nightfall, and how could Sydney have stashed Nate in his gallery when Nate was loose and on the streets when Sydney was miles away? You know that."

"And the Baker drowning?"

"Everyone is eligible for that. Petty was in Port Clyde that evening for a docents' meeting, Sydney says he was working late doing some special framing, Roger can't remember what the hell he was doing, Giddy was at her aerobics class so can't vouch for him. Nate Harwood was seen leaving Port Clyde in his boat after dark, and Marian was on North Haven. Now watch your step in all this muck."

"But what about Ruth Baker's fall—which may still be an accident?" Sarah lifted her feet high and pushed a clump of reeds aside.

"Harrison, Roger, Marian, Sydney were all on the island that noon, but only two were seen—by you—on that side of the island. Roger at the lighthouse and Petty off the trail. Next, we have the doorstop problem. How open is Sydney's shop and parlor? Can anyone walk in during the day and find doorstops for the taking?"

Sarah, struggling to keep her balance along the drier edge of the marsh, considered Sydney's security system. "The front door and the barn door—for deliveries—are open all day, but a little bell rings when they open and sounds in his workshop and in the Parlor Gallery. Both those rooms and Sydney's living quarters are off a hall that goes through to the attached barn. It's a regular maze, but I haven't seen any mysterious sliding panels or inglenooks. Sydney usually locks everything when he leaves at night, and he's got an alarm system. There's the basement—a real pit but absolutely ordinary."

"If Nate was killed at Sydney's shop there may be traces of blood or hairs. George and his lab team are having a second look. Now look out. It's really wet through here. Remember you've got a cold."

"I'm planning to cure it with a nice long swim in the cove."

"Marvelous idea, but if I said keep warm and out of the water you'd probably feel you had to swim to Port Clyde to keep me in my place."

Sarah suddenly laughed. The nail on the head. It was the first spontaneous expression she had allowed herself for several days. Now if he put out his hand . . . but he didn't. She smiled. "Okay, Dr. McKenzie, I won't swim to Port Clyde."

Swimming proved to be the popular activity of the early evening. Giddy floated far out in Tinker's Cove, Mr. and Mrs. Cobble/Cottle sported from the *Moondust III,* and Tina, her blond head bobbing rhythmically, did an easy crawl across the breadth of the cove. Even Elspeth had been in for a long dip and now sat in her faded blue bathing suit at the edge of the water.

Sarah walked over to her, trying not to notice that Alex had joined Tina and was apparently racing her to the yawl.

Elspeth looked up. "Sarah, should you be swimming?"

"It's good for a cold," said Sarah, sitting down. "I have a question. Mrs. Harwood's dress, the one she wore to the service. Were all her good ones locked up in the cottage so she was stuck with what she had in her suitcase?"

"But she had her nice new navy blue with the gray piping and tiny silver buttons with her. Quite smart, considering it was Marian's. She called it her wedding-funeral dress and said she wouldn't have to buy another for years. Nate was so tight with money." Elspeth shaded her eyes and peered across the darkening water. Tina was standing on the deck of the yawl, and Alex was swinging himself up on the boarding ladder. Elspeth frowned slightly, then stood up and pulled on a ragged terrycloth robe. "Well, nothing's simple, is it? And Marian, such an old friend and she hasn't been at all herself for days. Come on, Sarah, it's cooling off. Let's go up."

Later, back at the cottage, Sarah declined an offer to join an expedition to the harbor. "I've an idea I want to run down," she said.

* * *

Dressed and oil-coated against late-developing insects, Sarah climbed to the ridge overlooking the Harwood cottage. There was the clearing, barely visible, straight down below her. Sarah slid and scrambled down the decline and knelt down in the center of where she thought the fire must have been. In the failing light the area appeared completely flat, but there should be ashes. She reached out and gingerly ran her still sore fingers through the soft surface. Yes, there was a soft film and a tiny lump of something. Why hadn't she brought a flashlight? Or a bag? The never-prepared Ms. Deane. She crawled her fingers along the surface, picking up and discarding twigs and pebbles, putting a bent nail, a melted lump of something, and a piece of wire in her pocket, and finally, just before complete darkness, she added a small, cone-shaped object to her collection and departed.

The bathroom seemed the proper place for an examination of the found objects. Spread out along the edge of the sink, the wire, the nail, and what seemed to be a piece of melted plastic proved uninspiring. The cone, however, demanded further attention. The black film was stubborn and yielded at last only to an intensive scrubbing with toothpaste and nailbrush.

"Oh," Sarah said aloud, feeling suddenly sick. She dried the silver button and wrapped it in a piece of toilet paper and did the same for the other objects. It might not mean anything, she tried to tell herself. It might have been there for years, all summer at least. Try to think about something else and let it sink in.

She had just settled down in the cane rocking chair and checked off *Great Expectations* and *Black Boy* for the ninth grade, and was hovering between *The Red Badge of Courage* and *Lord of the Flies* for the tenth grade, when Alex banged on the door and entered.

"All right, Sarah, where did you sneak to?" He stood, back to the window, arms folded, and looked down at her.

"I followed up a guess. Information from your mother."

"Not a reliable source . . . unless her mind is on it."

"I think it was." And Sarah told Alex about the burned silver button, the fire, and Marian's all-purpose dress.

Alex was grim. "I'll put a call in to the police tonight. They'll have to move in on that clearing as soon as possible. I'm afraid it all ties in with something I squeezed out of Giddy."

"Which couldn't have been easy."

"I'm not proud of myself. I had to make Giddy mad, so mad that she blew up and defended Roger and let slip a few things. As I said, fidelity is one of Giddy's strong points, and she attacked me on the subject and dragged Roger in as an example."

"Fidelity? Roger?"

"It seems that Roger came back to the island after a soul tussle in Port Clyde to keep an eye on his mother. He was really worried about her. Self-protection lost out to filial loyalty. Of course, a good deal of his nastiness has had a family origin. But Marian had never turned against him, and there she was back on the island turning into a sort of robot. . . . Yes, I'm revising my opinion about her normality. She's borderline."

"I'll try to revise my opinion of Roger, but it won't be easy."

"Now I have a medical angle to work, some rumors to spread . . . not really lies. Just shake my head over Ruth's unfavorable prognosis. You see, if Ruth's fall was attempted murder, the person who did it must be pretty jittery. He knows she's not dead and may be afraid that she'll wake up and name names, so if I make a few gloomy remarks in public places, then the person might relax. Might even get careless and expose himself."

"Or herself," said Sarah, thinking of the burned dress. "But why not let drop that Ruth's conscious and set a trap outside the ICU? That's what happens in mysteries. You know, oxygen tubes being cut, doctors and nurses struggling with scalpels, and the murderer dressed up like a surgeon or disguised as a nun."

"Which is exactly what we want to avoid. Ruth's in enough trouble without staging a happening in the ICU. The nurses have orders not to let any strangers near her, and there's a Sheriff's Deputy on the floor."

"Then what do you think this relaxed and careless murderer is going to do? Go back to Captain's Head and be found having a good laugh?"

"Show an unusual interest in Ruth. Great concern but not so much alarm that he feels he has to go over to the hospital and try and pull tubes."

"Sydney's shown concern. He kept saying, 'Poor woman.'"

"Well, Sydney did know her and a lot of people who didn't have been saying, 'Poor woman.' I mean a continuing show of concern."

"Sydney suggested that his father's painting may have been the reason Ruth went to see Captain's Head."

"You said it. I didn't."

"Oh," said Sarah. "That is diabolical."

"Too diabolical, I think. Besides, no one's seen Sydney lurking at the cliff or near the trail. George has checked everyone he could find who was on Weymouth that day." Alex leaned down to ruffle Patsy's ears. "Hell, we may find out that everything that's happened is unconnected with anything else and it all reflects the rising national crime rate."

"Alex." Giddy stood in the doorway. "Amory Satterfield's had some sort of fainting fit. You're to go right over." Alex rose and without a word left the room, and Giddy made a face at his retreating back. "You creep," she said.

"Alex?" said Sarah.

"Yes, Alex. I've had it with him and told him so." Giddy threw herself down on Sarah's bed. "Though, you know, I'm beginning to think that I've been had, and that there was something funny going on in the scene I've just had with him. He went on and on admiring Tina."

"Which he is perfectly free to do," said Sarah calmly. She

picked up her school list, put a line through *The Red Badge of Courage,* and wrote in *Lord of the Flies* in a firm hand.

"All this slush about Tina. Such an intelligent, sensitive doctor, fine tennis player, so responsible. Yuck."

"All perfectly true, I suppose," said Sarah, crossing off *As You Like It* and substituting *Macbeth.*

"Now don't start being saintly or I'll abandon your cause," said Giddy.

"I don't have a cause," said Sarah. "Only my reading list and Ruth Baker."

"But, you see, the more I think about it, the more I'm sure that my dear cousin was working me over, pumping me. Making me say things about Roger. He knows exactly how to drive me out of my skull, and besides," said Giddy, pulling Sarah's quilt around her shoulders, "anyone can see that Tina's not his type. She's too bloody perfect. Alex doesn't go for really perfect people. They're so boring."

"Tina hardly strikes me as boring," said Sarah and then, deciding to move the conversation to where it properly belonged, asked, "Tell me, do you think Sydney Prior is mechanical? Does he fuss around with his car, change the oil, do things like that?"

"You mean did he drain the brake fluid from the Baker car? Well, I guess he knows a lot about his boat engine, but I've never actually seen him crawling around his car. He's awfully fat for that, and he wears those white suits, though, of course, he wears a rubber apron in the workshop, and I've seen him on his boat in one of those long coats . . . which hasn't much to do with getting rid of Tina."

"Giddy, for God's sake."

"Well, why not? She's a menace, and Alex just might start being really stupid about her with all that medical chitchat. I'm not thinking of anything drastic. Just move her off our mooring."

"Go to bed, Giddy, and leave Tina alone."

"You're reading *Mansfield Park,*" said Giddy, unwrapping

the quilt and rolling off the bed. "I liked *Pride and Prejudice* and Elizabeth Bennet, but that Fanny Price is something else. We had to read it last year in Introductory Lit. What a wimp. She just let that Crawford female walk all over her . . . "

"Good night, Giddy."

"So let Fanny be a lesson to you." And Giddy took herself off.

ELEVEN

Wednesday, Thursday, Friday, and Landing Day had arrived. Sydney's shop was thronged from opening to closing, and Sarah's investigations came to a halt. However, beyond dropping an extremely heavy framed reproduction of a Renoir on her instep, the three days were uneventful.

Alex, having decided that Amory Satterfield's lightheadedness was not life-threatening, ordered him to see his own physician. He then spent the last of the week shuttling between the hospital and the State Police trailer.

"No change worth talking about," said the neurosurgeon of Ruth. "Tracheostomy coming up. We can't keep her on the blower much longer."

"You've untaped her eyes?" asked Alex.

"The nurses have. Nothing to report. Don't give up. It's early days yet."

"A blank so far on Sydney Prior's place," said George Fitts, making a series of little x's across his pad. "Some stains from spilled solvents and varnishes, but nothing else, and they're from Sydney's own supplies. We're going in again to take samples from the walls, check for spattering."

"Have you gone over likely boats?" said Alex. "Sydney's *Tempest Queen,* for instance, and his old dinghy? Hello, Mike," this to the deputy investigator, who had just walked in.

"I have some news," said Mike. "Sydney sold the *Queen* to Tom Starkey over at Tenants Harbor. Tom's renamed it the *Honeybun* and taken the whole boat down right to the bare wood. Two new coats of primer and two finish coats, new bottom paint, the wheel revarnished. It's like new. He's had his eye on the boat for ages, made Sydney regular yearly offers. The old dinghy half sank by the dock and Sydney's had it broken up. Said rot had set in. Suspicious, I'd say, but those things do happen."

"Yes," said George, "but Prior's still clear for the Harwood murder, and the records show that he's bought four dinghies in the last ten years because he's never satisfied. And the lobster trap search is another dead end. No one is missing an old trap or any pot warp. But what's really interesting is the fire area on Weymouth. Three more silver buttons have turned up. That's going to mean another workout with Mrs. Harwood after we check up on the dress purchase."

"As for me," said Mike, "I've got the weekend off. First time this month, so, George, if you find any of Nate's blood on Sydney's antiques, will you hold off wrapping up the case until after the weekend? I've got the Arlington Million and Arlington Oaks to watch on the tube. Got me a little bet down. Devil's Rag and Blushing Bear, if you want a tip."

"No, thank you," said George. "I leave gambling to the mob."

"No rest and recreation for the State Police?" asked Alex.

"I have Sunday off," said George. "I plan to fish."

"What a fussy old maid," said Mike, as he and Alex left together. "I hope he falls off his boat."

"No, you don't," said Alex.

"No, I don't," said Mike. "If I got myself murdered, I'd sure as hell want George on the case."

They parted, and Alex walked over to Prior's Gallery, where he found Sydney shepherding Sarah out of the shop door and locking it. "The big weekend," he said. "Alex, may

I give you a ride over? Sarah and I are leaving a few minutes early."

Alex agreed. "Thanks. It will save me from being trampled by the Landing Day crowd on the ferry."

"Sarah," said Sydney, turning angrily, "there's George Fitts and Mike Laaka down at the dock. I cannot . . . I will not face them. Please go and tell them they may do as they like with my barn and my shop, but to leave my orders and workshop in one piece. The police spilled a tin of kerosene during the last search. All over the barn floor."

Sarah caught up with Mike and George, just as the latter was loosening the lines on the State Police runabout, and delivered her message.

"Landing Day," said George. "A public nuisance. The lab team will go through Prior's place again this evening, and Mike and I are going over tonight to Weymouth and supervise the exam of the Harwood clearing. Tell Mr. Prior that we'll be wanting to look through all the art school cottages and talk to the people there."

Once out in the harbor, Sydney opened the *Christmas Past* to full throttle, and the boat shot past island after island, leaving a boiling green wake behind, and then swung into Weymouth Harbor and came to a churning stop at the public landing.

"Sydney knows better than to charge into the dock like that," said Alex, after they had been left ashore and the *Christmas Past* had sped around Lighthouse Point in the direction of the Bucket.

"He's been in a rage all day," said Sarah. "He can't stand the police tramping around his shop."

"Sydney can take care of his own interests nicely. It's Marian Harwood I've been worrying about. I think I will, after all, have a talk with her. She must be frightened."

"With reason," said Sarah, as they began the walk up toward the post office.

"Yes," said Alex. "Another piece of trivia moving front

and center. And Roger may have a leading part in the script.'"

"I don't quite see why."

"Yes, you do. Go over it. Opportunities, motives. Oh, Lord, here's Mike."

"George has gone ahead," said Mike. "God-a-mighty, Sydney came into the harbor like a wild man, but I like that boat of his."

Sarah stopped in the path. "What does the name *Christmas Past* mean to you?"

"It's that *Christmas Carol* thing they do to death on TV every year," said Mike. "Ghosts and Scrooge."

"Anything else?"

"Matter of fact, she's a nifty filly, champion three-year-old a few years back. About the time I started watching the tracks. She's a gray with Grey Dawn II as her daddy."

"A horse?" demanded Sarah. "Christmas Past is a horse?"

"Yeah, and probably islands and coves and God knows what else. There's a Christmas Cove near Damariscotta. Now I've got to beat it, George will be stewing," and Mike broke into a jog and disappeared.

"It's a horse," said Sarah.

"Oh, hell," said Alex, "that's just Mike. He's horse-mad. Gets the *Daily Racing Form* and makes bets all over the country."

"So you don't think . . . ?"

"No, I don't think. Mike is just responding like a horse fan."

"I could go over to Sydney and try it out," said Sarah. "Say Secretariat to him and see if he twitches."

"Can you see Sydney on a horse? Or near one, or with any animal? I don't think he's ever even had a cat."

"But his father . . . or his grandfather. They were from Kentucky."

"His father was a working artist, and I never saw him near a horse. There's more in Kentucky than bluegrass and derbies."

"I still think it's worth following," said Sarah. "He may be a secret gambler or maybe Christmas Past is the title of a painting. A stolen painting. One he's made a lot of money from."

"Anything's possible," said Alex. "Go to it. And there's Marian Harwood ahead, let's catch up."

Marian was carrying a plastic bag with the red logo of the Weymouth store. "A chicken," she said. "Roger isn't eating well."

"Are you, Marian?" said Alex. "Eating well?"

"Pretty well. I wish they'd leave us alone. The police. They're coming again to talk. I've told them it's all over. All we want is peace . . . not to be bothered by the police. Roger is settling down, but," she added in her toneless voice, "he's nervous."

"Why is that, you think?" said Alex.

Marian shifted her bag to the other hand. To Sarah she seemed somewhat shrunken from the Mrs. Noah figure of two weeks ago. "Roger always was nervous," she said, "and now we're being bothered."

"If I can help," said Alex, "let me know, or I could find someone for you to see."

"Just not to be bothered," said Marian. "And sell the cottage. We don't need it anymore . . . just too much trouble."

"Why not wait on that idea?" said Alex. "Think it over."

"Then we could go away," said Marian, as if she had not heard him.

"My mother's right," said Alex, as Marian walked on toward her cottage. "She's heading for a crack-up."

"Or she's having one right now," said Sarah. "Her eyes are funny."

Elspeth was at the front of the house hanging the blue and white Weymouth flag from the front door. "The beginning of Landing Day," she explained to Sarah. "They'll fire off the cannon at sunset, about seven-thirty. Everyone goes to Lighthouse Point, except me. I've gone to sixty-four Landing Day send-offs, and I'm just pulling my painting into shape.

And, Alex, your father's coming home next week. I'm going to enjoy thinking of that."

"Look," said Alex, "can you spend time with Marian this weekend? I'm worried now. I think she's going to need you. Because of Roger."

"Roger? Why?"

"Oh," said Sarah in a low voice. "I think I see."

"All right, Alex," said Elspeth. "I'll go over after dinner."

Sarah followed Giddy and Tina along the shortcut path through Satter's Field, her mind still disordered by at least twenty conflicting ideas and wishes. Alex, silent, brought up the rear carrying a long-necked flashlight. As they converged on Lighthouse Point, Sarah found herself caught in a moving stream of people with blankets, six-packs, and coolers, and ahead, leading the way over a rise, she could see Sydney Prior and, to his left, above the crowd like a giraffe, Harrison Petty in a yellow sweater.

It was harder and harder for her to unravel one thread from this jungle of a case, but in the general tangle, Alex's linking of Roger with his mother made horrible sense. Taken alone, of course, the dress-burning and finding the silver button were only bits of circumstantial evidence, but if you added Marian's behavior to Roger's erratic course, why, you had something. Sarah, hastening along the rocky path, saw how two of the least accommodating strands of the case might be traced to the same root. Not Sydney, not Harrison, though he may have wished to have done it, but the Harwoods. Together.

Roger kills Nate. Where is not important. Out of sight anyway. With the doorstop, which is either grabbed on impulse—which means it was done at Sydney's—or somehow taken with malice aforethought. Most probably it was done at Sydney's. Nate had been trying all day to search his shop, and with Sydney gone, why not have a free look around without telling Giddy? The barn door would have been open, Giddy safely in the front shop. Roger sees his father go in and follows. After all, he is about to be exposed as a fraud, so why not try once more to make peace? They argue, Roger loses control—Sarah remembered the scene at the lighthouse, Roger with his hand lifted, his face twisted with rage. And Marian? She would never have followed Nate anywhere, she'd spent the afternoon trying to avoid him, but she must have gone in after Roger. The mother hen, Mrs. Noah, afraid of what might happen when her son's and her husband's tempers collided. She must have found them together, Nate just dead, Roger standing there with the befouled doorstop in one hand. Sarah could see it. Marian kneeling down, the skirt of her navy dress soaking up her husband's blood, then in shock, fleeing, her raincoat pulled around her. She catches the five-fifteen to the island and keeps to the cabin, raincoat on, trying to pull herself together. Once on shore she sees the groceries marked Harwood and asks Lem to take them to Fanny's. After all, she can't leave them there wilting and melting, announcing that something's happened to Nate.

And Roger? He disposes of the doorstop—didn't Alex tell her that Roger was seen later at the end of the dock *not* fishing? Not very bright, but he must have been rattled by then. He had his father's body to get rid of, the murder site to clean, his own clothes to change, and he had to be quick about it, because for all he knew Sydney might be right back or Giddy might turn up.

"Whoa up, Sarah," said Alex. He indicated a sign by her shoulder: WARNING: DO NOT GO BEYOND THIS POINT. LOWER TRAIL CLOSED. "It's too rocky and besides the best view is up here. They'll fire off the cannon just as the sun goes down."

"Alex," whispered Sarah, "I see what happened. Roger. He did it, Marian found them, got blood on her dress and took the boat back, and he got rid of the body."

"God, Sarah, you can't talk here. Come over behind that tree." He pulled her behind a large spruce, well away from the gathered crowd.

"No wonder Roger's been so edgy, almost hysterical,"

Sarah went on. "And Marian turning into a blank. Her son murdering her husband. And Roger was the only one who could have dumped the body that evening. He had access, you said, to traps and lines, and no one would have bothered about a dinghy being rowed out after dark."

"Yes," said Alex. "I've thought of all that."

"And naturally Marian wasn't thrilled about the furniture removal plan. Nate was dead. And Roger breaking into the cottage for his father's letters. He knew it was safe, but later, after hiding out, he was torn between escaping and staying near his mother . . . or near the scene of the crime in case he'd forgotten something."

"And Marian's fright about Nate's hat makes sense. I suppose it suggested that the rest of Nate was about to follow."

"But now we've put it all together, will the police listen?"

"I don't know. I'll get in touch with them tonight, but even with clear motives a lot depends on intangibles like Marian's nerves and Roger's temper. And it's not a crime to burn a dress, so unless Nate's blood type is found on a scrap of material, it's worthless. George is a stickler for hard evidence, so we'll have to wait."

"It may not be safe to wait . . . for anyone. But, still, how do Ruth Baker, the drownings, and the art thefts fit in?"

"I'm ready to say coincidence. Separate events that passed in the night, unless Roger was somehow involved. Think it over, maybe one of our bits of trivia can tie him in. Come on, let's go and join the crowd. The sun's going down. Ready for the cannon."

The enormous orange-red sun, flat as a plate, slipped behind the tree lines of the distant islands, the small brass cannon boomed, the sound ricocheted off the rocks and ledges, children screamed, a baby wailed, and cheering broke out. Sydney Prior, standing on a bench, raised both arms and called into the noise, "I proclaim Weymouth Landing Day to have commenced." A group at the base of the lighthouse burst into "The Star Spangled Banner," while a youth nearby lifted a bugle and wavered uncertainly into "Taps."

"Oh, there you are," said Tina. "Giddy and I lost you in the crush. I told her you were over this way."

Sarah looked at Giddy, who in the fading light had an expression very like that of the disappearing Cheshire cat.

"What's next?" said Tina.

"Singing, wandering around, drinking, blanket parties," said Giddy. "We've all done it a thousand times, but you might like to stay, Tina."

"No," said Tina, "I can live without this. I've gone through the Boston Esplanade Fourth of July."

The four moved away in single file, and Sarah, bringing up the rear, thought as she plodded back through Satter's Field, how this Landing Day weekend might perhaps be remembered in the future as the time when the son of an old summer resident was understood to have murdered his father and rolled him into the waters of Muscongus Bay.

As they reached the McKenzie gate, Sarah overtook the others and found Alex—once again—in a medical dispute with Tina.

"Are you absolutely sure?" she demanded. "Make your own examination. I use Q-tips up the nostril—I mean a really painful stimulus—and do it myself."

How vile, thought Sarah. But now Tina stretched out her arms, embracing the evening. "Let's forget medicine," she said. "It's too beautiful here." Tina in the gloaming loomed larger, stronger, more rose and gold than ever. Her figure and gestures suggested an absolute possession of the earth she walked on. Sarah, a visitor from another planet, moved away.

* * *

Landing Day proper began at daybreak with firecrackers and the cannon sounding from Captain's Head.

Sarah had gone to bed, leaving Alex to call the police,

bundle with Tina, argue with Giddy, or whatever pleased him. She had made a vow to put emotions into cold storage and try to regard all of the inhabitants of Weymouth as obscure and possibly dangerous fauna encountered on the way to somewhere else. She would spend the day in productive thought . . . alone. This proved to be easy. Elspeth, up at the first bang, rushed off with Giddy to help with the pageant costumes, and Alex ate a hasty breakfast, saying that he was going to help out for the morning at the first-aid tent.

"So you've got your Maine license now, have you?" said Tina, who had arrived at dawn.

"Yes, I'm all set, so I can do more than give advice."

Sarah, in spite of her vow, felt something congeal inside her. Alex to practice in Maine? Tina knew, and she, Sarah, who had thought him settled in Boston, had no idea of it.

"We'll be racing the *Moondust* this afternoon," said Tina to Sarah. "Want to come? My father's asked Alex to help crew."

Sarah tried a sincere voice. "Thanks, but I'll just walk around . . . watch the goings-on."

With a heavy thing inside her growing apace, Sarah fixed Patsy on his wire and made her way to the town center and over to the edge of a circle of people gathered around the historical society's flagpole. There in the middle, on a platform, stood Sydney Prior, a blue and white rosette pinned to the lapel of his white suit, and at his side Lem Wallace, who, in his doublet and hose, ruff and sword, looked like a fugitive from the first act of *The Tempest*.

Sydney was reading from a scroll in a somewhat ecclesiastical voice:

Know ye, good folk of Weymouth, that gallant Captain George Weymouth of Devonshire who stands now at my side first undertook his mission under the reign of her late majesty Elizabeth of glorious memory and does stand off Weymouth in his ship the *Archangel* on

> May the seventeenth the year of our Lord, sixteen
> hundred and five, and because of a most fearsome gale
> seeks shelter for his crew in what we people now call
> Sailor's Cove, and therefore sends in to the shore a
> boat for wood and game . . .

Sarah slipped away, pressed through a clutch of giggling girls
done up in gray stuff gowns and white caps, and took her way
down to the center of town. Here the shops were hung with
Weymouth banners, and every path was crowded with visitors
and newly risen ice cream and hot dog carts, while hard by
Clare's Diner a puppet show was enacting a moment in
Abenaki history. Sarah turned, uncertain of where to go next,
and saw Elspeth rushing by, saying, "I'm late," but Giddy,
behind her, stopped. "I'm helping Aunt Elspeth judge the
children's art show. Are you coming to the boat club buffet
thing? The food's not bad and afterwards there's the race. I'll
be in the *Peg* for the small-boat class. Alex, the rat, will probably be schlocking it up on the *Moondirt.*"

"*Moondust,*" said Sarah.

"All the same. Want to be my crew? No. Okay, I'll find
someone."

"Come on, Giddy," called Elspeth, reappearing by the
path. "Rachel will be wild."

It sounded like something out of *Alice,* and Sarah half-
expected Rachel to appear, shouting, "Off with their heads!"
Except that, despite surface whimsy and color, Weymouth
with its murdering son and floating father were from an another world. Was Roger still loose on the island? Had Alex
made his point with the police? Distracted by Alex's Maine
license, she'd forgotten to ask before he'd gone off for the
morning.

Almost from habit, Sarah continued her walk toward the
Ocean Trail. Reaching a point between the Pail and the
Bucket, she paused, looked over the water, and saw what
looked like a new line of fog lying across the horizon like a

folded gray blanket. Turning her sights closer to home, she saw that Sydney Prior's cottage rose just below her, its roof dappled with shade.

And Sydney? He was on that platform, busy with Landing Day mumbo jumbo, basking in the delights of being the founder of the feast. Go on, she said to herself. For though Sydney might not have killed Nate Harwood, might he not have been a little sticky-fingered when it came to other people's paintings? Maybe he needed more money, had a woman tucked off in some corner. Two women . . . or two wives. Sydney as a bigamist rather appealed to Sarah. Or had he been playing the stock market, buying long and selling short or whatever it was that people did? A share in Atlantic City slot machines, owner of a secret race track in Kentucky? Sarah hadn't entirely given up on *Christmas Past.*

She found herself at Sydney's side entrance, an arched lattice over which late roses straggled. And the door was open. How careless of Sydney. Or perhaps Sydney had nothing to hide.

This certainly seemed to be the case. The white kitchen, open shelves, the usual implements recommended by Julia Child, the dining room, equally disappointing, with its cherry table, its wildflower prints, an oil by August Prior of— wouldn't you know—Captain's Head, and a hooked rug that Sarah rolled up, thinking of loose boards and trap doors. A blank, too, on the living room, notable only for an Elspeth McKenzie watercolor and white slipcovers. Really, the whole place was perfectly open and in great contrast to Sydney's richly crowded Parlor Gallery. Sarah ran her hand behind pictures, under sofa cushions, inspected drawers, and then headed upstairs. Bedrooms, she felt, were better for keeping illicit objects. In the first, she frisked the furniture, then ran quickly over a line of framed photographs: a man in a Herbert Hoover collar holding a plump boy in a sailor suit, a woman, circa 1890, in a long sailor dress by the shore, an old gentleman in a wide-brimmed hat standing by a curricle, the horse in a high state of gloss, neck arched, one hoof lifted. A horse, said Sarah to herself, pleased, but then remembered that at the date the picture was taken, a horse was the only means of private transportation.

A clock radio and a bottle of cough syrup in the second bedroom suggested that the canopy bed was for the master himself. Sarah slipped her hands under the counterpane and pillows and encountered a folded pair of silk pajamas. Rolling her sleeves, she reached between the mattress and the box spring, thinking that this was the very place to conceal a stolen print or canvas.

And then the front door slammed.

"It's lucky I had extra programs made," said Sydney, his voice coming right up the stairwell. "More people here than ever."

"I feel a damn fool in this rig," said Lem Wallace's voice. "Can't believe they crossed the ocean in these outfits, all this velvet and lace."

"You'll make the best Captain Weymouth yet. You can handle a boat, which is more . . . " And Sarah hurled herself under the bed, hoping that the cover hung down low enough to hide her. The voices died to a mumble, and then Sydney, huffing up the stairs, called out, "Bring the *Archangel* as close as you dare. She only draws six feet. Tell the sailors to row in slowly. People want to take pictures, and the TV stations are covering it. I'll be on the beach to meet you."

"We've only rehearsed twice," shouted Lem from below. "Cross your fingers."

Here Sydney, whose feet were only inches from Sarah's chin, coughed and fumbled with the bedside table. "Go on ahead," he called back, "I'll bring the programs."

Sarah, frozen into position, heard Sydney go down the stairs, and then, after a pause, the door closed. Choking from dust mice, Sarah pulled herself from under the bed and in doing so dislodged a pile of magazines from the floor by the head of the bed. Nothing of interest. *Antique Digest, Art & Auction, Time, Horizon.* She turned her attention to Sydney's bedside table drawer. This revealed a roll of Tums, a cigarette holder, an open pack of Kools, and a small pad with a few odd —very odd—notations. In fact, they made no sense whatsoever. *Champagne, Oct 15? Young America—Med., Christmas Day?* (Christmas again! The man was obsessed.) *Queen Charlotte II,* then *12/21 Thomas A. Edison/Niagara/New Orleans/Molly Pitcher/Stuyvesant.* These were followed by *Dosage Index?—Mississippi Mud, Ragtime, Dixieland Band.*

Insanity seemed the only conclusion, unless with the last three names Sydney had now revealed himself as a jazz ragtime fan. Except she never remembered Sydney playing music in and around the shop. Sarah straightened, put the pad in the back pocket of her jeans, and closed the drawer. What in God's heaven did all these notations have in common? Art, antiques, Christmas, jazz, Thomas A. Edison? Back to square one. Well, okay, she'd thought of it before. Some paintings had absolutely daft titles. Homer's "The Nooning," and "Bright Circle" by Kandinsky, and something called "Tu'M" and "Broadway Boogie-Woogie" by Mondrian. Hah! Now she was on to something. Excited, feeling once more a useful member of the human race, she started down the stairs. Was this the missing piece that would make the Ruth Baker part of the puzzle into a whole? Queen Charlotte, Thomas A. Edison, and Molly Pitcher seemed strange partners unless you thought of portraits. The Nate Harwood murder seemed almost wrapped up, and right here was perhaps the thread that might make a noose for Sydney Prior. Pausing at the side door, Sarah considered for a moment that the names might be titles of pictures that Sydney knew were coming up for auction, but then dismissed the idea as not supporting her conviction of Sydney's guilt.

Now she had to fight an impulse to race around to the first-aid tent and tell Alex that, like Eliza Doolittle, she'd got it, by George, she'd got it. But no, it was almost noon, and Alex would be all tied up with the sailing race and Tina, and she suddenly saw that she would have to go to the mainland itself. To Sydney's shop, to his workroom, his Parlor Gallery, his living quarters. The police had been busy looking for bloodstains and human hairs and not papers with Mississippi Mud and Queen Charlotte on them. Even the art theft team, she understood from Alex, was more occupied with the how, when, where of the thefts than with such subtleties as the painting titles. And there was something else bothering her —that framed Renoir production that she'd dropped on her foot. Did that have an oddball title? But how could she get to Port Clyde with the *Robin Day*'s next trip not until one o'clock? She wouldn't be able to hitch a ride or hire a boat, because everything that could float would be circling Sailor's Cove watching for the arrival of the *Archangel*. She stared across the water, watching a little sloop heel over in a puff of wind and then right itself and swing over on another tack, working against the south wind. The south wind? Blowing right to Port Clyde. Well, why not? Giddy was using the *Peg*, the *Moondust* was over at the boat club, but the *Molly* must be at Tinker's Cove, idle and unwanted.

Swallowing qualms about first ocean solos and other people's boats, Sarah broke into a run and arrived panting at Tinker's Cove. Good. Giddy had left the sail on. It all went smoothly. There was the rudder lying along the floorboards, together with a paddle and two life jackets. What more could any seafaring detective want? Unlash the sail, pull the halyard, fasten the dinghy to the mooring. Now cast off, get hold of the main sheet, make sure the centerboard was up, just as Alex and Giddy had, now over those rocks, now let the sail out. The boom swung wide, the mast creaked, the old, much mended sail filled, and, sweetly rolling, the *Molly* took the wind for Port Clyde.

* * *

"What's this stuff?" said Giddy, dumping a spoonful of pink gelatin on her plate.

"Shrimp wiggle," said Tina. "It's terrific. Alex, eat up. You'll need your strength. My father's a tacking fiend. We grind winches like slaves."

"Where's Sarah?" said Alex, looking around. "Didn't anyone tell her about lunch?"

"I think she wanted to explore on her own," said Tina.

"You hope," said Giddy.

"Giddy, your claws," said Alex. For a moment he studied his well-filled plate and then abandoned it on a long table decorated with sailing trophies and ribbons. "I've been thinking about head injuries," he said.

"I know," said Tina, "and you said to leave it to the neurologists. Listen, I think we'd better skip dessert. My father wants to go over the boat with you and explain the jib changes."

"No," said Alex. "I can't, and I'm sorry. It's Ruth Baker. I've got to go to the hospital and try something. Look, Tina, find someone else. Half the people here are dying to race. Next time, maybe."

Tina shrugged. "If you must, you must." And then, staring at Alex's retreating back as he strode off down the boat club path, she for the first time showed a slight loss of cool. "Shit. Double shit," she said softly.

"He's impossible, isn't he?" said Giddy cheerfully. "I gave up on him years ago, but you know doctors. Compulsive as hell."

Alex pushed himself through the crowded paths and at the post office saw his mother hurrying toward him. Her face was anguished.

"Oh, Alex, it's Roger. He's confessed. Mike Laaka's come over and told me all about it. The police found a piece of Marian's dress that hadn't burned properly . . . with stains. They went to the house and picked up Roger, and he said he'd followed his father into Sydney's barn and his mother must have followed him. There was a sort of three-way argument, and Roger says something just snapped. He went into the hall and grabbed a doorstop . . . it's so awful . . . and hit his father. His mother was splattered by the blood."

"I'm sorry, Mother," said Alex. "I was afraid it might work out like this."

"Roger cleaned up with some turpentine he'd found in the barn and dropped the doorstop off the wharf, and then, after dark, took out a skiff and pushed the body off and, of course, Marian burned her dress. Roger said he came back to the island because he thought his mother was going crazy, which we all knew."

"Where's Roger now?"

"Down on the dock. The police are taking him over to the mainland, where that Sergeant Fitts is waiting. And Marian's down there, too, so I'll take charge of her."

Marian Harwood, wearing the same short green dress she had worn to her husband's service, stood, hands folded, next to a uniformed State Policeman, while Roger, handcuffed, hair neatly combed, shirt clean, stood in the stern of the police boat looking back at her.

"Anything I can do, Marian?" said Alex, coming up.

"No, thank you," said Marian. "All this trouble for nothing." She smiled and looked at some point past his left ear.

"Cast off," said the policeman. "Get this show on the road."

"Take it easy, Mother," said Roger. "Call Joyce. She'll come home and take care of you. Okay, Mother?" He used a soft wheedling voice that Alex had not heard since Roger's voice had changed. And Alex thought, looking at him, that he had dropped that mixed hangdog-belligerent look. In fact, Roger, at that moment in his life when he had presumably reached a low in degradation, seemed alert, confident, absolutely adult, and, well—unlikely word—proud.

"Mother," said Alex. "Get hold of Joyce Harwood as fast as you can. I have to go to the hospital—it may be something important." And he strode away toward the waiting *Robin Day*, rehearsing in his mind the complexities attendant on stupor and coma.

* * *

Piece of cake, said Sarah to herself as she swept into Port Clyde. Here and there it had been a little sticky—a near collision with the schooner impersonating the *Archangel* on its way to Sailor's Cove, and a close call with a sloop sailing right at her, its helmsman yelling, "Starboard tack," but now she steered for the center of the harbor, turned smartly into the wind, and let down the luffing sail. Better paddle in than try to make a landing at one of the public docks. The difficulties of sailing were overrated. It was just a matter of keeping the sail filled and not tipping over. Of course, the fog might cause trouble later, but she could always catch the ferry back.

She paddled an erratic course to the public landing, tied a double granny, and, pulling her blue bandanna over her head in a gesture toward disguise, moved quickly along the shore to the rear of Prior's Art Gallery.

The barn door was locked, as was every other door. To be expected. Both the searching police and Sydney would have seen to this. But there were windows. Sarah worked herself behind a quince bush and, after heaving without effect at several dusty cellar windows, lost patience, picked up a stone, and rammed it into the glass. It sounded like a thousand light bulbs hitting the fan, and she shrank back into the quince. Then, seeing that all of Port Clyde was not rushing upon her, Sarah began pulling at the broken glass and then, like a chicken going through its eggshell, let herself gingerly into the cellar, ending with both feet in the laundry tub.

The cellar was unlighted, but she found the stairs, climbed them, and was in luck. The master alarm system stood just at the head of the stairs, and Sydney had shown her how to disarm it for those days when she had to open the shop. The door was not locked, and she stepped into the small hall between the Parlor Gallery and Sydney's kitchen.

Where to start? The living quarters, certainly. But almost an hour later, Sarah had to admit that her search had told her little beyond that Sydney harbored an unparalleled collection of cough remedies and laxatives. The one interesting item was a folder showing a small fiberglass runabout on which Sydney had written, "Johnson 60 h.p.?" and underneath, "Plum Cake?" It was, she decided, a sort of Christmas fetish. Something repressed, now bursting out in boat names. Sydney's family, perhaps, had belonged to an austere sect that went in more for prayer than presents, or else Sydney as a child had been more deserving of a lump of coal than sugarplums.

Sarah now picked her way through the Parlor Gallery. The room, which in ordinary daylight appeared as a fine clutter of furniture and plate, now, lit only by the striped sunlight from the closed shutters, had an eerie quality. Deep shadows enlarged wing chairs into giant sitting vultures, tables became black edgeless pools, and a silver urn from some trick of ornamentation stood on its shelf like an elongated and helmeted skull. With a little shudder, she turned and made her way to Sydney's workroom. Here she had to risk a light, but the two windows were well screened by outside shrubbery.

The room was as she had seen it. The walls with their procession of boats, the bins of moldings, the trays of mat paper, and, set out on the long bench, glue bottles, hammers, nails, and the mat-cutting apparatus. Along the walls stood racks of framed paintings, each with a white tag neatly lettered with the owner's name and promised delivery date. And there was that monster painting that had tilted onto Sarah's instep last week. She winced in memory. She had thought those massive, curly white frames had gone out with the Victorians.

And did it have a title that fitted in with *Dixieland Band* or *Queen Charlotte*? Sarah walked forward and pulled the picture a short way out of the rack. It was Renoir's still-life study "Onions." Nothing much in that and not, she supposed, a widely popular painting. So why had Sydney put it in his collection of reproductions?

She remembered now that on the first day at work Sydney had told her that he carried only artists with a New England connection. Well, this might be a special order. Sarah pushed the heavy frame back and reached among the frames for another, smaller picture with an equally elaborate molding. Cézanne's "Card Players." But again, Sydney didn't sell Impressionists. Was this, too, a special order? Really, the frames almost swallowed up the picture, and both showed streaks of dust in the scrolls of the frame. Curious, Sarah lifted the tag on the Cézanne. "Mrs. Thos. Rolfe, July 17, $90." Well, Mrs. Rolfe was certainly late in picking up her painting. She quickly checked through six other pictures, New England scenes and prints. All early September dates. She returned to the Renoir. "Ms. Toney Black, August 3, $125." Searching, she located one more Impressionist, a Gauguin, this tagged for a Dr. Fager for July 28. More and more peculiar. Three special orders for French Impressionists. She pulled the Renoir entirely free of the rack.

"Onions" was backed with brown paper sealed along the border, with the oval red and gold sticker, "Sydney Prior Gallery—Port Clyde, Maine," centered at the top. But the picture had no screw eyes or picture wire. And Sydney always included these. She checked through the regular orders. All these had properly placed hardware plus a little plastic bag with the proper size of picture hook and nail—one of Sydney's "extra touches."

Okay, she could accept the three Impressionists as three special orders by forgetful customers—these last were legion. But the absence of screw eyes and hooks? No way. Sarah reached for the first tool that came to hand, an Exacto knife, and carefully cut out the brown paper backing. Underneath she found a rectangle of white foam, which she pulled out in one piece, coming face to face with a rough surface of masonite. But reproductions weren't mounted on masonite, were they? Or perhaps a heavy backing had been used because of the outsize frame. And damn, Sydney had used those miserable little nails to hold it in place. Sarah searched and found pliers and began pulling them out one by one. And then she heard it—a distant, heavy, ominous creak. Hell, the police. Hurry. Like a dentist gone berserk, she pulled nail after nail, pried the masonite loose, and turned the panel face up on the floor. Not Renoir but Bucket Cove in a waning light, the sky painted in broad strokes, a spruce shoreline, and, thrusting out through the silver water, the jagged outline of the weir. Below in the right corner in dark script, "E. McKenzie."

Sarah sank back on the floor next to the painting. "Night at the Weir," page nine of the Godding catalogue. And where was the Renoir? She turned the frame, and the onions looked stolidly back at her. The heavy frame held two pictures, Renoir over McKenzie. And how about the Cézanne? Sarah crawled over and grabbed the smaller picture, flipped it on its face, and then someone coughed, a dry, rasping little cough, the sort associated with a lifetime of smoking.

Sarah froze. Another cough and then shuffling footsteps down the hall. To the door. Which opened.

"Sarah. My dear. Oh, my, what a distressing sight. All my hard work." Sydney closed the door behind him, and from the floor Sarah found herself looking up at the bulk of her employer, his Landing Day blue and white rosette still fixed to his lapel. "And I thought you might have enjoyed our little historical celebration. We try to interest everyone in the Weymouth story. No, please, sit right there and do put down those pliers. I never let anyone use my tools, you know." Sydney took a step forward, one hand thrust into the pocket of his white jacket, the other circling the neck of a fruit-basket-shaped doorstop.

* * *

Alex didn't bother with the elevator. He took the concrete steps two at a time and, breathing hard at the nurse's station, identified himself. "Oh," said the nurse, looking doubtful—Alex, in sailing garb, patched shorts, and the oldest of sneakers, inspired little confidence. "Dr. Samuels isn't on today. I can try for Dr. Hopwood. She's in the hospital."

"Could you check the chart and tell me when you last looked at Miss Baker's eyes?"

"Let me call Dr. Hopwood," said the nurse.

"Fine," said Alex, "but look at the chart and then call him."

"Her eyes were untaped this A.M.," said the nurse, flipping over the pages of Ruth's chart. "Medication was given at the same time."

"I'll just go in and say hello," said Alex.

"She's unresponsive," said the nurse. "I'm beeping Dr. Hopwood. No one's supposed to go in there without one of the staff. The police left word. It's on her chart."

"I know," said Alex, exasperated. "I'm one of the people who brought her in here. Okay, call the police."

Ten minutes and three phone calls later, Alex stood by the head of Ruth's bed, the curtains pulled around them. He felt like a pirate about to storm a peaceful ship and drag its passenger back to the hazards of the mainland.

"Hello, Ruth Baker," said Alex slowly and distinctly. "It's Alex McKenzie. I'm going to take these bandages off your eyes."

Ruth, bound by her wires and tubes and bolts, did not move.

"I'm going to ask you some questions. Some simple questions and then some very important questions. If you want to say yes, will you roll your eyes up to the ceiling? If you want to say no, roll them down toward your feet." And Alex began to unfasten the bandages.

The eyelids, the cheekbones were swollen, the blue and purple fading into yellow. Ruth's eyes were dark centers set in pale gray circles.

"Is your name Ruth?"

The gray circles with the dark pupils did not move.

"Is your name Ruth Baker?"

"Is your name Ruth Baker?"

"Is your name Ruth Baker?"

And slowly the gossamer gray circles with the dark centers slipped toward the ceiling.

* * *

"And now," said Sydney—he had never sounded so pleasant—"because one can always trust the police to arrive when least wanted, I'll have to ask you to slip that picture back in its frame. Yes, that's it," as Sarah pushed Elspeth's painting back against the Renoir. "Now," said Sydney, "stand up and take that masking tape from the bench. We haven't time for nails. My hands, as you see, are otherwise occupied. Run the tape around the edges. . . . That's it. Now take the paper backing and tape it to the masonite. . . . I've always wondered why Elspeth prefers it to canvas. So stiff. But for my purposes, so easy to fit behind Monsieur Renoir. Those double frames are not simple, you know. Now my gallery sticker. Left-hand drawer in the cabinet. . . . No, not the hammer," as Sarah's hand slowed in its passage over that tool. "Thank you. There's something so finished about an object with a sticker. The police looked through every picture and never a second glance. However, the police are not interested in art, are they? But you, young woman, why did *you* look further? Come now, no silences, Miss Deane. This may be one of our last conversations."

Sarah came down in favor of buying time. Anything to pull her disordered wits together. "You don't carry French Impressionists," she said, "and I didn't see how all three could be special orders, and the tags were dated back in early August and July, and you didn't put in screw eyes and the picture hooks."

Sydney sighed. "This is the first time I've wished that Giddy had stayed on. I never let her in here and she never bothered to learn the inventory. I'm afraid you are one of my mistakes. I did hesitate in taking you on, because of the McKenzie connection, but I thought to refuse you might call undesirable attention to my shop. Now suppose," he went on, cradling the doorstop in his left arm, "you put the Renoir and Cézanne back in the rack and we both go to the parlor and discuss what is to be done with you. Ahead of me, please, but placing hands on your head. Splendid. Just as it's done in the movies. Now right in here while I get the light. The Queen Anne chair for you." Sydney lowered himself into an opposite wing chair and tilted a brass student lamp until the light hit Sarah full in the face.

"This doorstop is an awkward weapon." Sydney, balancing it on one knee, turned so the fruit faced Sarah. "Fortunately," he added, "I have in my pocket a little backup system. A citizen's right to bear arms, you know. What is the slogan? 'If guns are outlawed, only outlaws will have guns'?"

One part of Sarah's brain—the emergency center—told her to keep Sydney talking, and he loved to talk. The other part bent its efforts on enhancing sensory intake, which, with a light in her eyes, was difficult. Sarah cocked her head ever so slightly, moved her face the merest degree to her right, and tried to see what was at the edge of her vision. She had the impression of a jumble of tables, urns, bowls, clocks, tea services.

"I simply cannot risk a mess in this room," said Sydney in a thoughtful voice. "We'll make a plan here and take action elsewhere."

"Tell me," said Sarah, trying to nudge the conversation to safer ground, "about Mrs. McKenzie's painting."

"But that would unlock so many secrets," said Sydney. "And I, too, have read those mystery novels where a character confesses his crime to someone and then that someone escapes—not, mind you, that I consider myself a criminal. A victim, in fact. Of untoward circumstances."

"A victim?" said Sarah in what she hoped was an encouraging voice. "You?"

"Of course. Who could have dreamt that those poor dull Bakers would have gone right off the dock into the water? Only a small incident, a diversion, was planned. A few bruises, a concussion, a small fracture. Nothing more."

"Did the Bakers steal Mrs. McKenzie's painting from you after you had stolen it from her?" Sarah's voice rose in spite of herself.

"Is crime all you can think of, Sarah? No, no. The Bakers were meant to take their painting straight home to . . . what was their state? Missouri, I think. They paid cash, everything quite in order. A bargain price, so no receipt. People should stick to their plans. They had assured me, oh, several times, that they were en route home. It's a foolproof way of moving these, shall we say, 'special' sale items. I had to deal with their unexpected return immediately. I had to improvise, which I hate to do. I couldn't have Elspeth's painting being shown all around town by the admiring and much too talkative Bakers."

"So you drained the brake fluid," said Sarah softly.

"Let's just say I invited them to take tea, excused myself, and removed Elspeth's painting from their car. No time to plan properly. I think they received the impression that a rental cottage might be available at Lloyd's Wharf. I trusted that after their little accident, the Bakers would lay the loss of their painting to the uproar that would undoubtedly take place when their car crashed into Ted Bassett's bait house or into a tree. And I reminded them to wear seat belts. I had not the slightest idea that they would plunge straight into the harbor. In fact, I told them that the place was directly on the water. I was appalled. Absolutely appalled. No, Sarah, I am not the murderer of elderly customers."

"And Ruth Baker?" Sarah could hardly keep her voice level.

"Such a persistent lady. I regret that Miss Baker ever turned up."

"So would she if she could," said Sarah, losing control.

Her raised voice recalled Sydney. "We must now deal with your presence in my house . . . and, I may add, under my bed. Yes," seeing Sarah start, "I'd know those red jogging shoes of yours anywhere. So unsuitable for gallery work, but then I always said to myself, 'Thank God, it isn't Giddy.' Well, there were your shoes, so I waited outside in the garden until you left and I followed. To my distress, because a boat like that is simply not safe, I saw you take off in that tiny tub of the Harwoods, so, much as I regretted leaving Landing Day in the lurch, I came along."

"I didn't see you," said Sarah, remembering now that she'd been concentrating so hard on sailing that the Loch Ness monster might have been in her train.

"I kept my distance. Your course, though erratic at times, was clear. You hadn't found anything in my cottage, so you were going to Port Clyde. I listened to you rummaging around in the workshop and then, as you know, caught you redhanded, so to speak. To my chagrin, you've succeeded where the State Police have so lamentably failed. They, who wouldn't know a Winslow Homer from a Disney cartoon, just turned the pictures over and shook them."

"But the customers," said Sarah. Mrs. Rolfe, Ms. Toney Black, Dr. Fager."

"My own amusing little code. Surely you, who have been so interested in the *Christmas Past,* can guess."

"Titles of paintings," said Sarah promptly. "Portraits. Stolen portraits."

"Try again."

"Not horses? Because you're from Kentucky."

"Fair enough. If you had studied the sport of kings, you would know that Tom Rolfe, Black Toney, and Dr. Fager are stallions. I use different names in rotation. And Christmas Past is a favorite filly, a champion in her year. By Gray Dawn II out of Yule Log. I placed some extremely favorable bets on Christmas Past, and I am sentimental about the names of my boats, though I should have stuck to the sea names. I see that now. Another mistake," he finished sadly.

"Yes," said Sarah, "you should have been consistent. I would never have noticed. Are all the others horse names?"

"Of course. My father, my grandfather, all from Kentucky, with Kentucky interests. It was a little family joke, choosing champion fillies with water-related names. Why, Dewdrop goes back to 1885 and 1886, Blue Girl, 1901 to 1902, and on to Tempest Queen in 1978."

"And Queen Charlotte, Dixieland Band, Young America,

Dosage Index, all that," asked Sarah, forgetting that this was not an ordinary conversation. But her eyes were beginning to make out objects on the edge of her vision. An entire tea service sat on the table by her right arm. She moved an inch closer to the teapot.

"Stakes, horses, breeding terms. Things I must keep an eye on."

"I told Alex it might be horses, but he said you never rode."

"How very simple of Alex. My father, my grandfather, I myself have always had a lively interest in thoroughbreds, without always the income to support it. So our interest had to be a modest one. A stallion here, a brood mare there. A careful program of betting. But the money needed today, even for a stallion share . . . to join in a syndicate. Unbelievable. But you can't give up life interests because of money, can you? Landing Day, the art school, all precious to me, not to mention my gallery. Money already committed. I had to keep up with everything in my small way. And I was running just a little short, thirty, fifty, seventy thousand a year. A terrible worry. And now, my dear . . ."

"But Nate Harwood," said Sarah, feeling that perhaps Roger, after all, was somehow innocent.

"Sarah!" Sydney sounded truly shocked. "You cannot believe I killed Nate. Haven't I told you? I detest violence. I loathe being forced into taking physical steps. I look back on the Nate Harwood affair with revulsion. Imagine coming home from Portland after the most trying day and evening, the car breaking down in the middle of the night, and then, almost at dawn, finding that disgusting bloody thing on my floor. My hall floor."

"*You* found him!"

"Found him but did not kill him, although I have often been tempted."

"But you moved the body?"

"Would you have left such an object around the house? And I certainly didn't want the police to come snooping

around. I did the best under exceedingly difficult conditions
The lobster trap, the extra ballast, and the body. What a
weight. My back hasn't been the same since. A disk, I think.'

Sarah could not believe that this conversation was taking
place, that the cozy references to the body and the inconvenience of it all wouldn't be followed by an offer of tea and the
possibility of Sarah's purchasing some memorable piece of
silver or china. But she moved her feet and hips a fraction to
the right.

Sydney, without changing tone, returned to present essentials. "Now we must arrange for you. Another boat trip, I
think. Your last in the *Christmas Past*. Please remember how
well protected I am. Not only the doorstop, but my small
revolver, and though I dislike anything happening on this
carpet, I won't hesitate to use either weapon. Believe me."

Sarah believed him and moved four more inches to the
table by her side.

"Now," said Sydney, rising, "if you will bring your hands
again to the top of your head and stand up."

Instructions made to order. Sarah pushed her feet flat on
the carpet, no sudden movements, lifted and turned her head
slightly to her right, and brought her hands to shoulder
height. "Mr. Prior," she said in a soft questioning voice, and
at the same time moved her right arm in a strong sweeping
circle and sent the tea service for eight flying forward—teapot, tea cups, saucers, cream pitcher, sugar bowl, slop basin,
cake stand.

She had only time to catch sight of Sydney gaping like a
surprised flounder, then heard a report apparently next to her
left ear simultaneous with the jangle and crash of shattering
porcelain. She pushed the student lamp from the table, kicked
at a candlestand, and sent a huge rose medallion bowl smashing to the floor. Stumbling to the end of the room, she
reached the door and sensed rather than saw Sydney standing
amazed in the center of the wreckage.

Someone running for her life does not always choose her
route wisely. Sarah did not run down the street and into a

store and shout for help; she ran wildly down to the dock, scrambled over the lines and cleats and into the *Molly*, untied her, paddled the little boat to the middle of the harbor, and pulled up the mainsail, all without looking back. Then, as the wind caught the sail and the boat slid off at an angle, Sarah saw over her shoulder Sydney moving in a certain but unhurried way down to his dock and the waiting *Christmas Past*.

She turned the tiller toward the open sea and felt the wind dead ahead right in her face stalling the boat and luffing the sail. Damn, she'd have to let down her centerboard and tack, beat her way zigzag to . . . to where? Where did she think she was going, to Weymouth, Spain, Miami? Or? But now behind her she heard the steady throb of a diesel engine.

* * *

"License and registration," said the policeman, leaning into Alex's open window.

"It's an emergency," said Alex, trying to keep the fury out of his voice.

"License and registration," said the man, adding, "They're all emergencies, and you out-of-state drivers think you own the road. You were going over seventy."

Again a delay and a series of radio calls, and then Alex found himself free to exceed the speed limit as far as Port Clyde, where he found Deputy Investigator Mike Laaka racing toward Sydney Prior's gallery.

Lem Wallace had at first been annoyed at Sydney's defection and then openly disturbed. Sydney was necessary to Landing Day, so where the hell was he? The *Archangel* had dropped anchor and landed its crew, who, as rehearsed, had sunk to their knees to thank "Almighty God for His Divine Providence in watching over them, and for His Loving Care in blessing this island with abundant bounty." And then no Sydney to read, to proclaim, to give these events what Sydney liked to call "historical significance." Lem, sweating in his velvet doublet, swore loudly and then sent Mike on the double to the Bucket to check on Sydney's cottage and Sydney's boat.

Forty minutes later, in Lem Wallace's commandeered lobster boat, having been much hampered by the fog now rolling in over the whole stretch of ocean between Weymouth and Port Clyde, Mike landed and charged up the dock and toward Prior's Gallery.

"Sydney," yelled Mike to Alex, "he's gone. Off Weymouth."

"I've called the State Police," said Alex, running by his side. "George's men are on their way."

"So what do you know that I don't?" shouted Mike, as the two men rounded the corner toward the gallery driveway.

And Alex told him.

* * *

Sarah, crouching low with the idea of making a poor target, guided the *Molly* on a wavering course, all the while reproaching herself for not having paid more attention to Giddy's sailing lesson. The *Molly* seemed to be going nowhere, and tide and wind were at cross purposes. Panic had now subsided and cold sober fear taken charge. Idiocy to be out here, so why not turn right back to the harbor and, with the wind behind her, sail past Sydney to safety? Because he wouldn't dare shoot her in the middle of the harbor—or would he? Yes, she thought he would. Nothing to it. He could bring his boat right up to the *Molly* and put a shot into Sarah and then take the sailboat in tow . . . Well, there was no need to finish that script.

So it was out to sea, and Sarah, seeing a ledge ahead, turned away, forgetting that a jibe in a catboat can be hazardous. The boom came slamming over, and the *Molly*'s mast gave a great groan. Sarah, as she wildly pulled in the sheet, could almost hear Giddy say, "You turkey." And then, as she steadied the *Molly* on her new tack, Sarah saw that Sydney's big gray and white boat had closed the distance and was now, like a waiting shark, a short eighty or so yards off her stern, so close she could see that Sydney had pulled on his yellow slicker in response to the swirls of fog now coming over the water. Why didn't he come right in and finish her off? No, there were two lobster boats off her port bow, close enough to make Sydney cautious, but not near enough for Sarah to hail. When they disappeared, he could move in. All she could do was to sail back and forth like a big sitting duck. Well, how about the duck doing some thinking? There was the fog to hide in if she could somehow sail herself into it. Except Sydney could follow; he had all that new navigation equipment, radar, and other electronic marvels. His boat was big and for all weather. But wasn't that it? Sydney's boat was so big that it couldn't go just anywhere. Sarah remembered him, on the two trips to Weymouth, spinning his wheel and giving the rocks and ledges a wide berth. It was almost low tide now, and she had a little boat that *could* go anywhere, at least if the centerboard was up, but then it couldn't sail on a tack without the centerboard. Catch-22. Then, just as a welcome curtain of fog lowered over the *Molly*, Sarah saw the spindle for Old Horse Ledge off the port beam. She headed straight at it, gratified by an extra puff of wind. At the last minute, she came about and headed for a dusky line of rocks—Outer Shag Ledges, weren't they? It was a fog blindman's buff. Sarah felt the *Molly* graze a rock and float off with a shudder. She brought the boat about into a denser blanket of fog, but always behind her she heard the heavy thrum of the diesel, now slowing, now speeding up. How long could she keep this up? . . . And where was she, because hadn't she slipped by that same red and black lobster buoy twice? Why, she might end up right under Sydney's bow . . . in fact, there was that bow, pointing right at her through a rent in the gray curtain. Sarah jibed the *Molly* again, heard the mast groan, pulled up the centerboard, and with the wind at her back sailed straight at a blurred land mass that rose ahead. Now, with the water rushing under the boat, she knew this lethal hide-and-seek could have only one ending. Better to meet, or escape from, Sydney on land. A rocky beach loomed. Sarah bent her head, clenched her teeth, and held the tiller steady.

The *Molly* struck, shook herself loose, struck again. The boom swung over, the stern swiveled, the rudder jerked in the air; the mast of the *Molly* cried out and split; and the heavy gaff crashed to the deck. At the same time, across the space of water, came a great answering crack, a splintering and rendering followed by a slow sucking sound, as if some thirsty giant were sipping and pulling at the water. And then, in the eerie, fog-held silence, the creak of oars moving against oar-locks.

* * *

"My God," said Alex, fumbling at the light switch, "someone's let an elephant loose."

"Watch where you walk," said Mike. "There's china all over the place." He moved the spout of a teapot with his shoe. Alex leaned down and picked up a triangular shard from the rose medallion bowl. Two kimono-clad figures looked serenely out at him past the broken edge. "My God," he repeated. He turned the fragment over in his hand, whistling softly.

"Put it down," said Mike. "Evidence. You and your damn prints."

"Evidence?" said Alex stupidly. "What do you mean?"

"I mean," said Mike, "that you coming from the hospital with your hot news and me from Weymouth, both of us thinking that Sydney's our pigeon, well, here we find this place looking like a western bar after a free-for-all. Hell, maybe Sydney's just a middleman. Like I said, group crime. Because it looks like someone came after him."

"So we should look for another body?"

"I'll put in a call and put a rocket under the police. Don't leave this room." And Mike strode off, leaving Alex to contemplate the wreckage of what seemed to be a china service for a household of sixty. Odd, though, the debris seemed to be confined to a narrow area. It was as if a very small tornado had swept between that wing chair and the one opposite, hurling plates and cups and spinning tables. But two people fighting for their lives, wouldn't they have left a wider swath? And then he saw it. The blue and white patterned bandanna, the kind he'd seen so often around Sarah's head. It was by a foot of the wing chair, the knot still tied. And at almost the same time he saw the doorstop. The long-necked fruitbasket lying on its back by the chair.

Feeling suddenly sick, Alex knelt by the object and then exhaled. No visible bits of bone and flesh.

"Okay," said Mike. "George should be here any minute."

Alex pointed to the bandanna. "Sarah's," he said.

Mike nodded. "So what? She works here, doesn't she? Might have been dusting, taking a rest. If you're trying to say that Sarah may have been here today, throwing teapots at Sydney, forget it. I saw Sarah on Weymouth this A.M."

"That was A.M. This is P.M. Come on, let's help look for the bastard. The State Police are coming up the path."

But half an hour of professional searching of Sydney's shop, barn, and house produced nothing beyond the one path of destruction. The search, extended to the village, proved only that both Sydney's and Sarah's cars were in their accustomed places, but at the harbor one of the locals told Mike that Sydney's *Christmas Past* was on the high seas.

"Anyone else?" demanded Alex.

"Some cruisin' boats," said their informant. "And a dragger, the *Bonnie Bee,* and that crazy woman in the catboat goin' every which way."

"Catboat!" Alex almost yelled it.

"Yessir. Fourteen-foot gaff-rig thing. With that fog comin' in, didn't hardly make sense to go out in that little clamshell. I called to her but she weren't listenin'. Paddled out a ways and hauled up the sail. Boat's name's the *Molly*."

"Giddy?" said Alex to Mike. "But she's racing in the *Peg*. What the hell?"

"Naw," said the man. "I know Giddy. This was a skinny dark-haired woman."

"Come on," said Mike. "I've got Lem's boat. Let's go."

"Oh, Christ, look at the fog," said Alex, as he threw off the lines.

Mike nodded, took the wheel, and shoved the throttle forward; the big lobster boat took off like a heavy-duty missile, leaving the dinghies and skiffs by the dock rocking and banging.

"Gotta cut the speed," said Mike, as the fog wrapped around them. "Jesus, the whole U.S. Navy could be out in this and we wouldn't know the difference."

Alex alternately swore, took over the wheel, relinquished it to peer into the mist, and sounded the bell that hung from the bulkhead. Every now and then he shouted into the fog.

"Shut up," said Mike. "If Sydney's out there, you'll scare him farther out to sea or into doing something you don't want him to do."

"There's Old Horse Ledge again," said Alex irritably. "We've gone by it twice. Look, if Sarah's by herself, she'd try to tack back to Weymouth, but if she's being chased by Sydney, she may try to run with the wind. Let's try to the northwest of here, through McGee passage."

They saw the *Christmas Past* and the *Molly* at almost the same time. A sudden switch of wind rolled back the sheath of fog, and a line of low-tide ledges and a rocky beach rose into view like painted scenery.

"God, it's the *Molly* on the beach," said Alex. "She's lost her mast. Get in there."

"Look at Sydney's boat. Listed right over and half under. And some busted up. And I don't see anybody. . . . Where's his dinghy?"

"Sydney," said Alex, "can rot in hell. Get in to that shore."

"Can't. That's Bar Island and it shoals right up here. You'll have to wade in. Can't smash up a third boat, we may need it. Drop the anchor."

Seconds later, Alex swung himself into the waist-high water and plunged toward the shore. "Sarah," he yelled. "Goddammit, Sarah!"

* * *

Sarah had seen the *Molly*'s mast give way and in that second flattened herself on the floorboards so that the mast and gaff sliced down aslant the coaming, only the end of the gaff striking her shoulder. Head down, nose in the bilge, Sarah felt her whole arm flare in pain.

For a time she lay in the bottom of the *Molly*, covered by wet canvas and tangled lines, while the little boat tilted back and forth on the rocks. Then, with a sort of sigh, the *Molly* settled down in the shallows, and Sarah, holding her injured arm to her side, worked her head free of the sail and looked around.

The tide was still going out, and she could see that the *Molly*'s bow was resting like the head of a tired steed upon the low water point of the stony beach. All around the fog swirled and breathed. Sarah, now cold and wet, her shoulder pounding, heaved herself over the gunwales and into the ankle-deep water and began tugging ineffectually at the *Molly*'s painter. But the boat was stuck between two rocks. And where was she? She walked back up the beach and saw that the land rose in a knoll covered with brush and a few stunted spruce trees. At least it wasn't underwater at high tide, a small comfort.

And Sydney Prior? Sarah remembered that she was in peril, a proper target for a man with a revolver. Had that scream of breaking wood and that great crack meant that the *Christmas Past* had foundered and that any moment Sydney would be rowing toward her in the sturdy *Yule Log*, ready with a few well-chosen remarks about the inconvenience of an ocean chase? Then, having kept his powder dry, he would put several holes through her skull. Or, and somehow this seemed to be the most terrible picture of all, Sydney would wash in on the returning tide, fish-eyed and bloated in his white suit. Sarah, in an instinctive and crazy gesture, put her hands over her ears.

But nothing happened and, ashamed, she put her hands down and for a moment listened to the lonely double note of the foghorn and the sibilance of the water retreating over the rocks, then remembered the *Molly*—it had to be tied, because later on she might need that boat. She worked with stiff fingers, fastening the main sheet to the halyard and then tying one end around a large boulder above what seemed to be the high watermark of the beach. But as she was working the last knot, she heard at a distance the too well-known sound of a diesel engine. Closer, closer, sniffing around in the fog, next, silence and the sound of someone splashing through the water toward the beach. Sarah dropped her lines and raced away up the beach.

Then, "Sarah. Goddammit, Sarah!"

Alex! Sarah, heedless of a perhaps waiting Sydney with a waiting revolver, flung herself around, and, running and slipping on the sand, hurled herself at Alex, and Alex, arms open, took her into safe harbor.

In a tumble of words, she gasped out her story, her joy at finding him, her horror of Sydney, all the time feeling Alex holding her against him, kissing her cheeks, her forehead, her lips, smoothing her wet hair, and saying over and over, "God, I love you, I love you." But then, as he pulled her more tightly to him, Sarah let out a cry of pain, and Alex turned his attention to things medical. "I don't think it's broken or dislocated," he said finally, "but let's fix you up with a sling," and he was busy with the blue bandanna when Mike walked up the beach. "I see you've found each other and not Sydney. Lucky thing because I don't think either of you is paying attention. Now let's get back to the boat before we get plugged from behind a log—though I don't see his dinghy anywhere. . . . Alex—hey, Alex, Sarah, wake up, this isn't *South Pacific.*"

* * *

"It isn't usually such a muddle," said Elspeth to Tina, "but with Sydney taking off in the middle of the landing . . ."

"I had fun, anyway," said Tina. "*Moondust* coming in second and all. But Alex should have gotten back from the hospital."

"Typical of him," said Elspeth. "Off in every direction without any sense of time. And Sarah's missing, too. But what I need now is a long nap."

"You're not going to the square dance?"

"Gracious, no. I need peace after this sort of a day . . . and I've got to check on poor Marian Harwood, one of our neighbors. . . . She insisted on staying alone. But I'm sure you'll enjoy yourself, because we have a lot of energetic dancers on the island, although I'm afraid Alex isn't one of them. Good night, Tina." Elspeth closed the door, watched from the window as Tina walked down the path to Tinker's Cove, and then opened it again. The small procession coming up the road from the post office was closer now, and its members could be easily identified.

* * *

Dinner was over. In deference to the increasing fog and chill, a fire had been started in the living room and now sent a warm light over the faded slipcovers and rows of books.

Sarah sat, one arm in a sling and knees hunched, in a giant chair whose cushions through decades of use had formed themselves into comfortable hollows. Patsy snored at her feet.

"But has Mike called the Coast Guard?" said Elspeth. "He and Lem and one State Police boat can't find Sydney in all this fog."

"Yes," said Alex, "from Lem's boat radio." Alex was

standing up against the bookshelves, his elbow resting among a collection of shells.

"To think it was Sydney," said Elspeth. "And I was sure it was Nate. But why on earth? The Priors all had money, and I'm sure Sydney made a mint from the art school and his shop. And a murderer, too. The Priors have been on Weymouth for ages . . . and everybody trusted them. Oh, dear."

"Sydney had hidden expenses," said Alex. "And he was greedy. Or modestly greedy, as I think Sarah once said. Greedy people sometimes kill to keep themselves going in the style to which they've become accustomed. In Sydney's case, he was the Lord High Pooh-Bah of Landing Day, Mr. Art Supply, and Mr. Fine Art Dealer, and then he was into the thoroughbred game and that takes big bucks. Outgo exceeding income. And that new boat of his must have cost well over thirty thousand. And to think I told Sarah to forget horses."

"I finally did forget them," murmured Sarah. "I decided that the *Christmas Past* and the other names I found in his room were either a weird Christmas or jazz obsession or titles of stolen paintings." She heard her voice as from a distance, feeling like someone who has had a part in a demanding production and has been brought backstage in a numb and drained condition to discuss the meaning of it all.

"And as Sarah pointed out," said Alex, "Sydney had everything going for him to be in the art theft business. The view from the shop and a finger in every art pie. He knew which paintings were catalogued, which had been shown, and he knew about treasures without documentation, like that so-called Frederic Church from the library. And if there were small goodies lying around, silver snuffboxes and mustard pots, why, he'd slip them in his pocket and sell them, piece by piece, to the out-of-state people who came to the shop."

"He didn't need a middleman," said Sarah, rousing herself out of a near stupor from fatigue and the heat of the fire. "It was an almost perfect fence system. He just checked to make sure the buyers were on their way home to Kansas, or Texas . . . or Missouri, like the Bakers. He'd look over their car, their jewelry, judge their income, and then bring them back to the Parlor Gallery. I can just hear him going on about what a shame it was that they had to leave Maine, but would they be interested in some very special paintings he'd put away for very special people . . . the, the . . . " Sarah looked at Elspeth.

Elspeth nodded. "Call him any name you want."

"Everything for cash," said Alex. "No records, no income tax."

"So when the Bakers came back he had to kill them," said Elspeth.

"Yes," said Alex. "The whole scam in jeopardy."

"Not exactly," said Sarah. She frowned, trying to remember Sydney's explanation of the accident. "He didn't *plan* to kill them. I think he panicked. He offered them tea, went out and took the painting from the car, and at the same time drained the brake fluid from their car. He does know a lot about engines, what with all those boats, so I suppose he knows about automobiles, too. He told them about a rental cottage down by Lloyd's Wharf, because he knew the route took them uphill, then along the flat, and then when they'd made the turn, down that steep drive to the wharf. He said he thought they'd just steer into a tree or the bait house. Not to be killed—just injured perhaps—and everyone would think that the painting was lost or taken in the confusion. It was a stupid and terrible idea, and it killed the Bakers."

"In a way it did work," said Alex. "No one thought the painting was taken out of the car by the man who'd sold it, *before* the car went into the harbor. Only Ruth kept the search going and when she began calling garages . . . "

"And letting everyone know about it," said Sarah. "I'm sure that Sydney pushed her off the cliff—he almost admitted it—but what happened at the hospital? She was unconscious, couldn't speak."

"She still can't speak, but she's not unconscious and she did tell me that Sydney shoved her off Captain's Head. You see, something has been bothering me about her, but I don't see many neurological cases because we internists shoot them right along to the specialists. Anyway, I did some reading and thinking, and then Tina gave me a nudge in the right direction. Said to see for myself, try for a response."

"Get to the point, Alex," said Elspeth.

"There's an odd condition we sometimes see after brain injury, called the Locked-In Syndrome. Trauma or lesion can sometimes result in the patient being unable to move or talk and able to show they're aware of what's going on only by moving the eyes—usually on a vertical plane—up and down."

"But you said Ruth's eyes were untaped every day?" said Sarah.

"Yes, they were, but the staff probably missed this very specific, very limited eye movement. These patients are at such risk, and it's awfully easy to think of them as vegetables. But once I got hold of the idea, I had to try it out. I questioned her—roll your eyes up for yes, down for no—and she answered. Patients who stay in this state can be taught the Morse Code."

"Horrible," said Sarah. "You mean Ruth might have to lie in bed for the rest of her life doing S.O.S. with her eyes?"

"We can't tell yet. There have been recoveries, partial or complete. Not many, but some."

"Great," said Sarah bitterly. "If only I'd made it to Captain's Head sooner. And I must have been blind. How could I have missed a great blob like Sydney Prior? Or why didn't someone else see him? Even if he had on a disguise, everyone would know him."

"I have a confession," said Alex. "I realized it only a little while ago. An obvious fact and we all missed it. The lower shore trail."

"Which isn't on the map," said Elspeth. "Not anymore."

"For good reason," said Alex. "Three accidents in one summer about ten years ago. Visitors washed off in the surf. The trail marking was taken off the map, the old copies destroyed, and danger signs put up. That trail's only safe on calm days and only used now and then by residents or naturalists."

"So George Fitts wouldn't have known about it," said Sarah.

"The police only have the new map; I saw it in their office. I'd say Mike forgot about it like the rest of us. All Sydney had to do, once he'd primed Ruth with his father's painting, was to close the shop for the weekend, stay on Weymouth and keep an eye on boat arrivals, then watch from his cottage until Ruth went by on the regular Ocèan Trail, and make his way to the lower trail—it crosses the shore at Bucket Cove—and come up where that trail rises just east of Captain's Head to join the main trail. Don't forget that Sydney, like a lot of fat men, can be amazingly spry when he has to. He could wait behind a rock or some trees until the place cleared out and Ruth was alone. He was lucky, it was foggy that day, not many visitors around."

"And then," said Sarah, "he'd come out and say, 'Oh, Miss Baker, you've come to see the view in your painting. Right over here by the edge.' The murderer. I hope he's not drowned, I hope he's got Locked-In Syndrome and nobody untapes his eyes. Alex, I've got to go over and see Ruth."

"She's had enough for one day," said Alex, "but Monday she's being reevaluated and I'll go over with you. Now tell my mother about the interesting painting showing the Weymouth weir that was hidden behind a Renoir."

"How fiendish," said Elspeth, when Sarah had described her raid on Sydney's workshop. "But, of course, Sydney could do anything with a frame. And what a terrible risk, leaving stolen paintings just sitting there. Especially after the police got interested in the doorstop. He knew they'd be looking."

"A risk if the police had been looking for drugs or stolen jewelry," said Alex. "Then they'd have ripped the frames apart. But they were looking for stolen paintings and blunt instruments."

Elspeth shook her head again. "Two of our neighbors, murderers. I can't believe it. Two people on one small island. I dread telling Giddy."

"Tell Giddy what?" said Sarah, sitting up straight.

"About Nate Harwood. You've haven't heard, with all that's gone on, but Roger gave himself up. A complete confession. A boy we've watched grow up. Of course, it explains everything. So miserable for Marian. No wonder she's been going around in a fog, seeing Roger kill his father, her dress being spattered with Nate's blood."

Sarah nodded. Just as she'd thought. It made terrible sense.

"And imagine," said Elspeth, "he even described to Mike how he'd tied Nate up and after dark carried him out in a skiff and dumped him off Hupper's Island."

Sarah interrupted. "But he didn't. I don't think so, anyway. Sydney said *he* did. He said he found the body in the back hall when he came back from Portland and didn't dare call the police. He didn't sound as if he were making it up."

"Then why would Roger claim to have done it?" said Elspeth. "It's bad enough to murder your father in a rage, but then to tie him up and dump him overboard . . . Perhaps it's psychological. Roger feels guilty and wants more blame."

"He'll have enough blame to last a lifetime," said Alex. "As for being psychological, well, I won't even begin to try and understand Roger."

"I don't want to try," said Sarah, "but it is odd. . . . Anyway, Mrs. Harwood must have been dreading this for weeks."

"Yes," said Elspeth. "She's almost ceased to react. I'm not sure she even understands that Roger's been arrested. Or that he's confessed. She just talks in a rambling way about everything being too much trouble. Rachel is spending the night with her—even Marian can't say no to Rachel."

"So it's all over," said Sarah, "except for Ruth. I can't take it all in, but I'm sorry about smashing the *Molly*. I wasn't thinking when I ran away from Sydney, and sailing the boat on to that beach wasn't planned. I just wanted to bring Sydney into shallow water and wreck him."

"Giddy's a good teacher," said Alex. "You wrecked Sydney to the manner born."

"I can't bear to think of Giddy," said Elspeth, standing up and starting for the door. "I'm sure there's some old feeling despite this summer. She's at the square dance now, so we can put off telling her until tomorrow."

Sarah put her head back against the chair cushion. "There's still something . . . but I'm too tired to make any sense of it."

* * *

Giddy was the last to breakfast on Sunday morning, and everyone stopped talking when she appeared in the doorway.

"A conspiracy," she said. "What's going on, anyway? I heard last night that Sydney hit a ledge and is missing. I couldn't stand him, but I'm sorry."

"He's still missing," said Alex, "and so is his dingy. He turns out to be the man behind the art thefts, and Sarah here assaulted him with his own china."

"Wow!" said Giddy. "You mean it? Goody-goody Sydney? Well, I hope you ruined a whole tea set and trashed some of his precious antiques."

"I think I did. Desperation and self-defense. He had a gun. But I wish I'd done more. He drowned the Bakers and sent Ruth over Captain's Head."

"Wow," said Giddy again. "Oh, wow." She sat down suddenly at the kitchen table. "Sydney a murderer. And he's really missing? Well, I hope he stays that way. Wiping out the whole Baker family. And Nate, too, I suppose. Nate caught Sydney stealing. A triple murderer. Sneaking around with all of us. God."

"Not Nate," said Alex. "Sydney was away when Nate was killed."

There was a long pause while Giddy shook a box of Granola into a bowl and carefully dribbled honey over the surface. Then, without looking up, she said. "Not Roger."

"I'm afraid so." Alex sat down at the table next to Giddy.

"No. Absolutely no," said Giddy loudly. She poured the milk into her bowl up to the edge so that the milk trickled onto the table. "You've all been against Roger, and so have I, but he just couldn't have . . . "

"We're so sorry," said Elspeth, who was at the sink doing unnecessary things to already washed dishes. "We couldn't believe it at first either."

"If you couldn't believe it, why did you?" said Giddy furiously.

"Because he confessed," said Alex. "Because he explained the whole business and it makes sense—all but disposing of the body, but that's a detail, something after the fact. His mother apparently walked in on the murder and has been in shock ever since."

Giddy shoved her cereal bowl to one side. "I've got to see Roger."

"Later," said Alex. "He probably can only see his lawyer. I'll ask when I go over to see George this morning."

"Now," said Elspeth, "I've promised to read the lesson at the colonial church service. Landing Day isn't over yet, and we can't let down everyone who has worked so hard."

"Bullshit!" shouted Giddy, and then, seeing Elspeth's face, "I'm sorry, but you've got someone's whole life at stake and you're going to a Landing Day thing. Alex, I thought you'd understand. You know Roger."

"I'm afraid I do," said Alex, reaching for his jacket.

"Giddy," said Elspeth quietly, "why not go over and see Marian? She must be feeling pretty awful, and you'll be one of the few who really understand. I'll come over after church and stay with her. Sarah, do take it easy today."

Sarah found herself alone in the house, walking about in a kind of indefinable restlessness, her thoughts buffeted by a hundred ideas in conflict. Alex. Maybe telling her he loved her just happened in the heat of a rescue mission, because here he was off again and she was alone. Concentrate on something else. Well, Sydney Prior, alive, dead, or drifting, was of no consequence, but Ruth Baker was conscious. Almost. And she might get well. That was something to be cautiously cheerful about. And Roger. "The bond cracked 'twixt son and father." A terrible conclusion. Patricide. The definitive usurpation. And Giddy, so blinded by old loyalties, by childhood memories, that she couldn't see that the once favored boy had turned into a head-smashing killer. A loser, a guilt-ridden homicidal loser who, as Elspeth had suggested, had added to his confession by saying he'd dumped his father's body, because Sarah, the more she thought about it, found Sydney's account entirely believable. Was Roger, by heaping more blame on his head, atoning for letting his mother fend so long by herself, burning her bloody dress, losing her sanity?

Sarah shook herself. She had to get out. Take another walk, this time without the danger and fatality that so many of her Weymouth walks had brought. She slipped the sling from her arm—her shoulder, although fragile, was recovering —called Patsy, and set out. Perhaps her last walk on Weymouth. Fall was on its way, school starting next week. Already the hackmatacks were showing yellow, the white pines shedding last year's needles, and the late purple asters turning dry. She stepped quickly, propelled by a rush of unfocused energy, and made her way through the churchyard toward Satter's Field.

Landing Day had left its mark on the cemetery, the oldest section brave in bunting and flags, and at the entrance Sarah could see a procession moving forward, its leaders holding a large tricolor wreath. She escaped to the edge of the field and, as she paused to fix on some new direction, caught sight of Giddy stamping up a brushy incline, close enough for Sarah to see a scarlet face and fury in every step. Sarah raised a hand, thinking to call, and then lowered it.

No, Giddy wouldn't want anyone now. She would have to come to terms with Roger's guilt by herself. There she went, off south toward the lighthouse. Sarah was about to turn her own steps in the opposite direction when she saw Marian Harwood, leaning forward as if into a wind, hands held to her breast, walking steadily after Giddy. Oh, Lord, thought Sarah. She could see it. Giddy, sent by Elspeth to console Marian, had burst out defending Roger, saying God knows what. Giddy on the rampage, standing up for her childhood friend, Giddy losing control, shouting. And Marian, didn't she have enough to face without doing battle with Giddy? But the anger and unhappiness summed up in the passage of the two women across the field were almost palpable. Sarah, in a sort of abrogation of personal will, as if in pursuit of some unimagined disaster, found herself turning and following Marian, much as one might follow a fire engine or an ambulance.

Marian marched ahead, neither losing nor gaining on Giddy. She walked like someone who, if not deflected, might march off the edge of the world—or at least off Lighthouse Point. And there had been quite enough of that. Sarah quickened her pace so that she was only fifty or so yards behind the older woman. Now she could see that Marian carried something in both hands, just as she had going down the church aisle for the memorial service. And what did she want with Giddy? To say, Forgive him, he's my son, or forget him, he's a monster, not worth the trouble? Sarah remembered that Marian had been going on about everything being too much trouble. Now, perhaps living was too much trouble. Sarah dropped Patsy's leash and broke into a run, thrusting her way through a costumed group of children who were crossing the path on their way to some Landing Day event. There was Marian mounting the path to the lighthouse, holding the unseen object to her breast as a fleeing woman holds an infant. And Giddy? She had reached the top, where the wisps of fog circled the tower like smoke. Sarah saw her pull at the door and disappear. Of course, the lighthouse was open to the public for Landing Day, although no one was around because with the fog there would be no view. Sarah, now only a short distance behind Marian, was about to shout, so sure was she that Marian was going to walk into space, but Marian kept to the path and without hesitating also disappeared into the lighthouse.

Sarah stopped. Now that Marian was for the moment safe, could she intrude on Giddy's anguish, Marian's purpose? No, but at least she could station herself at the bottom of the lighthouse stairway, ready to give a comforting hand if Marian indeed was at the end of her small store of sanity. Unhappily, Patsy, who had galloped after her, chose at that moment to snuffle and whine into the corners of the stairwell, so that by the time Sarah had quieted the dog, she could not tell whether the echoing noise above her head had just begun or was the climax of a series of noises. Then, louder, a thud, the clang of something hitting the floor, and now Giddy—unmistakably Giddy—shouting, yelling, "No, no, no!"

Oh God, thought Sarah, Giddy's cracked up. "I'm coming, Mrs. Harwood," she called, hurling herself at the stairs. Up and around, up and around, every step reverberating in the hollow tower. Sarah could see it. Giddy, big, strong Giddy, Giddy with shoulders and arms built for women's crew, Giddy in her grief belaboring Marian Harwood, banging her against the walls as she might some crazed puppet. Shaking the life right out of her.

She saw Giddy first. Bloody-faced, flat on the concrete floor of the top landing. Marian Harwood leaning over her, hatchet in one hand, Giddy's arm straight up, holding Marian's wrist. Marian's other hand reaching for Giddy's arm. Giddy screaming, "No, no, no!" Giddy kicking with her feet, trying to upset Marian's balance. And Marian pressing forward, eyes set like glue, saying in a high, singsong voice, a counterpoint to Giddy's screams, "All this trouble, all this trouble." She did not see Sarah rising up the stairs behind her, did not even see Giddy. She was rapt, held, moved by some overwhelming inner storm.

Sarah reached the landing, leaped at Marian, dragged her back, at the same time feeling her resistance to anything but forward murderous motion. But even when Giddy, released and sputtering from the blood that welled from a gash above her eye, pinned Marian to the floor, she twice lost her hold. At last, Giddy gripping, Sarah prying finger after finger free, the hatchet clattered to the floor, its cutting edge thick with blood.

TWELVE

They sat in a circle under the apple trees in the warm September morning sun. It looked like a gathering of the walking wounded—Giddy with her swollen lip, her bruised face, and with a large gauze square anchored over one eyebrow, Sarah looking spent, her arm, now back in its sling, held close to her side.

"I don't see why you wouldn't do my stitches, Alex," said Giddy.

Alex shook his head. "You're lucky I didn't. Internists are out of practice. You might end with a big scar."

"Scars make for conversation," said Giddy. "You know, I got it wrestling with a crazy woman on top of a lighthouse."

"And that will be enough of that kind of talk, Giddy," said Elspeth, appearing with fresh coffee and a plate of raisin buns. "And I still can't take it in. Poor, poor Marian."

"Poor, poor Giddy," said Giddy. "She absolutely took me by surprise. I'd gone up to the lighthouse to get my head together, and I was almost finished when Sarah showed up out of nowhere."

"Not nowhere," said Sarah. "I followed you. I thought you might do something terrible to Mrs. Harwood. Because of Roger."

"But Marian Harwood," said Elspeth, sitting down and

shaking her head. "Always such a mouse, such a doormat. Never a raised voice. Not until she walked out on Nate. I suppose that's it. She just burst out and began *doing* things."

"Did she ever," said Giddy. "The doorstop, and the warming pan, and then the hatchet. We should have guessed after she brained Roger. The police should have. Aren't they supposed to put things like that together?"

"You can ask them," said Alex. "George and Mike are coming over this morning."

"I told them everything last night," said Giddy. "But what I don't get is why Mrs. Harwood let Roger take the blame and be arrested. To just sit there in her cottage mumbling and then to attack me because I said Roger wouldn't have done it."

"I think Marian was beyond making sense of anything by the time Roger was taken away," said Alex, "and I was awfully slow to see how far gone she was."

"Because you've never believed in psychology," said Elspeth.

"I just don't believe in amateur psychologists."

"But why did Roger confess?" demanded Giddy. "He's been doing some weird things, but to put his head on the block like that . . . "

"Here come Mike and George," said Alex. "Let's see if we can tie up those loose ends."

"And I'll leave you to it," said Elspeth. "I'm going over to pack up Marian's clothes."

"What *will* happen to Mrs. Harwood?" asked Sarah, after Elspeth had departed and George and Mike had found chairs.

"Psychiatric evaluation, first," said George. "Then we'll see. She's made a statement, a confession, if you can call it that. Questionable because of her condition. She's pretty incoherent."

"And Roger," said Giddy. "You're going to let him go?"

"On bail," said George. "He's admitted to being an accessory, concealing evidence—the doorstop—and lying to the police."

"Roger has been one big pain in the butt," said Mike.

Giddy turned, ready to explode, and Alex, feeling like some ancient father figure, held up his hand. "Let's clear up a few things first. Any word on Sydney?"

"Still a missing person, but we've picked up the dinghy drifting. Just a matter of time," said George, tapping a finger against his knee. "And the murders, interesting interlocking crimes."

Mike grinned, "Like the songs says, you can't have one without the other, foxy Sydney and crazy lady Harwood."

George frowned. "Not appropriate, Mike. But the cases were unusual. I'm afraid we have Sarah to thank for exposing Sydney Prior's secret activities."

"Alex and I were doing a trivia investigation. You know, like Harrison Petty being in such a dither about the stolen paintings, and the name of Sydney's new boat not matching the other boat names."

"Have you been concealing evidence?" said George.

"Christ, let her go on," said Mike.

"Mike gave me the clue even if I didn't really follow it up," said Sarah, thinking that the deputy needed a pat on the back. "You said Christmas Past was a horse. Sydney told me all about it when he was preparing for my last boat ride. All the Prior boats were named after champion horses . . . like the Tempest Queen."

"Wouldn't you know?" said Mike. "Old George here kept Sydney's shop as State Police turf, but if I'd seen those pictures I might have guessed. Trouble is I took up horses just a couple of years ago and some of those are before my time —Blue Girl, Ocean Bound. But hell, there was his dinghy, *Yule Log*, right in front of my nose. She's the dam of Christmas Past. And Sydney'd ordered that motor boat with the name to be painted on, *Plum Cake*. Yule Log is by Bold Ruler out of Plum Cake. Jesus, it was all so out of context, and every time I tried to talk Kentucky and racing with Sydney he gave me the cold shoulder."

"I like you humble, Mike," said Alex. "It suits you."

"And," said George, pressing the attack, "if Deputy Susan Cohen had been on her toes and not ruled the Baker car accidental, Ruth wouldn't have had to be her own investigator and scare Prior into pushing her off the cliff."

"Hey," said Mike, now quite red of face, "back up. I've got another admission. It wasn't Susie. It was her partner, Wayne Jones. Said he'd gone over the car properly, and he hadn't. Susie took his word. He's suspended without pay."

"And you've apologized to Susan?" said Sarah.

"Oh, sure," said Mike. "She's making me join NOW."

"Anyway," continued George, "we've got the final Harwood scenario roughed in. The attack on Giddy was just what we needed."

"Thanks a bunch," said Giddy.

"And Roger's revised account is plausible," said George. "He'd been having rows for days over the Brueghel copy and Nate's threat to make it public. After dodging Nate in Port Clyde that Friday—rowing out into the harbor—Roger changed his mind, came back, and followed his father in through the barn door into the back hall. Nate knew Sydney was safe off to Portland, so it was a chance to take another look for that order of his. Well, Marian Harwood followed Roger—she hadn't gone off to Spruce Head sightseeing—and found father and son in a shouting match. It was all too much and she reached for the first thing at hand, that dog doorstop. She'd climbed up those three steps to the inner hall and had the advantage of height. Nate probably died at once."

Giddy looked up. "I must have been in the front shop the whole time, but I didn't hear a thing, and I never went back that way."

"Roger says his father didn't even try to defend himself," said Mike. "Nate just turned and stared, little mouse Marian coming at him with a doorstop. She'd probably never so much as lifted a spoon to him all those years. Roger, too. He just stood there and didn't believe it."

"Like me," said Giddy. "I couldn't believe it. I saw her

coming at me and I just stood there, too. Marian Harwood coming at me with an ax."

"As you pointed out, Giddy, there was the warming-pan attack," said Alex, "but that made sense. An intruder in your house. And Marian is very strong, carries furniture, splits her own wood."

"Which no one thought of," said Mike. "It didn't fit in. Grade B thriller with complications. I suppose Marian started going into shock—or whatever it is she went into—right after she'd killed Nate. Didn't cope with the body, just hustled off leaving Roger with it all. Roger must have been in a fit, too, and all he could think of was cleaning up the blood and dumping the doorstop. He said he left the body because he couldn't just carry Nate into the streets of Port Clyde. And he couldn't call the police down on his mother."

"So Sydney got home just before dawn," said Alex, taking up the tale. "He had the traps, the pot warp, and knew that no one would wonder at a lobster boat out in the fog. All he had to do was find a dense patch, roll Nate over the side, sluice the decks, then order a new boat and accept a long-standing offer for the *Tempest Queen*, from someone who'd be stripping it down."

"And later wreck his dinghy and get a new one," said Sarah. "I suppose Nate's hat came off in the loading operation," she added. "The one Patsy found. That didn't help, the hat in one place, the body in another."

"And Sydney, without even knowing it," said George, "diverted suspicion by reporting the doorstop missing, which it certainly was. He also told us that some other objects were gone from his shop—including two paintings, and those might have been genuine red herrings."

"Okay, okay," said Giddy, who was shuffling her feet back and forth on the ground. "So you're letting Roger out on bail. When?"

George looked at his watch. "He should be coming in on the noon boat, about ten minutes. The lawyers want to see him at the cottage."

Giddy shot to her feet as if released by a spring. "Somebody should be there to meet him."

"Love's old sweet song," said Mike, as Giddy pounded away. "Powerful Katrinka and Roger the Dodger."

"Not so much love, I think," said Alex, "as the call of the underdog."

"And the misunderstood," said Sarah. "He *has* been abominable, but considering his home life and then the murder . . . well, it's almost Greek. Orestes has nothing on Roger."

Alex looked thoughtful. "The only time I've seen Roger happy in the last year was when he went off in handcuffs, taking the rap for his mother. He probably felt he was doing a Sydney Carton and making reparation for everything. But he overdid it by saying he'd dumped the body. I suppose that since no one had come forward to claim the honor, Roger thought it might add weight to his 'confession.' But he must have wondered just what had happened to the body."

"I think Roger was past wondering," said Sarah. "He was just racing around, hiding, leaving, coming back, worrying about plagiarism and his mother going bonkers."

"We're off now," said Mike. "We'll heat up the search for the other missing paintings, though they're probably scattered all over the country, or in Harrison Petty's bottom desk drawer."

George, ignoring Mike, stood up and shook hands solemnly with Sarah and Alex. "I may have to study up on race horses," he said, with an attempt at a light touch.

"I'm your man," said Mike. "The Woodward's coming up, then the Marlboro, the Futurity, the Ruffian, and the Jockey Gold Cup."

Sarah, who was not listening, shook her head. "To think that it was Sydney all along."

Mike laughed. "Beautiful mare, All Along, a real champion . . . and, oh, God . . . "

"What now?" said Alex, alarmed.

"My boat . . . my little wooden dory with the ten-horse . . ."

"What about it?" said George impatiently.

"I'm just like Sydney. My boat, her name's Miss Oceania. Miss Oceania is one beautiful filly, trained by Woody Stephens. Oh, Christ, how stupid."

"Mike won't forgive himself," said Alex, as the two policemen disappeared down the path. "Not for ten minutes, at least. Okay, Sarah, hurry up, we can catch the return trip to Port Clyde and go and see Ruth. I've got a tape deck and some cassettes, because she can listen even if she can't speak."

"Where's Tina?" said Sarah in a voice of studied detachment, as they boarded the ferry.

"Sailed. She has to be back at the hospital tomorrow. Said she'd see me there." Alex's voice indicated neither pleasure or pain.

"Good," said Sarah firmly. "I enjoyed meeting her." And this courtesy done, Sarah, as they looked back at the receding island, said, "It's so beautiful there . . . and it seems so tame. You'd never think, would you?"

"There's always been an undercurrent of rock-ribbed violence in New England," said Alex. "Northeast storms, Calvinism, isolation, inbred, long-lasting grudges against the soil, the sea, and your fellow man. But enchanting in its way. Habit-forming." He pointed. "Look over there. Giddy's found Roger." And Sarah saw two figures walking slowly along the harbor road, their heads bent in conversation. Giddy, with one hand in Roger's, the other flailing the air, was unmistakably exhorting, reproaching, and comforting her old friend.

* * *

Sarah and Alex left the hospital soberly.

"What sort of life is that?" demanded Sarah. "Listening to taped music and rolling your eyes up and down like window shades."

"It's something," said Alex, "and let's hope for more. Partial recovery anyway. I can arrange to have her sent to Boston for more tests later on."

"How about to Missouri?" said Sarah. "Wouldn't that be best? With her aunt and uncle."

"You're probably right. As soon as she's stabilized. Yes, home is usually best."

Yes, Sarah thought. Ruth had been *in terra incognita* too long—among strangers on a strange coast, now listening to strange voices.

Mike caught them on the Weymouth dock. "Sydney's been found."

Sarah felt a rise of nausea. "Where? How?"

"Washed in by McGee Island. Drowned. So that's that."

Alex, seeing Sarah's face, changed the subject. "Any more paintings found?"

"Two stolen watercolors. Double-framed behind some prints in his dining room, plus a stash of old silver in the life jacket locker of his *Christmas Past*, which we've salvaged. Clever bastard."

"No—murderer," said Sarah.

Rachel Seaver stopped Sarah and Alex as they came aboard the *Robin Day* for the return trip. "I've been to the dentist to see about my partial. Come into the cabin, both of you. There's room now that the tourists have gone. You know, I said to Lyda, who will not see anything plain in front of her nose, that there was something amiss with Marian . . . "

"Thanks, Rachel," said Alex, "but we're going to the bow." He took Sarah's elbow and steered her forward.

"Weren't you a little short with Rachel?" asked Sarah, leaning on the rail.

"I would have put Rachel in the bilge if I had to," said Alex. "Look, Sarah, time is running out. Vacation, if I can call it that, is over. I have to start back tomorrow, and you have to begin classes. In forty or fifty minutes, even with the fog, we'll be back on Weymouth, and there'll be Mother and Giddy and probably Roger, and Rachel and Lyda and God knows who else . . . "

"Yes," said Sarah, "and it's time for me to say how sorry I am for the way I've sometimes acted, some of the things I've thought . . . "

Alex interrupted. "Have you finished *Mansfield Park*?"

"What?" said Sarah, surprised. "Yes, I have, but I don't see . . . "

"How did it end? How did it come out?"

"Oh, fine for some, not so fine for others. Some people got their just desserts."

"Like life . . . except Ruth and her parents, and even Nate, didn't deserve what happened. So tell me, how is it coming out for us? For Sarah Deane and Alexander McKenzie? I tried to tell you back there when you were shipwrecked and I'll try again. I love you. I want you and I need you. I miss you when you're not there, and I miss you when you're being an efficient lady detective."

"That's one of the things I'm sorry about," murmured Sarah.

"Never mind it now. I'm going to practice in Maine. Do you think that someday you could live with me and do your teaching here . . . on an island, or on the coast, or in a marsh, or next to a shoe factory, or on top of Mount Katahdin, or damn well anywhere as long as we're together?"

"But what about . . . ?" said Sarah, and then stopped herself.

"If you were going to say 'Tina'—though I'm sure you weren't—let me say that Tina is a fine speciman of womanhood, but I don't want to live with a fine specimen. I want a slightly imperfect, aggravating, dark-haired English teacher from Boston who has an untrained Irish wolfhound, because I'm imperfect myself and also untrained—at least in saying I love you. Oh, Christ in heaven," shouted Alex, as Sarah looked at him without speaking, "come here." And Alex, forgetting Sarah's shoulder, pulled her to him into an enormous hug, so that her face rubbed against his raw wool sweater and the side of his chin. For a minute she fought against the pain in her arm, and then Alex relaxed his hold, bent, and kissed her, first lightly, then hard on her mouth. And Sarah, for once, without protest or doubt, kissed him back.

"Love," said Alex. "Remember. There's something going on besides murder."

"Yes," said Sarah, keeping him close. "I'd almost forgotten."

For a while they stood together, looking down into the dividing bow waves, and then Alex said, "The fog's thicker than ever. Maybe we can be marooned somewhere."

"I do like disappearing into it," Sarah said. "Not just because it saved my life, but," she added dreamily, "there's something mystical about it . . . all those islands turned to nothing. A whole world gone . . . " 'the great globe itself . . . shall dissolve.' "

"I've been missing those little nuggets of yours," said Alex, smiling down at her. "What was that thing you recited the day we went sailing? I liked it. Something about the ocean and how care becomes senseless there."

"It ends like this," said Sarah.

"Oh, to be there, under the silent spruces,
Where the wide, quiet evening darkens without haste
Over a sea with death acquainted, yet forever chaste."

"Yes," said Alex, "that seems right." He put his arm gently around her shoulder, and peacefully, without speaking, they watched as the *Robin Day* slid past the gray-veiled bulk of Captain's Head, past Lighthouse Point and Little Mote, between the dim outline of Abbott's Ledge and Mac's Mote, and into the shrouded harbor.